The Cromaboo Mail Carrier

Mary Leslie

Foreword by
Daniel Bratton

Introduction and Editing by
David J. Knight

Vocamus Editions
Guelph, Ontario
2016

Written by Mary Leslie
Public Domain

Cover design © Liz Morant
Cover photograph © David J. Knight
Foreword © Daniel Bratton
Introduction and Notes © David J. Knight

ISBN 13: 978-1-928171-25-6 (pbk)
ISBN 13: 978-1-928171-26-3 (ebk)

Vocamus Editions
130 Dublin Street, North
Guelph, Ontario, Canada
N1H 4N4

www.vocamus.net

2016

To my mother, Audrey Elizabeth Knight

Acknowledgements

Thank you to my parents and to Jeremy Luke Hill; Daniel Bratton for writing the Foreword and many fascinating conversations on Canadian Literary Heritage; Liz Morant for designing the cover; Andrew Vowles for an adventurous trip to Hamilton to locate the former Ocean House Hotel; Sona Mincoff, the Guelph Public Library archive staff, the Architectural Conservancy of Ontario Guelph/Wellington Branch and Scott McGovern for direct and indirect support during the process of preparing this new edition.

Preface

James Thomas Jones
(Mary Leslie)

In presenting to the public a few pen and ink sketches, thrown together in the form of a story, I can only hope that the reader may have as much pleasure in perusing them as the writer had in moulding them into shape. If this wish is realized, they will not have been published in vain, and will speedily be followed by other sketches, as a sequel to those now before the public.

If my readers take an interest in "The Cromaboo Mail Carrier," they shall renew his acquaintance in a new occupation – as "The Gibbeline Flower Seller."

J. T. J.
Guelph, Ontario, Sept., 1878.

Foreword

Daniel Bratton

David J. Knight is to be commended for bringing to light Mary Leslie's *The Cromaboo Mail Carrier*. With the exception of a facsimile edition recently published in the United States, this most unusual narrative has been out of print since its initial publication in 1878, when it was almost immediately withdrawn from distribution because of a lawsuit by the village of Erin, Ontario. The Canadian literary canon is in fact considerably enriched by the novel's reappearance, for it is arguably one of the earliest examples of literary realism in this country. Indeed, Leslie's work constitutes an important link between Susanna Moodie's *Roughing It in the Bush* (1852) and the "new realism" of the early twentieth century. In particular, it can be seen as a bridge between Moodie's book and Mazo de la Roche's first two published novels, *Possession* (1923) and *Delight* (1926), both of which have also been sadly neglected as notable examples of literary realism in English Canada.

Although Leslie was later touted as the first native-born Canadian female novelist, that distinction would seem to belong to New Brunswick's Julia Catherine Hart, who wrote *St. Ursula's Convent, or The Nun of Canada* in 1824. (Frances Brooke's *The History of Emily Montigue*, published in 1769, was the first Canadian novel, but Brooke was English, being nearly forty years old when she arrived in Quebec.) It has been fashionable since the heady days of Canadian literary nationalism to regard *Roughing It in the Bush* as a novel – or at least a "novelization" of Moodie's experiences in the backwoods of Upper Canada – and while there is certainly merit to such a view, a more salient connection between *Roughing It in the Bush* and Leslie's novel is both authors' experience of the primitive, at times barbarous, conditions of early and mid-nineteenth century rural Ontario. This focus also ties in with de la Roche's early fiction.

Regardless of whether we see _Roughing It in the Bush_ as primarily fictional or autobiographical, Moodie is clearly the protagonist, a role acknowledged by Margaret Atwood in assigning John Dunbar Moodie the part of "shadowy husband" in her _The Journals of Susanna Moodie_. The title of Leslie's novel implies that Robert Hardacre Smith, the Cromaboo mail carrier, occupies centre stage, as does the first of numerous shifts from third to first-person point of view, where the narrator remarks that Robert is "the hero of my story" (3). However, it is the older lady with whom he falls in love, Mary Paxton, who is at the heart of the narrative, for Miss Paxton is clearly the author's literary persona – a connection initially obscured by Leslie's writing under the pseudonym of James Thomas Jones yet reinforced not only by her bestowing her first name upon Miss Paxton but also by the notably intrusive inconsistencies in point of view.[1]

De la Roche's _Delight_ is of particular interest in having its female protagonist, Delight Mainprize, resemble both Moodie and Mary Paxton in finding herself at odds with a rowdy, raw, and unruly community that is completely controlled by men. From the backwoods of Upper Canada to the thinly disguised villages of Erin and Acton in the novels of Leslie and de la Roche, there is little forward social movement from the 1830s to the 1920s within these lawless backwater patriarchies.

Leslie sounds this chord in her opening, arguably the most striking paragraph in the whole novel:

> Cromaboo is the most blackguard village in Canada, and is settled by the lowest class of Irish, Highland Scotch and Dutch. It consists of seven taverns, six churches, and about one hundred shabby frame houses built on little gravelly mounds. Fights are frequent, drunkenness flourishes, vice abounds; more tobacco is smoked there than in any village of the same size in the Dominion; swearing is so common that it passes unnoticed, and there is an illegitimate child in nearly every house – in some two, in others three, in one six, – and the people think it no sin (1).

---

[1]Along similar lines, Leslie makes some curious observations for a supposedly male author. Consider, for example, how the narrator describes Dr. Meldrum's physical appeal to Mary Paxton's mother, who is also Meldrum's mother-in-law: "His healthy manly beauty pleased her, the very calves of his legs were in his favour" (162).

As the 1948 article from the *Fergus News* included in Appendix B observes – Leslie in fact resided in Fergus after living near Erin – this was "pretty hot stuff" for its time. Indeed, it remains a remarkable opening for any Canadian novel.

Still, this is very much the social setting of *Roughing It in the Bush*. Moodie and Leslie come down particularly hard on the Irish, though the Yankees get an equal drubbing in the earlier work. However, except for a few exceptional individuals almost inevitably possessing British origin and Anglo-Saxon virtues, both narratives present a rogues gallery dominated by uncouth, semi-barbarous men. Indeed, Leslie reminds us that the environs of Cromaboo were also primitive backwoods at the time that Robert Hardacre Smith, now in his early twenties, was conceived out of wedlock.

One gathers that conditions in the backwoods of Cromaboo would have resembled those detailed in the chapter on the charivari in *Roughing It in the Bush*. This practice, a French-Canadian custom, we are told, is described by one of Moodie's unpleasant neighbours:

> When an old man marries a young wife, or an old woman a young husband, or two old people, who ought to be thinking of their graves, enter for the second or third time into the holy estate of wedlock, as the priest calls it, all the idle young fellows of the neighbour-hood meet together to charivari them. For this purpose they disguise themselves, blackening their faces, putting their clothes on hind part before, and wearing horrible masks, with grotesque caps on their heads, adorned with cock's feathers and bells (Moodie 1852: 253-4).

She adds that the revelers then surround the house of the new-lyweds, beating on the door and causing general havoc until being admitted for a toast to the bride or receiving a payment to treat them-selves at the nearest tavern. Otherwise, trouble ensues. Moodie's neighbour details several instances of charivaris getting out of hand, including the riding on a rail of an escaped slave from the United States on a cold winter's night, this for his social transgression of marrying an attractive Irishwoman. He died as a result. On another occasion a bridegroom defended himself by shooting the leader of a charivari through the heart, thereafter having to depart for the United States as a marked man.

Mary Leslie, though situating her narrative nearly a quarter of a century after Moodie's historical setting, introduces her readers to a not dissimilar social environment. The narrator observes, "There were two honest men in Cromaboo, Mr. Llewellyn was one, and his neighbour John Smith was the other" (3): these are Robert's employer, who is the postmaster and proprietor of the Cromaboo mail-stage, and Robert's adoptive father. When John Smith approaches Mr. Llewellyn about hiring his son as driver of the stage, the Welshman confesses that, though they are neighbours, he has never really noticed Robert, for "I never do look at a man, woman, or child in Cromaboo, if I can help it" (Ibid). With such statements following on the heels of the opening paragraph, it is not difficult to see why Erin sued to prevent distribution of Leslie's novel.

Her claims, however, strike the reader as drolly hyperbolic. It is the particulars of the plot following Leslie's glib generalizations that most directly link her skewering of Erin with Moodie's damning depiction of life in the bush in eastern Ontario. After establishing a profanity-free coach – at some cost, involving heated altercations with a local Dutchman and well-to-do farmer – Robert Smith finds himself battling the cord-wood carriers on the road to Gibbeline, the fictional counterpart of Guelph, for they deliberately keep his sleigh from passing them. Punch-ups, whippings, and police charges follow, culminating in the poisoning of Robert in a tavern by the conniving group of wood-carriers. He barely manages to escape the fate of the black American in Moodie's narrative, hovering between life and death for several weeks.

Yet all this pales in comparison to a subsequent scene where Robert's coach, in which Miss Paxton is a passenger, is set upon by a group of thugs, one of whom calls out to him, "Now Bob, hand out the woman, and you shall have your turn with her" (26). The reader of Leslie's novel, set in the early 1850s, realizes that this explosive situation involves nothing less than the possibility of a brutal mid-Victorian gang-rape – right in the middle of the southern Ontario countryside! Fortunately, Robert courageously fends off the attackers, but the whole scene hangs in the air long after one has finished this chapter.

By the time we get to de la Roche's *Delight*, which drew upon some actual incidents from early twentieth-century Acton, where Mazo's father ran a hotel, we might expect rural Ontario to have moved on from the conditions described by Leslie and Moodie. Not really. The novel climaxes with an attack upon the heroine, newly arrived from England, by a vicious horde of local women, jealous of her good looks and natural sexuality. Readers might very well see this as a variant on the charivari, for de la Roche employs strikingly similar imagery in presenting this attack. When Delight is lured to a copse adjoining a lagoon (a landscape corresponding to Acton's Fairy Lake), she is met by the demented housekeeper of one of the local hotels, who has organized an all-female mob that mirrors the masculine violence of Moodie's and Leslie's narratives:

> The housekeeper glared at her and again uttered that strange deep whistle which came from her course lips like a spring of sweet water from rough clay... At the note every tree and shrub and clump of spiny undergrowth seemed to come alive. In every place that a woman could hide, there was a woman hidden. Like birds of prey, with skirts that flapped like flapping wings, uttering cries of rage and exultation they swooped forth.
>
> The sun had set. The bright space where the two stood became dusk as the other women gathered around them. For one instant Delight had seen their faces, transfigured by the last fiery glow, into strange burning masks, more like metal than flesh, with jewels for eyes. Now, as the shadows fell, she only saw them surging around her, blurred menacing darker shadows from the shadow (de la Roche 1926: 213).

Delight is spat upon, dealt vicious blows, and submerged in the water, until finally being rescued by the local men, who in this instance demonstrate civil virtue. Had de la Roche not so skillfully disguised the Acton setting – after her success with Jalna, she wrote its tanneries and rough itinerant labourers out of her life story – perhaps Acton would have legally pursued her the way Erin did Leslie! Indeed, when I visited Acton while working on a biography of de la Roche back in the early 1990s, some of the women in the old folks home by Fairy Lake had particularly cruel things to say about little Massie Roach, remarking what an odd girl she had been, hanging around corner stores reading books and exhibiting other aberrant behaviour, such as walking bare-foot on the newly-paved street. (Interestingly, David J. Knight has suggested that one of the settings in *The Cromaboo Mail Carrier*, the town of Bezar, might be based on Acton.)

Canadians of our own time tend toward self-congratulation concerning a perceived national politeness and civility, but these three books suggest that this attribute was not always in evidence. Even in my home village of Elora, just five minutes down the road from Fergus, where Leslie lived for a while on Tower Street, people remember a not-too-distant past when now artsy-fartsy Mill Street was a rough no-go zone for children, and some old-timers maintain that there was in fact far more violence at that time than there is today.

However, Leslie's presentation of this dark side of our collective mythology is to some degree mitigated by a spirit of satire that seems to belong to the eighteenth and early nineteenth centuries. Her gentle sense of irony ties her more to Jane Austen than Susanna Moodie, who while certainly capable of drollery, tends more toward Victorian earnestness, to say nothing of class snobbery. After all, upon leaving the bush, Moodie assumed a position of respectability as the sheriff's wife in Belleville, later spending evenings attending seances. Ditto for Mazo, who assumed a life of gentility after the success of *Jalna* in 1927, its fifteen sequels demonstrating an increasing devotion to United Empire Loyalism.

On the other hand, David J. Knight has told me that, during a subsequent residency in London, England, Mary Leslie not only demonstrated an interest in younger men but also indulged in the bottle. One cannot imagine Moodie or de la Roche enjoying a boy toy or good swig of gin at the local pub, signifiers of Leslie's choosing to live on the margins. She clearly possessed an "ex-centricity", to use Linda Hutcheon's term, that manifests itself in her tone – I know of no other voice in the Canadian literary canon quite like Mary Leslie's. One might go so far as to argue that, in addition to her startling shifts in point of view and use of romantic irony (a consistent undercutting of verisimilitude through authorial intervention), Leslie's cynical detachment from mainstream society makes this novel a prime candidate for postmodern revival. Certainly Mary Paxton's decision at the end of *The Cromaboo Mail Carrier* to open a garden nursery and have young Robert Smith move into her house, without any chaperone, is just one example of Leslie's endorsement of progressive social non-compliance.

Still, Leslie spent her final years in Toronto's posh Forest Hill, not far from where Mazo de la Roche finally settled. Her ex-centrism seems to have been more a rejection of narrow-minded provincialism and hypocritical assumptions of piety (masking the drunkenness, lechery, crudity, and violence alluded to in the opening paragraph of her novel) than an expression of social marginality. Indeed, the elegance and refinement of the authorial voice foreground what is perhaps most notable in *The Cromaboo Mail Carrier*, the way it bridges the eighteenth and nineteenth-century English novel of manners to early twentieth-century Canadian literary realism. As already suggested, Leslie's voice is much closer to Jane Austen's than to her Canadian literary predecessors or contemporaries, for she displays a sharp-edged wit and keen sense of irony unrivaled by any Canadian novelist of that time. On the other hand, her linking of human behaviour to social environment, frank treatment of human sexuality, and penetration into the hidden motivations that lie beneath the veneer of social convention establish her literary kinship with a whole school of twentieth-century Canadian writers: in his introduction to de la Roche's early short stories, Douglas Daymond identified Martha Ostenso, Robert Stead, Frederick Philip Grove, Raymond Knister, and Morley Callaghan as contributing, with de la Roche, to the development of realism.[2]

One should further mention that *The Cromaboo Mail Carrier* also reaches back to the sentimental novel of the latter part of the eighteenth century. Ironically and rather subversively, here the man of exquisite feeling, personal distresses, and over-reaching sorrow is Robert's biological father, Sir Robert Hardacre – who also happens to be a pedophile: "He was by nature a kisser and a very affectionate man, with all his faults; fond of young things, whether animals, birds or children; but especially of half-grown lad and lassies."[3] Lest it be argued that this is reading all sorts of twenty-first century post-Freudian implications into an innocent enough passage, one should emphasize that Sir Robert's love of half-grown lassies allowed him to seduce Robert's sexually naive fourteen-year-old mother, Nelly Connel. Upon finally meeting his son, now in his early twenties, he tells our hero:

> She was just a dear, innocent, ignorant child when I led her astray, feeling no fear in me, and not knowing why she blushed when I kissed her... Those dear, wild slips of Irish lasses are more really

---

[2] See *Selected Stories of Mazo de la Roche*. Ed. Douglas Daymond. (Ottawa: University of Ottawa Press, 1979), p. 16.

[3] *The Cromaboo Mail Carrier*, p. 174. Here we find a striking correspondence between Leslie's novel and Mazo's first realistic work of fiction, *Possession*, where the hero, Derek Vale, seduces Fawnie, an innocent young First Nations girl the same age as Robert Smith's mother, and is subsequently subject to a charivari. Of him the narrator observes, "He liked children, especially dark-eyed little girls" (de la Roche 1923: 51).

innocent and ignorant of evil than the children of any other nation
under heaven (199).

Of course Sir Robert, in the tradition of the reformed rake of sentimental fiction, now indulges in exquisite remorse at his defilement
of this innocent girl, but I wonder if I'm the only reader who feels
somewhat uneasy at the way he now revels in kissing his son fully
on the lips: "Robert, do you know I've been resisting a strong impulse within me ever since I saw you?... I have wanted to give you a
kiss." And then, "Do I tire you my son, do you wish my hands away?"
(196).

This is another way in which Mary Leslie seems so unabashedly
ex-centric, so completely disconnected from the pieties of her time.
Her caustic dismissal of her Erin neighbours in the opening paragraph seems curiously at odds with her eagerness to understand the
motivations of this aristocratic pedophile:

> A great admirer of beauty of any kind, and prone to express his af
> fection, without any restraint, by free caresses with his plump white
> fingers, or tender pressures of his full red lips, the very man to spoil
> a son or dear daughter by over much petting. A hearty rebuff, a
> sound box on the ear, would have been the greatest benefit to him in
> his youth, but unfortunately for himself and for others, he was too
> charming to receive any such check, and his attentions were all too
> acceptable (174-175).

Of course Sir Robert's affections are anything but acceptable to a
contemporary reader, who likely thinks he should have been horsewhipped or incarcerated for seducing Robert's innocent girl-mother.
Yet Leslie's ambivalent treatment of him as a character does not, I
would argue, detract from the novel; indeed, it contributes to the
complexity of the personality behind the shifting points of view, the
woman writing as a man, the woman who so clearly did not belong
in the narrow worlds of Erin and Fergus, Ontario. Here we return
to Mary Leslie's *voice*. What an intriguing woman she must have
been, with her barely muted sexual longings and clever subversions
of literary and social conventions.

To return to my Mazo biography: when I inquired of Timothy
Findley, who had been involved in the CBC television series *The
Whiteoaks of Jalna*, about de la Roche's place in the literary canon,
he made the following observation: "The way to discover if someone

has a place in a body of literature is to remove them. And if you take Mazo de la Roche out of the body of literature, the body of literature suffers." In Mary Leslie's case – with the exception of a few historical works she wrote along the lines of the twelve-volume *Lives of the Queens of England* penned by Susanna Moodie's sister Agnes Strickland – the author was immediately denied entry to the body of literature.

This is what makes it so wonderful that David J. Knight has chosen to give *The Cromaboo Mail Carrier* the life it never had. Few would contend that it belongs to the highest order of Canadian literature, but it is an important work both in its own right and also for how it connects to what came before and after it. Mary Leslie's distinctive voice – witty, ironic, and wickedly satiric – had been lost to us, and now it has been found! One can't imagine removing somebody from the body of literature who wasn't allowed into it in the first place, but now that *The Cromaboo Mail Carrier* is back in print, it has a chance to find its rightful place in Canadian literature. This is what Mary Leslie most assuredly deserved the first time around.

Daniel Bratton, Ph.D.
Elora, Ontario

Works Cited

De la Roche, Mazo. *Delight.* New York: Macmillan, 1926.

— *Possession.* Toronto: Macmillan of Canada, 1923.

— *Selected Stories of Mazo de la Roche.* Ed. Douglas Daymond. Ottawa: University of Ottawa Press, 1979.

Findley, Timothy. Personal interview. 21 July 1994.

Moodie, Susanna. *Roughing It in the Bush.* 1852; 1913. Toronto: Coles, 1980.

Introduction

David J. Knight

Mary Leslie (8 January, 1842 – 1 March, 1920)
Pseudonym: James Thomas Jones

I have lived with this novel and researched the details of Mary Leslie's life since 2013. I have never known a book that fictionalizes Guelph and our surrounding area, and provides a fascinating glimpse into former customs and the heritage of the built and lived environment. I thank Mary Leslie, an extraordinary woman and writer, for her offering to us.

As a child, whenever I found myself in a car or a truck or on my bicycle travelling down that little valley on Eramosa Road, just past Speedvale going East, and where it crosses wetland of what my friend Sona Mincoff and I call the "Slow River" (which eventually, lazily, joins the Speed River just West of Victoria Road), I always look to my right and there can be seen a low-lying bridge amidst the reeds and swamp grass. I now understand the importance of that little structure. It is the remaining evidence of the original course of Eramosa Road (at this point now Highway 124). I think of it as the "Cromaboo Bridge," or the "Gibbeline Bridge" as Leslie knew it, a place where the mail carriage crossed on its way to Guelph. I hope that little bridge is celebrated for the memory it holds of this Leslie novel.

While spending time with *The Cromaboo Mail Carrier* I delved into many aspects of Mary Leslie's life. With Daniel Bratton I have stood by her grave and understood her significance as a writer. When so much heritage is simply being erased in Wellington County, it is, I firmly believe, something of a miracle to encounter this novel. The following are a series of insights I have gathered from these researches.

While details of Mary Leslie's life story have been touched on by Greta Golick in her dissertation on *Frank Nunan and the Guelph Bookbindery* (2000) and Barb Mitchell's essay *Mary Leslie's Erin* (1994), the bulk of Mary Leslie's private papers reside at the Archives of Ontario.[4] An 1890 letter by her is also in the Guelph Civic Museum collection (Catalog Number: 1980.80.5.3). A comprehensive *Life of Mary Leslie* will, I hope, be the subject of some future publication.

Golick has pointed out that Leslie's attempts to establish herself as a writer met with "little support from her family, her local community, and the wider literary marketplace" (Golick 2000:123). Nevertheless, by 1937 in Guelph, Mary Leslie was touted by Guelph's local press as Canada's first female author of fiction.[5] In fact, Julia Catherine Beckwith Hart (1796-1867) is credited with that distinction, as she was born in Lower Canada at Fredericton in 1796 and published her first novel, *St. Ursula's Convent*, in 1824. However, since Mary Leslie was born in Eramosa Township, she can be considered an important early Upper Canada fiction writer, and her 1878 novel *The Cromaboo Mail Carrier* an important early fictional work by a Canadian female novelist.

Significance of Cromaboo

In *The Cromaboo Mail Carrier*, Mary Leslie provides the reader with tantalizing glimpses of urban and rural life in southwestern Ontario, in Guelph, Erin and Hamilton during the late 1860s. The main action is set in Erin (fictionalized as 'Cromaboo'), Guelph ('Gibbeline') and Hamilton. There is evidence[6] that Leslie may have started writing her novel in late 1867 or early 1868, shortly after her twenty-sixth birthday. These dates are also when she was visiting relatives in England and studying art in Amsterdam from 1867 to 1868. Therefore, the

---

[4] Mary Leslie fonds, F675, Archives of Ontario, Toronto.

[5] *Guelph Daily Mercury*; 29 October, 1937; cited in full in my Introduction of *Guelph Versifiers of the 19th Century* (Vocamus Editions, 2014:x-xi, and page 161).

[6] In a letter from Mary Leslie to her father, John T. Leslie, dated 12 January 1868 (F675, MU1715, file 6), she says "...I am trying to write a story," suggested by Golick (2000:123-8) to be *The Cromaboo Mail Carrier*.

initial draft for Cromaboo may have been written in Holland, but certainly continued at the Leslie homestead near Guelph upon her return later that year.

It can be calculated from various details in the novel that the story is also set in 1868, the year following Confederation. Even though the heroine of *The Cromaboo Mail Carrier*, Miss Mary Paxton, turns thirty-two in Chapter 3, thus older than Leslie, the work reads as a thinly veiled autobiography. The fascinating back-story Leslie provides the oldest character in the novel, Mary Paxton's aunt Mrs. Marshall, extends back to the early 1830s, before a church was yet built in Guelph. The earliest church in Guelph, St. Andrew's, was organized in 1831. In Chapter 36, Mrs. Marshall is said to have left England from Portsmouth at a time when "Scott was still alive and writing," and therefore before the Scottish novelist Sir Walter Scott's death on 21 September, 1832.

In Chapter 25 Mr. Hardacre recollects Ralph Oliver (the past fiancé of Mary Paxton), who "was the engineer of the first railway that passed through Gibbeline." The first train, carrying some of the Grand Trunk Directors and contractors from Toronto to Guelph, arrived in Guelph on Tuesday, June 10 of 1856. The main male character Robert Hardacre Smith is said to have been six years old at this time, and therefore born in 1850. In Chapter 24, Leslie has Mary Paxton fourteen years older than Robert Hardacre Smith, and therefore sets Mary's birth in 1836 and her thirty-second birthday in 1868. In Chapter 35, Dr. Meldrum says that he hears "there is to be a regiment quartered in Gibbeline." The Guelph Garrison Battery was organized as No. 1 Company of the 30th Wellington Battalion of Rifles in 1866. In 1871 this was made an independent unit and renamed the Wellington Field Battery of Artillery. Therefore, the scope of memory within the novel spans from the early 1830s to the late 1860s.

Leslie's choice of the name "Cromaboo" refers to the historic Croom Castle (also known as Castle of Crom) in Croom, County Limerick, Republic of Ireland. It was a fortress on a bend of the River Maigue (Irish: *Cromadh* = "Bend in the River") belonging to the O'Donovans and then, later, a principal residence of the Kildare branch of the Fitzgerald dynasty. The ancient war cry and motto "Crom a Boo" (Irish: *Crom Abu* = "Crom forever!") comes from this strategic fortress, and it is the motto of the Fitzgerald family. Leslie's choice of applying this name to the village of Erin, "Éirinn" being the dative case of the Irish word for Ireland, emphasizes the Irish roots of the Ontario settlement, although it is now mainly thought of as a predominantly Scottish enclave.

By assigning the name Gibbeline to Guelph, Leslie reveals her knowledge of the historical circumstance of the White Guelphs who provided protection to Dante while he was in exile at Ravenna. I have explored the same connection that may also have played a part in John Galt's choice of naming the new 1827 settlement Guelph in relation to his friendship with Lord Byron and that poet's reverence of Dante (see my Introduction to *Guelph Versifiers of the 19ᵗʰ Century*; Vocamus Editions 2014). The Guelph and Ghibelline factions in 12th century Italy supported the Pope and the Holy Roman Emperor respectively. By renaming Guelph as Gibbeline, Leslie anachronistically reverses the historic allegiance.

Leslie also seems to have given Acton the fictional name of "Bezar" (Chapter 24), perhaps an alternate spelling of *bezoar* (Persian for "antidote"), a mass of organic or inorganic matter trapped in the gastrointestinal system. Bezoar stones were collected because they were believed to be antidotes against any poison.

Aside from these place-name changes, she leaves intact and mentions several other Ontario locations: Hamilton, Mount Forest, Waterdown, Chippawa, Ostrander, the Credit Valley, and Eramosa Road. Several businesses are named, such as Murray's, a clothier in Hamilton. A number of hotels, inns and taverns are also named, including The Ocean House Hotel (Hamilton) which was built in 1874, expanded in 1876 and destroyed by fire in 1895. In Cromaboo/Erin the Harp of Erin tavern and The Royal Anglo-American Hotel are named, as is Mack's Tavern in Bezar/Acton, and Murphy's Inn, The Royal Hotel, Thompson's Inn, and The Great Western Hotel in Gibbeline/Guelph.

Original Reception of *Cromaboo*

Shortly after Joseph Hacking printed *The Cromaboo Mail Carrier* in Guelph in 1878, Erin town council apparently sued Mary Leslie and the book was pulled from circulation. Before this proscriptive decision, and luckily for us, the novel was bound in an edition of a hundred copies by F.T. Chapman at the Guelph Bookbindery and sent not only to friends and family members, but also to Canadian, American and British publishers. These included Smith, Elder & Company of London,[7] who, although unwilling to take a chance on a one-volume novel, replied by letter (5 December 1878) praising its "considerable power as well as literary ability," but agreed with the assessment of "friends" that it was "in parts, a little too outspoken" (Golick 2000:123-8, Note 471). The whereabouts of the various copies of Cromaboo that Leslie sent to London, New York, and other "Canadian towns" (Ibid.) is not certain. However, luckily, a few copies do survive, and the University of Guelph and the Guelph Public Library each have an original.

The Gibbeline Flower Seller

Mary Leslie promises in her Preface to *The Cromaboo Mail Carrier* that a sequel will appear shortly. This novel, *The Gibbeline Flower Seller*, was never published, although as Golick notes (2000: Notes 472 and 473), a proof sheet for a second volume of *Cromaboo* survives (F675, MU1711, Box 1) as well as Leslie's editorial corrections to random printed pages of the second novel (F675, MU1719, file 3). Beyond these items, Leslie appears to have abandoned the project.

Mary Leslie's Life

The 1901 Canada Census return tells us that Mary Leslie was born in Ontario on the 8th of January, 1842. However, the 1911 census says she was born in Ontario in July of 1842. Her death certificate states she was born at Leslie's Corners, Eramosa Township, in 1841, and that she was 79 years old when she died 1 March, 1920. She is buried near relatives at the Stone United Church Cemetery on Concession Road 4, Lot 13 (Eramosa Township), in the same plot as her sister Elizabeth Clarke (1840–1917). The unassuming grave marker has Mary's dates as 1841 to 1921. My preference is for the more detailed 1901 census. The information on Mary's death certificate was provided by her young nephew, Baptist La Johnston, detailing events before his own lifetime. Likewise, the grave marker appears to be a later addition; the 1984 transcription of this grave (Plot 22)[8] in this ceme-

---

[7]Smith, Elder & Co. began publishing in 1839. Beginning in 1841, they published *The London and Edinburgh Magazine*. Beginning in 1859, they published *Cornhill Magazine*. In 1847 they published Charlotte Brontë's *Jane Eyre*.

[8]Transcription by L.L., J.L., and T.J. French published by Waterloo Wellington

tery has Elizabeth Clarke but no mention of her sister Mary Leslie as seen at present; therefore, the present stone seems to have been a replacement after 1984.

Mary Leslie was the youngest daughter of John Thomas Leslie (1795–8 October, 1871) and Elizabeth (1801–1885). Elizabeth had been married to Thomas Griffin and by this union they had a daughter, Ruth Griffin (14 March, 1822–27 July, 1906), born in Shoreditch, London, England. Mr. Griffin died some time in the late 1820s.

Elizabeth Griffin was remarried to John Thomas Leslie in London. John grew up in London and entered into an engraving business partnership after 1817 as an engraver with Thomas Trimlet, variously spelled Trimlet / Tremlett / Trimblet. On the 6th of October, 1819, one James Russell, 19 years old, was indicted for stealing engraved knives and forks from the property of Thomas Tremlett and John Thomas Leslie. This case of grand larceny was heard at the Old Bailey Central Criminal Court in London on the 27th of October of that year (Reference Number: t18191027-88). John Thomas Leslie attended the proceedings and stated: "I am an engraver, in partnership with Thomas Tremlett; we live at No. 15, Oxendon-street, Leicester-square." Two apprentices and a servant of Leslie's also gave statements. Their names were William Brooks, John Walker, and Ann Beach. James Russell was found guilty and "transported for Seven Years."

In *Kent's Original London Directory* of 1823 Trimlet & Leslie are listed as engraver and printer, still at 15 Oxenden Street, Haymarket, London. An engraving of a heraldic shield of the Percy family dates to 1830 (Upcott *et al.* 1852:262) and was "engraved by J. Leslie, 15 Oxendon (*sic*) Street, Haymarket," printed by William Nicol, Shakespeare Press (Nichols 1866:267-268). The business partnership between John Thomas Leslie and Thomas Trimlet ended, and by 1842 *Robson's London Directory* lists Trimblet and Pemberton as engravers at 15 Oxendon Street (page 838).

In 1837 John Thomas Leslie and his wife Elizabeth, with her daughter Ruth Griffin, came to Canada. The homestead was located on Highway 24 (now 124) at the corner of Sideroad #7 and known as Leslie's Corners. This is now called Centre Inn. On 19 July 1838,

Branch of the Ontario Genealogical Society (Kitchener 1985), accessed at the Guelph Public Library in July 2015.

Ruth married George Sockett (1811–1860), and they resided in Er-amosa township. George Sockett was born at North Chapel, in the county of West Sussex, England (near Godalming). His father was Rev. Thomas Sockett, the Anglican Rector of Petworth who was a driving force of the important Petworth Emigration Scheme for Lord Wyndham, which sent around 1800 working-class people from the south of England to Upper Canada between 1832 and 1837. Ruth Sockett eventually lived in Guelph at Dublin Street, where she died 27 July, 1906.[9] A daughter married Robert Johnston of Guelph, and it is their son Baptist La Johnston who took care of Mary Leslie in her final days at his Toronto address of 271 Russell Hill Road.

Mary Leslie's older sister was Elizabeth Leslie, who was married to Charles Anthony Clarke. Charles "fought in the American Civil War, and returned to Soldier's Home in Washington DC in 1896" (Golick 2000: Note 479). He died "At the residence of his sister-in-law, Miss Leslie, Eramosa Road, on 7th October [1897], son of the late Commisary (*sic*) General Clarke" (*Guelph Daily Mercury* 8 October 1897). In 1911 Mary and her widowed sister Elizabeth were lodging in Rockwood at 148 Main Street.

Joseph Henry Hacking (1837 – 18 April 1895)

The working relationship between Mary Leslie and the Guelph printer Joseph Hacking is worth exploring in some detail. J.H. Hacking was the son of the pioneers William H. Hacking (born 1810, York-shire) and Margaret Tracey (born 1816, Irish). The Hacking family emigrated to Canada and settled in Whitchurch, County of York. They left Whitchurch and lived for five years in Guelph, between 1850 and 1855. William opened a pioneer store and was appointed as Guelph's first postmaster. Later, his son Joseph may have provided information and details of his father's postmaster role for Leslie's novel.

Joseph had an illustrious career in Canadian newspapers and printing industry. He was co-founder (with Thomas E. Hay) in 1866 of the *Listowel Banner*, and proprietor of that newspaper from 1866 to c.1872. Then he ran *The Guelph Weekly Advertiser* newspaper in

---

[9]Ruth Sockett's obituary in *The Guelph Daily Mercury* (28 July 1906) is incorrectly titled "Mrs. Robt. Sockett" while correctly referring to her husband Mr. George Sockett.

1873, in that year printing the *Directory of the Town of Guelph*. Hacking's Excelsior Printing House, Guelph (1874-1878) is described in an ad in the 1875/6/7 *Guelph Directory* as "First Prize winner at the Guelph Central Exhibition in 1874 and 1875 for the best specimens of ornamental and letterpress work." Hacking also founded the *Acton Free Press*, the first issue appearing 1 July 1875. He remained the proprietor of this paper from 1875 to 1878. He then founded *The Clifford Arrow* in 1878 and was proprietor from 1878 to c.1881. It was in this newspaper that Hacking printed the serial stories of Mary Leslie (writing as James T. Jones); *David Jones's Locker* (1879) and *Absolutely Her Own Mistress* (1881).

The Fortunes of Mary Leslie

It is difficult to substantiate any certain connection, but it is interesting to note that a serial story by "Mrs. Vincent Novello" was published in *Guelph's TriWeekly Advertiser* newspaper in 1854 entitled, "The Fortunes of Mary Leslie; A Tale of the Last War." This was previously printed in *The People's Journal* (Volume 1) in 1846. The renowned English musician Vincent Novello (1781-1861) married Mary Sabilla Hehl (c.1787-1854), and the 1854 inclusion of her story in the Guelph newspaper was presumably printed in remembrance of her, immediately following her death. They and their ten children enjoyed a London social circle that included the writers, musicians and artists of the day, including Charles and Mary Lamb, Leigh Hunt, John Keats, and Shelley. Perhaps Mrs Novello's Mary Leslie is a play on Mary Shelley's name. However this may be, and if Mary Leslie's family subscribed to the Guelph newspaper referred to above, when she was twelve or thirteen years old, it could be conjectured as an early influential inspiration to the young future novelist seeing her own name in a fiction title.

David J. Knight
Editor-in-Chief of Vocamus Editions
Guelph, Ontario

The Works of Mary Leslie as James Thomas Jones

The Cromaboo Mail Carrier. Guelph: Joseph Hacking, 1878.

The Gibbeline Flower Seller. Unpublished, c.1878/9.

"David Jones's Locker." Serial. *The Clifford Arrow* (1879); *The County of Wellington Gazetteer and Directory* (1879): 97.

"Absolutely Her Own Mistress." Serial. *The Clifford Arrow* (1881).

The Tobacco Box: A Christmas Story for Young Saints and Old Sinners. Epic poem. Unpublished, 1915.

The Works of Mary Leslie under her own name

Rhymes of the Kings and Queens of England. Unpublished, 1896.

Historical Sketches of Scotland, with an Account of Forty-eight of the Highlands Clans. Unpublished, 1905.

Works Cited

Golick, Greta Petronella. *Frank Nunan and the Guelph Bookbindery: A Documentary Investigation.* Dissertation. Toronto: University of Toronto, 2000.

Mitchell, Barb. "Mary Leslie's Erin: 'The Most Blackguard Village in Canada'." *Wellington County History* Volume 7. Wellington County Historical Society, 1994. Pp. 34-47.

Nichols, John Gough. *The Herald and Genealogist.* Volume 3. Nichols, 1866.

Upcott, William, Brayley, Edward William, and Thomson, Richard. *A Catalogue of the Library of the London Institution: The General Library. Additions from 1843-1852. An Index of Subjects. An Index of Authors and Books.* Catalogs. London: London Institution Library, 1852.

Appendix A

Article in the Fergus News Record
30 December, 1948.

"Think It Was Erin That Novelist Libelled"[10]

Mention has been made on this page of what is probably the first novel written in and about Wellington county. It has the strange title, "The Cromaboo Mail Carrier" and the book is rare and brings a high price – much more than a modern novel would. But the most amazing thing about this old book is the terrible picture it paints of the "Village of Cromaboo."

The location of Cromaboo has puzzled all who have been studying the book lately. Our own opinion was that the village was Erin and the Cromaboo stage was driven from Guelph to Erin. Others have reached the same conclusion. Frank Day of Rockwood, who knows Eramosa township and its history as well as anyone, finds many references to confirm this opinion. Some of these have been already mentioned on this page. He adds others. He says, "the big hill on the 3rd and the inns in Eramosa all seem to be described. The swamp attach tallies in time and distance with the 6th line swamp in Erin." Even the location of the farm of a German family in Erin is fairly accurate and only one letter in the family name was changed in the novel, which was withdrawn from circulation because it was considered libellous.

Mr. Day has the following to say about the suppression of the book: It would be interesting to know which families were responsible for suppressing the book, for there appears to be no reason for

---

[10] This newspaper clipping is appended to the scanned novel by the University of Alberta Libraries at Internet Archive.

shame in being a descendent (*sic*) of any of the characters. Most angels have a black feather in one wing and many of us would find in our family trees that some ancestor was hanged for sheep stealing.

Appendix B

Article in the Fergus News Record
30 December, 1948.

"An Old Novel"[11]

One of the pleasures of the Christmas season was the opportunity to read a novel, written seventy years ago about people and places in Wellington county by a writer who spent her later years in Fergus. The name of the novel is a rather strange one, "The Cromaboo Mail Carrier," and we never knew that such a book existed. This page has often dealt with books about Wellington county, and we thought we had heard of most of them. There are few novels in the lot. Fred Jacob wrote two novels, based on life in Elora in his youth. "Yon Toon o' Mine," written about Fergus by James Black Perry, was almost a novel but could more truly be classed as a series of sketches of his native town. The other works were mostly poetry, or history, or sketches, or short stories, or even books of sermons and family trees.

This book was brought to our attention by the King's Printer in Toronto, Baptist Johnston, who loaned us a copy of the book and sent the following explanation:

> I am forwarding to you, under separate cover, a copy of "The Cromaboo Mail Carrier," written by my great-aunt, Mary Leslie, in the 70's, under the nom de plume of James Thomas Jones. It relates chiefly to the Guelph district and Hamilton. Some of the characters were so thinly disguised that my Aunt was threatened with a law-suit for damages, and on that account the book was withdrawn from circulation. Her old house, I believe, still stands. It is on the Eramosa Road,

---

[11]This newspaper clipping is appended to the scanned novel by the University of Alberta Libraries at Internet Archive.

three miles north-east of Guelph. She died at our house on Russell
Hill Road, Toronto, about 1921.

That sounded interesting and the book lived up to advance no-
tices. Miss Leslie lived in Fergus in our youth, we think on Tower
street, near the bridge. We knew her as the author of two books, one
about the Kings and Queens of Scotland, the other on English history, with prose and verse and illustrations, and nicely bound. Miss
Leslie used to sell these herself and nowadays they are considered of
some value, because they are scarce. We did not suspect that Miss
Leslie had once written a novel that was libellous and to which she
would not attach her own name.

Mr. Johnston says that Miss Leslie disguised her characters rather
thinly. We can quite believe it. Mary Paxton, heroine of the story, is
probably Mary Leslie herself. If so, she must have had some angry
relatives, including the doctor and a minister or two. The hero is
the driver of the mail stage from Gibbeline to Cromaboo. We would
not know about the characters, for the book was printed in Guelph
in 1878, which was 70 years ago, but the names of the places are
easy to guess. Gibbeline is Guelph, of course. (The Guelphs and the
Gibbelines were warring families in Italy long ago.) The Gibbeline
Stage Road is undoubtedly the Eramosa Road from Guelph to Erin.
Overton would be Everton.[12] But Cromaboo eluded us for a while.
The name itself meant nothing but the evidence soon piles up. It
was on the Eramosa road, 20 miles from Guelph, on the Credit Valley
Railway. Its chief tavern was "The Harp of Erin." The doctor lived
on an island in the river. A high gravel hill rose beside the village –
and so on. It must be Erin, as it was 80 years ago. But listen to the
opening paragraph of the first chapter of the book:

> Cromaboo is the most blackguard village in Canada, and is settled
> by the lowest class of Irish, Highland Scotch and Dutch. It consists
> of seven taverns, six churches, and about one hundred shabby frame
> houses built on little gravelly mounds. Fights are frequent, drunken-
> ness flourishes, vice abounds: more tobacco is smoked there than in
> any village of the same size in the Dominion; swearing is so common
> that it passes unnoticed, and there is an illegitimate child in nearly
> every house – in some two, in others three, in one six – and the peo-
> ple think it no sin. Yet, even in this Sodom, there was at the time of
> which I write, a Lot.

---

[12]Overton is not mentioned in the novel.

That's pretty hot stuff. We couldn't believe that Erin was ever like that. Later, the writer changes the picture a bit. The number of taverns is cut to two; churches to two or three and a few, very few, decent characters emerge.

The novel interested us greatly. It follows the old pattern of the time, when a great deal of class distinction survived in Canada. In those novels, at least, the illegitimate son of a titled man was superior to an honest workman. The servant could not sit at the same table as his master. Children of ten or twelve became servant girls. No decent young lady went out with a man unless she was chaperoned – and so on.

The old novel is not expertly done, by modern standards. It contradicts itself in spots. It has extra characters that clutter it up with their stories. The story does not end, either happily or unhappily, and is not complete. Obviously Miss Leslie planned a sequel, and she says that in the introduction. Perhaps the hot reception her first novel received discouraged her, and made her turn to history afterwards, or perhaps she wrote it and never had it printed. Anyway, this adds an interesting chapter to the literary history of Wellington county.

The Cromaboo Mail Carrier

A Canadian Love Story

by

Mary Leslie

(writing as James Thomas Jones)

1878

"The theme is old, even as the flowers are old
    That sweetly showed
Their silver bosses and bright budding gold
    From Eden's sod,
And still peep forth through grass and garden mould
    As fresh from God.

Worldling, deride it not, for it is well
    Even for thee
That in this world some heavenly things do dwell.
    All may not see
Day's regal beams, but even the blind can tell
    How sweet they be."

               – Merrick[13]

---

[13] These verses are ascribed to James Merrick (1720-1769), but are actually by James Hedderwick (1814-1897); "New Verses On An Old Theme."

Chapter One

"This boy is forest-born."
– *As You Like It*[14]

"Firm his step as one who knows
He is free where'ere he goes;
And withal as light of spring,
As the arrow from its string."
– Lord Houghton[15]

CROMABOO is the most blackguard village in Canada, and is settled by the lowest class of Irish, Highland Scotch and Dutch. It consists of seven taverns, six churches, and about one hundred shabby frame houses built on little gravelly mounds. Fights are frequent, drunkenness flourishes, vice abounds; more tobacco is smoked there than in any village of the same size in the Dominion; swearing is so common that it passes unnoticed, and there is an illegitimate child in nearly every house – in some two, in others three, in one six, – and the people think it no sin.

Yet, even in this Sodom, there was at the time of which I write, a Lot. He was a Welshman by birth, a gentleman by station, an honest man, a learned man, a Christian; his name was Owen Llewellyn. He was the village postmaster and the proprietor of the Cromaboo mail-stage. A man of long pedigree, and great class-prejudice, yet a

---

[14]William Shakespeare, *As You Like It*: Act 5, Scene 4.

[15]Richard Monckton Milnes, Lord Houghton, "Flight of Youth" (1833). Leslie's 1878 edition incorrectly has "Lord Haughton."

kindly man, large-hearted, clear-headed, fearless as a lion and obstinate as a jackass. He had lived in Cromaboo for six years before he became the proprietor of the mail-stage; he came as engineer for the new Government Gravel Road, and had not served the contractors a month before they quarreled with him. The Board met in Toronto and their engineer met them by appointment, and they told him his sins. He took too much pains, they said; he did his work too well; they feared to lose by the contract; they only wanted a road that would last twenty years or so, he was making one that would last a hundred; they could not legally break their contract with him, but if he persisted in going on as he had begun they would never employ him again.

"If you were so foolish," said he, "as to take the contract too low, and are so dishonest as to wish me to slight my work that you may gain by it, that is your affair; I, at least, am an honest man, and to my own Master I stand or fall; I shall do my duty whether you employ me again or not."

He kept his word, and they kept theirs; the main line through the Township of Cromaboo is the best gravel road in Canada, and the engineer was never employed again; but a friend in the Government bestowed the Cromaboo post office upon him, and he bought a piece of ground on the outskirts of the village, and built a house and lived in it in spite of the wishes of the inhabitants. Finding the profits of the post office too small to live upon, he started a small general store and throve in it a little to his own astonishment, for the people of Cromaboo disliked him and he disliked them, but with this difference, they respected him, whereas he despised them utterly. There was no quarter between them, they annoyed him continually and he annoyed them; he told them their sins when they came for their newspapers and tobacco, and they in return gave him impudence and oaths; he hated their ways and they hated his; they threatened to destroy his property, but feared to carry out the threat; he threatened them with the law and the judgment of God if they didn't mend their ways.

Mr. Llewellyn was a married man, and his wife was insane; she hadn't one bee in her bonnet, but a whole swarm; a hundred vague suspicions and foolish fancies haunted her daily, and though not dangerous, she was very troublesome. Many a man would have placed her in a lunatic asylum, but Mr. Llewellyn never shirked a duty; he had taken her for better or worse till death parted them, and though it was a bitter bargain, he stood to it like an honest man, and never once ever thought of getting rid of her.

He had a niece who kept house for him and helped take care of his wife – a dark, bright, plain little girl, brown as a Brazilian nut, quick as a flash of lightning. As obstinate and fearless as her uncle, she was more courteous, and therefore more popular, especially with the men. Good temper is infectious, and innate refinement will tell upon the most uncouth nature. A woman can lay down the law with less offence than a man, and make harsh truths more palatable; her smiles soften her words, and occasionally contradict them. Mr. Llewellyn's custom was partly due to his niece, partly to the fact that he gave twelve months' credit.

Ah! times are changed. Now the great Credit Valley Railway passes through Cromaboo, but at the period of which I write such a thing was not dreamt of; a rough uncovered wagon ran between that village and the great town of Gibbeline[16] and was called the Cromaboo Royal Mail Stage. Even that was an improvement upon the old way of carrying the mail on horseback; a poor post boy had to be frozen to death on a bitter winter day before the wagon was instituted, so slow is progress even in Canada. The first contract had just ended at the time when my story commences and a new contract was offered by Government to the lowest tender. Two Cromaboo tavern keepers competed for the honor of carrying the mail, but Mr. Llewellyn put in a lower tender and the office was bestowed upon him. Great was the anger of his rivals, bitter the discontent of Cromaboo at his appointment, many the threats and ill wishes expressed.

He bought a large open three-seated spring carriage that would accommodate nine passengers comfortably, with a good rack behind for baggage. A large, light, comfortable sleigh, good buffalo-robes, good oil skins, two strong piebald ponies, a double reflecting lamp, and a musical tin horn, completed the new arrangements.

The first driver hired by Mr. Llewellyn was in the interest of the enemy; he fed the horses on peas to injure them, and pocketed his master's money; he was dismissed at the end of a month. The second

---

[16]Leslie's fictionalization of Guelph, Ontario, Canada. The choice of name is an echo of the medieval Ghibbelines, the Italian faction supporting the Holy Roman Emperor. The Guelphs (*Guelfi*) supported the Papacy.

also in the pay of the enemy, was dismissed at the end of a fortnight, having lamed one of the ponies, kissed all the female passengers, and smoked in their faces to disgust them from riding in the new coach; and finally asked Miss Llewellyn to marry him. Driver the third ran away on the third day, after overturning the Royal Mail and breaking the pole and the lamp. The fourth mail carrier was Robert Hardacre Smith, the hero of my story.

There were two honest men in Cromaboo, Mr. Llewellyn was one, and his neighbour John Smith[17] was the other. John Smith was the father of my hero. He was an Irishman, and could neither read nor write; he did not know the first rule of arithmetic; he had never heard of grammar or seen a map; he sometimes drank more than was good for him, and could swear as well or ill as any man in the village; but he never told a lie, and was thoroughly reliable; he did a good day's work for his wages, and always kept his word. He admired his aristocratic neighbor for his pluck, he respected him for his learning, he admired him for his honesty; and Mr. Llewellyn in return had a kinder feeling for John Smith than any of his neighbours. So when he strolled into the shop, pipe in mouth, on the evening of the disaster to the Cromaboo mail coach, and said –

"Sure ye might take Robbie on thrial for a month; he's honest anyway, the crather, and won't injure your horses and pocket the fares," – Mr. Llewellyn promptly accepted the offer, and closed the bargain by saying, "Send him in, that I may see him."

"Why havn't ye seen him a thousand times?" said John Smith. "Every day in the year ye see him when he's at home."

"I have never seen him in my life," returned Mr. Llewellyn, with perfect truth, "for I have never looked at him. I never do look at man, woman or child in Cromaboo, if I can avoid it."

"Well, it's you that's the quare[18] man entirely, Misther Llewellyn, never to look at Robbie," said John Smith; "it's your loss, I'll make boold to say, as ye'll think when ye see him." And away he went to fetch his son, and in a few minutes they entered together.

A greater contrast could hardly be; the father tall, raw-boned, coarse featured, wiry, dark; the son a small slight lad of nineteen,

---

[17] At the time of publication, in 1878, Leslie's choice of character name – John Smith – is interesting, as a John Smith was proprietor and editor of the Guelph *Herald* newspaper.

[18] quare = remarkable or strange.

light of foot and graceful. He was encased in a very shabby old military great-coat, once grey, now nearly white, one scarlet shoulder-knot gone and a red woolen comforter tied round the waist by way of sash; very bright, bonnie and picturesque he looked – the pleasure of his new appointment shining in his face. A very intelligent face; I wish I could bring it before you, my reader, as it came before Mr. Llewellyn. I will try. Brown eyes, fair closely-cut hair, inclined to curl, short but regular features, white even teeth, a smile that is very sunshine; all surmounted by a ragged hat with half the rim gone. His new master looked at him keenly, critically.

"Can you read and write?" he asked.

"Yes, sir," said the lad, in a remarkably clear, pleasant voice.

"Sure it's he that's the scholar," chimed in his father, proudly, in a rough, coarse bass, that was like the hoarse croak of a crow after the sweet pipe of a canary.

"Write your name," said Mr. Llewellyn, putting a sheet of paper on the counter.

He wrote in a bold clear hand, "Robert Hardacre Smith."

"I dislike double names," said the old gentleman, "but it's sensible in this case, as Smith is so common, to distinguish you from other Smiths."

"I never saw a Smith like him," said the father.

"How far have you got in arithmetic?" went on Mr. Llewellyn.

Robert coloured; it cost him a great effort to say "no furder than long division, sir."

"Can you speak the truth?"

"Yes, sir." The colour deepened.

"Is the world round, square or oblong?"

"I wouldn't presume to say," with a gleam of white teeth and a slight laugh. "I lave that to the decision of scholars like yourself, sir."

Mr. Llewellyn returned the smile, and at that moment his niece entered the shop with a bright "good evening" to both the Smiths. Each returned it civilly, and the father said, "Where's your manners, Bob? Sure ye might doff ye're hat to the young leedy."

For the first time in his life, Robert uncovered his head in token of respect. He removed the ragged hat quietly and without embarrassment, and stood with it in his hand. The smile died on Mr. Llewellyn's lips; he looked at the lad again and again, with less of liking at each glance; it was not the kind of pate[19] he expected to find under that ragged beaver. It was a peculiarly shaped head, not unlike that of Sir Walter Scott, and when uncovered it made the boy's face look graver, more manly, less pleasing; there was power in it of some kind, that struck Mr. Llewellyn unpleasantly, and gave him a new feeling; and Robert's absolute calmness, under his new master's gaze, was an offence to the aristocrat. He resumed his catechism.

"I know your father is an honest man," he said, "but you –."

He paused. The lad flushed, and lifting his eyes, looked steadily and gravely into his face.

"If you doubt me," he said, "you had better not employ me."

The tone was not impudent, but quiet and resolute, and Mr. Llewellyn did not dream of the effort it cost poor Robert to renounce the occupation he looked forward to with pride and pleasure.

"You are not like your father," he said, doubtfully, "not in the least."

"Faith, sir, he's a dale bether looking," said John Smith, "it's like his mother he is, and ye needn't be quarreling with the crather for that, not that I blame ye for being suspicious, seeing how ye've been trated, but ye may take my word he's honest, and I wouldn't lie to ye. And for ye, Bob," laying a heavy hand on his son's shoulder, "don't be throwing away a good chance for a bit o' pride; if the masther doubts ye, just live it down, and prove ye're bether than he thinks."

Robert looked up in his father's face with a smile, half fond, half humorous; "Better than I look!" he said.

---

[19]pate = head, especially the top of the head.

Chapter Two

"Courage ! - there is none so poor,
None of all who wrongs endure,
None so humble, none so weak,
But may flush his father's cheek
And his maiden's, dear and true,
With the deeds that he may do.
Be his days as dark as night
He may make himself a light."

– Barry Cornwall[20]

So Robert was engaged, and no Chancellor ever mounted the wool-sack with a greater feeling of pride and power than Robert Hardacre Smith felt in mounting the front seat of the Cromaboo mail stage, the day after his promotion. Never did Prime Minister assume his new position with a stronger sense of the responsibility and importance of it; never did nun or priest take solemn vows or holy orders with a firmer or more honest intention of doing their duty.

The lad was a quick observer, and especially quick where women were concerned, for they were interesting to him, and he was indifferent to nothing regarding them. He was a great admirer of beauty, and a better judge of it than he himself knew; no little grace, no point of attraction was lost on him, no trifling charm ever made in vain. All women were ladies to Robert; he studied them, came to quick and correct conclusions about them, and was civil or saucy as he thought it pleased them best. Sometimes he affected to sympathise with them,

---

[20]Bryan Waller Procter (Barry Cornwall), "Courage": Stanza 3.

sometimes he did it sincerely, sometimes he laughed at them, but always in his sleeve; – whatever he did or left undone, they liked him, one and all.

He soon saw that swearing was displeasing to some of his fair passengers; he had heard so many oaths himself that no curse however dreadful shocked him, or gave him the least offense; but if it offended the women it would injure the stage and detract from its respectability, therefore he would have no swearing in his coach. Having made this resolution, he proceeded at once to put it into execution.

"I am not a-going to have no swearing in this yer coach, Joe Shenker," said this newly-fledged despot to an old Dutchman, who, because he had no match to light his pipe, had relieved himself by a royal blast of oaths. The outraged Dutchman replied by a still more offensive volley. He was seated beside the driver, who by a sudden and dexterous shove, threw him off his balance and out of the sleigh. Touching his horses with the whip, he called out "Good day to ye, then; I charge nothing for the mile's ride," and left him sprawling in the snow. By a kind of retribution, called poetical justice, Joe Shenker had to walk four miles facing an east wind before he got a chance ride.

"You have lost seventy cents by that, Bob," said a gentleman occupying the back seat.

"And a deal o' bad company, Mr. Meldrum," was the reply.

"So bad that I don't mind paying you half the money for disposing of him," pursued the gentleman.

"No sir, thank you all the same," replied our Cromaboo hero, strengthened in his resolution to have no more swearing.

The next case was a more difficult one; the offender being a well-to-do Cromaboo farmer who made use of an expletive that brought a flush of shame to the cheeks of a stout young girl who sat between himself and the driver. He was a giant in comparison to Robert, who suddenly drew up, and asked him civilly to get out and raise the check rein. The man saw through the manoeuvre.

"You think to serve me as you did Joe Shenker, Master Bob," said he, "but –." Here followed language too offensive to repeat.

"Am I the master of this yer coach or you, Mr. Bonnycastle?" asked Robert, with dignity.

"You think you are, I suppose, Bob Smith," with another offensive expression.

"I *am* and will be," said the despised Bob, quietly and sturdily.

More abuse on the part of Mr. Bonnycastle, which so frightened the girl between them that she exclaimed, "Oh! do let me out."

Robert dismounted at once and helped her down, calling out as he did so to the driver of a load of hay behind them, "Will ye kindly give this lady a lift?" The sleigh stopping, he ran back to carry her bag and help her mount the new conveyance; in the meantime Mr. Bonnycastle drove on, and our hero had half a mile of hard running before he could overtake the stage. The rest of the passengers jeered at him – they were all men – and enjoyed the fun of conquering "little Bob." He resumed the reins and said not a word, but as soon as they reached Gibbeline he hailed the first policeman he saw, and gave Mr. Bonnycastle in charge, summoning his fellow-passengers as most unwilling witnesses against him. Poor Mr. Bonnycastle was like a great blue bottle fly caught by a tiny little spider; he made a great deal of noise, he swore great oaths, but alas! they only told against him, he was fined five dollars and costs. When Robert returned to the stage office, he found the girl waiting to pay her fare.

"Not a cent, Miss," said Robert, "I'll pay your fare to the master out of my own wages, and I'm very sorry it's been so unpleasant for you." She was only a servant maid, but his knight-errantry was not lost upon her – he had made a friend for life.

He was never again troubled with swearers, but now came a battle with the cord-wood carriers. A load of cord-wood is an awkward thing to turn out on a narrow road, and in vain Robert blew his horn, and called out civilly for half the track; they never budged an inch; they were insolent or willfully deaf. Three times was the Royal Mail upset in the soft snow without any damage to anything but the tempers of the passengers. Robert took his resolution. On his next journey to Gibbeline he overtook seven teams of wood, all in a row; he blew his horn and called out for half the road. No notice was taken; he attempted to pass the first team and upset. He had but one passenger, a stout burly man who helped him right the sleigh; they crept on perilously near the ditch till they came to the last team, here they upset again. They picked themselves up as before and drove on. Three of the men were known to Robert – one was his own elder brother, John James William Smith; he noted the faces of the others.

"I should like to thrash every wood fellow between this and Cromaboo, and if I was as big as you I *would* do it," said the indignant mail carrier to his passenger.

"No you wouldn't, Robbie," returned the other, good naturedly, "you wouldn't have the *will* then; it's the little fellows that are so hot."

As soon as Robert reached the town he went to the market with a couple of policemen and waited for the offending wood carriers. He gave them all in charge, and all were fined and cautioned against a second offense.

"What do ye mane, ye unbrotherly little divole, ye?" asked John James William Smith, angrily, as he paid his portion of the fine.

"I mane to have half the road as long as I'm driver of the Cromaboo mail," was the reply.

On his return trip, with the same passenger and two women, he overtook the seven empty wood-racks on their way home; in vain he blew his horn; they kept him behind them for an hour walking their horses on purpose to irritate him. At last after a war of words, one of the wood-carriers sprang off his sleigh, and pulling Robert from his seat, struck him with his whip. The blow was returned, but our hero was by far the weakest of the two, and would have got the worst of it had not John James William joined in the dance, forgetting his recent injuries and proving the truth of the old proverb "blood is thicker than water."

The Smiths came off victorious and shook hands on the victory, but the mail was behind time that night and the driver had a black eye; however, when Mr. Llewellyn heard of his adventures he commended him, and his young mistress treated him like a hero as he was, and dressed his wounds with her own dumpy aristocratic little fingers.

The next day he overtook seventeen wood teams in a string; one only turned out for him – his brother, who happened to be tail of the party. The rest kept on their way, and he was forced to dawdle behind them for three hours, as the roads were far too bad to risk passing without half the track, especially as his passengers were all women. The Cromaboo mail was too late for the train, and the Gibbeline postmaster – who was a bit of a martinet[21] – threatened to

---

[21]martinet = one who demands absolute adherence to rules.

report Mr. Llewellyn. Robert took the sixteen offending wood-men before the Police Magistrate. They were fined two dollars each and solemnly warned not to offend again. Robert asked if he might be allowed to say a word to them before they were dismissed, and permission being given, thus spoke Robert Hardacre Smith:

"I am heart-sorry, my men, to take money out of your pockets, and I know some of you need it bad enough; but I'm not strong enough to thrash ye all round, and so subdue ye, so I'm forced to thry the law. I have a right to half the road as ye all know, and understand me once for all, *I will have it.*"

No one who heard him could doubt that he meant what he said; there is power and dignity in truth, even though he who speaks it happens to have a ragged coat and a black eye; the wood carriers having had a taste of the law, tacitly admitted they were conquered, for ever after they sulkily gave way for the Royal Mail.

Time would fail me to tell of all the victories achieved in the first month by our Cromaboo hero, how he charmed the women by singing hymns or comic songs, as best suited their feelings, and put out the pipes of the men, his own included – and I am sorry to say he loved tobacco – as soon as a petticoat took possession of the stage. At first he had everything his own way, but as time passed, a reverse of fortune came that nearly ended fatally. Robert went to the blacksmith's one Saturday night at e'en to get a shoe re-set; opposite the blacksmith's stood the most roaring disorderly tavern in Cromaboo, and as usual a crowd of half tipsy fellows had gathered about the door, and they called out to Robert to come and have a drink. He had had several squabbles with more than half of them during the last thirty days, and he thought one glass with them might mend the breach, and place them on good terms again; he did not wish to make enemies for his coach and its master, and as yet he knew not the evil of half measures; he crossed to the Royal Anglo-American and went in to be treated. He stayed no longer than fifteen minutes, and drank only one glass, but it made him feel deadly sick, and when out in the air again he felt worse instead of better. He thought he should be all right when once in the sleigh and on his way home, but as soon as he mounted his seat he lost consciousness, and the horses took him home without his knowledge, and stopping suddenly he fell out face downwards before the shop door.

Mr. Llewellyn, who was looking out for him, pronounced him

drunk, and said he would dismiss him, touching the prostrate figure slightly with a scornful foot; but his niece knelt down and turned up the boy's face.

"Not drunk," she said, "but dying!" and springing up, she ran for his father and dispatched him for the doctor, and returning quickly with his mother, helped carry the lad into the house. The doctor came, applied the stomach pump, and pronounced it a serious case of poisoning. He stayed with Robert till the daylight dawned, and so did the lad's mother and Miss Llewellyn; it was a sad and anxious night.

As for John Smith and his son John James William, they went together to the Royal Anglo-American and sobered the jolly inmates by telling them that if Robert died they should all be hanged. All denied having done anything to injure the lad, though some of them looked guilty enough, and they separated and sneaked away when the Smiths were gone, and two or three of them were not seen in Cromaboo for many days after.

In a fortnight Robert was in his seat again, very pale indeed, but more determined than ever to do his duty, and neither take or give quarter; prouder of his post than ever, and happier in it, for had not his master shaken hands with him, and said, "I have perfect confidence in you, Robert?" had not his young mistress made gruel and sago[22] for him with her own hands, and shed tears when she thought he was dying? had not Dr. Medrum thought it worth his while to sit up with him? had he not fresh proof that his father and mother loved him?

Mr. Llewellyn had driven his own coach during the lad's illness, and had received good evidence of his servant's honesty, as well as his tact and popularity with the women, and an obstinate belief in him took possession of his prejudiced Welsh head, a kindly warmth for the boy kindled up in his old Welsh heart.

It leaked out in time that the dose Robert had swallowed had been mixed for him by a disreputable veterinary surgeon, who had unintentionally made it too strong, being more accustomed to compounding doses for horses than men. His object was to make Robert appear drunk and have him dismissed.

---

[22] sago = a starch derived from the pith of tropical palm stems, especially *Metroxylon sagu*, and used in making puddings.

So ends the chapter. Do not be discouraged, my reader, and give up the story. I promise you a *bon bouche* for desert, though you have begun your repast with simple bacon and beans. I promise to introduce you to the most fashionable people. I promise you romance, adventures, love-making, in galore, and finally orange blossoms and wedding favours; kisses – blessings – only have patience.

Chapter Three

"The sweetest lady that ever I looked upon."

– Shakespeare[23]

A NEW influence was brought to bear upon Robert, the strongest and most subtle that ever touched his life. This is how it happened. I have said Robert was fond of the ladies, but most of all did he love them between the ages of five and seven. He was intimate with many little girls between Gibbeline and Cromaboo; they felt at home with him, and told him most important secrets about pet cats, puppies and dolls; they gave him their confidence and their kisses, and he gave them sweetmeats and kisses in return, and occasionally free rides for half a mile or so, on condition they should sit on his knee. The tavern-keeper in Gibbeline,[24] where the stage put up, had a little daughter who watched eagerly for Robert, and never let him leave without a flirtation and a romp. One stormy March day, as he was donning his great coat for a start, this little lassie came running in, and challenged him to a game of romps, by exclaiming, "You don't *dare* to take me to Cromaboo, you don't!"

"Don't I, though?" retorted Robert, "I'll button ye into my coat this very minute," and he chased her with the skirts extended in each hand and a great deal of noise, of course.

"I want the Cromaboo stage," said a clear, sweet voice, near him as with flushed face and coat-tails spread wide he pretended to try and corner the little runaway.

---

[23]William Shakespeare, *Much Ado About Nothing*: Act 1, Scene 1.

[24]In Leslie's original 1878 publication this is misspelled only here as Gibberline.

"I'm not the stage, but I'm the driver," said Robert, rather flippantly, before he saw the speaker. A well-dressed lady stood before him; two soft, grave eyes met his and regarded him doubtfully; he was not shy by nature, but he dropped his coat-tails and blushed violently.

"Beg pardon, ma'am," he said, "are you going by the coach?"

"Yes. Will you call at the Royal for me, if you please? You will ask for Miss Paxton."

"Yes, ma'am."

"You won't forget?" looking as if she thought he would. Indeed he was not likely to forget what he thought the prettiest face he had ever seen, but he only said "no ma'am."

He called for her, ensconced her in the best seat, and took furtive glances at her as he went along. Her face was shaded, not concealed, by a large grey cloud; he thought it good to look at; he had never seen a face that interested him as this did. She only rode four miles, and then got out at a large plaster house that stood on a high bank above the road. She had a great many parcels, and Robert carried them in for her. She thanked him, and no expression of courtesy ever touched him so much, though it meant absolutely nothing, for courtesy was a habit with her, and in this case she thought it his duty and felt no gratitude. He charged her twenty cents, and she paid without haggling, to his surprise, for his fair customers generally badgered him to take off a cent or two.

She asked if it would be too much trouble for him to blow his horn when he passed, as she might often take advantage of the stage. He promised to do it, with pleasure, and he did blow most faithfully the next time and many times, before the lady came again. He wished she would come out, and never passed the place without thinking of her, but this interest was all on one side, for our hero had left no distinct impression on the mind of Miss Paxton.

Her sister asked her during the evening what sort of a person the new driver was, and she answered wearily, "a civil lad enough, and I think nice looking, but really I hardly know. He was playing very noisily with a child when I first saw him, and I thought for a moment that he was a tipsy fellow, like the last, but that was a mistake."

At last Miss Paxton gladdened Robert's eyes by appearing, and made three trips in succession to the town, going and returning with a very anxious face. She had but a vague idea of the driver, and took more interest in the spotted ponies than she did in him. He observed her keenly and thought about her constantly; he thought her face looked almost hopeless sometimes, but would brighten up and become smiling and gracious when any one spoke to her; he felt sure she was good and kind, but he soon found out that her civility, so far as he was concerned, was nothing but civility; she did not know his name or care to know it, she scarcely saw him, never looked at him when she put the money into his little rough fist with her slender white fingers; she was not as other women to him, and he felt her indifference with a little pain. Once he mentioned her to Miss Llewellyn – he had described her at full length to his mother the first time he saw her, and mother-like she had taken a great interest in her.

"Has she been on the stage?" said Miss Llewellyn; "I wonder they don't keep horses. Do you know, uncle, I should so much like to visit Miss Paxton, only I couldn't call without being asked; it would seem like intrusion."

"I dare say she would be glad to see you, my dear," remarked the old gentleman.

"She is always very polite when I meet her, but they are so rich, and we –."

"*We*," said her uncle, taking up the unfinished sentence, "are people of good education, descended from a line of princes; I should think Miss Paxton might be proud of your acquaintance; for her father, though a man of good birth, was only a London tradesman. When I meet her again, my dear, I will see if I cannot bring about an intimacy; she is a very pretty, well-informed girl, and I often have a chat with her."

This conversation took place at supper, and Robert, who was seated at the foot of the table, took in every word, and wondered in his heart if Miss Paxton would be glad of his little mistress' acquaintance; hoped she would, as then perhaps she might come to Cromaboo.

The mail was crowded the next morning, and Miss Paxton came running out as it passed; there was only one place available, the front seat, between Robert and another man. Her face expressed both hesitation and repugnance as she got in, a fact not lost upon our hero, who stepped over the dash-board and sat upon it with his legs outside.

"That is a very uncomfortable seat, I am afraid," said the lady, in a faint protest against a proceeding that made her much more comfortable.

"Yes, ma'am, but the day is mild and four miles isn't far."

The response struck her with its novelty, and though she said no more at the time, she felt the lad's gallantry and thanked him when she got out.

Mr. Llewellyn was with them, and sat beside her when they returned, and had a long chat with her. He got upon his favourite hobby, the siege of Babylon, and the lady felt very much bored, but kept up an appearance of interest with a power of endurance that belongs to no living thing under heaven but a polite woman. Robert thought she looked "tired like," and guessed truly that in spite of her civility she was glad to say good bye and get away.

She was his sole passenger on his next trip, and, in his opinion, looked upon this occasion as beautiful as an angel, and when he put her down, by her own request, at a private house in a side street, his pride in her was such that he proclaimed her arrival by a royal blast of his horn that brought all the people in the neighborhood to their windows. Miss Paxton felt annoyed at being announced like a mail-bag.

"It's a very good thing, no doubt, to be able to blow one's own trumpet," she said, "but there is a time for all things; you have made every one look at us."

"Let 'em look," replied Robert, "it's a beautiful sight and costs 'em nothing."

She did not understand him in the least; she thought he meant that his coach was "a beautiful sight," and was glad to shut the house door between herself and the staring faces.

Miss Paxton was far from being a happy woman; few people had more pretty cares and small harassing troubles than she; yet she ought to have been happier, for she hated nothing that God had made; she was not wicked at heart or in life: she tried to do her duty.

That afternoon she was crossing the railroad, wearily, with a large paper parcel which looked heavier than it was; she was far more tired in *spirit* than body, for to-day had been a day of failures; her face looked almost hopeless as she turned into the railway track and met Robert face to face. She did not see him, but he saw her, and like Sir Walter Raleigh, he felt there was nothing to fear in a "pretty-faced lady;" so he called out cheerily, "You're a long way from where I set you down, Miss Paxton."

She started; the familiarity of this address annoyed her exceedingly, even though she had very little of what Mr. Thackeray calls "the snob" in her composition; she wouldn't take a liberty herself, and she didn't like others to presume with her. She stopped perforce, for the way was narrow, and looking the Cromaboo mail carrier steadily in the face, really saw him for the first time. He had thrown off his ragged, but picturesque top coat, and was arrayed in dirty mole-skin; he had a large bag on his back; his brimless hat was set on the back of his head; his brown eyes met hers deprecatingly, modestly, the scarlet lips parted, the white teeth gleamed in half a smile; he guessed her thought, as well as if she had spoken it.

"Won't you let me carry your parcel?" he said; "it's more for the like o' me to carry than you." Her heart smote her with a sense of shame; she felt much as she would if she had tried to drive away a poor dog, and it had suddenly wagged its tail and rubbed against her.

"No, thank you," she said; "I think you are burdened enough."

"Oh! but do, now," urged Robert, "I am used to burdens." His voice had a plaintive sound; he held out his hand for the parcel, and in a minute was marching off with it under his arm.

"Poor boy," she thought, with a sigh, "you are not the only one used to burdens."

He had gained a great victory and was not entirely unconscious of it, he had killed her indifference forever. She took an interest in him from that time, and observed him as keenly as he did her, but being more conventional and polished, and withal a woman, this watching did not appear palpably, and Robert was quite unconscious of it, though he felt that her indifference had vanished, that she greeted him with a bright smile of recognition, and soon learned his name; never before had it sounded so sweetly in his ears; it gave him an odd kind of thrill whenever she uttered it.

There was a little up-stairs parlour in the Great Western Hotel where she took up her abode sometimes, and from the window watched the unconscious Robert bring out his horses and fasten them to the sleigh. A desire took possession of her to see how he behaved at table, and accordingly she condescended to dine at the Western. She sat near him, though at another table, and observed him and he never saw her, never thought of seeing her in that place; it was much

as if Queen Victoria had slipped in and taken a snack at some obscure London chop-house, where her faithful subjects would never
look for her. She lay *perdu*[25] within three feet of the unsuspicious
stage driver, who was quite "at his ease in his inn," and ate his dinner heartily. Scrawling in his little account book while he waited for
the pudding, and smiling over it well pleased for it was what he called
"a big day," much luggage and many passengers. When he rose, the
waiting maid said, rather pertly, as she took his money, "You owe me
a cent, master Bob."

"There it is, my dear," said he, "and a kiss for interest," suiting the
action to the word, and slipping away swiftly, having dexterously
avoided a box on the ear.

From the little parlour above, Miss Paxton watched them settle
their matters, as he brought out his horses. The damsel attacked him
with a broom, but he dodged with great agility, keeping the horses
between himself and his fair enemy, running under their bellies, and
peeping over their backs, his white teeth gleaming, his curls blowing,
for she had knocked off his hat in the first sally. The lady was too far
off to hear a word, but she saw that he succeeded in mollifying the
offended maiden, for the affair ended in the transfer of a flower from
his button-hole to the bosom of his fair adversary, and she actually
let him pin it in.

It was quite a different Robert whom Miss Paxton addressed ten
minutes later in the high street, and asked if he had room for her. Of
course he had, and very respectful he was as he helped her in.

"I hope you didn't walk, Miss Paxton," he said, courteously; "I
blowed and blowed, as I passed your house this morning."

On his next trip, Miss Llewellyn and Miss Paxton were both in the
stage, and had a thousand civil things to say to each other, greatly
to the edification of the driver; and the next time he passed, Miss
Paxton ran out with a basket of beautiful spring flowers to be taken to
Miss Llewellyn, with her compliments; and after that, Robert was the
bearer of several little three-cornered notes, and finally a fat kitten
in a commodious basket; and when things had got thus far, Miss
Llewellyn called on Miss Paxton, and spent a couple of hours, while
the stage was in Gibbeline, and the ladies kissed when they parted.

---

[25] *perdu* = a soldier assigned to extremely hazardous duty.

But it is time that I described Miss Paxton – "Miss Mary," as she was called in the neighbourhood. We have nothing to do with her at her best in her rosy brilliant youth, but we wish the reader to see her as Robert saw her, on a sweet May morning; her two-and-thirtieth birthday, though he knew it not. The gate swings open, and the lady slightly stooping to avoid the acacia boughs, appears before us, smiling brightly and walking with a light firm step towards the Cromaboo mail carrier. She wears a crisp muslin, dotted with tiny, delicate lilac roses, a black lace tippet, pointed before and behind, reaching to the waist and fastened to the bosom by a knot of fresh dewey brilliant pansies; white lace ruffles about her throat and wrists, a lilac ribbon, but no jewelry; a black stringless bonnet, with a wreath of May across the forehead, and a silver grey veil floating far behind and around her, forming a soft cloud-like background to her face. A very fair face though a little sunburnt, bearing a certain resemblance in its soft thoroughly feminine beauty to Gainsborough's portrait of the ill-fated Perdita[26], but more intelligent and therefore more charming. Smooth, abundant fair hair, arranged in a large loose knot at the back of her head, large deep-set eyes with certain changeful lights in them, looking now blue, now grey, now almost black; long dark lashed, a perfect mouth and chin, a sharply cut, handsome profile, a self-possessed easy manner. See her and you will pronounce her a little too thin for a beauty, a little too old also, for there is a crow's foot at the corner of the sweet mouth, yet a lovely woman, a dainty little lady, immaculately clean, sweet, fair and attractive, in spite of rude old Time with his scythe and hour-glass.

Does my coarse pen and ink sketch give you a true idea of her? I fear not, for Bacon says, with reason, "that is the best part of beauty that a picture cannot express." She holds a bunch of cow-slips and violets in one hand, and the scent of them gives Robert an odd feeling; it is with a little reluctance that he takes the grey-gloved hand in his little rough fist to help her in; and he thinks the red cheeked lasses in the stage look coarse and common beside her; he has the dust of twenty miles upon him, and fears in his heart she will think him coarse and common too; he wishes she could see him in his Sunday clothes, yet is not without a consciousness that "a man's a man for a'

---

[26]Thomas Gainsborough (1727-1788), an English portrait and landscape painter. He painted the portrait of the actress Mrs Mary Robinson: Perdita, in c.1781.

that," and even a mere mail carrier may be worthy of all respect.

They had been singing songs before they took Miss Mary up, songs comic and sentimental, and one of the girls urged Robert to begin again, "Come, go a-head, Bob," said she, "Give us another song."

"Oh! yes," chimed in Miss Paxton, "sing again, please."

That which is called instinct in a dog is genius in a man, it is an unerring innate knowledge untaught and not to be learned. Robert's genius taught him that comic songs would be unattractive, perhaps offensive, to Miss Paxton; he therefore started a hymn, "Rock of Ages," and the girls, though they wondered at him, joined in. They sang several hymns, and finally a temperance song, "There's nothing like cold water," which made Miss Mary ask, "Are you a total abstainer, Robert?"

"No, ma'am, I am better than that," he replied, "I can take it or leave it alone."

"I am afraid," said Miss Paxton, "you will think it impudent of me to ask so many questions; but are you a member of the Church of England?"

"No, ma'am."

"Better than that?" asked the lady, with a smile.

"I am a Methodist."

He had just lifted her out and she stood upon the pavement. "A Methodist!" she repeated, as she took the bouquet from his hand, "I never knew a Methodist before. I hope your method is a good one," and making him a little bend, half saucy, half patronizing, and wholly graceful, she walked away.

Chapter Four

"When toils and troubles have been borne,
And disappointment stings;
When we have learnt to doubt and mourn,
And Hope has tired her wings;
When we look backward with a sigh,
And memory brings a smart –
It may be summer in the sky,
'Tis winter in the heart!
When lonely homes and hearts are ours,
Though we be in our prime,
And spring embroiders earth with flowers –
Oh! this is winter-time!"

–H. E. Hunter[27]

THE house in which the Paxtons lived was a cheerful and charming house to look upon, as the summer advanced, and to Robert the sight of it was like an oasis in the desert. The verandah in front was covered with climbing roses of three colours, virginia creeper matted the back to the very roof, trumpet honeysuckle was trained up one side and sweet-briar up the other, making the house a very bower of sweetness, delightful to the eye and grateful to the nose of the passer-by.

The garden in the rear was large and nearly square; a purple lilac hedge divided it from the orchard on one side, a white lilac hedge protected it on the other, a thorn hedge closed it in at the back, and the house, a large and commodious one, sheltered the front and formed

---

[27]H. E. Hunter, "Our Seasons," *The Sunday Magazine* (1874): 751-752.

the fourth square. This garden was one long succession of beauty, from early spring till late in autumn – from the coming of the first snow-drop till the November blast nipped down the last aster and pansy. There did thousands of lilies-of-the-valley rear their graceful heads; there did great peonies flourish and expand in jolly glory, as large as cannon balls; there did oriental poppies display their fiery magnificence; there did periwinkles open myriads of blue eyes under the hedges, and creep into the orchard grass.

And that orchard of three acres, planted as it was on a gentle slope, with a brook babbling at the foot of it, a closely-cut sweetbriar hedge all round it, clumps of balsam and tamerack at the four corners, mountain ashes drooping by the water – no wonder people checked their horses as they drove down the hill beside it, no wonder they crawled slowly up, inhaling the sweet scents and rejoicing in the shadowy, dewey, emerald hill side; no wonder the school children helped themselves plentifully to sweet briar, and looked longingly at the snowy blossoms, or the red and yellow apples, as the case might be, and occasionally risked the thorns and entered on forbidden grounds.

The house was built on a high bank, and only a slight strip of ground divided it from the Queen's highway, clumps of snow-ball grew beside the gate, Scotch roses peeped through the pickets and bloomed on the outside, a gigantic locust drooped graceful branches and waved its pea-like, trailing blossoms above the fence, dog-roses crept down the paths and blossomed close to the dusty wagon track.

But though a blooming paradise without, it was very different within; it was like a lovely flower with an ugly grub in the heart of it, destroying its very life; for bitter discontent, envy, disappointment and avarice flourished and grew rank inside as the roses did without. The owner was that most unlovely thing in the whole world – a grossly selfish old woman. Like her home, she was picturesque and pretty; a delicately fair, somewhat bent old woman, a wearer of pretty caps and gowns and muslin handkerchiefs; tyrannical by nature, dictatorial in speech, always delivering herself *ex cathedra*.[28] With her resided two daughters, all that remained to her of six children. Her eldest daughter was a clergyman's widow, who had returned to her father's house without a penny. She was a good looking, haughty

---

[28] *ex cathedra* = by virtue of or in the exercise of one's office or position.

woman, with a fine figure, a large Roman nose, dark hair, and like her
mother – a talent for ruling and laying down the law. Two people of
this disposition are not likely to agree in one house, especially when
one is wholly dependent on the other, as in this case, for Mr. Paxton
had left his widow sole proprietor of everything as long as she lived,
at her death to be equally divided between the two daughters. He
did not consider them of age, as long as their mother remained, or
entitled to power in anything. This might have answered very well
had Mrs. Paxton been an amiable old lady, but she was quite the reverse, and bitter and continual were the squabbles between her and
her eldest daughter, Margaret Hurst, who considered she had a perfect right in her father's house; who would rule and did in the sense
of having her own way in a negative fashion, for if she couldn't gain
her point and manage the household, she was like a naughty boy
who wouldn't play, or a gibbe horse who would lie down in the har-
ness and do nothing. She occupied her time in reading, eating and
sleeping; she did not even darn her own stockings or crimp the frill
that she wore about her neck.

Mrs. Paxton's reign was a paradox, for it combined the opposite
qualities of dullness and confusion. She was avaricious, and therefore kept but one little maid, who being dull and slow, was cheaper
than a quick, efficient girl would have been.

She thought her daughters ought to do the work of the house,
and would have made them do it if she could; she gave them as little
money as possible, and that grudgingly; too feeble to work herself,
she could find fault with those who did not do it to her liking; she
could not sweep down a cobweb, but she could scold if she saw one;
she could not collect the rents or look after her own business, but she
could express her anger and discontent if it was not done properly.

Mary, with the assistance of the little maid I have mentioned, did
everything; she was private secretary – for Mrs. Paxton would not
write her own letters – and woman of business, and house-keeper,
and dressmaker and cook; she did all the ironing of the establishment and might have done the washing if she had not rebelled. This
standing up for one's own rights is always a hard task for an amiable
woman, and to oppose Mrs. Paxton was to incur her dislike, for she
regarded a person who differed from her in opinion as either a fool
or a knave. She would have liked to make her daughters obedient
drudges, and was always holding forth on the duties of children to

their parents, laying especial stress upon obedience, but she did not consider that parents had any duties towards their grown-up children; it was quite right that they should take care of them in infancy, but as soon as they grew up they should work for their parents and strictly obey them all the rest of their lives.

Mrs. Hurst was very like her mother in one particular, though she wouldn't work herself she was a keen and excellent critic upon the performances of others. Like her mother, she would not wear a gown unless it fitted her perfectly, but they differed in some of their peculiarities. Mrs. Hurst would not eat anything unless it was perfectly to her taste, whereas Mrs. Paxton would eat what she professed to dislike and grumble all the time. Breakfast was always a stormy meal; Mary took hers with Dolly at seven, Mrs. Paxton and her daughter had theirs together at half-past nine or ten. Toast, oatmeal porridge and fried potatoes were always served for these two ladies. Mrs. Paxton liked her porridge thin, Mrs. Hurst thick, so two jorums[29] had to be prepared in separate pots; Mrs. Paxton liked her potatoes cut in large pieces and warmed through, Mrs. Hurst liked hers cut very small and fried very brown; again, Mrs. Paxton took buttered toast and the fair Margaret dry; Mrs. Hurst took sugar with her porridge, which Mrs. Paxton considered great extravagance as she took nothing but salt.

The old lady was always jibing at her daughter for rising so late. She regarded it as disgraceful in a young person, though she herself had never got up earlier at any time of her life except upon one occasion, when she had been known to rise at six to see the morning glories, but then it was only in a dressing jacket and petticoat, and she went to bed again for her morning nap. She had seen the sun rise once when she was traveling, and Margaret had once seen the morning star, when as the parson's wife she had sat up with a sick person of note in her husband's parish; and they sometimes boasted of these things among their kinsfolk and acquaintances. Both mother and daughter nursed their injuries and fostered them and would not let them die, but Mrs. Paxton, though always in a chronic state of bad temper, was never in low spirits, whereas Margaret constantly bemoaned the death of her two boys, whom she had lost when they were infants, and would weep about them for days at a time.

---

[29] Jorum = a large drinking bowl. Leslie has spelled it "joram."

Mrs. Paxton looked back upon the deaths of these children with great satisfaction. "I have enough to keep without them," she would say, complacently, a remark which her eldest daughter never forgave.

Five years had passed since the death of Mr. Paxton, and his widow had been queen bee of the establishment ever since, and Mrs. Hurst the drone. Mary had grown rapidly older in those five years; she was not at all well and not at all happy; she had the whole responsibility of the household upon her shoulders, and was in a constant state of anxiety, not from want of faith in her mother and sister, but from a too perfect faith in them, built upon long experience; she knew if it was possible to do or say a disagreeable thing, they would do and say it.

We have it on divine authority that it is not possible to serve "two masters," but Mary Paxton served two mistresses, whose wishes were directly in opposition to each other, and both ladies were alike in considering it "their duty" to speak their minds to their relatives; Mrs. Paxton called it telling the truth, Mrs. Hurst called it "dealing faithfully" with them. They were polite and kind to the outer world, though they kept it rather at the staff end, and did not indulge in much society. Both had hobbies, Mrs. Paxton's was a love of flowers and a love of her carpets – she would not admit a ray of light to the two best rooms, except upon the most state occasions – and above all a love of money, that "root of all evil." Mrs. Hurst had a love of theology, she called it a "love of God and zeal for the truth as it is in Jesus." Woe to the person who moved her Bible, her concordance, her hymn book, her sermons, her tracts; and equal woe to the unlucky urchin who was caught stealing Mrs. Paxton's roses; she would bear malice forever, though he took but one poor bud. I should have liked to introduce these two ladies to the Reverend Laurence Sterne,[30] it would have cured him of the foolish idea that a hobby is a mark of amiability in man or woman.

Miss Mary did her best to enter into the tastes of her mother and sister, she worked for them unremittingly; they were on her mind morning, noon and night; yet she did not please them, and she felt she was imposed upon, but saw no way out of it all. She disliked the

---

[30]Laurence Sterne (1713-1768) was an Anglo-Irish novelist and an Anglican clergyman. He published many sermons, but is best known for his novel *The Life and Opinions of Tristram Shandy, Gentleman* (1759-1767).

life, but no honorable mode of escape presented itself; her mother was so old and feeble and her sister as helpless in a different way, that it seemed to her like a shabby little treason to desert them; to re-form them was impossible, as well try and change a cockroach and a mosquito into a lion and a dove; their strengths lay in their weakness; so she lived on wearily with them from day to day. A new discomfort had been recently added to her life, that of extreme nervousness. Mrs. Paxton was exceedingly fond of her newspaper, and always read all the horrors at full length; Margaret would not listen; so Mary stayed perforce, and not to make her mother too angry by seeming neglect, while the old lady enlarged and dwelt upon all the little disgusting details with the greatest gusto. The poor girl stood the murders and suicides with tolerable equanimity, but the fashionable crimes for the last six months had been housebreaking and indecent assaults upon women; these she could not forget or cast off; she tried not to dwell on them, but every night came back the thought of how helpless they were if attacked – only three women and a child in the house. Some-times she would not sleep at all; sometimes she had worse dreams than ever Richard the Third had.

"When the tale of bricks is doubled, Moses comes," and a deliverer was on the way to Mary Paxton, though she knew it not.

One night she stood at her bed-room window watching the ris-ing moon, now nearly at the full; she was weary in body and hope-less in mind; her grief was not stormy but it was deep; tears stole down her cheeks in a dull, slow way; the dreariness of her loveless life was breaking her spirits and injuring her health. She sat full three hours without moving, except to wipe the tears away; then she closed the curtains and slowly undressed, first fastening the win-dow securely, afraid to leave it open, though the night was sultry. She opened her Bible at random: "Thou hidest thy face, they are troubled; thou takest away their breath, they die and return to their dust."[31] She turned the leaves hastily: "The waters wear the stones; thou washest away the things that grow out of the earth, and thou destroyest the hope of man; thou prevailest forever against him and he passeth; thou changest his countenance and sendeth him away."[32] Again she turned the leaves: "When He giveth quietness, who can

---

[31] Psalm 104:29
[32] Job 14:20

make trouble? and when He hideth His face, who then can behold Him, whether it be done against a nation or a man only?"[33]

She shut the book with a sigh that was almost a groan, and knelt down and prayed, and rose again uncomforted; but let us hope the petition was not unheard and unheeded. We shall see.

Being utterly worn out, she was asleep almost as soon as her head touched the pillow, and for a long time her sleep was sound and undisturbed, but towards the morning it was broken by a vivid dream. She was with Robert in the stage, his sole passenger and sitting beside him, and he looked at her as she had never seen him look, sullenly and reproachfully. Words were added to looks; he said "You should not despise me, for but for me you would have been like that," and he showed her a picture – a photograph. The subject was a dead, half-naked woman, all exposed that is usually concealed, her face ghastly and distorted with fear, the glazed eyes starting from her head - and this woman was *herself.*

She woke with a cry of horror. It was a lovely, still summer morning, the sun had not yet risen, the pipe of an early bird alone broke the silence. She raised the window and let in the sweet morning air; she thanked God it was only a dream; then bathed her face and began to dress; she would not lie down again, though it was so early, and risk another dream.

At that very moment, twenty miles away, the Cromaboo mail carrier was dreaming too. He saw a lovely dove with a standing ruff of feathers round its beautiful neck, like one he had seen in a traveling menagerie as a little boy, and it was frightened and fascinated by a rattlesnake that was just going to spring at it. With a sudden blow he killed the snake, and the bird flew to him and nestled in his bosom. He felt it warm and soft; his caressing hand touched it, when the ruthless voice of his master awoke him to the duties of the day, and, as Bunyan says, "it was a dream."

---

[33] Job 34:29

Chapter Five

"When the tale of bricks is doubled, Moses comes."
— Old Jewish Proverb[34]

"I am a man of war and might,
And know this much' that I can fight,
Whether I'm in the wrong or right,
Devoutly."

— Sir John Suckling[35]

THE bustle of the day began, and Mary forgot her dream till the stage horn recalled it to her mind, and Robert appeared on the balcony with a bright tin pail in his hand, and a note from Miss Llewellyn. The pail contained wild strawberries, and was sent to Mrs. Paxton with Miss Llewellyn's compliments; the note was for Mary, inviting her to Cromaboo for a day or two, and saying Robert would call for her as he returned from Gibbeline. She showed the note to her mother and sister, saying, "I *should* like it, very much; I do not feel well, and I long for a holiday."

"Really I see no necessity for such a visit," replied her mother; "if you go there, you must invite the girl back, and I'm sure we have acquaintances enough already. If you are not well, you should take a camomile pill – as for a holiday, young women never required a holiday when I was young."

Margaret saw no necessity for the visit either, but she would not side with her mother, so she said nothing.

---

[34]This line appeared in *The Church School Journal* (1874): 16.
[35]Sir John Suckling (1609-1642), "A Soldier".

"I think I will go," said Mary gently, after a pause. "I can stay till Wednesday."

Mrs. Hurst could hold her peace no longer. "Oh! you had better stay longer when you are away," she said, satirically, "and what good fairy do you suppose will cook the dinner and finish the ironing?"

"And who is to wash my feet?" asked Mrs. Paxton in a crushing tone.

"Dolly will cook and do the plain ironing, if you will act good fairy and kindly superintend her, Margaret, – the starched things can wait till I return – and I will wash your feet right away, if you like, mother."

"I do not like, it's not a proper time to do it; it must be done just before I go to bed," returned the old lady, sharply.

"Then Dolly will do it for you, mother; I must go now and pack up a few things," and she quietly left the room. As she opened the door, she encountered Dolly herself.

"You're never a-going away, Miss Mary," she said, "and leaving me all to do, and the old missis and Mrs. Hurst so cross – what shall I ever do? I call it real mean; don't stay long, will you?"

"I shall stay till Wednesday," replied her mistress as she went up stairs; "and whatever you do, you will never do well so long as you listen at doors, Dolly?"

Both Mrs. Paxton and her daughter were seriously displeased with Mary, but they chose rather to quarrel than agree about the offender, and kept up a war of words till the stage arrived. Robert came to carry our Mary's traveling bag, and observed the parting between the ladies with a good deal of interest.

His fair passenger wore a neatly-fitting silver-grey dress, made of some shining, lustrous material, with a standing ruff of lace at the neck, and a black hat shaped like the Scottish Queen Mary's cap, and worn back upon the head in the same fashion; it was ornamented with a scarlet ribbon and a few rose buds. As she turned on the steps to kiss her haughty sister, a graceful movement of the head, a look in the face half proud, half fond, half shrinking, a gleam of sunshine on her dress that made it shimmer, brought suddenly to Robert's mind the beautiful dove of his dream, and it tickled the lad's vanity, and was a happy remembrance to think it had nestled in his bosom for protection.

They were soon seated and off, and the rapid motion, the fresh air and the courtesy of her fellow-travelers did Mary good before she had gone a mile; her spirits rose – "sweet is pleasure after pain." She felt free, and began to enjoy herself and everything with the simplicity and heartiness of a child. She chatted gaily to the doctor at her side, and the priest who sat opposite, till one forgot his debts which were just then pressing rather heavily, and the other his hard vows and antipathy to heretics; both dropped conventionalities for the time, and were natural men and gentlemen, conversing with a sweet, intelligent woman; and the driver – nobody thought of him, but he listened with keen pleasure, and now and then took furtive glances at the speakers.

They paused for a few minutes at various post offices on the road, but did not stop till they reached Ostrander, a village within six miles of Cromaboo; here they stayed an hour to rest the horses. The sun was just setting as they drove up to the inn door. The priest, a strong, active young man, was the first out of the coach, and extended his hands to help Miss Paxton.

"I wonder at you, good father," said she, rather mischievously; "you will have to do penance if you touch the hand of a woman and a heretic; all the village is looking at you – what will it think?"

"*Honi soit qui mal y pense*,"[36] returned his reverence, gallantly, as he set her on the ground.

Robert forgot his prudence and his place. "What did he mane by that Frinch?" he asked of the other gentleman.

"He meant," said the doctor, laughing, "In for a penny in for a pound." The priest and the lady joined in the laugh, as if they thought it a funny translation; but Robert felt humiliated, and thought bitterly of his own ignorance, as he marched away with his mail-bag. He was sure it was not a true translation, and a sudden fit of anger and jealousy raged in his heart, against both gentlemen.

The priest remained in Ostrander, and as it happened the doctor went no further, having received information that two bailiffs waited in Cromaboo to pay their respects to him; so Robert and Miss Mary set off alone. She sat beside the driver by her own desire, and put on her water-proof cloak at the request of Dr. Meldrum, and with his assistance, before starting.

---

[36] *Honi soit qui mal y pense* = "Shamed be he who thinks ill of it."

It was dark when they left the inn, but the moon soon rose. Mary, who had seen Robert's vexation at the foreign quotation, tried to be conversational, and made a pleasant remark or two; but though he answered respectfully, he did not seem inclined to talk: so she soon relapsed into silence. After a mile or two they entered a wood and lost the light of the moon; the road was excellent, thanks to Mr. Llewellyn, an inclined grade for two miles running through a pine swamp. Robert urged the ponies to a very rapid trot, and as the cool air met them, and the fresh sweet scent of the forest, Mary enjoyed a greater sense of freedom and happiness than she had experienced for many a day. It seemed almost like a flight, and brought to her mind a picture she had seen of the retreat from Waterloo; she did not mention this, however, thinking perhaps her companion had never heard of the great battle; but she said, "I feel as if I were running away, Robert," and she felt indeed as though she were leaving her troubles far behind her.

"You are not afraid, Miss Paxton," asked Robert.

"Afraid! No – what should I fear? I am enjoying myself very much; I am happy."

"What would you do if robbers set upon us? You wouldn't seize me and hold down my arms, I hope," said Robert.

"What a mere boy he is," she thought, with a little disdain. "You want to frighten me," was all she said.

"Oh! no, ma'am," replied Robert, touching the horses with the whip, and urging them faster, twisting the reins as he spoke round the hook on the splash board. "You have faith in my driving, I hope."

"I suppose you know what you are about," replied Miss Mary, "but you have no mercy on the ponies; you are worse than a woman. Shall I take the lines?" she added, seeing that he had abandoned them and was sitting with one hand in the breast of his coat and his whip in the other.

"No do not touch them, please; they are all right," he replied.

On the ponies went faster and faster, but never breaking out of a trot; they were nearly through the swamp, the trees were further apart, the foliage less dense; the moon began to glimmer through the boughs and shone bright on the road before them; they were rapidly approaching a little ascent at the end of the swamp, when tall figures sprang out of the woods on either side, and two of them seized the horses' heads and tried to stop them, while a third sprang on to the step of the carriage at Robert's side, and called out, "Now, Bob, hand out the woman, and you shall have your turn with her."

He was answered by a stinging blow across the eyes from the mail carrier's whip, and at the same instant another man climbed into the carriage behind, and seizing Mary round the waist tried to drag her back over the seat. She screamed and struggled, and Robert pulling a revolver from his breast, turned and shot the man almost as soon as he had touched her; she felt his grasp loosen, he reeled and fell into the road. As quick as a flash, Robert fired again at the man he had struck with his whip, who though blinded with the blow he had received, still stood on the step and clung to the coach, with fearful oaths at the driver. He fell, too, and the ponies, now furious with fear, freed themselves from those who held them, and breaking into a gallop, dashed up the hill before them. All seemed to pass in an instant; Robert replaced his pistol, seized the reins, and with some difficulty pulled in the horses, and reduced their pace to a trot again; their blood was up and they were not easily quieted. They had gone a mile before they were pacified enough to let him attend to his passenger. At first she had turned cold and trembled violently, but hysterical sobs and a burst of tears relieved her. "Oh! do not stop," she panted, as the pace of the ponies moderated; "they will pursue us."

"Not they," said her escort, soothingly, "we are quite safe now; you needn't be afraid. I settled two o' them and Bonnie another, and the other fellow won't feel like following us, I think. Hush! hush! don't cry, dear Miss Paxton – Miss Mary – I may call you Miss Mary?" He touched her slightly with his left hand and her fingers closed on it with a nervous clasp and held it tremblingly.

"You brave, good boy," she said, "but for you where should I have been? How can I ever thank you enough? You have saved life and honor." Her hair had fallen down and a soft mass blew across his shoulder and touched his cheek.

"It was only my duty; I should ha' been a blackguard if I hadn't defended you. Don't cry any more," said he, coaxingly; "do try and quiet down; I'll walk the ponies and give ye time. See, there's houses on each side, and we're quite safe; them lights away off to the left is Cromaboo."

She tried to command herself and presently succeeded; the hand that held his trembled less, and she gently withdrew it.

"Robert," she said at length, "You expected those ruffians – you knew they would attack us?"

"I thought it likely, Miss Paxton, but was not quite sure. They have been hiding in the woods for more nor a fortnight, and twice, when I went through alone, they spoke to me, and said the next time a woman passed on the stage they would have her. I have had several with me since, but men, too, always. I noticed one o' them lurking around and watching whenever I passed. When Miss Llewellyn spoke this morning of having you to see her for a day or two, I thought it a pity to disappoint two ladies for fear o' them dirty blackguards. I was sure Mr. Meldrum would be on the stage to-night, and two honest men in a good cause, and one o' them a gentleman, would, God helping them, be more nor a match for four o' the like o' them."

"But when the doctor said he was not coming, why did you not speak – why did you run the risk? Robert, it was very rash; you might have been murdered and I –" she shuddered and did not finish the sentence.

"I borrowed a revolver and loaded it myself, and counted the odds and thought I could do without him," returned her defender, coolly.

Mary thought of the fearful odds, and shuddered again. There was a long pause.

"You will have to tell some magistrate," said the lady, at last, as the horses walked slowly on.

"Miss Mary," replied Robert, "I've pulled ye through so far, though I am but a boy, as you say – will ye trust me still further? Will you let me judge what is best?"

"Perhaps," she replied, doubtfully. "Well, Robert?"

"I want you not to tell a single soul about it, and neither will I."

"Why!" she asked, quickly turning a startled face upon him, in the moonlight.

"For your sake. Just think o' meeting them nasty rascals in a court o' justice; a lady like you can't think o' the things they might say, dirty vermin as they are; and to have it put in the papers, and all – just think."

Mary thought of her mother and the delight such an account would give the old lady; she would say it was a punishment from Providence because she had disobeyed her mother in coming to Cromaboo. "It is very king of you, Robert, to think for me, and I shrink from it, but that is cowardly; these men ought to be punished; they will bear malice, and if we let them go free, they will murder you, my poor boy."

"More like I have murdered some o' them," he said, "and if that's so, it must come out, and it will be better to own up at once; but I hope it's not so bad as that. I wasn't particular about my aim with the first fellow when you cried out; but I shot the second in the arm only. I'll send my father and brother to-morrow to see the extent o' the damage. They will not speak when I bid them be silent, and Chip can go with me on Wednesday."

"Who is Chip, and why do you call him that?" with a touch of impatience.

"My brother John James William, because he's a chip o' the old block. I'll take them fellows to the hospital on Wednesday, if they need it, and you must wait till Friday, Miss Paxton."

Another pause.

"Well, Robert," she said, at last, "I do not know what to think about it, or how to act; I will let you guide me in this matter. I will do as you think best."

"Thank you," said the lad, softly. "If you say you are not well, and very tired, Miss Llewellyn will let you go to bed at once, for she's kind to sick people, and used to nervous folks all her life. I'm very sorry you've been frightened, and prouder than a king to have fought for you; I wouldn't change places with the Prince o' Wales, this night," and he lifted her hand to his lips and kissed it. "If I say all right, at breakfast to-morrow, you may make sure there's no danger o' them scoundrels losing their lives."

Another pause, broken by a brisk chirrup from Robert, and "come pets, come bonnie." Thus urged, the ponies broke into a trot again that soon brought them to Mr. Llewellyn's door, where the old gentleman himself stood, in seedy black frock coat and red skull-cap, waiting to receive his guest.

"I am very glad to see you, my dear Miss Paxton," he said, shaking hands with her, warmly, as soon as Robert had lifted her out. "My house is as rough as a barn, and hardly fit to ask a lady into, but you are heartily welcome, and I hope it is not the last time, my dear, that you will do us the honour," and he gave her his arm, and conducted her through the shop to the room beyond.

Chapter Six

"Whatever passes as a cloud between
The mental eye of faith and things unseen,
Causing that brighter world to disappear,
And seem less lovely and its hope less dear;
This is our world, our idol, though it bear
Affection's impress or devotion's air."

                                        – Cowper[37]

I T was as Robert predicted; Miss Llewellyn saw that her friend was
very tired and nervous, and soon conducted her to her room, and
bade her good night. She fastened the door, and after more tears and
thanks to God for her deliverance, lay down and fell asleep. This
time no ill-dreams haunted her; she slept soundly, sweetly, till the
cock crew, a cow bell began to clang, and the sun peep in at the little
window. She lay still for a few minutes, looking round at her room;
it had a sloping roof and was almost as small as a ship's cabin; it
was a spotless little room, well scrubbed, well white-washed. The
washing-stand was a small wooden fixture fastened to the wall, with
a roller beside it for a towel; the basin and jug were tin – silver could
hardly have been brighter – and a cocoanut shell contained the soap.
The dressing-table was a large wooden bracket; a noble looking-glass
hung above it, the only costly piece of furniture in the room. There
was a corner cupboard, and a chair made out of a barrel; the bedstead
was a common stub covered with bleached calico sheets, and a gay
patchwork quilt that was quite a work of art, so complicated and

---

[37]Leslie attributes this verse to William Cowper (1731-1800), but in fact its author
is unknown.

beautiful was the pattern; a white muslin curtain covered the tiny window. All these things were noted approvingly by the great bright eyes in the bed, till they presently grew drowsy again and closed in another nap.

By and bye they opened, brought back to life by voices under the window.

"Now look here, Robert," said the sharp tongue of Miss Llewellyn, "if this is the way you keep promises, I'll never trust you again. You said if I invited Miss Paxton for a day or two, you would help me in every way, and give me time to entertain her; and this is a fine beginning. Where have you been for the last hour and a half?"

"Hush!" said the other voice, so softly that it was like the cooing of a dove after the cackling of barn-door fowls, "you will wake her, and she was very tired. I have been fishing – look."

Mary slipped softly from the bed and cautiously peeped behind the curtain. Miss Llewellyn was concealed in the doorway, but Robert stood full in the bright sunlight with a basket of trout in his hand; his bare feet thrust into old shoes, his trowsers rolled to the knee, a ragged old swallow-tailed coat upon his back, and a coarse straw hat, very much on the back of his head.

"What beauties!" said his little mistress, somewhat mollified at the sight of them, "but who is to cook them, I should like to know?"

"I will," replied the offending Robert, promptly, "and get the breakfast and all, and then I'll mind the shop while you are at it; maybe Miss Paxton wouldn't like to sit down with a servant."

Miss Llewellyn was entirely pacified. "Well, you are a good boy," she said, "only you shouldn't go away and not tell me where you are going, for then I don't know what to think."

"How could I tell you then, and you in bed?" said her servant with a half-saucy, half deferential expression of face that ended the argument.

Half an hour later Miss Paxton was summoned to her breakfast, and appeared in a delicate lilac dress and white muslin apron, a cap of light lace upon her head. She said she felt much refreshed and looked herself again.

The dining-room – used as a kitchen during the winter – was very large and clean; there were corner cupboards and shelves innumerable, ornamented with bright tin and clean crockery; there was a large fire-place filled with fresh evergreen from the forest, and a long table stood in the centre of the room, covered with a snowy cloth, and a breakfast to tempt the appetite. Steaming coffee, sweetened with maple sugar, and surmounted by a thick foam of cream, white bread and brown, fresh pots of butter, noble new potatoes, served in their jackets, Robert's trout fried to a light crisp brown, and a deep dish of strawberries and Devonshire cream "to top up with," as a school-boy would say.

Mr. Llewellyn was seated, but rose to receive his guest, and introduced her to his wife, and he did not sit down again till he had said grace. The garden door stood open, and a bird outside amended his benediction with a loud carol, and the breakfast began.

While they are thus pleasantly occupied, I will try and give you an idea of Mr. Llewellyn and his wife. The old gentleman was about the middle height, but stooped in the shoulders, which made him appear shorter. He was very thin, and his hair and beard were iron grey; he had a noble forehead and broad crown to the head, deep sunken grey eyes and high cheek bones; and he spoke in a clear, sonorous, somewhat dictatorial voice. His wife was a tiny, well formed little woman, a stealthy little woman, quick and cat-like in all her movements, with a pair of bright eyes that never met yours by any chance, and the deep voice of a man. She ate rapidly, indeed rather savagely, as if very hungry, occasionally uttering deep sighs; she spoke but little, and made her remarks abruptly and apropos of nothing. The husband's face looked honest; the wife's as double and deceitful as it was restless.

"What has become of Robert?" asked Mr. Llewellyn, when he had helped the ladies to fish.

"He thought Miss Paxton might object to sit at table with a servant," replied his niece, "he is minding the shop."

"What nonsense," said her uncle, "there will be no customers for a couple of hours, and the fish will be cold for the boy. Do you consider it *infra dig*[38] to sit at the same table with Robert, Miss Paxton?"

"Not with Robert," replied his guest, "he is not vulgar or even common-place; he would never take a liberty; but I would not sit at the same table with every servant, Mr. Llewellyn."

The old gentleman looked much pleased. "That is just my feeling," he said, "as a general rule I like to keep these people beneath the salt,

---

[38] *infra dig* = beneath someone's dignity

and in their proper places; but Robert is Robert, and quite another thing – call him in, Lavy."

"It is the man after all, not his class or occupation, that makes the difference," said Miss Paxton.

"I hate them all – low creatures," exclaimed Mrs. Llewellyn, abruptly.

Robert came at the summons of his little mistress, and took the vacant place between the two young ladies, with a modest good morning to Miss Paxton. Clad in a clean linen suit, he did not look unfit to sit there.

"How are the ponies this morning – have you groomed them yet?" asked the master.

"Yes, sir, they are all right," replied the lad with a hearty emphasis that disgusted his old mistress, and made his young one think, "He must be nervous."

Miss Paxton's heart gave a bound of relief; the fish were sweeter after that; the very sight of Robert, looking quite at his ease and as fresh as the morning, re-assured her as much as that hearty "all right," for he could not be like that, she thought, if the men were dead or in danger. She was glad she had taken his advice. She felt free and happy.

Breakfast over, Lavinia asked her guest to excuse her for a couple of hours, and having seated her in a rustic chair under a large apple tree in the garden, with a cushion at her back and books and papers, to pass the time, she left her. Mary did not take up a newspaper or open a book, but leaning back against the great trunk of the tree, enjoyed a quiet reverie. Thought succeeded thought, and scenes glad and sad came back without an effort; old pleasures made her smile; old sorrows brought tears brimming to her eyes, and presently one bright bead rolled down her cheek and fell on her dainty little apron.

It happened that Mr. Llewellyn, who had been to feed his chickens, issued from a side gate at that very instant and stood before her. Though a little deaf, he was far from blind; he saw the sad expression of face, he saw the tear, and he acted according to his nature. Being a kindly, honest man, with little tact, much learning; and not much knowledge of human nature, the spirit within him led him to say, "What is the matter, my dear?" and to lay his hand on hers as he spoke, "Is it some little pensive imaginary grief, or a real trouble? Do you know the one infallible remedy for all sorrows, great and small; the only true source of happiness in this life and the one to come?"

"I am not always happy. I have many troubles." Her large eyes met his, gravely, as she spoke. "I know no remedy for the evil there is in the world – I should like to know what you think of it."

The words of this speech were true, but it was partly dictated by politeness, partly by a desire to gauge the old man and see what was in him.

"Are you in harmony with God?" he asked.

"I do not understand you, Mr. Llewellyn; what do you mean?"

"Have you no will but God's will? Have you brought every thought into captivity to the obedience of Christ?"

"No, indeed," said Miss Mary.

"Then, that is the trouble; that is the difficulty, my dear; that, and that alone. Your will must be honest, uncompromising, entire. You must believe with your *whole* heart, not acknowledge the divinity of our Saviour with your head merely. Outward circumstances have nothing to do with our happiness, absolutely nothing; if we are in harmony with God, we are happy. You must mortify every corrupt affection, and all are corrupted by the fall – and God tells you how to do it. Walk in the spirit, and ye shall *not* fulfill the lusts of the flesh, for blessed are they that keep His commandments and seek Him with the *whole* heart; they also do *no* iniquity, they walk in His ways. *Seek and ye shall find,*" said the old gentleman, with great emphasis; "all power and salvation is of God, and the being whom He calls is free, the will He appeals to is free; when the sheep hears His voice and recognizes it, that is the day of His power. I counsel you, my dear, to make no delay, but to buy gold tried in the fire, that you may be rich, and white raiment that you may be clothed."

"Buy!" said Mary, rather tremulously, "how can I buy that for which God will accept neither money nor price? Purity, peace, holiness, righteousness, with what are these to be bought?"

"What are God's conditions?" returned Mr. Llewellyn, promptly. "We cannot pay in that which is valuable, for we have nothing of worth to offer; but we *can* tender our corruptions, and that is what God will accept as a full equivalent for eternal life. Wash you, make you clean, put away the evil of your doings from before mine eyes, He says, but with the whole will, absolute and unflinching, it must be, as with the prodigal son, or we shall remain impure forever, and *therefore* separated from God – the only source of every blessing. Let the wicked forsake his way and the unrighteous man his *thoughts*, and like the prodigal he is at once harmonized with God, he has come to himself, to a right state of mind, and this is all God ever did or will require. The prodigal was not even permitted to utter his repentance to the full; the *Father knew* it, and that was sufficient. Having once got right thoughts of God, Miss Mary, – God is *love*, and love guides us well – once believing that, I do not see how *you could* be unhappy. I can understand a man of strong passions, whose will is in harmony with God, but whose appetites and propensities are all at variance, having to agonize to enter in at the straight gate, when the seed of God's spirit having taken root is pushing out the weeds of the fall, when the refiner's fire is burning out, and the fuller's soap washing off the filth of sin; but *you*, my dear –." He paused.

"I am no better than the worst," said Mary, "I am often very discontented, very wicked, and I can't help thinking my circumstances have something to do with it."

"They haven't the least thing in the world to do with it," said the old gentleman, earnestly. "The kingdom of God is *within* you; once in harmony with God, you will be happy anywhere, no matter what the circumstances. God's ways are ways of pleasantness. *All* power is of God, our *sufficiency* is of God; but remember, the branch cannot bear fruit of itself, except it abide in the vine; no more can ye, except ye abide in *me*, says God. Behold I stand at the door and knock, if any man hear my voice, and open the door, *I will* come in to him. But you must have done with idols. The creatures of God are good and to be received with thanksgiving when they help instead of hindering us in the way of holiness; but when they absorb our thoughts and affections so as in any degree to shut out higher and holier things, they are idols. We may make an idol of our severest cross – a very ugly idol, too – and worship it by refusing to think of anything else. To blame circumstances for our own failures, is to upbraid God, who never makes mistakes, and who loves us and knows what is best for us. Where God reigns, *there* is His kingdom; he giveth power to the faint and to those who are without strength; those that wait upon the Lord shall *renew* their strength. Think upon these glorious promises, dear Miss Paxton, and take courage; think of God and his perfection, not of your own little peccadillos, and you will be happier – nay, happy altogether. And now, if you will excuse me for leaving you, I will take my wife for her daily stroll. Lavy will be here by and bye." So saying, the old gentleman turned to depart.

"I am grateful for the trouble you have taken with me," said Mary, "and I will try and do better. I will think of what you have said."

"No trouble," replied the old gentleman, with a wave of his hand, "it is a pleasure to set people right when they are wrong." And so he left her.

During this lecture, Mr. Llewellyn and his guest had been under the eye of a watchful observer, even Robert, who from a little window at the end of the shop, had seen Mary Paxton take her seat under the tree; had seen the absorbed gravity of her face, had seen that she did not move to take up book or paper, had seen the bright tear roll down her cheek, had seen his master's lecture though he could not hear a word, had watched her lips quiver and her eyes brim over, and felt so very much annoyed with Mr. Llewellyn as the cause of the tear, that his indignation took the form of words, though he had no one to hear and sympathise but a big brown dog.

"It's like eating a peck o' sawdust to listen to him," he muttered, "for all he's a scholar," and when he saw the lady was alone again, he put a favourite book of his own into the mouth of his dog, and sent him across the garden to her. Trip marched away with great dignity and laid the book in her lap. It was an old volume of ballads, bearing on the title page the name "Robert Hardacre;" a silken thread marked the song, "O! tell me how to woo."[39]

"Who sent you?" asked Mary, patting the dog's great brown head, and looking about her. Not a sign of life appeared in all the large garden, or at the windows of the house. Trip wagged his tail, but revealed nothing. She turned the book about and opened it with some curiosity, and glanced from one ballad to another, not without pleasure, till Miss Lavinia joined her; then she showed her the book and asked from whence it came.

"Oh! from Robert, I suppose," replied the young lady, rather coldly, as if the fact did not please her; so Mary changed the subject, and the respective merits of tatted and crochet lace were discussed with energy, if not with sincerity.

---

[39]Sir Walter Scott, "O! Tell me How To Woo," *The Complete Works of Sir Walter Scott* (Volume 1); *Minstrelsy of the Scottish Border* (1833): 174.

The atmosphere grew more and more sultry as the day advanced; the ladies talked languidly at intervals; the evening closed in at last, and nothing more worthy of note occurred.

Chapter Seven

"And like the dying swan, it ends in music."[40]

MORNING came, and with it the jolly sound of the stage horn. Miss Lavinia had the previous evening pressed her guest to stay a day or two longer, and she had accepted the invitation, though she heard Mrs. Llewellyn groan loudly when it was given. She could not from her window see the coach depart, but she asked Miss Llewellyn, at breakfast, if there were many passengers.

"Only Chip, Robert's brother," replied Lavinia, "it's quite a new freak for him to go to Gibbeline by stage."

We will leave the young ladies to the enjoyment of each other's society, and follow the coach. At Ostrander, it picked up Dr. Meldrum, who was rather surprised at the sight of four ill-looking fellows whom he did not know, three of whom were badly wounded. One who had his collar-bone broken by Bonnie's foot, asked the doctor to look at his wound and relieve him if possible, and if he couldn't to blow his brains out. Dr. Meldrum examined the hurt and told him the bone could not be set till the swelling was reduced, and declined to commit murder. By the time they reached Mrs. Paxton's, all three were in great pain from the jolting of the carriage. The doctor went in, instead of Robert, and Mrs. Hurst, who opened the door, saw he was a gentleman, and asked him into the parlour, where her mother was seated. The old lady knew him, having once consulted him about rheumatism; she received him civilly, and he asked after her health

---

[40]This quotation is perhaps a paraphrase of a line from "IV. Enigma 66", by Mr. Ja. Payne, of Croyden ('And like the dying swan, my latest breath shall sing a requiem'), according to C. Hutton, *The Diarian Miscellany* (1775): 142.

with great courtesy, and begged to be introduced to her daughter. This ceremony over, he told them he had a message from Miss Paxton, who desired her love, and was enjoying herself so much that she would not return till Friday.

"I only gave her leave to stay till to-day," said the old lady, crossly, which caused Mrs. Hurst to say, with great sweetness, that she was glad dear Mary was enjoying herself, and hoped the change would do her good.

Dr. Meldrum turned to the old lady and said, with great gallantry, "if you are so sorry to lose your charming daughters for a day or two, Mrs. Paxton, what would you do if you lost them altogether?"

"I should be very glad," she answered sourly, "but that is quite another thing, there is no such good fortune in store for me."

Dr. Meldrum now changed the subject, and told the ladies he had a very sick man in the stage, and he would be much obliged to them for a little whisky for him – if he was not asking too much – as there was a danger of the fellow fainting before he reached the hospital. Mrs. Paxton grudgingly ordered her daughter to give him a glass of whisky, and Mrs. urst was much concerned for the poor man's soul, and hoped he was in a proper frame of mind, and gave the doctor a tract for him along with the whisky. When the gentleman returned with the empty glass, Mrs. Paxton said she would like to consult him about her health, as she had hear of his skill, and was feeling far from well; she asked him if he could dine with her that day week. He of course said he should be most happy, so with mutual civilities they parted.

Through the doctor's influence – to whom Robert confided the whole matter – the sick men were admitted to the hospital without question, and the other man was shipped to the States by the Great Western Railway, Robert and Chip clubbing to pay his fare. Our hero gave a word of parting advice.

"You've got a free ticket to the other side, my man," said he, "and I've told the officials to keep an eye upon you, seeing you are a person o' consequence. When you get across the border, you'd better stay there, and never return to this y'er country, or it'll be the worse for you. We could sleep in safety in our beds before such gentry as you came about."

That evening, Robert was the bearer of a three-cornered note from Mrs. Paxton to her daughter, which we will take the liberty of reading over the young lady's shoulder.

> Dear Mary: –
>
> You are laying yourself under an obligation to those people by stay-ing so long. You had better ask Miss Llewellyn to come for a day or two, *As soon as possible*, and then we shall have done with the thing. *And come home on Friday.*
>
> Your affectionate mother,
>
> Pricilla Paxton.

The last command was underscored as showing the imperative mood in which it was written.

Mary had been a good deal alone that day, as Miss Llewellyn had to attend to the shop; but the next day Robert, being at home, Lavinia was more at liberty to entertain her guest, and made herself very agreeable and amusing. In the afternoon, they climbed the high-est hill in the neighbourhood to make a joint sketch of Cromaboo, Lavinia drawing the houses, and Mary, who had a taste for foliage, dotting in the trees. Mary noticed that if she made any allusion to Robert her new friend instantly became reserved, and that frank and open as she was on other subjects, she would not speak of him. This was rather a disappointment to Mary, who would have liked to know more of his family and himself, but she could not with politeness ask questions on a subject that was clearly unpleasant to Miss Lavinia.

Both had enough of the spirit of the artist in them to take plea-sure in what they were doing, and to those who love it, sketching is a refreshing, soul-reviving work, that sets thought in motion and pleasantly, too; the most innocent and happy work that ever mortal chose as a trade to earn bread by, the most pleasing occupation for the man or woman of leisure. I love to see children sketching, if it is only a tiny fellow with a slate, provided his heart is in the business, and he is quite absorbed; I know he is happy, that the little creating brain is at work, and the small hand trying to execute its commands.

Lavinia had finished her part of the sketch, and was now occu-pied in turning the heel of a white cotton stocking, and Mary was remarking the repose and dignity of the large elm she was drawing, when the top of it suddenly swayed in the wind, and the maples un-der which they sat shivered – though a minute before there had not been a breath of air to stir a leaf – and a low growl of thunder suc-ceeded, followed by a rushing wind. A minute later great splats of rain fell on the sketch book. The ladies scrambled up books, camp stools, and knitting, and ran down the hill with more haste than dignity, a furious wind facing, impeding them, and driving the rain in their faces. In a few minutes they were wet to the skin, and were forced to proceed more slowly by the weight of their garments; peal following peal, the lightning almost blinded them; the windows of heaven were open, and the rain descended in torrents; however they got home safely at last, but the sketch of Cromaboo was ruined, the knitting lost on the road, and the fair artists themselves, as the phrase goes, "as wet as drowned rats."

The commotion within doors was scarcely less than that without; Mrs. Llewellyn was screaming, wringing her hands, and declaring a second flood had come and that the earth would again be destroyed by water. In vain her husband assured her that the next time it was destroyed it would be by fire; she refused to be comforted and screamed louder than ever, "I would rather be drowned than burned." This she repeated again and again till the storm subsided.

The builder of the house had arranged the chimney so beautifully that the rain poured down in torrents and flooded the dining-room floor; the brown dog howled in fear and consternation at every peal of thunder, and the cat brought her kitten in her mouth and placed it in Miss Llewellyn's wet lap, as if she would say, "Let us all die together." The storm lasted an hour, then rolled away in the distance; the sun shone out brightly, and behold! a magnificent rainbow, perfect in itself and its reflexion, to lovely arches of soft, bright colour that spanned and glorified Cromaboo. Then the sun disappeared, the black clouds became grey, the rain softened to a gentle drizzle, and the air grew chilly. The disturbance within doors subsided as the storm ceased, Mrs. Llewellyn was persuaded to go to her little parlour and have her shoes and stockings changed; her husband sat with her to keep her company; the young ladies went to their bed-rooms to change their dripping muslins for warmer garments; and Robert, Trip and the cat were left in undisputed possession of the dining-room.

Robert, when left alone, exerted himself nobly to make the room habitable again. He turned Trip out of his kennel with small ceremony, carried Puss and her baby back to their box in the kitchen, and mopped up the floor with a vigor and skill that soon made it tidy, removed the evergreens from the chimney, except one small tree which he piled round with chips and lighted to dry the floor. Very pleasant the fire looked on the chill ending of a day that had begun with almost tropical heat.

Then he put a fire in the back kitchen stove and the kettle over it, and set out the cups for tea, when, considering his duties over for the present, he retreated to the shop, to be called back presently by his little mistress to make toast and boil eggs while she prepared a junket under the superintendence of Miss Paxton, who had made many a one, and volunteered to teach her young friend. While thus engaged, the ladies compared notes about cooking, Miss Lavinia asserting with great energy that the Brazilian mode of preparing fruit for the table was superior to all others, and the only proper method on the face of the earth. She was born in Brazil, and had lived there as a child; that to stew it in copper, tin, or any kind of metal, was to spoil it, and make it unfit for human food.

"It should be covered close in an earthen dish," she concluded, "and never touch metal, and so should any preparation with milk. I love cooking," added the little lady with a gentle sigh.

"And I detest it," said Mary; "I would be content never to taste poultry again rather than prepare it for the table, as I have done for the last five years. Ah! if ever I have a cook, I'll not quarrel with her if the toast is a bit burnt, or the porridge too thick or too thin."

"I would not quarrel with her, but I would dismiss her," said Lavinia; "badly cooked food is simply disgusting. I have taught Robert to cook since he came here; he could not boil a potato even, or cook an egg; but now he knows his duty pretty well."

"It is not my duty," said the lad, in his gentle distinct voice; "I was not hired to cook, I do it of grace to save you."

The eyes of the ladies met, both smiled and Lavinia flushed scarlet; but Miss Mary only lifted her eye-brows and said, "Ah! Robert, I see we must use words with discretion when in your company, weigh them well, and give them their exact meaning."

"It is better always to do that," he replied gravely.

"True, O! Robert," said Miss Paxton, "but who can always be wise? Not I for one."

"Well, I always try to say what I mean," remarked Lavinia, sharply, "and I mean what I say."

"So do I," said her servant, "but then somehow one changes, and may not mean to-morrow the same as to-day. I remember when I thought a briar rose the most perfect rose in the world, but then I had never seen any other."

"You are a sage," said his young mistress, rather scornfully, "but your philosophy is too deep for me; it goes beyond cooking."

After this, conversation flagged until all were seated at the table, and even then it took the form of a dialogue between Mr. Llewellyn and Miss Paxton, and Lavinia was unusually quiet and taciturn. Robert said but little, and Mrs. Llewellyn not one word during the meal, though she ate greedily.

Miss Paxton asked if there was a Sunday School in Cromaboo, and if Mr. Llewellyn was a teacher.

"There are Sunday Schools here," he replied, "and I was once a teacher. I had a class of young men and women, but failed to interest them, and gave it up. They came to seek amusement, not to seek light and truth, and to flirt in a coarse way and enjoy each other's society. The power of God was so strong in Goldsmith's pastor that those who came to scoff remained to pray, but there was no such power in me; I could not melt nor purify them; not one chord of sympathy vibrated to my touch; I felt God did not bless me in my work, and gave it up, leaving them to go their own gate; leaving them as I found them, dense in ignorance and gross as to morality."

"But the little children – could you do nothing with them? They surely are capable of improvement."

"Undoubtedly they are, my dear, but I have unfortunately no talent for instructing little ones. I believe if ever Cromaboo is a better place, it will be brought about by the children, and I wish I had a talent for bringing down my ideas to their comprehension; but others may come who have what I lack, and children are quick to learn and imbibe ideas imperceptibly, and reason at a very early age. Robert has a little brother who could reason in a way that astonished me, when he was scarcely three years old. His father indulges in the habit of swearing – which is one of the minor vices of Cromaboo – and though fond of children, he is not kind to animals; indeed it by no means follows that the love of children includes the love of pets; a fact which ought to make phrenologists blush for their ignorance, when they class all these little amiable peculiarities into one bump. But to come back to my story. – John Smith invariably calls cats devils. Little Tommy was brought into the shop by his mother, one day, and I showed the child two kittens to amuse him. 'Baby devils,' he cried, in great delight. I thought my deaf ears had deceived me, so I put my head close to the little fellow and made a sounding-board of my hand. 'What did you call them, Tommy?' I said. 'Baby devils,' he responded, tenderly stroking them and laying his head against them. Some instinct, not inherited from his father, made him love the little things."

"The dear little creature," said Mary, "what a pity he should not have a good example."

"Oh! you mustn't be prejudiced against Robert's father, he is a white lily in comparison with some of his neighbours. Tommy is better off than any little man in Cromaboo, for he has a good mother as well, to say nothing of Bob here."

The mail carrier's face flushed with pleasure. "Oh! Tommy don't consider me much of a blessing," he said, "he is often very jealous of me. One day when mother said, 'I'm very proud of my son,' meaning me, he got off his little stool and stood before her for full a minute, and then he said, 'I thought you had two sons, mother.'"

"Tommy and his mother seem to have forgotten Chip," said Mary.

"Chip is my father's son, not my mother's, Miss Paxton."

"I believe character is formed in the first twelve years," resumed Mr. Llewellyn, "and there is great truth in the old Scotch proverb, 'thraw the woodie while it's green, between three and thirteen,' but the purest Sunday-school teaching is often counteracted by the bad example of home, when the home is a mere sink of corruption. I often think nothing would ever reform Cromaboo but a great fire that would burn the old birds and their nests of bugs and fleas together, and leave the little children to begin a new town."

"I am sorry Cromaboo is such a bad place," said Mary, thoughtfully; "it seemed to me such a pretty pastoral little village, as I sketched it from the hill; each little white dwelling looked like a home, an abode of peace and innocence. I thought of 'Sweet Auburn,' and mentally quoted:

'Sweet was the sound when oft at evening's close
Up yonder hill the village murmur rose.'[41]

Ah! who can judge from appearances?" and she sighed.

---

[41] Oliver Goldsmith (1728-1774), "The Deserted Village" (1770). Sweet Auburn is the name of the deserted village in Goldsmith's poem.

Mr. Llewellyn laughed outright and Mary fancied she detected a subtle, observant half amused look on Robert's face, that led her to think he was taking the length of her foot.

"If you could hear 'the village murmur' on a fair day, from that very hill as I have," said Mr. Llewellyn, "you would think it anything but sweet; it's a chorus of oaths, screams and drunken songs, rising higher and louder as the night advances; you would stop your ears and run down faster than you did from the storm to-day, and be glad to shut the door between yourself and the foul world outside. But Robert will give us some music and make us forget our bad neighbours, now we have done with the tea-tackle."

Mrs. Llewellyn started up at this, and ran about the room with a sudden restlessness that made Mary think she took especial interest in the music, and Robert opened the melodeon,[42] not without the demur that perhaps Miss Paxton did not care for music.

"I love music," said Mary, and mentally added "*good music*," for she expected but a poor performance, and settled herself in her chair with a determination not to look bored whatever her feelings might be.

The rough fingers touched the keys, and Mrs. Llewellyn's restlessness[43] ceased as by magic; she sat down, leaned her face on her hands and listened. His touch was good; he played a soft minor, and sweet and plaintive harmony filled the room, not discord.

Truly music is a wonderful thing, and the power of it is inexplicable when we consider that after all it is but regulated noise. It can unlock hearts and bring the dead to life, and restore in all their freshness half-forgotten faces and events which had grown dim with time. Does its power lie in its truth, or is it but a sweet and potent falsehood, a gracious answer to the longing within us, promising much but never paying; a sympathizing unseen presence that twines about the heart and insinuates love and joy, never to be realized? It is certainly something – this blending and dividing of sounds – that wins our confidence, touches our conscience, melts our hearts, throws us off our guard, and turns us inside out. I have sometimes thought that beautiful music is perfect truth, and therein lies its power to make us honest for the time; it unmasks our motives to ourselves without

---

[42] melodeon = a small accordion of German origin.

[43] The 1878 edition has "restleness," which I take as a mistake for "restlessness."

saying "by your leave," it is a ray of light direct from God himself, showing us the innermost thoughts of our hearts.

Mary's first thought as she heard Robert play was, "He is not offensive," but as the melody swelled and sank and died almost away, only to revive in sweeter and more thrilling harmony, it begun to tell upon her; her heart was stirred, her large eyes brightened, her hands trembled, though she sat very still, and by and bye great tears came rolling down her cheeks.

Robert thought of but one hearer, and performed but for one person; so after playing for twenty minutes, he turned to see the effect of his music. He was startled – shocked.

"I have made you unhappy," he said, on an impulse of compunction, "I have given you pain." He was sorry as soon as the words had left his tongue, and felt he should not have spoken.

"No! *pleasure*, Robert, pure unalloyed pleasure. People sometimes cry from joy as well as sorrow, you foolish boy. Is Robert your pupil in music as well as in cooking, Miss Llewellyn?"

"Oh! no, he could play when he came, as well as he does now; but by ear; he does not know a note."

"Is it possible?" said Mary.

"I know G and D," said Robert, lightly touching the keys in question.

"That is not even the alphabet of music," remarked Mr. Llewellyn.

"He understands the whole language of music, alphabet or not," said Mary. "Play again, Robert, play again, – Miss Llewellyn longs to hear you and so do I; play, and ease our hearts."

He did play again; he played back happy memories, old scenes, sweet words, dear faces; he played till nine o'clock, when he struck into 'God Save the Queen,' and having scattered Her Majesty's enemies with voice as well as fingers, – a loyal outburst in which the young ladies assisted, – he rose and closed the instrument.

"It isn't late, my lad; it's only nine," said the master.

"To-morrow is stage-day, sir, and Miss Paxton is going; she will be tired if we keep her up late."

Mrs. Llewellyn groaned loudly; but her husband said "to be sure, I had forgotten, – you are a thoughtful boy, Bob," and Miss Lavinia offering no opposition, they all separated for the night.

Chapter Eight

"Leave a kiss within the cup and I'll not ask for wine."

– Ben Jonson[44]

SOFT was the air and bright the sunrise, fresh and clean and without dust the dry baked roads of yesterday, as Robert and Miss Paxton turned their backs on Cromaboo. For once his master's interest was not paramount with Robert; he was glad he had no other passenger that the one beside him. They had scarcely left the village when Mary began to question him eagerly.

"Now about those horrid men, Robert – are they much hurt, and what have you done with them? I have longed to ask you."

"Three in hospital and one gone to the States," he replied. "The one Bonnie trod on is pretty badly hurt; his collar bone broken and some ribs – he may die yet, but I hope not – and the one I shot in the arm has a slight wound. The third fellow isn't much hurt either, 'twas fright made him let you go; the bullet lodged in his neck and one of the others got it out with his pen-knife. I must see them off to the other side as soon as they are out of the hospital."

"Did you know that man was suffering all the first day? Did your father or brother do anything for him?"

"Took them all some food," replied Robert, "and as for his suffering, serve him right, I say; a deal too much is made of such like rascals. If every honest man set his face against them, instead o' petting them up for their sins and signing petitions for them when they are condemned to be hanged, Canada would be more like it used to

---

[44]Ben Jonson (1572-1637), "To Celia".

be. Why I've heard mother say, when she was young a woman might sleep with the doors and windows open and be safe, or walk in the dead o' the night for miles, and never a hand raised but to help her on her way, nor a heart wish her evil, nor a tongue say worse nor 'God be wid you,' – that's as it should be."

"I hope we have done right," said Mary, thoughtfully, "it seems scarcely fair to the Yankees to send such men among them."

"Oh! *that's* nothing," returned her companion, lightly; "they are always sending us rubbish in the way o' pedlars and showmen and the like; let 'em look out for theirselves – they're well able – and maybe them fellows will behave better after this lesson. I wouldn't trouble about it, Miss Paxton, they are not worth a thought of yours – they are not worth a hair of your head – nor the whole nation o' Yankees either."

"You are a thick and thin youngster, Robert, to be so bright and careless when you knew that man you had wounded was suffering and in want of help; I felt sure by your face and manner that they were very little hurt."

"I meant you to think so," said Robert, quietly, "it wasn't fit them nasty vermin should spoil the whole o' your visit; 'twas bad enough that they frightened you."

"Had you any difficulty in getting them into the hospital?" asked the lady, after a pause.

"No, ma'am; the authorities are bound to take in them that apply. The men know they committed a crime in attacking the mail, and can't understand why I don't prosecute; they know they are quite in my hands and will be quiet for their own sakes, or tell some lie to satisfy the curiosity of the surgeons."

He did not mention the help and influence of Dr. Meldrum, partly because he thought she might feel annoyed that he knew of the adventure, and partly because he was secretly jealous of him, and did not wish her to take an interest in him.

They trotted on, in silence, till they reached the swamp.

"This is the place," said Miss Paxton, looking about in a startled way, "I can't help feeling nervous."

"You needn't fear," said Robert, soothingly, "there's nothing in the whole length and breadth of the wood to harm you, this morning. I cannot trot faster because it's up-grade. Look at that squirrel – he's running a race with us – and hearken to the birds."

"I know it's foolish to feel nervous," she said, "I'll try and think of something else. Tell me about your music, – how did you come to play so well? I will try and bend my attention to what you may say and catch courage from you; you look calm enough, but you would if you were going to have your head cut off."

Robert laughed. "I don't know about that," he said, "I'd put a good face on it if my mind was made up to go through with it. I didn't feel calm the other night, only determined to do my duty, come what would, and to get the better o' them, – but about the music, Miss Paxton" –

"About the music, presently Robert, – you talk of duty – was it your duty to deceive me deliberately about that wounded man, who may yet die, you say, by saying 'all right?'"

"Yes; Scripture plain, its every man's duty to bear his own burden," said the lad, promptly, "and not to put it on the shoulders of a delicate little lady. You trusted the whole thing to me, and you shall have no more trouble in the matter, if I can help it. I wouldn't have told you about the rascal's danger now, but I'm afeared he may die out o' spite like, and 'twould startle you more to hear it on a sudden. I have but one care in the thing, and that's you, and I don't wish the man to die and make you unhappy; for himself I don't care, he's not as respectable as Bonnie."

"He is not fit to die," said Miss Paxton, "he's a poor ignorant wretch, I suppose."

"He can read and write well, he knows more nor I do, and the learning's been wasted on the like o' *him*, while I – I am ignorant."

There was an intense bitterness in the last words that startled his hearer, and moved her heart to a sudden thrill of pity for the boy beside her. She touched his brown hand kindly.

"You ignorant – no, Robin Adair,[45] you can play – come tell me about the music."

The touch of the fingers, the name she had given him – for he knew the old song well enough – brought a blush of pleasure to his face, a smile to his expressive mouth, and a quick warmth and tenderness to the brown eyes, as they turned upon her gratefully, that startled and touched her in a different way.

---

[45] "Robin Adair" was a popular ballad of the nineteenth century.

"There's not much to tell," he said. "I can never remember the time when I couldn't sing and whistle, but I never tried to play on an instrument till I went to live at Mack's tavern at Bezar. I just had to set the tables, cut wood, and keep the fires up, so I had plenty of time to myself. They had a melodeon. I tried to play and the landlady liked to hear me, and encouraged me. I lived there a year and played every day; twas the only pleasure I had; my heart was in it. My next place was the church parson's, in Cromaboo. Mrs. Johnson, his wife, had a small organ, and let me play when my work was done; she said it soothed her to hear me. She took great pains to teach me part singing, and she taught me several hymns and temperance songs. She used to knit warp stockings for her children, and it's a nasty job to wind warp. She said she would give me a lesson in singing for every ball I wound. I generally got one every day. I stayed there nigh upon two years, till they left Cromaboo; the wages wasn't much, but learning is better than money. Mrs. Johnson lent me books, and I had to read the Bible twice a day, in turns with the children, and she was good at accounts and taught me to cipher in the winter evenings. When I left, Mr. Llewellyn took me to drive the stage, and that's all, Miss Paxton."

"*Multum in parvo*,"[46] said Mary, "you took to playing as the birds take to singing, I see." After a long pause – "Have you a Bible?"

"Not of my own, ma'am, but I can have the loan of one, any time; they are as thick as peas at Mr. Llewellyn's, and at the parsonage we read the Bible every day, and at the tavern there was a Bible in every room, according to law, and my mother has two, one for show and one for use."

"Robert, I want to give you something; not as pay – your bravery is above reward – but to mark my sense of gratitude for a great deliverance. I think I will give you a Bible."

"I should prize anything you gave me," he replied simply, "but if I might choose a gift it would not be that."

"It is the best of books, Robert."

"It is; but I would not choose a book. You see my bravery is not above reward," with a smile.

"Well, name what you would like, if it is anything within my means you shall have it."

---

[46] *Multum in parvo* (Latin) = "much in little," i.e. a great deal in a small package.

"I hardly like to, Miss Paxton; I would not offend you for the world; in one sense it would not cost as much as a Bible, and yet it might cost you more."

"Don't be mysterious," she said, "I am not a touchy person, or prone to take offense where none is meant. I have no idea what you would like, but I will not refuse, if I can help it."

"Will you," he said, "because I am your friend, though only a poor fellow – because I fought for you, and because I would die for you cheerfully – will you give me one kiss?"

They emerged from the swamp as he spoke, and the sun shone full upon his face as she looked at him; his shy, deprecating, coaxing, smiling bonnie face. She was half vexed, half amused, and wholly astonished at the request.

"No, you silly boy," she said, "what good would that do you? You must have the Bible."

"I will not have the Bible, if I may not have the kiss," he said.

His under lip protruded obstinately, his face took a sullen expression; the horses walked slowly on.

"Now, Robert, don't be unreasonable," said the lady.

"I am *not* unreasonable," replied the quiet, persistent voice at her side. "I know the reason of the thing quite well, it's because I'm an ignorant fellow and a servant, that you refuse me. If the Prince of Wales had done half as much for you, and asked you to honour him with a kiss as payment, and he would feel more than rewarded – as well he might, Prince though he is – you know you would not say no to *him*; you wouldn't call him silly, or think him impudent; you would not despise *him*."

The truth of the words struck home, and the reproach in the lad's eyes brought her dream to her mind with the suddenness of a flash of lightning.

"I do not despise you," she said, "but you are a *very silly* boy, and a very sentimental boy, and a very saucy boy, too; to tell me so plainly what you think of me; but you shall have the kiss if you like," and she turned her pretty pale face towards him and offered her cheek. His sullenness flashed into sunshine in a moment; he gave her no time to reconsider the matter, but removing his ragged straw hat reverently, he pressed his lips, not to the offered cheek, but to the smiling rosy mouth that had just given him permission. There was a passion in the lad's kiss, with all its tenderness, that made her blush like a rose, and look really beautiful for the moment; and a feeling of embarrassment and shyness was succeeded as instantly by a sense of keen annoyance, as a man got over the fence near them and shouted out "stop stage."

Robert drew in his horses, whispering earnestly at the same time, "Don't be vexed, he did not see us; he was looking the other way – I was watching him."

"What's your fare to Gibbeline?" asked the new comer.

Robert stated it, and the man climbed in. After what had passed, conversation was impossible; they could not chat on general subjects, so they were silent; Robert, intoxicated with that taste of perfect bliss, yet fearful that he had offended past pardon, was restlessly quiet. Mary, annoyed with herself, that she had been so weak as to permit such a liberty, and more constrained than she would have thought possible a day ago. So they sped along silently, in the fresh bright morning, passing green corn-fields, patches of wood and meadow land, log houses, frame[47] houses, and as they advanced, brick and stone houses, surrounded by orchards and gardens, till they came to the old home embowered in roses and honeysuckle.

Robert lifted Miss Paxton down, threw the reins to his passenger and ran up the steps with her valise.

"I asked too much," he said in a low voice, as he held the gate open for her to pass through; "what gave me such pleasure, gave you pain; I took too great a liberty – forgive me – it was not manly in me."

"No," she replied, "it was very boyish; if you were a man I could not forgive you or myself either; but you are only a naughty presuming boy, and I'll try and forget it as soon as I can. The Bible will be a far better gift for you."

She tried to be dignified, but blushed in spite of herself, as she met the bright brown eyes, a fact that brought a beaming smile to the rogue's face. "The Bible would never equal that kiss," he thought, but he did not say so. She did not offer to shake hands, so Robert could only remove his hat and bow as he said good morning. He had a delighted feeling that he had not been born in vain, as he ran down the steps and mounted his seat again.

Once within doors, Mary was surprised to find things better

---

[47]The 1878 edition has "frome."

than she expected; Mrs. Hurst was quite alert[48] and good-tempered, telling her sister they were going to have quite a little dinner party on Wednesday next, Miss Llewellyn and Dr. Meldrum were to come.

"It is all arranged," she said, "and it will make quite a break in our dull life. I feel sure Mr. Meldrum is a gaudy man, by the way he received the tract I gave him."

He had not impressed Mary in that way, but she was glad her sister was pleased. As for Mrs. Paxton, she received her daughter sulkily enough; she did not know her motive for staying two days longer than she had given her permission, and regarded it as flat rebellion. It surprised her, for she did not think Mary had so much spirit left, and she considered it better to pass it over this time without comment, though she was angry at heart.

---

[48]The 1878 edition has "elert."

Chapter Nine

Thou knowest no less but all; I have unclasped
To thee the book even of my secret soul."

— *Twelfth Night*[49]

WEDNESDAY came and with it Mrs. Paxton's guests. Spinach was a specialty with Mrs. Paxton; a dish of spinach with poached eggs and toast she would say was "food for a queen." She would plant spinach in the fall to have it early in the spring, and in the spring, and again in July, to indulge in it as late as October. She was also fond of asparagus, and had it every second day as long as the season lasted, and woe to the unlucky household if the drawn butter happened to be too thick or too thin, it would anger her for twenty-four hours. To-day it was just right, however, and she remarked graciously to Dr. Meldrum that she considered these vegetables "particularly wholesome," a sentiment in which he politely acquiesced, thinking in his heart, no doubt, they were for the consumer, but how about the cook when the thermometer stood at ninety in the shade? And then to be expected to sit down to dinner and do the amiable and make conversation, – he thought it too bad, and would rather have had a salad or a sandwich to eat in his hand, and the pretty provider as cool and comfortable as himself; but nothing of this mental commentary appeared in his clear, handsome face.

The third course was apple pudding, another favourite dish with Mrs. Paxton; every day all the year round it was served at her table; the russets lasted till the early summer apples were ripe in July. Never by any chance was a cold dinner served in that house, for

---

[49]William Shakespeare, *Twelfth Night*: Act 1, Scene 4.

though Mrs. Paxton and her eldest daughter were fond of a salad, they differed unhappily about the dressing, and a salad was the signal for a dispute that generally ended in a quarrel; so Mary avoided it as she would the apple of discord.

Mrs. Paxton was never a great talker at meal-times; a dinner she considered was made to be eaten, not talked over, and the little Brazilian was rather shy among so many strangers, so she said little, but thought of her uncle, who if his tea was hot, never inquired whether it was strong or sweet, who could eat very queer butter without grumbling, who always gave the tit-bits to his wife, and thanked God heartily for lettuce and cold bacon, reverently removing his skull-cap, and standing to his grace; here there was no pretense of asking a blessing, neither God nor the cook were thanked for the good things provided, for Mrs. Paxton pronounced such ceremonies "all gammon,"[50] chiefly it must be confessed to annoy the parson's widow.

Mrs. Hurst and the doctor had nearly all the conversation to themselves – for Mary was too tired to talk much – and said very civil things to one another which neither quite meant, and had a walk in the garden afterwards, while Mary superintended the dishwashing lest Polly should break the best china, and Mrs. Paxton gave her little guest a long dissertation upon the cultivation of bulbous roots. By and bye the ramblers returned, and Mrs. Paxton expressed a wish to consult the doctor on the subject of her health, so Margaret left them and went up stairs, and the younger ladies strolled off into the orchard to watch for the stage and have a chat.

Mrs. Paxton explained her various ailments at great length to the doctor, who listened with patience, felt her pulse, gently pumped her as to her age, and the age of her parents when they died, her general habits and other matters of no importance to the reader, and he came to the conclusion that she would hardly last two years longer, perhaps not one; that the flowers she so much admired would soon be growing above her; but of this he gave no hint; he said soothing things and promised a little stimulating medicine and pronounced her "a wonderful old lady," an opinion which entirely fell in with her own. In the meantime Mary and her new friend had strolled to the bottom of the orchard, and were seated under the shade of a large

---

[50] gammon = misleading, deceitful, or nonsensical talk.

apple-tree, leaning their backs against its trunk, and lazily watching the brook.

"How tired you look," said Lavinia. "Do you always do the cooking?"

"Yes, since my father died. We have had seven hand-maidens in the last five years, left-handed, inefficient bodies every one of them, who couldn't do the commonest thing without teaching. They had to be taught how to pick peas, to dig potatoes, to clean vegetables and knives; things that would come by nature to a smart girl; they could not even wash dishes or sweep the back kitchen in a tidy way." And she sighed.

"You do not keep a cow?" said Lavinia.

"No, if we did I should have to milk it half the time myself."

"You have a feeling face," remarked Lavinia, presently, "and now I know some of your troubles. I feel more courage to confide in you; I think you might help me by advice, or at least by sympathy. I have never had a young lady for a friend, – of course uncle loves me, and auntie too, sometimes, but mamma died when I was a child, and there's no one amongst those Cromaboo people with whom I can associate."

"*Pourquoi pas*? If one may inquire."

"They are all of a lower class, and they are so dreadfully immoral; nearly everybody."

"What of the Smiths?" asked Mary.

"Mrs. Smith is a good woman and above her class in many ways, but she cannot write her name, and her husband is still more ignorant, and their eldest son is a *dreadful* fellow," with great emphasis.

"In what way?" inquired Mary.

"He is a farmer in partnership with a German named Root, and people say they have the house-keeper in partnership too. She has never married, but she has four children, some like Chip, and some like the other man. Is it not too disgusting? I am sure Robert believes it, for he will never take money from Chip, or money's worth, although he likes him; and Mrs. Smith feels as I do about it, and though the children come to her house sometimes, she will not have the woman. The Cromaboo people in general don't feel the immorality of these things; they call it 'a misfortune' if a girl has a baby and no husband, or say she has been very unfortunate, as if it was entirely an accident."

"Poor things, they couldn't express it better," said Mary, "it is a misfortune that may lead to the loss of their souls, for when evil is begun who can tell where it will end. We cannot say how great a misfortune is a life brought into the world sinfully. But Robert – what of him? He is good, I hope."

"He is good, but he is a willful, strange boy; what do you think of him, Miss Paxton?"

"I like him, and think him no ordinary lad," she replied, simply and frankly. "I take an interest in him; I should like you to tell me all you know of him. He seems very complying in manner," said this foxey, fair lady; "is he determined, do you think – has he any decision of character?"

"He will lay a plan and carry it through with the pertinacity of a bull-dog," replied Lavinia. "Even when taken by surprise, and put upon his mettle, he will have his own way in spite of obstacles that to others would be insuperable. I will give you an example. The first clergyman we had in Cromaboo was a *horrid* drinking man," – the little lady held up her hands most expressively, – "and the next wasn't there long before he was suspended for seducing a woman of thirty, or she did him – she ought to have been suspended, too, from a rope – but the third was really a *good* religious man, but harsh and with no tact; he would tell people their sins right up to their faces in their own houses in the *plainest* language. He used to call it 'speaking the truth in love.' They hated him for it, he was very unpopular, just *detested*. At last some of them laid logs across the road, one dark night, to trap him. His buggy upset, and he broke his thigh in two places, and dislocated his shoulder. He lay there all night, and John Smith found him in the morning when going to his work, and carried the poor little man in his arms to the parsonage, and sent Dr. Meldrum to set the leg, and Robert to take care of the horse and help Mrs. Johnson. They hired him for a month, but he stayed till they left Cromaboo. The house is on an island, and the only way to get at it was by a strong narrow bridge the drunken parson had built. It was in the spring, and there was a great freshet,[51] and the first Sunday after the accident – only it was design, not accident – the whole population of Cromaboo, men and women, assembled on the river bank, tore up the bridge and cut off all communication with the main land. Robert

---

[51]freshet = a spring thaw resulting in snow and ice melt.

had gone home for the afternoon, and had on his Sunday clothes –
he is very proud of his best clothes- -"

"Does he look well in them?" asked Mary, interrupting her, "best
clothes are a severe test for a working man."

"He looks like a gentleman, as much at ease as in his rags."

Mary inclined her head approvingly. "Go on with the story," she
said.

"Well, when he got to the bank he was met by shouts and sneers
of derision, and advice to swim. 'I had better go home,' he said, quietly, and turned back. There is a little cone-shaped hill further down
the river, covered with scrub on one side, but perfectly bare at the top
and bare towards Cromaboo, where a steep, straight path descends
to the edge of the stream. Twenty minutes after, Robert was seen on
the top of this cone, deliberately taking off his clothes and making
them into a parcel. He held them on his head with his hand, and holding his hat aloft in the other in salutation to the people of Cromaboo
and to keep it from the water, he ran down the steep path dressed
as Adam was before the fall, waded into the river and through it, in
the eyes of his fellow-citizens and in spite of their teeth, for he was
too far off to pelt, though near enough to be seen very plainly. He
retired among the tamaracks, donned his garments again and presented himself at Mrs. Johnson's back door, calmly apologizing to
the frightened little woman for being ten minutes too late."

Mary laughed, a ringing, musical laugh that startled a cat-bird in
the tree above them and set him scolding.

"If I had not known Robert was an Irish boy before, I should have
guessed it now," said she.

"How do you know he is Irish, – did he tell you?"

"I know from the way he speaks, and the way he wears his hat,
it is quite national, he only wants a shelalah[52] to make him complete.
Tell me more of his battles?"

Thus encouraged, Miss Lavinia related Robert's exploits with the
wood-carriers, the smokers, the swearers, and finally the attempt to
poison him, at which her companion looked grave and startled.

"There is one thing I wished *particularly* to tell you about Robert,"
she said in conclusion, with a blush and a sigh, "though I am afraid
you will despise me for it, – I – I am engaged to him."

---

[52] shillelagh = a cudgel with a strap, associated with Ireland and Irish folklore.

The large eyes that were looking into hers, widened with surprise at this statement. "Do you mean that you are engaged to be married to him?"

"Yes, though it may never come to that, and I am more than half ashamed of it; but it's so dull where we live, and we never see a gentleman, – really there is *no* chance of getting a beau in Cromaboo, and we have been so much thrown together, Robert and I. Of course I know it is a great condescension on my part, and I wouldn't have it known for the world."

Mary regarded her keenly, but was silent.

"I believe uncle would turn me out of doors if he knew," she went on, "and I see you disapprove of me for loving Robert."

"If you loved him would you feel it a condescension to be engaged to him?" said her companion, breaking into a smile.

"Why of *course* it *is* a condescension," replied the little Brazilian, with energy, "he is a very ignorant lad of mean origin, and I am descended from Prince Llewellyn; he is quite uneducated, but for all that he knows things from intuition, that some men would never learn in a thousand years; he has nice feelings, and little courteous ways."

"I am sure of that," assented the other lady. "Tell me – that is if you don't mind – how it all happened. I am trustworthy."

"I feel *sure* you are," said Lavinia. "It was when he was ill it began. I helped his mother nurse him, and at first we thought he would die, and I took to petting him, and got to have an interest in him I hardly know how. I used to watch him when he was asleep, and he had such an innocent weary look when his eyes were closed, and it seemed so cruel to have him suffering because of those wretches. His face was quite close to mine one day when I was putting a pillow under his head, and he kissed me and said he loved me, and I couldn't be angry, he looked so pinched and pallid, but I told him he had forgotten his place, and he said he had at once and forever, for he should always love me, and then he kissed me again. It is so hard to deal with ignorant people, Miss Mary; you see he didn't know any better, poor fellow; he doesn't know enough to understand making love as a gentleman would."

"Upon my word," said Mary, "I think he does understand it pretty well. He's an impudent young rascal." The memory of that extorted kiss smote her with a sense of anger against Robert.

"It's nice to be loved even by an ignorant boy," proceeded Lavinia, "but pleasure always brings pain. Robert is so cold to me lately and changed, and doesn't kiss my hand and pay me compliments as he used to. It is too humiliating to think he is getting tired of me, after I have lowered myself to accept his attentions. If I thought there was any chance of getting cousin Harry for a husband I would break with him at once."

"So that is the extent of your love," said Miss Paxton. "And who is cousin Harry?"

"He is the most perfect gentleman I know – he lives in Hamilton – but I am so plain I am afraid I have no chance with him, and I wouldn't be an old maid for the world, and Bob really is a dear dainty little fellow – how I wish you could see him in his Sunday clothes."

Miss Paxton shrugged her shoulders. "He is better than nothing for a husband, aye? Poor Robert."

"You needn't pity him," said Lavinia, rather tartly, "I would make him an excellent wife, and it isn't every person in his station gets such a chance. Do you know, Miss Mary, I am half afraid of you, and jealous of you, and that made me tell you what I have. Robert thinks so much of you that – I may be a fool to tell you – but I am jealous of you."

"Of *me*," said Miss Paxton, rather proudly, "setting aside other differences, I am nearly old enough to be his mother; I thought you spoke to me because I had a feeling face."

"But you have influence with him, and he likes and admires you," persisted Lavinia, "and as for the difference in age, Queen Elizabeth had her Essex even at seventy, and you know how Mary loved Phillip of Spain."

Miss Paxton laughed till the tears rolled down her cheeks and the cat-bird began to screech with alarm and vexation.

"You have drawn more than one nail out of my coffin," she said, as she wiped her eyes. "I feel the full force of the compliment, but really you do me too much honor. Those women were queens, you foolish child, and Essex did not love Elizabeth, nor Phillip Mary. The love was all on one side in both cases; and Elizabeth condescended, as you do, to receive the addresses of her servant, who was just an ambitious young hypocrite as I hope your Cromaboo Adonis is not, my little friend, for your sake."

At that moment they both caught a glimpse of the stage crawling slowly up the hill. The sight of it seemed to sober the speaker.

"Let us go and speak to him," said Lavinia, and they walked slowly across to the sweet briar hedge and waited.

Robert sprang out of the coach when he saw them and came into the shade of the orchard, and said the green hill side looked just like paradise; and so it did to him – hot, dusty and tired as he was. He thought Mary looked better, cooler and more beautiful than he had ever seen her. Never before had he seen her in a plain print dress, or felt so keenly the distance between them, for she only bowed with quiet gravity and said "good afternoon," and not another word during the interview. Lavinia contrasted unfavourably with the pale beauty by her side; she seemed to the eyes of the faithless Robert smaller, darker and plainer than usual. She sympathized with him for looking so weary, and sent a message to her uncle.

He left them with a dissatisfied feeling; the distance of Mary's manner was not lost upon him, and he half suspected that the young ladies had been comparing notes about him.

Chapter Ten

"He either fears his fate too much,
   or his deserts are small,
Who dares not put it to the touch,
   and win or lose it all."

– Montrose[53]

D R. MELDRUM was one of those lookers on who are supposed to
see most of the game. He was a man of leisure without family
ties. Like Mary Paxton, he hated nothing that God had made, and
so far had in him the elements of a happy man; but unlike her, he
loved nothing. He had his predilections for certain things and people
as others have, but they never amounted to a stronger feeling than
liking. He liked the lower animals well enough, they amused him;
but he would not get up in the dead o' the night to attend a sick dog
or cat, as Mary would. He liked men and women well enough to be
greatly interested in them, but put his liking for them in the balance
with his self-interest, and *you would see.* He really loved to study
human nature, and had a great knowledge of the world, but often
failed in his object and missed his point from want of sympathy with
his subject.

A man must have the element of conceit in him before he can understand a vain nature; he must love before he knows the meaning
of the word; he cannot fathom the mystery of hatred till he hates;
he must be ill before he knows how to feel with the sick. Mr. Meldrum had once been very ill, and that made him a much better doctor

---

[53]James Graham, 1st Marquess of Montrose (1612-1650), "My Dear and Only
Love".

than he otherwise would have been; but he had never loved, never hated, and therefore failed to comprehend a thoroughly passionate nature, or a very warm hearted one; half the people he knew were *terra incognita*[54] to him from a want of sympathy.

Looking for a word in the dictionary will never help to convey a meaning to the mind; either you know intuitively, or experience teaches, or you never know it at all. Dr. Meldrum had never been jealous, had never coveted his neighbor's wife, or his ox, or his ass, or anything that was his, – what need had he to covet? Was he not a fine-looking man in the prime of life, with a good profession, when he was not too lazy to practice, perfect health, and a certain annuity? Let me remark by the way, my reader, that a certain annuity, however small, adds much to man's peace and lengthens his days. Let the world wag as it would, he got his dividend quarterly. The only care he ever had was debt, and as the years passed it scarcely weighed upon him; he got used to it, he avoided duns, slipped out of the way of bailiffs, lighted his cigar with his bills sent in, and slept none the less soundly. His oldest acquaintance had never seen him in a bad temper, and no story however touching, no thought however exquisite could bring tears to his fine hazel eyes. He had buried a sweet wife and two little children, but these events never impaired his appetite, or destroyed his rest, or moved him to more than a sigh, though he liked wife and children too, in his way.

He was a pleasant man to meet, gentle in voice, courteous in manners, a man whom you could not pass with indifference, a man with a presence. Nearly six feet high, active, strong, graceful, with a well-shaped head, good features, a slight black mustache. He was the son of a church of England clergyman, and had a liking for the established church as a highly respectable institution, and he often went to church and was fully aware of the good effect his practice had upon his reputation; but he had no greater knowledge of true religion, no stronger love for Christ our Saviour, than the horse he rode so gracefully.

He admired beauty in a cool way, and liked women better than men; could be unselfish in small matters to please them, and preferred a married life to a single one; indeed, as soon as his wife died he had determined to marry again if he could only find a suitable

---

[54] *terra incognita* (Latin) = "unknown land."

match, but five years had passed since that sad event and he was still a widower.

His opinion as a professional man had weight with his fellow practitioners,[55] and not without reason, for he was a clever surgeon. The sight of suffering, the sound of groans never discomposed him; his pulse never quickened, his heart never failed at the responsibility of his position as an operator; on all occasions he had his wits about him. If he undertook a case he was never careless, and carried it through if possible, but there were few cases he *would* undertake, and his rival practitioners[56] liked him none the less for that; then he never disparaged another doctor or criticized his mode of treatment; this gave the finishing touch to his popularity.

When sent for to prescribe for an old toper suffering from delirium tremens – "Dying, is he?" said Mr. Meldrum, "Bah! 'tis the best thing he can do. Send for another doctor, I'll have nothing to do with him."

"Mrs. Higgs is very ill, sir," said another applicant, looking into the surgery door one morning.

"Then she must just get well the best way she can," said Mr. Meldrum, calmly.

Sometimes a person was answered plainly, "I won't come; get Gregor," his rival practitioner[57] in Cromaboo.

Thomas Meldrum was a noble-looking, intelligent mortal, as he sat on the verandah of the Royal Hotel, Gibbeline, the evening of Mrs. Paxton's little dinner party. He was puffing a cigar, and reading a copy of the last will and testament of the late John Paxton, which he had procured from the Register office, for the sum of fifty cents. He read it twice over carefully, guessing rightly that the testator was imbecile from illness or old age, when he left such unlimited power in the hands of his wife.

He had made up his mind some time ago that he would either marry Miss Paxton or her sister, and he wished to know the exact amount of their property – hence his present proceeding. Margaret had four thousand pounds left to her, and Mary three thousand and

---

[55]The 1878 edition has "practioners."
[56]Ibid.
[57]Ibid.

the place where they lived, which was justly considered by her father as equivalent to a thousand pounds.

The doctor folded the document, and turned the thing over in his mind, and balanced it this way and that. He thought the money preferable to the house and land, charming as the place was, but then Miss Mary was decidedly more attractive than her sister, though that lady was undoubtedly good-looking and affable; but it was just possible that Miss Mary might refuse him, whereas he felt pretty certain that Mrs. Hurst would accept him. He decided after some thought to ask Mary first, – judging rightly that she was too honourable to tell tales of him – and to offer himself to Margaret if she refused him. The old lady, he reasoned, could not last long, so the sooner he married the better; her death might put off the wedding if he delayed too long, and then who could tell what might happen? Having mentally arranged his plan, and settled all in his mind, he went to bed and slept soundly.

The next evening he hired a comfortable buggy and swift horse and drove up to the Paxton's. Fortune favoured the brave, Mary was alone mending a large basketful of the family stockings; her mother was taking a nap and Mrs. Hurst and Lavinia had gone for a walk. After a few remarks he asked her if she would take a drive with him. She was tired as usual from overwork and the proposal was tempting; she thought it kind of him and said so.

"Kind to myself," he replied, with a smile.

She hesitated, and said if she went it must not be far; he promised to turn back when she pleased, so she threw a light shawl over her shoulders, and put on her hat, having first tripped into the back kitchen to charge Dolly to take care of the house while she was away.

They drove rapidly down a side road which was skirted by trees on either hand. The doctor soon slackened his horse's pace, and Mary was inhaling the sweet evening breeze with a feeling of thankfulness for this little respite after the day's toil, when her companion began his operation as coolly as he would his amputation of a leg or an arm.

"Miss Paxton," said he, "you must know, I think, that I have a great respect and admiration for you?" He did not say love, because he had decided not to exceed the truth lest she should see through him and disdain him.

Her bright eyes looked into his rather vacantly, her face flushed a little.

"I beg your pardon – it's very rude of me – but I was not attending," she said. "Will you kindly repeat your remark?"

He did repeat it as calmly as he had said it at first. Her eyes widened with surprise, the flush on her cheek deepened.

"I never thought about it," she said.

"Will you think about it now?" asked Mr. Meldrum with a smile. "I have been married, as you know, and cannot profess a passionate love for you, but if you will honour me with your hand, it shall not be my fault if you are unhappy. I really like you very much; I would help you, take care of you and cherish you all my life."

"Liking and respect are not enough in that relation," she replied, with a sharpness that startled the calm doctor. "If you do not love me, you have no right to ask me to marry you."

"Pardon me," said her admirer, "I thought you were a lover of truth."

"So I am," she replied, "but truth in this case is the reverse of complimentary; if I married you, respect for me would soon die, and liking turn to aversion, even if I loved you, and I don't, doctor. I like you just well enough as a friendly acquaintance, and till this evening I respected you."

"That is very bitter," said the doctor gently, and not quite unmoved by the reproach; "is it not enough to say no, without saying it harshly?"

She was polite by nature, and the reproof touched her.

"Pardon me," she said, "I am afraid I am very rude, and I am sure you meant it kindly, but it's just horrible to marry without love, and leads to more evils than unthinking people can dream of; only all do not think as I do on this subject – more's the pity."

"If a man has been unhappy enough to lose his wife, is he to live alone forever?" asked Mr. Meldrum, pathetically.

"Yes," said the lady in all earnestness, unless he loves some one as well as the first wife; but let us talk of something else and forget all about it. I shall never mention it to anybody, for I am altogether ashamed of it, and – and you ought to be."

"I do not think that," he said, "but I will try and forget it."

"*And forgive,*" said the lady looking up in his face with a little tremour about the mouth. He was mollified, her words had stung him a little and he had felt more hurt than he would have thought possible a day ago.

"Oh! I don't bear malice," he said truly, "never did in my life, – don't agitate yourself, pray. Shall we turn back? Let us be friends, and as you say forget all about it. I didn't mean to vex you, so don't be vexed. The flower is beautiful and I may admire it, I suppose, though it isn't to be mine, and I had no idea it could be anything but sweet till I unintentionally drew out the vinegar."

"Now you feel relieved by that, don't you?" said Mary, laughing, and feeling relieved herself; "drive faster, please, it is so pleasant to meet the fresh air."

He did drive faster, the horse seemed to fly over the smooth gravel road, and they were at home in a few minutes. He handed her out at the gate; he shook hands with her; he left his kindest compliments for Mrs. Paxton and Mrs. Hurst, not forgetting our little Cromaboo friend Miss Lavinia; he lifted his hat gracefully as he drove away; returned to his hotel at a rapid pace, read the papers for an hour or two, indulged in a light supper and a cigar to aid digestion, and finally went to bed and slept as soundly as he had on the previous night.

The next day he took the field again. Having come to a temporary arrangement with his creditors he thought it time to return to Cromaboo, and on his way called at Mrs. Paxton's. When Dolly opened the door, he declined to come in, but hoped the ladies were well, and left a very beautiful bouquet with his compliments for Mrs. Hurst.

"Them flowers is for Mrs. Hurst with Mr. Meldrum's compliments," said Dolly, putting her head into the parlour where the three younger ladies were seated. This struck Miss Paxton as so irresistibly funny that she broke into her ringing musical laugh. The windows were open, and the sound reached the doctor as he mounted his horse; it moved him to a smile and a muttered "deuce take the girl," but created no feeling of anger.

"Really, Mary, I must say I think your mirth's very ill-timed," said Margaret, who had flushed with pleasure as she took the bouquet from Dolly's hand.

"Pardon me, Maggie, it is very rude of me, – what beautiful flowers," and Mary slipped from the room as she spoke and ran up stairs, concealing a second merry bubble of laughter till she was out of hearing. She could laugh now; the exciting events of the last week had coloured and warmed her life, and set her up like a tonic. Mrs. Paxton's sharp, ill-humour did not tell as of old, nor did Margaret's complaining spirit weigh so heavily upon her; the expression of her face had changed, her cheek had a colour, her eyes were brighter; she thought of Mr. Llewellyn's words and took comfort from them; she determined not to make idols of her crosses, and prayed for the recovery of the sick wretch in the hospital, and had faith that he would be healed, and prayed to be guided out of all her perplexities, and felt less perplexed as she rose from her knees each day.

Her step had a spring in it, her voice a new tone, the cobweb tyranny of home was broken forever.

Chapter Eleven

"O! woman, in our hours of ease,
Uncertain, coy and hard to please,
And variable as the shade
By the light quivering aspen made.
When pain and sickness wring the brow
A ministering angel thou."

– Scott[58]

THREE weeks passed, and Robert saw nothing of the Paxtons, though he blew his horn lustily whenever he passed the house. The fact was that Mary had thought over Lavinia's story and avoided him on principle, though it cost her some trouble to find a neighbour willing to carry herself and her parcels, for the township of Gibbeline is as civilized as old England, and the kindly savage custom of giving rides and picking up passengers has long passed away; now to carry a neighbour, or a neighbour's basket, is to place him under an obligation to you, and in return if you ask for a ride, you may meet with a refusal, though there is plenty of room in the conveyance, and your legs are weary.

It was a long three weeks to Robert, and when at the end of that time he caught a glimpse of a muslin dress at a window, as the stage crawled slowly by on a sultry afternoon, he blew his horn at a venture on a sudden impulse, and stopping the horses sprang out. Shall I call it chance, or was he favoured by Providence? Mrs. Paxton and Mrs. Hurst were both taking a siesta, and Dolly crimping her hair. Robert, as he ran up the steps, heard the beloved voice calling softly to Dolly

---

[58] Sir Walter Scott (1771-1832), *Marmion* (1808).

to come down and open the door, and the heartier response of the hand-maiden:

"Oh! law, I couldn't, Miss Mary; I hain't got no frock on."

There was no help for it, Mary had to confront the mail carrier herself.

"I have been wishing to see you, Miss Paxton," said he, removing his ragged straw hat, "to tell you about the fellow in the hospital – he is out of danger."

"Indeed! – I am very glad," said Mary, though she knew it already through Dr. Meldrum, who had satisfied all Margaret's civil inquiries about his hospital patients as calmly as if he knew nothing of Mary's particular interest in that one; he was too generous a man to annoy her by seeming to know anything of that painful business, and he gave all requisite information in her presence without rousing her suspicions.

"Has he any money?" asked Miss Paxton, after a pause, "will it be any expense to get him out of the country?"

"I think he has a little," returned Robert, "but anyhow it shall be no expense to you. I think you suffered enough in the fright."

"If you advance what is necessary I will pay you again," said Mary, who knew in her heart she must ask her mother for the money, who would certainly grudge, perhaps refuse her, and want to know the why and the wherefore of such an extraordinary proceeding. Yet she could not stoop to take money from this lad, it was humiliating enough to borrow it for a time, after the kiss and Lavinia's revelations.

"You have taken a great deal of trouble for me," she added a little stiffly, feeling anything but at her ease under the boy's brown eyes.

Robert saw the embarrassment in her face, the effort at dignity, and partly guessed her feeling, but also partly misunderstood it, and felt more flattered by the little nervous flush of her cheek than he would if he had known what she really thought of him at that moment.

"It's a pleasure, not a trouble, to do anything for you," he said, his eyes adding too plainly because I love you – "may I have a rose?" There were hundreds of beautiful blossoms about them.

"Oh! certainly, as many as you like."

"Would you pull one for me?" in a slightly hesitating voice.

"Oh! you are welcome to any – to all – a handful if you care for them," said the lady.

"I do not care for one unless you pull it," in a very low voice and without looking at her.

"I should prick my fingers," replied the lady, without a smile and without moving an inch.

A slight sigh from the mail carrier, followed by a reproachful glance, and "Good afternoon, Miss Paxton."

"Good afternoon, Robert, and many thanks for your kindness in this matter," still very stiffly.

So he left her standing amid her roses. Ten minutes later he met Mr. Meldrum on horse-back, and the sight of him roused a fierce pang of jealousy in the boy's heart; she would not refuse to pull a rose for him, he thought.

Three more weeks and Robert saw nothing of Miss Paxton, but it by no means follows that she saw nothing of him. Not once had the stage passed unobserved by her since her adventure in the Cromaboo swamp. Behind her muslin curtain she noted the driver and his passengers. She noted the bright young face looking up at the house eagerly day by day, and then turn away disappointed when nobody came out. And Robert, too, made his remarks, and had his own thoughts, very troubled and jealous ones, about Miss Paxton. Four times had he seen Mr. Meldrum's horse tied at Mrs. Paxton's gate when he passed, and three times had he met the doctor not far from the place; yet no one was ill in the house to form a pretext for such visits. He began to hate that calm gentleman.

One morning Mary Paxton thought the horn had a different twang – it was feebly blown – and from behind her curtain she saw the stage and Mr. Llewellyn driving, but no Robert; the next day there was a new driver. She felt troubled and conscience-stricken, she hardly knew why. Was he ill, or had he left Cromaboo, and without his Bible? After all he had behaved nobly to her, had she been right to snub and avoid him? She thought of him that day, and dreamt of him that night. Two more stage days and no Robert; Monday in the following week and no Robert. She felt very anxious, and even wrote a note to Miss Llewellyn, but on consideration thought it undignified and burnt it. On Wednesday she watched eagerly for the stage, and looked out boldly in the hope of seeing the bright young face; but no, he was not there.

She went down stairs with a heavy heart, and as she passed the front door saw Mr. Meldrum tying up his horse at the gate. She went on to the verandah and waited for him.

"I am going to appeal to Miss Paxton's kindness," he said, gracefully uncovering his head – "dear Mrs. Hurst, you look as fresh as your roses," as that lady appeared at the open door, "and I am delighted to see you, because you always take a right view of things. My time is limited, and you will pardon me for entering on my business at once. Bob Smith, the mail carrier, is ill of a fever, and I am attending him; he is not delirious, but seems troubled in mind and talks in his sleep, and last night he mentioned Miss Paxton's name in a way which led me to think – that –" he hesitated.

"That he is troubled about his soul," suggested Mrs. Hurst, in a gushing tone.

"Precisely," replied Mr. Meldrum, suavely; "you ladies are so quick that you see our thoughts before we express them – and Miss Lavy is anxious for her servant, and I for my patient – his mind once at rest I should not despair of his recovery – and we are going to ask Miss Mary to spend two days in Cromaboo, and see Bob and soothe him about his little religious difficulties, for you know the poor fellow is a Methodist, Mrs. Hurst."

"Sad indeed," said Mrs. Hurst, "I fear he has very little light. The fever is not infectious, I hope?"

"Oh! no, or I would not allow your sister to go, and so risk the precious lives of you two ladies. He is at his father's, and Miss Paxton would stay with Miss Llewellyn – by the bye I have a note from her. I would be glad if you could go by the stage to-day, Miss Mary – business detains me in Gibbeline till the evening, but I will return tomorrow."

Mrs. Hurst had the temerity to say, without consulting her mother, that there would be a bed at his service, and a stable for his horse, if it would be any convenience to him; and he replied that it would be the greatest pleasure in the world to have ladies' society instead of spending the evening alone at the hotel, so with mutual courtesies they parted for the present.

Miss Lavinia wrote:

> "Oh! do, do come at once. I believe Robert is dying; he talks of you in his sleep, and Mr. Meldrum says you are the only thing that will do him good. I am so troubled and worried.

Ever yours, L.L.

Thus urged Miss Paxton made ready and departed, notwithstanding her mother's opposition; and that evening she might have been seen tripping over John Smith's threshold, in all the glories of a light print dress, her head covered with a pretty large structure in the form of a cap, composed of lace and pale blue ribbon, and designed to make her look antiquated, and impress Robert with the great difference in their ages. In that day Lady Dufferins[59] and Dolly Vardens[60] were unheard of, and only old ladies wore caps. It was so light that she didn't feel it on her head, and a slight puff of wind had disarranged it, and made it the most coquettish head-gear in the world before she peeped in at John Smith's door, with a soft "Excuse me for not knocking, – you are Mrs. Smith, I suppose, – how is Robert?"

"No better, thank you ma'am," said a tall woman coming forward, "will you come in please, you are Miss Paxton, I know, Mr. Meldrum said you would come, but I haven't told Robbie. I thought it would excite him."

The first thing that impressed Mary about Robert's mother was that she was bolt upright; she was rather tall, and she looked very tall from being as inflexible and unbending as the kitchen poker; the next thing that struck her was her likeness to her son, and the strange length and blackness of her eye lashes, – Horace Walpole[61] would certainly have called them "half a yard long." She spoke with propriety, making few grammatical errors, and using no vulgarisms; her hair was thick and black and wavy, with a sprinkling of grey in it; her forehead low; her features sharp and handsome, but haggard, anxious, sunburnt; her eyes habitually half-closed, and more than half concealed by their long lashes, but opening unexpectedly now and then, with a sparkling blackness that astonished the beholder.

---

[59]Helen Selina Blackwood, Baroness Dufferin and Claneboye (1807-1867).

[60]Dolly Varden is a character of Charles Dickens' 1839 historical novel *Barnaby Rudge* (1840-41), set in 1780. A Dolly Varden costume was a woman's outfit, inspired by the novel, briefly fashionable from 1869 to 1875 in Britain and North America, consisting of brightly patterned, usually floral, dress with a polonaise overskirt gathered up and draped over a separate underskirt. A Dolly Varden hat was a flat straw hat trimmed with flowers and ribbons.

[61]Horace Walpole (1717-1797), English art historian, man of letters, antiquarian and Whig politician.

"She is like Jeal or Judith,"[62] thought Mary, as she softly sympathised about Robert's illness in an undertone, "and her voice is sweet
like her son's."

John Smith's house is a fair sample of all the houses in Cromaboo,
and is therefore worthy of a description. John Jibb, the village builder,
erected them all on the same plan; the front door opened into the
room of the house. There was a bed-room on one side with three
windows in it, and on the other a room with no window at all; at the
back a shed which contained the stove in summer, and above all a
large room with a sloping roof, which Mrs. Smith had converted into
a best parlour by covering the floor with a rag carpet, and decorating
it with cheap pictures, half a dozen chairs, and a melodeon. I have
been told that this style of architecture is not peculiar to Cromaboo,
but that in Mt. Forest and even Listowel[63] there are many houses built
on the same plan. The outside was clap board, well white washed to
the roof. The dark room was shared by John Smith, his wife, and little
Tommy, the one with the three windows was at present occupied by
Robert. Everything was clean, but it was clearly the house of very
poor people. Mrs. Smith was dressed in a derry gown and her hands
were distorted with labor.

"I am very sorry Robert cares so much for me," said Mary, after
they had discussed his illness, "but love never lasts long with a boy
of his age, that is one comfort."

"Faith, that depends upon who the boy is," answered the sick
lad's mother, – it was wonderful how like her son she was when
she smiled, in spite of the difference in age and complexion, – "but I
don't wonder he likes you. He's asleep now, but it never lasts long
with him; would you like to see him and he not see you? Then come
softly," – and she led the way to Robert's room. There was only the
bed on which he lay, and a rough little table with a glass of lemonade
on it, a chair and no furniture. Two of the windows were darkened
with green paper blinds, the other partly darkened, but there was
light enough to see the sick lad's face which was turned towards
them. Mary was struck with its pinched, altered appearance, the

---

[62] Judith is the central character of the deuterocanonical *Book of Judith*, in which
she beheads the Assyrian general, Holophernes.

[63] Mount Forest (Wellington North) and Listowel (North Perth) are small communities in Ontario. Joseph Hacking, the Guelph printer of *The Cromaboo Mail Carrier*,
came from Listowel.

eyes were sunken, the cheeks flushed, the hand which lay outside the cover very thin. Though the women made no sound, their presence disturbed the restless sleeper, and his eyes opened upon the face he loved best in the world, regarding him half tearfully, and altogether compassionately. He gave a little cry, and extended his hands, but in an instant covered his face with them and burst into tears. Mary left the foot of the bed and moved round to the side. Mrs. Smith quietly left the room.

"I am sorry to see you so ill, Robert," said Mary, "*dear* Robert."

After a few hard sobs, he lay quiet; he moved his hands from his face and looked at her. She took his wasted hand in hers, and his weak fingers closed on it as if he would never let it go.

"I have longed to see you – I know you are vexed with me – I have so much to say," his voice shook and he broke down again.

"Well, take your time, do not over-exert yourself," said Mary, gently patting the hand she held; "I am not going away in a hurry, and I am not vexed with you, my poor, dear boy – see I have brought the rose you coveted."

He took it in his trembling fingers and pressed it to his lips.

"I shall never part with it," he said, "and now I have seen you, I am content to die if it's God's will."

"You have youth on your side – you must try and bear up for your mother's sake, dear Robert; she would be heart-broken if she lost you."

"Her love isn't enough, it doesn't satisfy; if I thought you didn't like me I would rather die than live - even your pity is very sweet, and I know you do not love, you only pity me." His voice died to a whisper at the last words.

"Pity is akin to love," said Mary, with a smile and a sigh.

"Aye, and akin to contempt as well," replied the invalid.

"Not mine, Robert," said the lady with spirit, "I wouldn't travel twenty miles to see a person for whom I had a contempt.[64] I like you very much, much more than you deserve, considering the way you have acted to Miss Llewellyn. You are a very, very naughty boy, and I want you to get well that I may give you a good scolding."

---

[64]Therefore, Cromaboo is situated 20 miles from Gibbeline, as is Erin from Guelph.

"I didn't know that there was such a woman in the world as you, when I spoke to Miss Llewellyn – I didn't know what love meant, I didn't think I should ever care more for another than for her. I love you so that I think of nothing else. I shut my eyes to dream of you; I wake to think of you all day long. I told Miss Llewellyn so last night. I was very sorry to pain her – I like and respect her very much, but I never could care for another as I do for you, Miss Mary. You are my one thought." He ceased, exhausted.

"You may see some one yet you love better," she said, with a little comic shrug of the shoulder, "may God grant it. And now Robert, I forbid you to say another word; you have talked too much for your strength already. You may look at me, and I shall hold your hand till you go to sleep."

"Sleep! I scarcely sleep at all," with a weary shake of the head.

"My poor boy," in a tone of the greatest compassion; "how parched your lips are – would you like a drink?"

"I would from your hand – I would take it if it was poison."

"Mrs. Smith!" raising her clear, bell-like voice. His mother was there in a minute. "Just lift Robert, please, while I give him a drink, and shake up his pillows and make him comfortable, and then he *must* go to sleep."

"My faith, it's that he needs," said the mother, as she lifted him tenderly.

"Yes, you *must*, sir, if you love me," in a bright, imperative way that made him smile. "I shall sit and hold your hand and croon to you softly, and you must go to sleep, your life depends on it. Do you think your mother wants to lose her bad boy, and I the last beau I shall ever have, now I have come to wrinkles and a cap?"

"I thought it was a beautiful new bonnet," said Robert, looking at her head-dress with great interest.

"Go to sleep this minute," and taking his wasted hand in both hers, now that his mother had shaken his pillows into order, she began softly crooning Rousseau's dream.[65] Already his spirit was quieted, his cure had begun; he had spoken his mind, and she did not wholly despise his love; she admitted she liked him very much;

---

[65] Jean Jacques Rousseau, "Days of Absence, Sad and Dreary," *Le Devin du Village* (c.1752). This aria was commonly known years afterward as "Rousseau's Dream." Leslie's 1878 edition has "Rosseau's dream."

she did not disdain to hold his hand and sing for him; he felt her fingers, he heard her voice, and it soothed him, exhausted as he was with the excitement of the last twenty minutes. He closed his eyes to please her and the hymn grew fainter in his ears, though he was still conscious of the hand that held his, but presently that consciousness ceased; he slept, and soundly. Not till he had slept an hour did she attempt to withdraw her fingers, and then very cautiously. Presently she crept out on tip-toe to the kitchen, with her finger on her lip. Mrs. Smith went out into the still night – for it was night now – to speak to her.

"Sure you must be stiff and tired," she said, "sitting there so long."

"Well, a little – but I *do* think he has taken a turn for the better; his face is not so flushed, and his hands are a little damp. How anxious you must be for your boy."

"She has another boy," said a childish voice at her elbow, and looking down Mary saw a ragged dark-eyed urchin beside her. She gently pulled his nose, and again addressed his mother.

"How many nights have you sat with him, Mrs. Smith?"

"Faith, every one since he's so ill – could I trust what I love better than life, to another? Smith, and Miss Llewellyn and Chip have watched him sometimes in the day."

"Would you trust me to sit with him to-night, Mrs. Smith, and take a good rest?"

"No, my dear, thank you," with great decision, "pray for us both, if I may make so bold as to ask you; and then go to sleep like a lamb and come back refreshed in the morning. Good night to you, miss, and God bless you."

She turned and stalked into the house. Some women walk and some women waddle; Miss Paxton tripped or glided as the case might be; to-night she glided the softest bit of light in the darkness; but Mrs. Smith always stalked swiftly and steadily, like a woman with a purpose.

Chapter Twelve

Olivia – "What kind o' man is he? What manner of man?"
Malvolio – "Of very ill-manner; not yet old enough for a man
   nor young enough for a boy."

– Twelfth Night[66]

I DO not know what an author could do without a wife; a sailor, a
soldier, a lawyer, a tradesman, might get on very well without
one – pardon me, fair ladies, for saying so – but not a parson, for
who would make soup for the old women, and read to them, and
help with the Sunday-school, and manage the sewing society, and tell
the parson his faults, and play the church organ without pay? Not
a doctor, for ladies object to consult unmarried doctors; and above
all not an author, for how could he describe the bed-room chats, the
twilight confidences, between young ladies, were it not for the wife
of his bosom?

On this best authority I know that Lavinia and Mary took off their
dresses, and put on loose jackets and brushed each other's hair, and
cried a little over their pet sick boy, and agreed that he was a very
perverse, naughty boy, but a very dear boy for all that, and if he died
– "But he *won't* die," said Lavinia, "I feel *sure* he will get better, I feel
as if I really couldn't live if he died; I have so much to bear already;
but you are tired, dear, and would like a little supper, and I will tell
you my troubles afterwards;" and she kissed Miss Paxton and then
they had a little supper, and – tell it not to the Dunkinites[67] – a little

---

[66]William Shakespeare, *Twelfth Night*: Act 1, Scene 5.
[67]The later Scott Act (Canadian Temperance Act of 1878) was based on similar
legislation known as the Dunkin Act (the Canadian Temperance Act of 1864, named

wine and water, with a little nutmeg and sugar in it, but weak, my temperance people, very weak, and home-made wine at that; so do not think evil. This they took with some thin ham sandwiches, and they sat upon the bed-room floor and chatted as they ate and drank.

"I think there never, never was a person so troubled as I am," said Lavinia, emphatically. "You know this place of uncle's is mortgaged to cousin Frank for four hundred dollars, and uncle has always paid the interest punctually till this year, but now times are so bad, and it is so very hard to get money, that uncle sent me to Hamilton, just to make a friendly visit to cousin Frank and his wife, and tell them all about it, and ask them to wait a little; and do you know when I knocked at the door, and asked for Mrs. Llewellyn, she was not at home to me, though I saw her face at the window. I didn't know what to do; I went to the Royal Hotel and stayed there, and wrote a pathetic letter to cousin Frank telling him all about it, and begging him to call on me; he made no reply for two days, and then he wrote a cold, brief note enclosing five dollars, and sent it by the Hamilton stage driver, telling me I had better go by stage instead of rail, as it was cheaper, and to go *at once*, and he would pass over the interest for this year."

"Too bad," said Mary – "and cousin Harry – what of him?"

"I saw him pass the hotel twice, but he never looked up, or came. Uncle was *so* much hurt, at their conduct, only he is a Christian or he could not forgive it. Do you know I *couldn't* stand taking money from them. I told Robert the whole thing, and borrowed the interest, and the five dollars from him and sent it to cousin Frank, and we have never heard a word from any of them since."

"That Frank Llewellyn is a selfish little puppy," said Miss Paxton, indignantly.

"Oh! *do* not say that, it hurts me to hear you say that, he is my cousin, you know, and he is so handsome and a perfect gentleman in manners; I'm sure you would think so if you knew him."

"I *do* know him," said Miss Paxton, "no one better. I stayed in Hamilton after a severe illness ten years ago, and he condescended to offer me his hand, his little jeweled hand, and his heart, which is as hard as a stone and no bigger than a marrowfat pea. You look

after Christopher Dunkin), passed in 1864 by the Province of Canada, which gave the power to communities to enact prohibition.

astonished – doubtful – I will describe him, I will convince you. He has dark, sleek hair, parted in the middle, and curling at the ends. I dare say he puts it in curl papers, tongs could never make that kind of ringlet – and great eyes like a girl; indeed he is altogether rather like a girl dressed in man's clothes for a lark. He often wears prunella[68] boots, because he has a corn, and carries a cane; he had a very little mustache when I knew him, twelve hairs on one side and thirteen on the other, for I counted them once when I sat beside him in a sleigh; he talks about 'our profession' and 'the legal profession,' and 'the bar,' and says 'I give you my word of honour,' in every sentence; he dresses in the height of fashion and wears little kids[69] that just fit his little hands, – I wonder he doesn't wear a flower in his hat, it would become him, or a little scarlet wing, – but he doesn't; he wears a glossy stove-pipe hat with a little looking glass in the crown of it that he may see himself in church when he casts down his eyes devoutly, and covers his face at the opening prayer; he worships but one god, and that is himself; he has a single eye to his own perfections; he is insufferably insolent and patronizing to his inferiors in station, and stares into the eyes of pretty women till they long to knock his head off – at least he did in my day, – he dances divinely, he strums a little on the piano, and professes to be a connoisseur in music, wine and tobacco, and above all in women. 'I hope God will forgive me,' he says 'but I never could endure an ugly woman, I give you my word of honour,'" and here she imitated the absent Frank with such success that Lavinia laughed in spite of herself, and said, "That's just cousin Frank, and it's a great shame of you to make me laugh at my own flesh and blood, but I really cannot be angry with you. How I wish you could see his wife."

"I hope she's a tartar; I hope she henpecks him well," said Mary, laughing too, "and pulls his hair when she curls it, and stamps upon his little embroidered slipper till he squeaks again. He should be embalmed when he dies in his velveteen coat, and his little shining pointed boots that turn up at the ends, and his most touching neck-tie. What a wonderful little figure he would be to turn out of a stone coffin and astonish our descendants."

---

[68] prunella = a strong heavy fabric of worsted twill, used chiefly for shoe uppers, clerical robes, and academic gowns.

[69] kids = kid gloves, made from young goats-hide.

"What a shame," said Lavinia, but she laughed too. "I shall never be able to look at him again without thinking of it."

"Ah!" said Mary, "if I had taken this little sprig of fashion to my heart, and worshipped this little idol as he worships himself, Mrs. Frank Llewellyn would never have turned you from her door," and she held out her hand to Lavinia, "to think what we have both lost!"

They were quiet for a little while, and the night grew darker.

"I wonder if Robert is still asleep," said Lavinia at last. "Ah! if he only loved me as he loves you, – will you ever marry him?" in a very low tone.

"Marry him! do you think I am cracked outright? No, never. I am quite sane, my dear, I assure you; but I like him very much. I should be very sorry if he died."

"I should be just heart-broken," said Lavinia, "I wouldn't care so much about his loving you if I had a chance with cousin Harry, but I am sure I have not. I am sure if it was anybody but you I should hate you; I couldn't – I really *couldn't* stand his marrying one of those horrid, coarse Cromaboo minxes; I think I should do something to her if he did."

"Cousin Harry, as you call him, was at school when I was in Hamilton," said Mary, "and I never saw him; is he like his brother, a little pocket Adonis?"

"No, he is not at all like Frank, not so han –" she hesitated.

"Pretty is the word," suggested her friend.

"Well, pretty, then; but more manly and simple in manner." Another long pause.

"I wonder," said Lavinia, presently, "if Robert gets better and knows you will never marry him, if – if I could win back his heart? Would you be vexed if I tried?"

"No, indeed," said Mary, with a smile.

"He gave me this tiny locket with his hair in it; he *should* not have tried to make me love him and then changed his mind."

"No, indeed," said Mary again, this time very gravely and thoughtfully, and presently she added, "let us say our prayers and go to bed, my dear." And they did.

Chapter Thirteen

"There is no earthly pleasure here below
Which by experience does not folly prove,
But among all the follies which I know
The sweetest folly in the world is love."

– Sir Robert Aytoun[70]

ROBERT had indeed taken a turn for the better. He slept soundly till the second cock crow, and though as weak as a baby on waking, the fever had left him. Lavinia cooked his breakfast herself, his mother propped him up, and he ate with an appetite, fed bit by bit by Miss Paxton's slight fingers.

Mr. Meldrum came in about ten in the morning, found his patient in a light sleep, and complimented Miss Mary upon being a better doctor than himself; he came again in the evening, found Robert awake and thought him greatly improved. Miss Paxton staid with him till nearly ten, and promised to look in in the morning before the stage left and say good bye. Peep of day found her at John Smith's door, where Robert's mother met her with an anxious face.

"My faith! I think he's worse again," she said in answer to Mary's inquiries, "he's had a restless night, and is low and doesn't want to lose you."

"Did you sit up with him?"

"No, I wish I had. I lay down for awhile, and being tired I never woke till an hour ago."

Miss Paxton paused for a minute in the kitchen, and then entered the sick room with a cheerful face.

---

[70] Sir Robert Aytoun/Ayton/Alton (1570-1638), a Scottish poet.

"Well, Robin Adair, how are you this morning?"

"Are you going to leave me?" he said, taking her hand beseechingly.

"I must go to-day, dear Robert, but I will come and see you again."

"When I am dead," he said, and his lips quivered.

"My poor, dear boy, I am very sorry to leave you. I am not going of my own will, I *must* go, for I promised, you know. You are low-spirited from want of sleep, you must cheer up, we cannot do without you, Robin."

Here the stage horn sounded a clear, loud blast, as if it would say, "hurry up there."

"I *do* care very much for you, dear Robert," she said with great tenderness, really frightened at the sudden pallor in the lad's face as he raised his head from the pillow.

"I shall never see your face again if you go," he said; "will you give me one kiss, the first and the last? Do you care enough for me?"

The stage horn blew again louder than before. She stooped and kissed him hastily, and turned to go, but Robert suddenly sat up and stretched out his arms towards her, and the same instant fell back in a dead faint.

"The stage is just going, Miss Paxton," cried Mrs. Smith.

"Oh! do, for heaven's sake, come here, I believe he is dead," cried Miss Paxton.

"The Lord preserve us all," said the mother, rushing in and plucking the pillow from beneath her son's head, "go for water this minute."

She did go and encountered Lavinia at the doorway. Water was brought, vinegar was brought, feathers were burnt, smelling bottles produced, and Tommy Smith pulled out of bed and buttoned into his breeches before he knew he was awake, and dispatched for the doctor, – and through all the stage-horn tooted unremittingly.

"Oh! do, for goodness' sake, send that horrid man away with his horn, it's like the last trump," said Mary, impatiently, as the light began to come back into Robert's eyes, and Lavinia ran out and said "drive on." Thus released, the man took the horn from his mouth, whipped up his horses and trotted gaily away and Miss Paxton was left behind.

Tommy found Mr. Meldrum from home, he had gone to assist a little body into this weary world on this pleasant summer morning, and the hubbub had subsided, the sun was high in the heavens, and Robert in a sound sleep, before he entered John Smith's door. He found Mrs. Smith watching her son, with a haggard face, and the young ladies whispering together in the outer room. He felt his patient's pulse, watch in hand, and then beckoned Mrs. Smith away from the bed-side.

"Come up stairs all of you," he said when they reached the kitchen, "we can speak there without disturbing him."

With that they all adjourned to the best room and sat upon four of the state chairs in solemn conclave.

"What's all this fuss about Bob?" asked Mr. Meldrum, when they were seated, "his pulse is equal, and there is no return of the fever, – he is weak of course, but that we must expect."

At this they all began at once and told him their morning's experience, and then at his request told him separately.

"Well, I'll tell you what I think about it all," said the doctor when they had finished. "He kept himself awake all night thinking that Miss Paxton was going, and making up his mind that she should not go if he could help it, and when the tug of war came and he saw she was determined, he made himself faint, as a *dernier ressort*,[71] and got his own way at last."

"Heartless!" exclaimed Lavinia, indignantly, "I don't believe it."

"You are talking sheer nonsense," said Miss Paxton sharply, and with sparkling eyes. "How *could* he make himself faint, poor boy?"

"By sitting bolt upright suddenly," replied the doctor, calmly, "I told him yesterday that he would faint if he did, that in his weak state he must change his position gradually. Oh! he is a fox."

The young ladies exchanged glances, and Mrs. Smith opened her black eyes with a sudden flash of intelligence.

"Faith, I'm glad you think him no worse," she said, "but you judge him hardly, sir, sure he forgot what you told him, and everything when he saw the young lady going."

"I don't believe it, ma'am," said the gentleman, with great imperturbability.

"I judge Bob in this by myself. I shot myself by accident when I was about his age, and was carried into a house, – the nearest of course, – and there happened to be nobody at home, but one most

---

[71] *dernier ressort* (French) = last resort.

compassionate young lady, afterwards my wife. I was weak from loss of blood, and she was naturally shocked and concerned at the sight of a gory man, whom she, in her ignorance, thought dying. My friends left me in her care while they went for a doctor, six miles away, and it was a new and delicious experience to have her about me. I thought it a lucky shot, and revived wonderfully under her care, but as soon as I grew better she left me, and went to a distant part of the room with her sewing. Then I closed my eyes as if it was all over with me, and groaned. Back she flew like a little white-winged bird, she dabbled me with vinegar and water, she wetted my lips with wine, she unbuttoned my collar and loosened my necktie, and chafed my hands with her little plump white fingers; she gently raised my head, and then fearing she had done wrong, tenderly lowered it again; she felt my pulse, she even laid her hand upon my heart, and was frightened at the rapid way in which it thumped under her touch. No, no, Mrs. Smith, I do not judge Bob hardly, but *correctly*; I excuse him, but I call him a fox, and I think Miss Paxton would do well to rebuke him for his selfishness; her word would have weight, where yours or mine would fail."

The doctor's little narrative inspired both young ladies with a desire to fly at him and box his ears, but their indignation took the form of silence and Mrs. Smith of speech.

"Sure, men are selfish, one and all," said she; "I never knew one to better another, when they come to fall in love, as it's called, and I suppose Robbie will be like the rest. Happy the mother that can lay her son in a child's coffin before guile and deceit enters his heart."

She spoke with a bitterness that reminded Mary of Robert when he said, "I am ignorant."

"You take it too seriously, dear Mrs. Smith," said Mr. Meldrum; "he must fall in love some time or other, you know, and I'm sure his good angel led him to Miss Paxton."

He was quite unconscious that he gave Lavinia pain by this remark, but Mary knew it, and guessed that his words, for some reason she could not understand, pained Mrs. Smith also.

"You really talk too much, Mr. Meldrum," she said; "much you know about love, indeed, – and you forget the last word is a woman's prerogative; it is for women to talk and men to act. Now don't say another word, but go home and get your dinner, and then mount your horse and ride to Gibbeline, and make the best excuse you can for me to Maggie and mamma – I know they will be very angry with me for staying. Say we feared a relapse and death; that will be quite true, for I really thought for a moment the boy was dead, – they don't know as we do what a perfect humbug you are – pardon the word – and they will believe all you say. Be off, if you are a man, and not a word more, but if you are an old woman, doctor, you will not do as I bid you, I know, but stay and talk for the next hour."

Mr. Meldrum laughed, rose, laid his hand upon his heart, bowed and departed without another word.

Saturday came, and Robert was decidedly better, and on Sunday he was so much stronger that he was dressed and removed to a rude couch in the outer room, and his father came home from his week's work and his brother to spend the day with him. Not till Chip had gone for the night, and Robert was in bed again, and John Smith in his dark room snoring lustily, did Miss Paxton and her friend peep in to see the invalid. He had been watching for them eagerly, and gave a hand to each with a smile.

"I am better," he said.

"Well enough to take that good scolding I promised you?" said Miss Paxton.

"Perhaps," he replied, with such love in his eyes that it drove Lavinia into the next room to talk to Mrs. Smith.

"Robert," said Mary, seating herself lightly on the side of the bed, "did you really think you were dying, the other morning, or did you bounce up in bed on purpose to faint, and so frighten me and detain me whether I would or not? That is the doctor's view of the matter."

Robert's jealousy blazed up at once; "He is no friend of mine," he said.

"Come, tell me the truth, now," laying her hand on his as she spoke.

"I *couldn't* part with you," he said, putting her fingers to his lips, "I felt very ill, and I was desperate; I thought if I *must* die, let it come when you were with me; it is death when you are away."

The lady rose and took a turn or two about the little room, and then came back and touched his cheek with her fan, and earnestly addressed him:

"Robert, the love that is exacting, selfish, unreasonable, would tire out the patience of even a saint, much more a poor sinner like me. If you deceive me for your own selfish ends, you will kill my love for you even in it's birth." Then seeing his face grow pale under her words, she added more softly, "God alone is never tired of us, however foolish we may be we cannot win His love by our importunity; you should think more of your Creator, and then you would think less of His creature; you should pray not to be selfish, my poor boy, and not to make an idol of me. Your feeling for me half frightens me," – and here she touched his head with a caressing hand, – "you must not make an idol of me, or deceive me again. You *were* very ill, or I couldn't excuse you; but I know all sick people are selfish. Dear as you are to me, I would rather see you dead than selfish and hard." She had begun the lecture in sharp earnest, but now tears trembled in her eyes, and the tenderness of her tone half contradicted her words. "I will send you some good books, – you will read them, will you not, to please me? – and the Bible."

With her soft hand smoothing his hair, I fear he would have promised to read it in the original Greek, if she had asked him. She read him a chapter there and then, and promised to mark verses for him, that she hoped would comfort him, and then she shook hands with him warmly and kindly, but gave him no kiss, and told him positively she would not come in to say good bye in the morning. He kissed her hand with a sigh, but did not remonstrate, and he knew when he heard the horn in the morning that she was gone.

She did send him the promised Bible and certain good papers called the *British Workman*,[72] and a publication, then in its infancy, called *Good Words*,[73] and he read them all faithfully, and really enjoyed some things in them, though I fear if Mr. Llewellyn had sent them he would have pronounced them "as dry as saw dust," and never looked into them twice.

And he grew stronger, day by day, he thought more and more of the last interview with Miss Paxton and her words; she had said he was "dear" to her, her eyes looked lovingly at him even when her words were the sharpest, and when she touched his head, surely it was love, not pity that prompted the action. "Yes," he thought,

[72] *The British Workman* was a broadsheet periodical, published monthly between 1855 and 1892 in England, with the aim to "promote the health, wealth and happiness of the working classes."

[73] *Good Words* was a monthly periodical in the United Kingdom from 1860 to 1906, directed at evangelicals and nonconformists, particularly of the lower middle class.

"without vanity, this is love, but I am younger than her, and mean in station, and she will not allow the feeling even to herself," and in this thought he misunderstood her and did her injustice; it was love indeed she felt for the sick boy, but the love of an old bird for a callow young one, the love of a mother for her grown up son, the love of a big sister for her younger brother, and she was not at all ashamed of the feeling, warm and strong as it was, for it was not the love of a woman for the man she would marry, or anything like it.

Chapter Fourteen

"Marriage is the foolishest act a wise man commits in all his life."

– Sir Thomas Browne[74]

"Conjugal love seems never old or stale, but ever sweet; it multiplieth joy, it divideth sorrow, and here in this sorry world is the thing likest heaven."

– Charles Reade[75]

A s ROBERT grew better he began to feel keenly that it is impossible to escape the consequences of one's actions, that as a man sows, so indeed must he reap. His love-making to Miss Lavinia, sweet in the bud, was bitter in the fruit, and perplexed him much and made him very uncomfortable, nay even retarded his progress towards health. That young lady, as we have seen, was quite unwilling to give up her quondam[76] lover, until at least she could secure a better; and she began the process of winning back his heart, by writing little notes while he was still in bed, and sending them by Tommy; because on paper she could express feelings she had not the courage to speak of to his face. Tommy was charged to tell nobody about these *billet doux*,[77] but give them to Robert when no one was present, and Tommy was loyal, but with the best intentions he occasionally let the cat out of the bag. Once his brother Chip seized

---

[74]Sir Thomas Browne (1605-1682), English polymath and author.
[75]Charles Reade (1814-1884), English novelist and dramatist.
[76]*quondam* (Latin) = former.
[77]*billet doux* (French) = sweet letter.

him, as he was speeding along like a lap-wing, with a note squeezed tightly in his little fist.

"What have ye there?" he asked.

Tommy bit and scratched like a little wild cat, – "You're not to know, I won't let you see it, – it's a love letter for Bob," he said, struggling and screaming to get away.

Chip gave a great roar of laughter, and let him go, but didn't fail to tell the joke to his acquaintances, and ask his brother where his love letters came from.

The next evening Tommy stole through the kitchen in such a very sly and mysterious way, that he attracted the attention of the whole family, and a spirit of mischief impelled Chip – who had come in to ask after his brother – to seize him again. Tommy fought as before.

"You're not to see it – I won't let you see what I've got, Chip."

"Will you let me see it, Tommy?" said Mr. Meldrum, who happened to be present.

"No I won't, – it isn't for you, it's for Bob, all by himself."

Then Chip related yesterday's experience, and the doctor's face still wore an amused look, when he went in to feel his patient's pulse. Robert was greatly annoyed, yet knew not what to do, but Tommy helped his brother unconsciously. When Miss Lavinia gave him another note with a warning not to let anybody but Robert know where it came from, "No I won't," said Tommy, very earnestly, "for then everybody would laugh at you."

"Why do you say that, you urchin?" asked Miss Lavinia, sharply.

"Because they laugh at me for taking them, and Bob for getting them."

"*Who* laughs? Have you *dared* to show them to anybody but Bob?" said Lavinia, in a tragic tone.

"Chip and father and Mr. Meldrum did last night," and Tommy told his adventures.

She did not send the note, but took it herself, and finding Robert asleep, placed it in his unconscious hand. His mother saw it there, and a kind womanly feeling for Miss Lavinia prompted her to take it away, till he woke, least others should see it too. She gave it to him herself, and noted that he received it with an impatient sigh; in truth he was half minded to tell his mother all about it, but a sense of honor held him tongue tied. His love for Miss Paxton was no secret to her, and never did another sympathise with a son as this one did with hers; she was nearly as much in love with Mary as Bob himself, and her sympathy comforted him greatly.

As soon as he was strong enough, he spent an hour or two at the Paxton's, while the stage went to Gibbeline. Miss Lavinia went with him, and also Dr. Meldrum, and greatly marred the pleasure of the visit, yet did not wholly spoil it either, for he saw the inside of the quaint old house, the beautiful garden, the verdant grass, and had his dinner under the orchard trees, and Miss Mary served him with her own hands, and gave him a white rose for his button hole. Mrs. Hurst gave him a tract, and greatly puzzled and confused him, and brought the blood to his pale cheeks by saying she was glad her sister had shown him what a sinner he was, and the way to life eternal; even Mrs. Paxton's stony old heart was touched by the sight of his wan face, and she advised him to wear flannel drawers, and graciously gave him a rosey-cheeked apple with a worm in it, and pronounced him "a pretty boy."

He took back a little basket of cherries which Mrs. Paxton sorely grudged, and a great bouquet of flowers for his mother. Poor boy, he was glad at heart, though still a little weak in body when he resumed his duties, and it was with a thrill of joy that he saw the old house loom in sight, and a hope that Miss Paxton would run out to speak to him, a hope as instantly succeeded by consternation, dismay, despair, for there stood two cabs in the yard, and another at the gate, with bunches of white ribbon at the horses' ears, *wedding favours.* For a moment his heart stood still, then anger and jealousy made him hot all over; he took his horn mechanically and blew a loud and piercing blast, but it did not relieve his feelings, and no more unhappy creature existed on the face of the globe than Robert as he drove into Gibbeline. But if he had received a blow, he had given one back, for never had stage horn tooted at a more unfortunate moment than his tin trumpet on this particular occasion. Thomas Meldrum and Margaret Hurst were just plighting their troth to each other in the presence of a Rural Dean and a select company of guests, and the sound of Robert's horn made Margaret angry on her wedding day.

Poor miserable Robert could not keep away from the railway station, he *must* see Mary's face once more, and there he felt sure he would see it, for did not all newly married couples go to the Falls? He felt sure she had married Mr. Meldrum; in his heart he called her cruel, yet loved her none the less. Mr. Meldrum had looked elated lately, and Lavinia had spoken mysteriously of some particular event when she went the day before yesterday to stay at Mrs. Paxton's. How glad he had been to get rid of her worrying attentions, little dreaming the cruel truth.

When at length the cab with the wedding favours arrived, and he saw Mr. Meldrum get out, though he had expected to see him, he turned sick and faint, and with difficulty staggered to a seat, "because things seen are mightier than things heard," as Tennyson says truly. He kept his eyes fixed on the cab with a kind of fascination; a lady in dark grey stepped out, whose strongly marked features and dark rosy cheeks were quite unlike Miss Mary's. Her gait was firm and proud. She saw nothing so insignificant as Bob Smith, the Cromaboo mail carrier, but her husband was not so oblivious of passing things; he saw his patient and smiled, and when he had disposed of his bride for the present, by leaving her in the waiting-room, he came back and laid his hand on Robert's shoulder.

"It's kind of you to come and see me off, Bob," he said, "but you are a foolish fellow to try your strength so much; you are not strong yet and you look quite ill. Why did you waste your breath in that tremendous blast this morning? Mrs. Meldrum is quite out of temper with you. You must have known they wouldn't want to send for butcher's meat and groceries on a wedding day. I left a message for you at the Western from Miss Paxton; you are to call as you return for Miss Lavy, and a piece of brides' cake to dream on – we all know who *you* will dream about," he said, with a good humoured smile.

Robert poured out congratulations and good wishes, his heart smote him for his past ill-will to the doctor, who patted him on the shoulder, and said, "I wish I could leave you looking more robust Bob," and immediately after hailed the wedding cab, as it turned to depart, and sent him back to the Western in it royally.

This marriage was considered by all parties concerned a particularly happy event; Margaret was pleased because she was tired of a subordinate position, and wished to lord it over a house of her own once more; her husband was pleased because he had a handsome wife in possession, and four thousand pounds in prospect; Mrs. Paxton because she had one the less to board and clothe; and Mary saw her sister depart with a sigh of relief, and felt secretly grateful to the doctor for removing one of her burdens; she knew far better than he what he had undertaken. Lavinia was pleased to be bride's maid, and Robert was pleased that the doctor was married, and so out of his way; the Rev. Paul Moorhouse, of Cromaboo, being a bachelor was pleased to let his parsonage to Mr. Meldrum and remove into lodgings; Dolly was pleased to get rid of one of her mistresses, and above all Mr. Meldrum's creditors were pleased to hear [that he] had married a lady with money, not knowing as he did that the money was only in prospective; and Mr. Llewellyn said it would increase the respectability of the place, and was glad for his niece's sake. All Cromaboo was on the tip-toe of expectation, when, after a week's absence, the newly married couple returned, and took possession of the parsonage.

In the meantime Robert went on improving in health and getting more and more troubled in conscience, and perplexed in mind with regard to his little mistress, who paid unremitting attention to his comfort, prepared little choice dishes to tempt his appetite, and left nosegays and notes upon his pillow daily, now she had him in the house again.

Towards the end of October, Mary Paxton went to Cromaboo to spend a few days with her sister. It was singularly fine warm weather in spite of the prophets who predicted an early fall and a hard winter; and when warm in Cromaboo, it is sultry in Gibbeline, and insufferably, unendurably hot in Hamilton. To Hamilton we must now remove the scene of our story.

Chapter Fifteen

"She may be handsome, but a handsome proud face is but a handsome ugly one to my thinking."

– Leigh Hunt[78]

> "He that high growth on cedars did bestow,
> Gave also lowly mushrooms leave to grow.
> We trample grass and prize the flowers of May;
> Yet grass is green when flowers do fade away."

– Robert Southwell[79]

M RS. FRANK LLEWELLYN was a person of very handsome exterior, a very strong will, and very little common sense. She had a passion for domineering and ruling all who came into contact with her. She had few relatives of her own since her father's death, and those she entirely ignored, and devoted her energies to her husband's family, who all acknowledged her sway, except the Cromaboo Llewellyns. Those near yet distant relatives were a continual trouble to Mrs. Frank.

"The girl," she would say, "is not fit to be seen in decent society, and the old man is shabby looking and peculiar in his ways."

His wife she had never seen, but when she heard that her mind was affected, she said she ought to be placed in a lunatic asylum, and offered to pay for her there.

Mrs. Frank's money was strictly settled herself, and her husband was the highest paid servant in her establishment, and censorious

---

[78]James Henry Leigh Hunt (1784-1859), English poet and writer.

[79]Also known as Saint Robert Southwell (c.1561-1595), English poet and Roman Catholic priest of the Jesuit Order.

people said the most ill-used; yet to do him justice, he would not have served her for money alone, he was proud of her beauty, and liked to hear it said that he had married "the belle of three cities," the finest woman who ever entered Hamilton as a bride; and it was not entirely the love of money that made him her slave, though no doubt the lucre had a little to do with it, and had he carried the purse he would have made a fight for the ascendancy, but it would have come to the same thing in the end, and she would have conquered.

Mrs. Frank had no wish to be cruel or despotic, she thought she ruled her relatives for their own good, she wished them to be fashionable in exterior and highly respectable in conduct; she loved propriety and objected to eccentricities in dress or manner. Before I had the honor of an introduction to this lady, her brother-in-law Harry gave me a description of her beauty and qualities.

"By George, you know," he said, "Eleanor will have everybody about her crack and tip-top, you know, or else she won't tolerate them; and don't you know nobody feels inclined to stand at bay and face her, they just feel somehow they must give in, and they do, you know. She doesn't walk, she sweeps and sails about slowly, looking like Juno, and if she doesn't like people, she looks through them and over them, somehow. Excellence of some kind she expects from all her acquaintances, no mediocrity for Eleanor. 'I can't put up with ugly, stupid people,' she says, with a toss of her head, 'unless they are *very* rich.'"

"How is she affected towards you?" I asked.

"Oh! she endures me because I'm Frank's brother, but she's glad he hasn't another brother like me; '*one* of that sort is enough,' she says. She takes me under her wing, or rather under her thumb, like the rest of his relatives, all but the Cromaboo people, you know, and they're more than she can stand," said this frank, young gentleman.

One sultry afternoon, towards the end of October, Mr. Frank Llewellyn steamed across the Burlington Bay to the Ocean House,[80] where his wife was staying for fresh air; he expected to enjoy a good dinner in the company of a handsome, languid woman in muslin and lace, who would be too much overpowered by the heat to say much

---

[80]Burlington Bay is now called Hamilton Harbor, at the western tip of Lake Ontario. The Ocean House Hotel was built in 1874, expanded in 1876 and destroyed by fire in 1895.

more than "how very warm it is;" and he was thinking of a trip to Portland, late as it was, and reckoning the probable expense in his mind as he entered the hotel. Blessed is he who expecteth nothing. He found the wife of his bosom transformed to an energetic fury, arrayed in a linen travelling dress and hat, who, valise and umbrella in hand, confronted him at the door of his apartments, with the sharp question, "When does the boat return?"

"In half an hour, but what of that?" said Mr. Frank, "I want my dinner."

"You will get it in two hours, in Gibbeline," said the tall lady, with stern decision; "we are going to Cromaboo."

"Going to the devil," blustered Mr. Frank, "you are mad, Eleanor."

"Don't be insolent, Frank," returned the lady, "*I* am going to Cromaboo; if you don't choose to escort me, I go alone. I have heard that that hateful Lavinia is going to make a horrid low marriage with a creature of the meanest origin, a fellow who drives the stage, and I *won't* stand it. I *will* make uncle stop it."

"But are you sure?" said the husband, quailing a little before her vehemence.

"*Sure!*" with great scorn; "will you go with me, or will you not?"

"I am sorry about Lavy," remonstrated Mr. Frank, "but really –"

"Sorry, she ought to be put in the penitentiary," said his wife, stamping her foot emphatically, "*that girl* was born to be a disgrace to the family."

Mr. Frank said much, very much; he talked till they heard the sound of the whistle, which indicated that the little vessel was getting up her steam.

"I am going, do as you like, Mr. Frank Llewellyn," said the lady, taking up her valise, "it's *your* relatives I wish to benefit, not mine," and she sailed out at the open door. Her husband followed, not meekly indeed, but still he followed; they got on board and steamed back to Hamilton; they took a cab and drove to the station; they were soon in the train and off. In vain Mr. Frank urged his wife to tell him her reasons for thinking so ill of Lavinia. She was for a long time sulky and silent; not till they had retired to her apartment for the night did she open her heart to him, and then not fully. She told him indeed what she was going to do, but she gave him no reason for her conduct, that she said he would hear in time. She would give her reasons to Mr. Llewellyn in his presence.

"I *will* break up the establishment," said Mrs. Frank, "and make your uncle send his wife to the lunatic asylum, and I'll pay for her there as I offered to when I first married you, and he refused, – *now* he shall *not* refuse, and he shall live with us; I'll get him new clothes and make him look respectable, and as for *that girl*, I'll give her two hundred dollars a year if she will live in the States, and give up this hateful match, and never see the fellow again, or come to disgrace us in Hamilton with her little vulgar plebeian presence; and if she refuses we'll cut and disown her forever."

She stopped to take breath, and pull out sundry hair pins, and loosen her dark hair with a toss, and throw it over her shoulders. Her husband doubted her power to do all this; he knew his uncle was an obstinate man, notwithstanding his courtesy to women; he knew that he loved Lavy, and loved his wife, but he quailed before the handsome termagant,[81] who sat on the bed-side in her white drapery, scowling upon him as he paced the room in his shirt-sleeves, and tapping her bare foot as he turned to look at her, with an imperious "well?" He did not dare to tell his mind to her.

"You are excited, my dear," he said, nervously, "you had better go to bed, I think."

He would tell her what he thought of her scheme in the morning, he said to himself, and stop the visit to Cromaboo; but Mrs. Frank Llewellyn did not sleep well, and her temper was as bad in the morning as it had been on the previous night; he had not the pluck to try and dissuade her from the journey, and went meekly at her bidding to tell the obnoxious Robert to call for them before he left Gibbeline. He carried it with a high hand in speaking to the mail carrier – who had no idea he was related to the master – it was a relief to him to bully somebody, and he detested Robert as the cause of his present annoyance. Robert did not like the little gentleman, but was disposed to be civil to Mrs. Frank when he saw her in consideration of her great beauty. He gave them the back seat to themselves for the present; three passengers were sitting opposite to them, and two in front with the driver. On the bridge[82] they came upon a young girl with a large basket on her arm, and she hailed the stage. It was

---

[81]termagant = bully.

[82]This bridge may refer here to the Eramosa Bridge (formerly also known as the Strickland Bridge), in Guelph (Gibbeline).

Mrs. Paxton's hand-maiden Dolly, not in her ordinary working garments of blue or brown derry, but in holiday attire; her gown of three
different colors, her hat adorned with both flowers and feathers, her
hair frizzed, scratched and puffed in a dreadful way. Bad taste in
dress was an unpardonable sin in the eyes of Mrs. Frank Llewellyn,
and she determined not to have "such a creature" sitting beside her
if she could help it, as she calmly surveyed poor Dolly through her
double-eye glass.

"The old misses told me to go home by stage," said Dolly, blushing
and much flustered by the sight of so many people looking at her.

"All right," replied our hero, "plenty of room in the back seat;
make room for this lady, please," turning as he spoke, and addressing the aristocratic occupants of the best seat in the coach. Eleanor
looked at her husband as if she would say "speak."

"I will have no one in this seat," blustered Mr. Frank, "there's no
room."

"There's plenty of room," said the cool, sweet voice of the driver.

"I object to being crowded," said Mr. Frank, "I would rather take
a cab and drive to Cromaboo."

"All right, sir," replied Robert, "then out with you, please, the lady
waits on you."

Mr. Frank did not expect to be taken at his word so promptly,
especially as Eleanor carried the purse.

"What would the cab fare be?" he asked, still in a blustering tone,
but a little crest-fallen.

"Seventeen dollars, and one by stage," was the answer; "this lady
must go, but she is not going far."

Eleanor did not care to spend so much, so "the lady," got in
with an uncomfortable sense of putting everybody about, and Mr.
Frank squeezed himself into a corner, and Eleanor gathered up her
draperies and sat almost on top of her lord, as if poor Dolly had been
suffering from itch, small-pox or other contagious disorder; so they
rolled along till they came to Mrs. Paxton's, when Mr. Frank and his
wife had the seat to themselves once more.

In due time they arrived in Cromaboo, and Robert stopped at his
master's door to throw in the mail bag before taking his passengers
to their several destinations.

Mr. Frank dismounted and helped his lady out, feeling in his heart
that now came the tug of war.

"Your fare, sir, please," said Robert, who felt not the slightest curiosity as to where they were going. Mrs. Frank turned haughtily to the driver, and without a word placed in his hand four American fifty cent pieces. "Thank you ma'am, but this is Yankee money, – eight cents more, if you please."[83]

She had always passed it at par in Hamilton, where the tradesmen knew her and honoured her, and got it out of her in some other way; she looked upon Robert's demand as another insult from this presumptuous low creature, so she glared at him disdainfully with her dark eyes, but offered no more. Had she not honoured his poor conveyance by riding in it, – was she not his master's kins-woman? – a fact not dreamt of by the offender, – and therefore she ought never to have paid her fare at all.

Robert tossed the coins in his palm, and turning to the other passengers with an impudence worthy of a London cabman, said, "Well, I didn't think such a very good-looking woman could ha' been so mean like," and he mounted his perch without further haggling and drove on.

Shall I describe how this tall magnificent lady and her timid little lord came suddenly upon their uncle in his shabbiest coat, and oldest skull-cap, how they caught Miss Lavinia dyeing woolen yarn for her uncle's stockings, and startled Mrs. Llewellyn out of a sound sleep, causing her to tare about the house like a frightened cat? No, I will draw the veil, and leave all this to the reader's imagination; suffice it to say that half an hour later a flying post in the form of little Tommy Smith came pelting across the green in font of Dr. Meldrum's house, with a note for Mary Paxton, begging, imploring, entreating that lady and Mrs. Meldrum and the doctor to dine at Mr. Llewellyn's at eight that evening, as cousin Frank and his wife had arrived unexpectedly, "And I am sure," wrote Lavinia, "that Eleanor is angry with me, as she would not let me kiss her, and she used to turn her cheek so graciously, and she says I am 'a dirty creature' for dyeing yarn. Oh! *do, do* come at once."

The note was read aloud and Mrs. Meldrum remarked that it showed how very little respect Lavinia had for *her* judgement, to

---

[83]Either at the time the story is set (1860s), or at the time Leslie was writing (late 1870s), the exchange rate was such that $1.08 American dollars equalled $1 Canadian.

have written to Mary instead of herself.

"You may go if you like," she said in a crushing tone to her sister, "and Thomas may escort you if he pleases; *I* will go when I am properly invited, not before."

Mary did like to go, and Thomas was pleased to escort her, and consequently they were soon strolling through the village in the light of the setting sun, – a misty Indian Summer sun, – to the place of rendezvous; little bare-footed Tommy trotting far in front of them to herald their approach, his teeth occupied, and his heart gladdened with a large apple turnover.

Chapter Sixteen

"I could a tale unfold, whose lightest word
Would harrow up thy soul."

– Shakespeare[84]

"A man can scarce allege his own merits with modesty, much less
extol them;... but all these things are graceful in a friend's mouth
which are blushing in a man's own. I have given a rule where a man
cannot fitly play his own part; if he have not a friend he may quit the
stage."

– Lord Bacon[85]

E LEANOR was pleased to see Mr. Meldrum notwithstanding her ill-
temper, for she had always admired him for his good looks and
good manners, and the sight of his gentle sister-in-law was most welcome, too, after the first glance, for she was pretty, she was dressed in
the most exquisite taste; the softest and most spotless white muslin
floated about her, only relieved by a bright ribbon at the throat, and
a moss rose-bud in the bosom. She had a gentleness of voice and
softness of feature that, in Mr. Frank's opinion, betokened weakness
of nature. She looked like a person who would be shocked at any impropriety and easily managed. The fact was that when Miss Mary's
voice was the gentlest, her heart was at its hardest, her mind in its
most determined mood, as those most intimate with her well knew.
She was not by any means deficient in moral courage, though cow-

---

[84]William Shakespeare, *Hamlet*: Act 1, Scene 5.
[85]Francis Bacon (1561-1626), *Essays, Civil and Moral*: 27.

ardly enough in a fire, or a scene like that in the Cromaboo swamp. She was not at all afraid to face an angry or unreasonable fellow-creature, her mind once made up; she could do it in cold blood, so to speak, without flurry or nervousness, and had from a child fought other people's battles better than her own.

Eleanor thought that being highly respectable people, Mr. Meldrum and Miss Paxton must feel with her, and the first compliments over, and the new arrivals seated, she opened fire at once, with the full conviction that they would both be on her side, and think entirely as she did.

"Uncle," she said "we have come to see you on very unpleasant business, we hear that Lavinia is about to form a low marriage, and we come to remonstrate, and beg you to put a stop to it. I speak the more freely before Miss Paxton and Mr. Meldrum, delicate as the subject is, because I am sure they will sympathise with me entirely."

The old gentleman heard, but he could not believe his ears, he thought they had deceived him, as in the case of the "baby-devil."

"I beg your pardon, my dear," he said meekly, "but I have grown very deaf on the right ear; will you be so kind as to sit on this side of me and say it again."

She changed her position and spoke with such clearness and sharpness that there could be no mistake this time. "I hear," said he, "but I fail to comprehend, – what do you mean? Explain, if you please."

"I hear," said Mrs. Frank, raising her voice to a high pitch, "that Lavy is engaged to the mail carrier, Bob Smith, and I call it a disgrace to the family. Everybody talks of it – it is all over Hamilton."

"You have heard, Eleanor, what is not true," said Mr. Llewellyn, with dignity.

"But it is true," persisted Mrs. Frank, "she let him kiss her as he lay sick in bed, and the girl who was helping his mother heard the word love ever so many times, and *I believe* it, uncle; and she sits beside him in the stage whenever she can, and people actually call her 'the conductor.' The boy is nice enough, I dare say, for his station, but he is dangerous for all that. It is *dreadful* presumption to make love to Lavy, and as for her, I've no patience with her; that girl was born to be a disgrace to the family."

"If I thought it possible – but it's not possible," said Mr. Llewellyn; "I'll call Lavinia."

"Oh! don't, please," pleaded Miss Paxton, laying her hand on his arm, "you'll only hurt her feelings very much and spoil the dinner. She isn't in love with the boy, and he isn't in love with her I know; it's all a mistake, I assure you."

Mr. Llewellyn felt a little comforted, and sat down again.

"Pardon me, Miss Paxton," said Mrs. Frank, with dignity, and "looking through her and over her," as Harry would have expressed it, with her great black eyes, "but she is in love with him, and he said he was in love with her in the presence of a person I believe."

Miss Paxton laughed. "It is not possible for even an Irishman to love two ladies at once," she said, "and Robert loves me at present, he told me so ever so many times quite lately. He did love Miss Lavy in the spring, and he loves me now, and may love somebody else before the winter."

"The impudent little low dandy," broke in Mr. Frank, with great indignation.

"I can't quarrel with you, sir, for calling him little," said Miss Mary, turning to him, "and he is a bit of a dandy on Sundays, and he is lowly, but only as the lilies of the valley and the violets are, and we never reproach them for their origin, or enjoy their sweetness the less because they grow near the earth; but I set down my foot against that word impudent. Robert is not *impudent*, he is modest, and he has tact and gentleness, and a sense of honour, and those are qualities that go far to make a gentleman. I have known many "gentlemen," so-called, with only a decent education – no merit of their own – and a little conventional outside polish, and not half the worth of Robert Smith. I don't despise his love, poor boy, though it be fleeting as a spring blossom. I have been loved by worse men, and coarser men, though in a better station; I don't blame Miss Lavinia for valuing him, it may be a little too highly, but I deny that she loves him. She loves herself as yet better than any man in the world except her uncle. It is natural she should like Robert, the young like the young, and there is no one here in her own station to compare with him. It would do her a great deal of good, Mr. Llewellyn, to see a little pleasant society, and make her happier, too," here she turned to Mrs. Frank and looked her steadily in the face, with eyes that, soft in the beginning, were now as bright and keen as a hawk's. "I wonder that *you*, who take such an interest in her welfare, do not ask her to Hamilton, and introduce her to the *bon-ton*[86] of that great little city; you who treated her so kindly the last time she was there on her uncle's business. And Mr. Frank, too, was extremely considerate upon that occasion to his young kinswoman, his own flesh and blood; your conduct leads one to look for special favours for Lavinia from both of you."

Mr. Llewellyn could have taken Mary in his arms and kissed her, Mr. Meldrum opened his brown eyes in the twilight, and was greatly amused and interested, but Mr. Frank was extremely nervous, not to say frightened, not knowing how his Eleanor would take it, and dreading a scene; but that lady had less of the lion in her than the cat, and declined to give battle, when confronted by a person who did not fear her. Her paws became velvet at once, and she said suavely, "I shall be happy to entertain Lavinia for a week or two, if you will give me the pleasure of your company too."

Miss Paxton was a novelty to her, she admired her for her beauty, and forgave her for her plainness of speech. She was surprised at her spirit, and unwilling to do battle with such an opponent. "It will help you to forget this troublesome Robert," she added with a gracious smile.

"Oh! I have no wish to forget him," said his defender, returning the smile, "and I seldom leave home, thank you all the same for your kind invitation; it would be base ingratitude even to try and forget him, for he saved my life once, and I should like to tell you all the story, because I fear Mr. Llewellyn will be prejudiced against his good servant after what you have said, Mrs. Llewellyn."

All expressed themselves very willing to hear, and listened with different thoughts to her account of Robert's prowess.

"Very rash," commented Mr. Frank, when she had ended, "he should have given information to the police at Gibbeline, and not have passed through the woods without a sufficient force. You might both have been murdered; and he was still more culpable in not bring-ing the rogues to justice."

"No, Frank," said his uncle, "you're wrong there, no gentleman could have acted with greater delicacy or finer feeling when the ad-venture was over; it would never have done to bring a lady into a Police Court; but he was wrong, entirely wrong to lead her into such

---

[86] *bon-ton* = decent society, from the French phrase, *le bon ton*, meaning "good manners."

danger. Still, to do him justice, I believe I should have acted as he did at his age. Young fellows are so rash and hopeful."

Mr. Meldrum had never quite approved of Robert's conduct in the matter, but he would not lose the opportunity of propitiating his sister-in-law, so he said, "I suppose we must judge Bob by his success, as we do Napoleon when he crossed the Alps; forgive him for risking so much, since he came off victorious; but if any harm had come to his charge, I must say I should have a different feeling; I should vote for hanging him up along with the rascals who attacked him."

"Oh! dear, I winder you didn't die of fright," exclaimed Mrs. Frank, "and as for keeping it secret, I'm sure I should have told everybody, and roused the whole country, and I never could have forgiven that boy for leading me into such a pickle."

"Miss Llewellyn desired me to tell you that dinner is ready," said the gentle voice of Robert at the open door. There was a pause broken by Mr. Llewellyn when the lad's retreating footsteps had died away.

"Robert has always taken his meals with us," he said nervously, "but I hesitate about asking so many guests to sit down with a servant, even though he isn't an ordinary servant."

"I think if the person with the longest pedigree doesn't object that nobody else has a right to," said Miss Paxton. "My father was descended from Dame Sprott, who won the King's Knowe by kilting up her coats and running like a deer, while Robert Bruce ate the boiling butter brose she had set before him."[87]

Courage is infectious; Mr. Llewellyn returned the smile, but shook his head at her as he replied, "Frank and I can trace our origin to more noble people than Dame Sprott, I think."

"Oh! but you haven't heard half I have to say," returned Mary, quite gravely; "here is Mr. Meldrum; well, his great uncle's mother's second cousin is the half sister of The O'Callaghan, Lord of Sismore, and she told my sister that Mr. Meldrum is descended from King Brian Barroo, and she has his pedigree on parchment right away back to the time when it was the fashion for great Irish gentlemen to bite each other's noses off. I think King Brian died before Prince Llewellyn was born, so if Mr. Meldrum doesn't object to sit at the

---

[87] A battle in 1309 between Robert the Bruce and forces under Sir Walter Selby took place near the cottage of a soldier-herdsman named Sprott (Charles Norton Elvin *Anecdotes of Heraldry* (1864): 15).

same table with Robert, it is not for us to put on airs. She has the parchment at home," she added, seeing Mr. Frank was about to make a protest.

"We will take your word for it, my dear, and not wait for it," said Mr. Llewellyn, patting her on the shoulder. "Take my arm, Eleanor, and forgive me for placing you at the same board with this naughty Robert, whom I forgive for his presumptuous gallantry to these two young ladies, because he is the happy occasion of bringing you under my roof. Come, Mr. Meldrum, – Frank, give your arm to Miss Mary, and believe me, fair ladies, both, it is only when I have such guests as you that I sigh to think that the ancient power and grandeur of my family are gone forever."

They proceeded in great state to the dining-room, to find a delicate repast awaiting them, and Miss Lavinia and Mrs. Llewellyn in their best clothes, and to learn that Robert had gone to take tea with his mother, and so lost the honour of dining with so many people of gentle blood.

Chapter Seventeen

"Those many had not dared to do that evil,
If the first man that did the edict infringe
Had answered for his deed."

– Measure For Measure[88]

"Corin – I partly guess, for I have loved ere now.
Silvius – No, Corin, being old, thou cans't not guess,
Though in thy youth thou wast as true a lover
As ever sighed upon a midnight pillow."

– As You Like It[89]

WILL it be believed that three hours after Mrs. Frank's arrival in Cromaboo, that hostile lady was seated peaceably in her uncle's garden, watching the great hazy full moon rising in all its fiery glory, and conversing quite good temperedly with Lavinia and Mary about appropriate costumes for St. Andrew's ball in Gibbeline? Will it be believed that she had promised – nay proposed – to come to Gibbeline and chaperon these ladies to the ball in question; and had invited them most affably to spend the following fortnight in her house in Hamilton?

She had eaten a good dinner, and felt pleasantly weary after it, and her ill-temper had spent itself for the time; Mary Paxton was a novelty, and she was willing to put up with Lavinia for her sake; she would take the girl up for a little time, she thought, and see if anything could be made of her; there must after all be something in

---

[88] William Shakespeare, *Measure For Measure*: Act 2, Scene 2.
[89] William Shakespeare, *As You Like It*: Act 2, Scene 4.

her, or she could not have attracted such a woman as Miss Paxton; so she was insufferably condescending and patronizing to her dark little kins-woman, and really very polite and pleasant to Lavinia's friend.

The three gentlemen who were smoking their cigars together on the veranda in front of the shop, fell to talking over Robert and Miss Paxton's adventure in the Cromaboo Swamp. Mr. Frank was so delighted that his Eleanor was in a good temper again, that he was quite jocose and satirical in his way.

"If he had laid an information against those fellows," he said, "I don't suppose they would have had a very severe punishment, after all, even if they had succeeded in their purpose; it requires a great deal of influence to get hanged now, you know; in fact if a fellow wishes to get hanged he may commit manslaughter, and indecent assaults without number, and rape, and all that sort of thing, and yet not succeed after all; the feeling of the public is against it; they are so tender-hearted, you see, they won't have severe punishment for anything, so if a man wants to have his neck stretched he must just do it himself."

"It is too true, Frank, and God knows it is not a subject for mirth," said the elder Llewellyn, sadly. "It is a shame and disgrace to the country we live in that indecent assaults on tender women and little children are not visited with a more severe punishment. Mercy is misplaced in such cases, for what is the law for but to protect those who are without a protector."

"Oh! you know they make quite heroes of the fellows who do such things, they do really," said the lawyer, "they tell about their families in the papers, and their pious bringing up, and their poor old mothers, and all that sort of thing."

The calm voice of Mr. Meldrum broke the stillness that succeeded this remark. "You remember the case last year in Gibbeline – the – well I suppose I must call him a man – who committed a rape upon a little child of five? He was condemned to be hanged, and four hundred people signed a petition to get the sentence commuted, and succeeded in their purpose.[90] As this is the age of presentations, I almost wonder they had not presented the fellow with an address."

---

[90] In the entire novel, this is Leslie's sole footnote; simply "A fact."

"And a tea-pot, or butter-cooler, or something of that sort," chimed in Mr. Frank, "and congratulated him upon his presence of mind in trying circumstances – it will come to that soon."

"I have sometimes thought that if a special jury of married men was chosen, men with daughters of their won, it might make a difference," said Mr. Meldrum. "I once had a little daughter of my own, and can partly understand how a man would feel whose child had been do injured. Very young men should not be jurymen in such a case."

"Juries may condemn," said Mr. Frank, "but the public feeling is against hanging."

"I don't know that it would make much difference," said Mr. Llewellyn, answering the doctor, and ignoring the last remark; "I have had neither son nor daughter, and there's Bob, a mere boy, would be a very severe judge of a villain of that calibre. You know Dr. Johnson[91] says that 'young men are the most virtuous,' Mr. Meldrum."

Mr. Frank drew himself up and looked very irate and virtuous at this. "By George, you know," he said, "if any fellow should insult my Eleanor, I should think as little of shooting him as I would a crow."

It happened that the other gentlemen lifted their eyes at the same time, and being very near together their glances met through the soft moonlight and the tobacco smoke; the remark struck them both in the same way, and they smiled.

"I am greatly puzzled about that boy Bob," said Mr. Llewellyn, after a pause; "one would almost think the fellow had gentle blood in him, and yet his father is a coarse Connaught peasant, and the mother a straight-backed, good kind of common-place woman enough, but nothing more. Now in this affair with Miss Paxton, Bob has acted like the Chevalier Bayard[92] even to the love-making, which is certainly presumptuous in the highest degree, considering his station. I remember an occurrence that took place last winter in Gibbeline on a Fair day that struck me at the time as most gentlemanly in Bob.

---

[91] Samuel Johnson (1709-1784) - "...Sir, young men have more virtue than old men; they have more generous sentiments in every respect" (James Boswell, John Wilson Croker, and John Wright, *The Life of Samuel Johnson* Volume 2 (1846): 231).

[92] Pierre Terrail, seigneur de Bayard (1473-1524) was a French soldier, generally known as the Chevalier de Bayard, and, by his contemporaries, as "le bon chevalier," or "the good knight."

Some roughs jostled a poor old woman, and pinned a large piece of dirty paper to the back of her shawl, and he removed it in a minute deftly and quietly, so that she never knew of that insult, and helped the feeble old creature safely across the slippery street and beyond the reach of her tormentors; and then he returned and made a speech to those gentlemen, which contained a great deal of right feeling, and bad English enough to set one's teeth on edge. Where can he have got his little niceties of feeling, his delicacy of thought?"

Perhaps Mr. Meldrum could have told, but he only calmly puffed his cigar and listened.

"You make too much of the puppy," said Mr. Frank, "he's remarkable for nothing but self-will and forwardness."

"I must speak to him about his conduct to these ladies," said the uncle, "and tell him it's entirely reprehensible."

"Talk of the angels," said Mr. Meldrum, as a light firm step approached, and in a moment Robert appeared, and would have passed them but that his master stopped him. "I wish to speak to you Bob, before you go to bed."

"All right, sir," – very respectfully it was spoken.

"Why not now?" said Mr. Meldrum, "and Frank and I will join the ladies." They were old college chums, and it was Frank and Tom between them.

"I shall be happy to join the ladies," said Mr. Frank, "but I tell this young man before I go that I consider his conduct to me to-day highly insolent and offensive."

"I ask your pardon, sir," in a very clear distinct voice, "if I had known you were related to the master, I would have behaved quite different."

"You at least knew I was a gentleman," said Mr. Frank, with great dignity.

"I didn't know it, sir," in too low a voice to reach the old master's ears, and looking Mr. Frank in the face with the greatest simplicity.

"I *am* a gentleman, fellow," said Mr. Frank, in a thundering tone.

"Come, come Frank," said Mr. Llewellyn, "an apology should be accepted whether from peasant or peer."

"It's kind in you to tell me," the boy went on in the same low key, "you see when a gentleman doesn't show as he's a gentleman in face or dress, or manners or the like, he ought to be ticketed 'gentleman' for the benefit of such ignorant fellows as me; 'twould save a deal of misunderstanding."

"You are an insolent low rascal," said Mr. Frank, shaking with anger, "and I have a great mind to chastise you."

"I like a great mind," said Robert, in the same gentle monotone, which implied as plainly as anything could "come on and try."

"No, no Frank," said Mr. Llewellyn, who could hear his nephew's sharp tongue well enough, "he has been much to blame about the young ladies, but leave him to me; I am his master."

"Really, I can't defend you, Bob," said Mr. Meldrum, drawing the lawyer's arm through his own, and leading the trembling excited hero away, and wondering in his heart what Miss Paxton would think of her "modest" boy now. "Consider, my dear Frank," he said, "it would never do for a person in your station – a Llewellyn – to fight with your uncle's servant. I would not do him the honour."

"True," said the irate little hero, who was not sorry of a hole to slip out of, "he is quite beneath me."

"Entirely, entirely," said Mr. Meldrum, soothingly, "let us talk of something else," and they strolled towards the ladies, who were at the extremity of the garden, and too far removed from Mr. Llewellyn and his servant to hear a word that passed.

"I have heard an account of you to-day, my boy, that greatly surprises me," begun the master, "and I consider your conduct in many particulars highly improper, though I commend you for your conduct in defending Miss Paxton, and especially in not letting her appear in a Police Court, which must have been very painful to her feelings. But, Robert, what excuse can you make for offering yourself to these two young ladies? It is inexcusable, for they are entirely removed from you in rank and station."

Robert changed colour as his master spoke, and forgot all about Mr. Frank in a minute, but he answered at once.

"I love Miss Paxton,- - I told her so, – I did not ask her to marry me; and about Miss Lavinia, – I – " he hesitated.

"Not to confuse you," said the master, with a smile, "let us deal with one young lady at a time; go on about Miss Paxton."

"Well, sir, I know I am much her inferior in every way, but I cannot help admiring what is beautiful, and loving what was made to be loved. I never dreamt there could be such a woman in the world till I saw her. She is like a fairy."

"A what?" said the master.

"A fairy, sir," raising his voice a little.

"A fairy, you foolish boy; much you know about fairies. She is no more like one than I am. Why, she is as tall as yourself," with a kindly, tolerant smile, "and fairies are not a span long. She is not even beautiful, her features are by no means perfect."

"Her imperfections are lovelier than other people's perfection – that is if you call perfection a straight nose and regular features – her character shines through her face and would make an ugly one pretty," said the boy, with a great flush in his own; "and she is fairy-like," returning the master's smile as he spoke; "look at her now," pointing to the distant white-robed figure, "see her as she raises her arm to pluck a leaf, and turns up her face to speak to the tall lady from Hamilton. She has a cloud about her; them 'clouds,' as they are called, are just coarse wraps and drag around them to keep them warm; but look at the cloud on her, how it floats about her face, half concealing, half revealing, as a soft white cloud covers yet scarcely hides the moon; how it softly coils about her waist as if it loved her; not sticking to her as weeds cling to a wet log. She is fairy-like; much you know about fairies, sir – them little things you speak of is imps."

"She is not so much like Queen Titiana as you are like Bottom the weaver, Bob."[93]

"Who is he?" asked Robert, in all simplicity, "and where does he live, sir? I never heard of the man."

"Miss Mary has heard of him, ask her some day. There is a glamour upon you, my poor boy, you see what I do not see. I see a sprightly, attractive, good-looking lady, who is quite thirty, I am sure; you glorify her into an angel. This is love, Bob, I admit; but love is a dream of youth, and unlike other dreams its effects do not pass with the night; the vision indeed is gone, but the consequences remain. Try to realize it and you will find it impossible, but it may curse your life and the lady's till you drop into the grave at three-score years and ten. You should pray against all unholy desires, and foolish desires are unholy, and wrong. You should, for Miss Paxton's sake, fight against this feeling in your heart. You should strive against it as unmanly; for if people knew of it, and knew that the lady forgave you, and regarded your impudence leniently, good-naturedly, as she does,

---

[93]These characters are from William Shakespeare's *A Midsummer Night's Dream*.

they would say that old fools were the worst of fools, and perhaps give her a great deal of annoyance and pain. She is as much beyond your reach as yonder moon, my lad, as much above you as the Queen – don't look at *her*, but look at me and *attend* to what I am saying. Tell me what you would see if you looked at Queen Victoria?"

Robert regarded his master with a puzzled expression, but answered truthfully: "I should see a dumpy, little, old lady that I'm bound to take off my hat to, because she's a good woman and our Queen."

"You would see the highest lady in the land, Robert, the descendant of kings and heroes, through whose veins runs the noblest and purest blood in England, whose pedigree can be traced for a thousand years; now if I should fall in love with this lady, and ask her to marry me, what would you think of me?" asked the old gentleman, with energy, and quite unconscious of saying anything ridiculous, as he waved his cigar with one hand, and rubbed up his red skull-cap with the other.

"I should think you an old fool," was on the tip of Robert's tongue, but the remark did not pass his lips; he merely looked at his master in silence.

"Miss Paxton is as far removed from you in station as the Queen is from me; her ancestors were wealthy and influenced people three hundred years ago, when yours were mere hewers of wood and drawers of water, un-noted and unknown."

"It is nothing to her credit that she is well-born," said Robert, speaking slowly, as if he were weighing each word, and regarding his master steadily, "and it is no disgrace to me that I come of a low family; these things are ordered by God, we have nothing to do with them."

"I admit it, my lad, and I do not speak to pain you, but for her sake and yours. You should regard her with veneration, as something out of your sphere, and beyond you; if you indulge in unholy desires – if you wish to take her in your arms and kiss her – in a word to have her for a wife – your love is no better than the love of a cat for a lark; it can never soar up to heaven and sing with the lark, but if the foolish bird stoops within its reach, it can pull it to the earth and destroy it. Love that is worth the name is unselfish, and I see nothing unselfish in your love for these young ladies; you have done positive harm to my niece, for it has reached Hamilton that you kissed her when you were ill, and her relatives believe it and think less of her. They came on purpose to speak to me about it to-day. Is it true that you kissed her?"

"Yes," said the guilty lad, and it was not without a great effort that he told the truth. So do the ugly effects of our pleasant peccadillos rise up when we least expect them.

"It was very wrong, Bob, very unmanly; a gentleman would never have done it, especially as things were then; it was taking an unfair advantage of my niece's generosity, for she could not box your ears, or have you dismissed when you were too weak to lift your hand to your head; it was a very mean action."

"I am very sorry I did it, sir," said Robert, truly, "and doubly sorry that Miss Lavy has been annoyed about it; it was entirely my fault, not hers."

"I fully believe *that*," replied the old gentleman, with dignity; "my niece would be above encouraging such attentions from a servant;" – Robert looked down at his boots, and it is greatly to his credit that he did not even smile at this juncture – "if I thought otherwise I would dismiss you at once, though it would put me to great inconvenience to part with you."

"Mr. Llewellyn, I never meant to annoy Miss Lavinia, never thought to do her harm; it was only a kiss after all, and your folks are very uncharitable to make so much of it; I did it from gratitude, because she had been kind to me," – the gentle simplicity with which he told this fib nettled the master – "I always kiss my mother when she pleases me very much, as a warm kind of thank you."

"It is one thing to kiss your mother, and quite another thing to kiss my niece; in the last case it is an unwarrantable liberty, in the first a mere meaningless habit. I never kissed my mother but when I parted with her for a long time – a number of years. I think your mother a sensible woman in the main, Bob, but she is very foolish to encourage you in so much kissing and slobbering; it is a habit like smoking or drinking and will grow upon you. I can understand kissing a baby every day, but a lump of a lad in his teens," said this severe old gentleman, "is quite another thing."

"I am as much my mother's son now as I was when I was first born," replied Robert with some heat.

"True, Bob, but you couldn't wear baby clothes now, and you should put away childish things; all things are good in their season;

a little child may call his mother ma, and commit no offense against good taste, but it is a ridiculous expression in the mouth of a fellow six feet high."

Robert thought a kiss never out of season, but he bit his lips and refrained from saying so.

"It is natural you and I should regard things and people differently," said Mr. Llewellyn more quietly after a pause, "we are different in age, in station, in education. You have told me how you regard Miss Paxton, and I see in her a lady whom you have it in your power to injure very much by your selfish love. I do not know in what light you see my niece, but I see a girl of my own flesh and blood, very dear to me, – whom you have injured in the eyes of her relatives by your presumption and ill-manners. You start – it was only my wife fleeting by like a hunted hare to hide herself in the darkness. *You* see in her a weak, shabby, crazy old woman; I see Christ suffering in one of his members, a dear immortal soul who will one day sing the praises of God in perfect happiness. You see and despise the poor maimed grub, I see in perspective, and with certainty, – for she is a believer, – the glorious butterfly."

"You think too hardly of me, sir," said Robert, "I have never despised Mrs. Llewellyn. God forbid that I should. A slight crack in the skull, or a sunstroke might make me as queer any day. And about the young ladies, I know I have been to blame, but I will think of what you say, and try and command myself. I never saw it in the light you do."

"Pray, Robert, pray," said the old man, earnestly, laying his hand on his servant's shoulder, "no man can withstand temptation in his own strength, he can do it only with the help of God. If you cannot get over your fancy for Miss Paxton without, you must leave this part of the country for her sake; and I would willingly part with you Bob, though I should miss you sorely."

"You are very kind I am sure, sir," said Robert, rather ruefully, and there is no telling what expression of penitence he would have added, but at that instant Miss Lavinia burst in upon them with more haste than dignity. "Oh! Robert, run at once, that horrid old pig is in the kitchen," she exclaimed, "and upset the pot of water the beef was boiled in; I meant it for soup to-morrow;" so Robert escaped, nothing loathe, and a soft musical laugh broke from his lips, as he whacked poor piggy with a great corn broom, and nimbly avoided the greasy water that flooded the kitchen floor.

"How do you account for little Bob's fine feelings?" asked Mr. Llewellyn, as he shook hands with Miss Paxton at parting. "Can you solve what to me is a great puzzle?"

"Why, he is an Irishman," replied the lady, gaily. "Did you ever know an Irishman who was not of 'a hoigh' family? I never did. There is a gentleman in every Irish family, and Bob is the one in this."

"My dear, you speak too lightly of that word *gentleman*."

"Not at all, sir; I could prove my words in this case, only Mrs. Llewellyn is yawning and longing to be rid of us. Good night, and many thanks for a very pleasant evening."

As they were going home, Mr. Meldrum told his sister-in-law of the squabble between Mr. Frank and Robert, just to see what she would say. She was delighted. "The dear boy," she exclaimed, "he deserves a medal. That Frank Llewellyn was always a horrid little puppy."

"I fancy Bob is improving in grammar," remarked Mr. Meldrum, presently. "Have you been instructing him?"

"I told him I would cut his acquaintance if he did not give up 'this yer' and 'that there,' and I have not heard him use those expressions since."

"He has given up smoking, too; by your advice, I suppose?"

"Well, I spoke to him about it," she admitted, "I detest smokers."

"Do you detest me?" he asked.

"No, indeed, what an idea! But you are not offensive, you never intrude your tobacco. I like you very much, *for a brother*," with emphasis on the last words.

"Thank you; and Bob likes *you* very much, you have great influence with him; but do you look forward to the end of all this? *He* evidently hopes that you will one day be his wife."

"Others have had the same hope," said the lady coolly, as she tripped across the little bridge before him. Mr. Meldrum considered this remark a little, and thinking rightly that it meant "mind your own business," he said no more.

Chapter Eighteen

"Glorious Apollo from on high behold us."

– Old Song[94]

"By the holy cross of St. Andrew."

– Old Scottish Oath[95]

THE band was in full force, a screaming tenor followed by a chorus of twenty voices, sang "Glorious Apollo, from on high behold us,"[96] as Mr. Meldrum entered the town hall, at Gibbeline, on the night of St. Andrew's ball.[97] The concert was nearly at an end, and after a few Scottish ballads and "Auld Lang Syne," the band proceeded to scatter the Queen's enemies, and the benches were removed for the ball. Mr. Meldrum strolled about with his hands behind him, glancing at the mottos on the walls, till his eyes were suddenly arrested by a young man in a kilt; a bright intelligent, rather stout, and not very good looking young man, who was evidently not a Scotchman, and very clearly felt ill at ease and uncomfortable in his gala dress.

Mr. Meldrum's face wore a smile of amusement, as he crossed the room, and passed his arm through that of the new comer.

"Good evening to you, Harry," he said, "I hoped you would be here to-night; I must compliment you upon your taste. Which clan do you honour with your countenance?"

---

[94]"Glorious Apollo" was composed by Samuel Webbe Sr. in 1787, originally for the London Glee Club.

[95]Unknown source.

[96]See note 94 above.

[97]The old City Hall of Guelph, November 30th.

"Oh! it's a fancy tartan," returned the young gentleman, "and by George, you know I am glad of your countenance, Meldrum, for I feel like an ass in this petticoat; but Eleanor would have it, you know, and threatened a passion if I didn't give in, said it was national, and all that, and Frank is so afraid of her that he begged me to humour her, and hang it, you know," he concluded, with a good deal of complacency, "I don't mind showing my legs for once if the girls don't mind it."

"And Frank, – has he turned Highlandman?" asked his friend.

"Oh! *he* couldn't, you know, by George, with his spindle-shanks, but Eleanor made him try it on. He's like the Queen of Spain, he's got no legs."

"I wished to see you very much," said Mr. Meldrum, leading his young friend to a quiet corner, "to tell you of a chance of making your fortune. There is an heiress coming here to-night, and if you are the clever fellow I take you to be you will improve the opportunity."

"Who is it?" inquired his young companion, eagerly, "I want money in the worst way, – is she young and good-looking?"

"Pretty fair as to looks," said the doctor, "with as much sense as the generality of women, and not more willfulness; you can manage her, I make no doubt if you try, and it's not too much trouble, give her her way in small things and you have your own in great."

"But who is she?" said Harry, "I'll marry her if she isn't too horrid, and the money is enough. What is her dot, as the French say, and what is her name?"

"Lavinia Llewellyn is her name, and her dot is about thirty thousand pounds sterling."

"Do you mean my cousin, the little brownie of Cromaboo? You are chaffing me, – where is the money to come from?"

"From the Brazils, where she was born; her maternal aunt is just dead; I had a letter from my brother Jack about it, – you shall have it presently to read, – asking me if I knew of such a person as Lavinia Llewellyn, and begging me to try and find her out. Ah! we are short-sighted mortals, – if I had not married four thousand pounds in the summer, I would have married thirty thousand in the winter, and you would not have had this chance; but I am no dog in the manger, and it is really a great fortune for Canada. I answered Jack at once, giving him full particulars, and referring him to your brother Frank. I have not spoken to anyone about it, and I will not to a single soul. You are the only person in the secret, and if you play your cards skillfully you may carry off the prize; but let me tell you, master Harry, your family have treated her vilely, – in fact every Llewellyn of you all, except your uncle Owen, – and if you don't make sure of her before her good fortune is publicly known, in fact marry her, – your chance is gone forever. A much more stupid woman would see through your motives, if your attentions began after."

"I don't know much about the little thing," pondered Harry, thoughtfully; "but she is very plain, and my sisters say she is a mischief-maker, and Eleanor can't bear her."

"They will sing another tune in a month or two," returned Mr. Meldrum, "and she is not *very* plain, my young friend; her face is intelligent, and she has a pretty little figure; she will no doubt have many brilliant opportunities even if she loses Mr. Harry Llewellyn."

"Her taste in dress is simply awful," said Harry, quite seriously, "I saw her in this town, last summer, in a bright scarlet scarf, and a green gown, and blue flowers in her hat, – I give you my word of honour."

"I shouldn't wonder if *all* the ladies wear them next summer," said Mr. Meldrum, with a placid smile; "it will be called the Llewellyn costume, or the Cromaboo toilet, and if that comes to pass, even you, Harry, will not think it so very awful."

"Are you sure Frank doesn't know of her fortune?" asked Harry.

"Quite sure."

"Then what the dickens made them take her up and invite her to Hamilton, and bring her here to-night?" exclaimed Harry, much puzzled, "they can't bear her; I could hardly believe it when I heard it."

"My fair sister-in-law, Mary Paxton, made them," said Mr. Meldrum; "she has a way of managing people when she is not too lazy to exert her authority. She is one of those 'gracious women' who retain honour as strong men do riches. If she had Miss Lavy's money, with her beauty and good qualities, she might marry a bishop."

"That's a hard hit at the clergy," said Harry. "I have heard Eleanor rave about her; why didn't you marry her yourself, Meldrum, since you admire her so much?"

"For the very good reason that she would not marry me, but this is *entre nous*,[98] and not to be repeated."

"I understand," nodded his friend; "is Mrs. Meldrum coming to-night as well as her sister?"

"No, she is pious, and doesn't approve of St. Andrew's balls, and sic like vanities. Look to the door; here – if you are a sensible fellow – comes Mrs. Harry Llewellyn."

Sure enough, there entered Miss Lavinia, leaning upon Mr. Frank's arm, and arrayed in a sweeping robe of soft, white muslin, with a sash and shoulder-knots of Marie Stuart tartan; her hair curled and tied in a queue with a bit of plaid ribbon. Pretty she was not, but very bright, animated, pleased and happy.

"I never saw her look so nice," said cousin Harry.

"Many a plainer girl has been thought passable, especially with thirty thousand pounds," commented Mr. Meldrum; "you must get Miss Mary to choose her gowns and petticoats."

Mrs. Frank came behind, looking queenly, but rather cross, in velvet and lace, and by her side Mary Paxton, in a plain white silk, without any ornament but a tartan sash across the shoulder.

"She's a beauty," said Harry, decidedly, "is your wife as handsome?"

"Neither so nice nor so nice-looking," was the reply.

"You missed it that time, Meldrum – I shall ask her to dance."

"Only once," said his mentor, "if you are wise, and every other dance with Lavy. If you make her jealous, or doubtful of your good faith, it's all up with you. Of course I know you would prefer Miss Mary with three thousand pounds, but it's hardly likely she would take you after refusing me, you see."

"No, I suppose not," said Harry, rather ruefully; "do you know a beauty like that makes a fellow regret being so common-place and all that sort of thing; and, by George, you know, I hardly know how to set about love-making in the other quarter, either, I've laughed at her so, almost to her face; but hang it, it's only trying, after all, and if I lose her I shall be no worse off," so saying, he crossed the room and shook hands with his cousin, and told her he was very glad to see her, and asked her how many dances she was engaged for. His manner was rather theatrical, but Lavinia was too happy to be critical.

---

[98] *entre nous* (French) = between ourselves.

"I can't dance anything but a polka," she said, "and there is only one on the programme."

"Put me down for that, please," said cousin Harry. "Would you like to see the national emblems, and all that? If you will do me the honour," and he offered his arm and carried Miss Lavy off, to the amusement of Mrs. Frank, who thought he was going to make fun of her.

"It's really very good natured of Harry," she said, complacently, to take her off our hands. "How nice his legs look."

Mr. Harry obeyed his adviser to the letter, and made the best use of his time; he had no rivals, and monopolized his cousin without opposition, sticking to her like a burr the whole evening, taking her into supper, and seeing that she got her favourite dishes, – she was a connoisseur, and not one of those ladies to whom one dish is the same as another, – and finally helping her on with her wraps and escorting her to the carriage when she left. Then he joined his friend and they walked to the Royal Hotel together, through the falling snow.

"By George, I'm tired through," said Mr. Harry, confidentially, "but she's not a bad kind of girl either, Meldrum, only you know one may have too much of even a good thing. Hang it, you know, nobody asked her to dance but me. I thought you might, you know."

"I," said Mr. Meldrum, laughing, "I am not a dancing man, and besides Miss Lavy is not a dancing woman either. I *did* ask her when you left her for a minute to look for the kind of ice she liked, and she said she would rather talk to cousin Harry. Go to bed and rest, my boy, your fortune's made; every night of your life may be like to-night, you lucky dog you, henceforth and forever."

"I don't know that the money is worth the sacrifice," said Harry, with a yawn.

"Oh! you'll feel differently when the tailor sends in his bill," replied his friend; "are your legs cold?"

"Let my legs alone, and tell me about that Bob Smith, Meldrum. Is there any truth in it, or was it only spite in Eleanor to say Lavy cared for him."

"I think there was something sentimental between them, and thirty thousand pounds would no doubt quicken the fellow's affections," said the doctor, judging Robert by himself. "He would be a formidable rival if he entered the lists, for though he doesn't understand English, he understands love-making, and has a way with him that women like. He's a pretty little fellow for his inches, and there's worth in him, he has a will of his own. I think he has only been play-ing at love-making with Miss Lavy, but if he was once thoroughly in earnest you would find yourself nowhere, my young friend; so make hay while the sun shines, and if you succeed Harry, take my advice, and never admit to a soul that you knew of Lavy's good fortune be-fore anyone else. Don't, for the sake of justifying yourself, tell Frank or any living creature, or your domestic peace will be at an end. Stick to it that pure love and nothing else was the motive; they may guess that you're lying, but they can't prove it, except myself, and I will never tell tales."

"By George, you are a cool fellow, Meldrum," said the doctor's pupil, "and an awful hypocrite."

"You had better give up George, and swear by St. Andrew in fu-ture," replied his friend, as they turned into the Royal. "Good night to you, Harry, or rather good morning, and my benison[99] upon you."

---

[99]benison = a blessing.

Chapter Nineteen

"The proof of the pudding is in the eating."
– Vulgar Old Proverb[100]

IT had dimly dawned upon Mr. Meldrum, during the first three days of his second honey-moon, that he had made a mistake in his marriage, and as days rolled into weeks, and weeks into months, the unmistakable fact stared him in the face that his choice had been a very unhappy one. He had put himself to school again under a stern mistress, and was learning things daily hitherto not dreamt of in his philosophy. He had always lied occasionally when it suited his purpose, and now he was obliged to lie habitually to avoid daily domestic fracas. Never when he lied voluntarily, had he felt humiliated, but now that necessity forced him, he began to despise that useful weapon called falsehood, as a hateful and mean one.

A prophet could not have convinced him, three months ago, that he would invent stories, and tell falsehoods, blacks as well as whites, to escape from sleeping with a handsome woman, his wife; that he would absolutely prefer the kitchen floor with the crickets and black beetles for bed-fellows, to the soft couch of that very good-looking woman. A white-robed angel descending straight from heaven could not have made him believe it. If anybody had told him three months ago that he would ever desire to lay violent hands on his wife, box her ears, shake her out of her clothes, or throw her out of the window, he would have considered it the wildest dream, an accusation beneath

---

[100]This proverb is at least as old as the 14th century. In 1605, William Camden stated it in *Remaines of a Greater Worke, Concerning Britaine* as "All the proofe of a pudding, is in the eating."

contempt. Then he did not think it possible that those inferior pretty creatures could put him out of temper, or occasion a deep feeling of anger, or even annoyance, by anything they could say or do. Now all that had changed, he felt he was as other men are. He was surprised at himself, he had such difficulty in commanding his temper when conversing privately with his wife, and this new phase of his nature rather shocked him by its novelty; it was as if the peaceful domestic pussy on his hearth had suddenly risen in his face a large and fierce tiger. Mrs. Meldrum did not care to please her lord and master, she did not scruple to be rude to him, she openly despised his tastes, and above all she was determined to rule, change and convert him into what he was not by nature, and never could be. She was on unknown ground with her husband's character as much as he was with hers. In the first month she hinted at his faults, – and who so immaculate as to be without them? In the second she told him of them plainly; in the third she advanced further, and if they did not quarrel every time they met, it was only because it takes two to make a quarrel. During the honeymoon she had made a great effort to rise and breakfast with him, but she soon gave it up and went back to her old habits, and her lord found her absence a relief, though he professed to regret it. She began to realize fully that he was related to her and for life, and she discovered that it was her duty to be faithful with him, as she had always been with her mother and sister and first husband. In the first month of their union she would answer if he spoke, she would look at a book or a picture if he would ask her; *now* she said peevishly or snappishly, "I *won't* be bothered, Thomas, I can't look at the thing."

She never doubted the affection of those she snubbed, but considered it only a natural tribute to her many virtues and good qualities, and good looks; it never occurred to her that affection may be wounded, nay killed outright, by cruel stabs of the tongue, or starvation. Her husband had told her he loved her; she felt sure he would love her forever, when the fact was he had only profaned the word in using it, and admired her person in a cool way, and her cash with rather more warmth of feeling.

A thousand disagreements had occurred in that quarter of a year, negative on the husband's part, for he said little or nothing, positive on the wife's, who expressed herself very freely. She would have bed-curtains, and draw them close about her, she would sleep in a soft smothering down bed in the hottest weather; curtains looked "respectable," she said, and she had never been accustomed to sleep on a board; in vain the doctor pleaded the unhealthiness of the practice. She had her own way. The husband liked the broad sunlight streaming across the house from room to room; the wife liked darkened rooms, and would have blinds down and curtains drawn, and the merest dim gleam to guide people on their way. Mrs. Meldrum loved a warm room, her husband liked a somewhat chill apartment and plenty of fresh air; these things were only a difference of taste, but alas! Margaret judged her neighbours, scandalized and found fault with them in no measured terms; in fact said what she thought of them, and she thought very ill of everybody, while Thomas, her husband, seldom thought of his neighbours, and never spoke harshly of them, and so this practice of his wife's annoyed him greatly. The doctor put on his religion with his Sunday coat; the doctor's lady wore hers all the week, it entered into every thought and action of her life; everybody was wrong and she would set them right; she was sent to do a great work and she must do it, and as charity begins at home, her husband was the first to be attended to. His shirts, stockings and puddings were matters of indifference to her, but his character and behaviour was what she had at heart.

Mr. Meldrum's creditors had been extremely lenient as yet, having heard that he had married a rich lady, but all patience has its limits, and as Christmas drew near they wanted their money, and bills flowed in. The doctor, according to his custom, lighted his cigar with them, and when hardy duns made personal visits he always happened to be out of the way; but though he could escape his creditors he could not escape his wife, who as yet dreamt not of his liabilities. At last her eyes were opened. A bold grocer from Gibbeline – the small Cromaboo traders had given up trusting him long ago, knowing how impossible it was to get money from him – asked to see Mrs. Meldrum, and presented his bill of one hundred and fifty dollars to that lady personally, telling her if it was not paid within a week he should be obliged to take legal proceedings. If Margaret had possessed as much money she would have paid him, but she had only ten cents left in her purse, so she promised to pay him in two days, and dismissed him with a feeling of anger and humiliation. At dinner she told her husband in a solemn and awful tone about the visit of the tradesman and his threat.

"Take legal proceedings, aye?" said Mr. Meldrum, calmly. "*You* take the liver wing I think, my dear, with plenty of stuffing?"

"Thomas, I have promised to pay that man in two days," said his wife.

"Glad to hear you have so much money, Maggie, but I think you might spend it to better advantage. Shall I give you tomato?"

"Is that your only debt?" asking Mrs. Meldrum, ignoring the question of tomato.

"By no means," replied her husband.

"How much do you owe?" was the next question.

"Can't say, I'm sure," replied the doctor, truly; "never trouble myself about such things, and if you are sensible you will not trouble yourself either."

"I am an honest woman," said his wife.

"Never doubted it," with a half smile, and a slight shrug of the shoulder. A pause.

"What will that man do if he is not paid?" asked Margaret, at last.

"Sue me, I suppose," said her husband, as he poured out a foaming glass of ale, "and I must pay the bill, with costs, when I get my quarterly dividend."

"I have never broken my word, and I'm not going to begin now, you must borrow the money and pay the man in two days, as I promised," said the lady.

"Bah! to what purpose?" replied Mr. Meldrum, "it will only make more expense."

"I am an honest woman," with great emphasis.

"I think you made that remark before, my dear," said her husband, going on quietly with his dinner.

"I say that debt must be paid, and every debt we owe must be paid. I will not eat food that isn't paid for, or wear clothes that are not paid for. I would rather starve," said Margaret, in a high dictatorial tone, and with an emphasis. "I have passed my word and I *will* keep it."

"It will be better not to pass your word in future, Margaret, unless you have the money in your hand," said her husband, with provoking coolness.

"What *is* your income? I ask *that*? What is your income and I will live within it, – you shall never have reason to complain of *my* extravagance."

"I shall never have the inclination, my dear. My income is two hundred a year, besides what I gain in my profession, which isn't much, for those who owe me light their pipes with my bills, I dare say, as I do with theirs, – at least they seldom pay, and I never sue."

"Then you ought to sue," replied Margaret, "it's your *duty* to sue, and pay your debts as an honest man, and a man of honour. I thought I had married a man of honour, and a man of means," with great bitterness. Her husband made no reply, and there was a long pause. "Tell me the people who owe you, and I will collect for you," she presently went on. "I will not live in this loose dishonourable way."

Mr. Meldrum, who had made but half a dinner, and that with bitter sauce, as we have seen, rose from the table, and stood upon the hearth; his tone had changed from coolness to icy coldness as he answered, "Thank you, I prefer to do my own business, Margaret, and I would advise you for the future to mind *your own*, if you have any, and not to meddle with my affairs. I wish you good afternoon," and he left the room and the house.

It was a natural speech, but impolitic and foolish, considering the person to whom it was addressed; it roused all the combativeness and obstinacy in Mrs. Meldrum's nature. Shall I fear a man whose breath is in his nostrils, she thought; does he dare to threaten me? I will know what is owing to him, and make the people pay. I am his wife and have the right to know, and a right to see that his creditors are paid, it is my duty. Having once arrived at that point, she never receded, but proceeded at once to put her intention into execution. Chance, – or shall we call it mischance, – led her past the parson's lodgings, and she decided in her perplexity to call and lay the matter before him. "I will consult him," she thought, "he is a man of Gaud," for so she pronounced God, to her husband's great annoyance. In his heart he felt more like a critic than a husband towards Margaret, but he was willing to live peaceably with her, and did not positively dislike her, though he possessed not that love which is blind to little faults and failings. She had chosen unluckily a very bad adviser, for Mr. Moorhouse was the only man in Cromaboo who really disliked Mr. Meldrum, and owed him a grudge.

Mr. Moorhouse was by nature, a very grave man, and took all the duties of life most seriously, and though a well-meaning man he was narrow minded, and particular about trifles, thinking more of his cloth, and dignity of the pulpit, than the weightier matters of the law.

He did not regard his parishioners as a shepherd regards his sheep, but looked upon them rather as a harsh school teacher might look upon his naughty troublesome boys and girls. He took a very severe view of his fellow-creatures, and was disposed to keep them up to the mark with the rod of wholesome correction; he *talked* about taking the low place, but he carried it with a high hand in all dealings with them. This being the case, the fact of Mr. Meldrum being so much in debt was nearly as offensive to the parson as to Margaret herself, because the medical gentleman was a communicant, and his debts gave an occasion of scandal to the dissenters. Once Mr. Moorhouse has the, – shall we say the moral courage or the hardihood, – to advise Mr. Meldrum to pay his debts for the sake of his moral character, and the church to which he belonged.

"Are you prepared to advance the money and discharge them all?" asked Mr. Meldrum, eyeing his adviser with some curiosity.

"Certainly not," was the reply, "you ought to pay your own debts; I have no private means, nothing but my salary, and if I had I should consider it a sinful waste of money to lend to you."

"Then go to Jericho with you, Mr. Parson," said his parishioner, with cool, good humoured insolence, "and keep your impracticable advice for the pulpit; it's your privilege to talk nonsense there, and we who go to church are bound to listen to you; but advising me to pay my debts without giving me the means of doing it, is as silly as advising me to grow a foot taller, or change the colour of my eyes."

Mr. Moorhouse remembered every word of this speech, and I grieve to say bore malice, though he never omitted the doctor in his private prayers; but when Mr. Meldrum offered to rent the parsonage he wisely insisted upon having the money in advance, and said it was against his conscience to help him further into debt, at which remark the doctor laughed, and though it was a good-tempered laugh, it had a sting in it for the clergyman, and it was not without a little envy that he heard of Mr. Meldrum's marriage with a rich lady, aggravated, no doubt, by the fact that the Rev. Paul Moorhouse had not been asked to perform the ceremony; but when he heard the lady was pious and a great supporter of the church, he gave a sigh of satisfaction, and said he trusted the Lord was dealing with Meldrum for his good. He took an early opportunity of calling on them, and had a long conversation with Mrs. Meldrum, her husband excusing himself for leaving him, on the plea of urgent professional business.

When Mrs. Meldrum, in her perplexity, called on him, she found a most sympathising listener and a very bad adviser. He counseled her to look over her husband's accounts, and be resolute in collecting his debts and paying his creditors; he addressed her as if she were a martyr, and in shaking hands with her at parting, he said, fervently:

"Blessed are they that are persecuted for righteousness sake; if your husband is angry, Mrs. Meldrum, you must just be patient, and pray God to change his heart."

Mrs. Meldrum felt much encouraged and cheered by the clergyman's approval, and the next day, her husband being away, she examined his accounts; an easy matter, as he kept nothing locked but one small drawer, containing old letters, his first wife's portrait and a lock of her hair. This little private sanctum raised Margaret's curiosity, but she made her[101] best use of her time notwithstanding, and made out several bills, and the next day presented them in person, telling the people plainly they must pay at once to save expense. Then she called upon her husband's creditors in Cromaboo, ten in number, and told them they should be paid as soon as she could get the money, and that she knew nothing of these debts when she married Mr. Meldrum, and speaking of him with anything but respect. The last person upon whom she called was Mr. Llewellyn, to whom the doctor owed twenty dollars. She sat very near to the old gentleman at his request, and shrilly poured her remarks into his best ear. Robert, who was at work in the next room, had the benefit of them also.

"Is that all you have to say, Mrs. Meldrum?" asked Mr. Llewellyn, at last.

"That was all," and Mrs. Meldrum professed herself very sorry to have to say it.

"You ought to be sorry," said Mr. Llewellyn, emphatically, "and I hope for your own sake, as well as your husband's, you will never say such things again to man or woman. If you do, you will be like the foolish woman spoken of by Solomon, who plucketh down her house with her own hands. Mr. Meldrum is careless in money matters; but I see in him no other fault, and I have known him for ten years; you might by gentleness win him to a sense of his error, never by the course you are pursuing; you will only lose the respect of all sensible

---

[101]The 1878 edition has "...she made she..."

people, and bring your husband into contempt. If you had the money in your hand, I would not take it from you, because it would humiliate him. I hope you will pardon me for speaking so plainly, and if you have disagreed with your husband, my dear, go home and make it up with him, and tell him what you have done, and be guided by him in future. Think of what I have said, and forgive me for saying it; you know I am old enough to be your father."

"I hope I am Christian enough to forgive all my enemies," said Margaret, with sparkling eyes. "I will pray for you, Mr. Llewellyn; I thought till now you were a friend."

"Flatterers are the worst friends," replied the old man, sturdily, "and a woman cannot injure her husband without injuring herself. You injure him by acting without him, and making a cipher of him; it is reversing the word of God, which says a wife should obey her husband. He may not be willing to be set wholly on one side, and in that case you will make a great deal of domestic trouble for yourself."

This was the only rebuff Margaret ever received, and it had no effect in changing her purpose. She was bent on victory, even with Mr. Llewellyn. Half the money was owed for stage fare, and the first time she saw Robert she offered it to him. She never dreamt that he had been an ear witness of the scene with his master, and there was so much simplicity in his bright, young face that even when he declined to take it, she did not suspect him.

"Thank you, ma'am," he said, taking out his purse, but suddenly he paused, as if a new thought had struck him, – "I guess you had better settle it with the master, any time when you are passing, as Mr. Meldrum said there was another claim, and I couldn't give you a receipt, and it might make confusion. There's no hurry; it's as safe as if 'twas in the bank, with Mr. Meldrum, – I wish you good day, ma'am," and he lifted his hat and drove on.

The very evening Margaret had visited Mr. Llewellyn, she had called on John Smith and presented a bill for ten dollars, which he owed her husband. She told him with scant ceremony to pay the money speedily. He was very respectful, but it was an unexpected summons, and he scratched his head in much perplexity.

"Faith then," said he, "I'm heart sorry to kape his honour waiting, but I'll bring it up to-morrow, ma'am, widout fail – I'll borrow it of Chip and Robbie – the divole a word can I read, ma'am, and it's no use laving the scrap o' paper. If you'd be plazed to come in and sit down, ma'am – it's a poor place, but you're welcome – I would go to Robbie at once, maybe he could lend me the whole sum."

But Mrs. Meldrum said to-morrow would do, and walked home, having set a sharp thorn in John Smith's nest for that night.

The next day was a hard one for Margaret; she visited nearly a score of houses, and left bills, and some people, far from being grateful for the attention, were rather uncivil; only one paid, an old woman, who said she would have Dr. Gregor the next time, as she thought it was sharp practice to ask for the money before the year was up.

As Margaret reached the little bridge that connected the house with the mainland, she met her husband. He was walking, and had been, she knew, to see a man who had been injured in sinking a well. "How is that man?" she asked, as they met.

"He is dead," was the calm reply, as Mr. Meldrum held the gate open for his wife to pass through before him. Margaret stepped onto the bridge and looked back over her shoulder at her husband, as she asked "was he a believer?"

"Can't say, I'm sure," he replied, with the greatest indifference, "he was a Scotchman and a Presbyterian."

At that instant they both caught sight of John Smith striding rapidly towards them. Margaret knew his errand, but Mr. Meldrum thought somebody was ill, and cried out, "What's the matter, Smith? Nothing wrong with the wife or Tommy, I hope?"

"Sure it only this bit of a bill," replied John Smith, as he pulled his fore-lock to Mrs. Meldrum. She was almost the only woman in Canada to whom he would have shown such a mark of respect, and it was not for her own sake that he did it, but because she was Mr. Meldrum's wife and her father's daughter, for he had known Mr. Paxton, and remembered him kindly. John Smith handed Mr. Meldrum the account his wife had made out, and a dirty ten dollar bill along with it, saying, "Faith, it's I that am sorry that it wasn't paid before, and that your leedy had the trouble of asking for it." He spoke very civilly, but with a certain constraint.

Now it was that Mr. Meldrum was seized with a desire to push his wife into the brook, and give her a sousing. He had as great a respect for Smith as he had for the Archbishop of Canterbury, and his feeling for him was far nearer akin to love, than the feeling he had for his Margaret. Had he not known him for twenty years, – had they not roamed the woods together in search of game, when they were both younger? Many an old memory had they in common, and many a jolly tramp they had taken together. Had not Smith nursed his dead children, and made his wife laugh even in her last illness by his queer Irish bulls? He knew the history of Smith's courtship and marriage, and had brought seven children into the world for him without charging a penny; he had stood beside him when some of those junior Smiths were nipped in the bud by King Death, and laid in their last resting place. He had lent him money, and had borrowed money from him at a pinch; there were a hundred kindly memories between them. He turned his back upon his wife to avoid temptation, and laid his hand upon the shoulder of his old acquaintance.

"You are hurt, Smith," he said; "you think I have forgotten old times?"

"Well, sir, if you had asked me yourself 'twould be different, but I take it a little hard that you sent the leedy."

"I never sent her, man; she went of her own accord; she's a – a very troublesome and meddling lady. I would never dun you, Smith – I would rather put money in your fob than take it out; put it back as a present for my godson Tommy, and I'll scratch the account out of my book. Mrs. Meldrum doesn't know what a very old friend you are, – I will tell her," and he put his white hand in John Smith's with a hearty kindly pressure.

John Smith had a big heart, and he was an Irishman, and there-fore his feelings[102] were quick; he had been much hurt, and now came a reaction; he felt the hand shake a great honour, and fairly blubbered, as he thanked and blessed the doctor. But we must leave what followed for another chapter.

---

[102]The 1878 edition has "fellings" rather than "feelings."

Chapter Twenty

"You never know a man till you have been on shipboard with him,
Nor a woman till you have married her."

– Lord Byron[103]

M R. MELDRUM and his wife did not exchange a sentence till they
were in the house. Margaret sat down wearily, and loosened
her shawl and took off her bonnet. Her husband stood on the hearth,
leaning easily against the mantle-piece; the room had a cosy, home
look, the wood fire blazed brightly, but neither of them thought of it.

"What is your connection with that man," asked Margaret, "and
why should you forgive him his debt when you owe so much? You
said you would tell me."

Mr. Meldrum felt it a difficult thing to tell; before his marriage he
would not have hesitated a moment, but now he did. He thought, perhaps justly, that he could not make her understand him; she would
regard his reasons as sentimental, perhaps foolish; he felt they were
foreigners by nature, and he was trying to command himself and
curb his temper; he was so chafed that she had the temerity to dun
Smith. This difficulty in keeping down his anger, made his face as
immobile as if it had been cut in marble, and his tone of the iciest, as
he answered his wife.

"I have known him intimately for twenty years, – he is strictly
honest, and would have paid without dunning, as soon as he got the
money," – he paused, and Margaret looked at him as if she expected
more, – "He worked as a day labourer for me for three years," – another pause, – "His son Bob is the first child I ever helped into this

---

[103] George Gordon Byron (1788-1824).

world," – another pause, a very long one, broken at last by the same cold, measured voice, but this time with a touch of sarcasm in it.

"When you go dunning again, Peggy, you will please to omit Mrs. Scott, whose husband is just dead, as I have told her I will charge nothing for my services."

"And you will please not to call me Peggy," returned his wife, tartly, "I detest the name, and think it an insult. It is easy to see that you care more for widow Scott than you do for your wife or your creditors."

"My creditors are all men, and it appears, Peggy, that my wife is pretty competent to look after her own interests. Widow Scott, – poor woman, she did not dream of being a widow three days ago, – has no property, but seven small children, and she mourns for her husband, but my Peggy would be a happy woman if she could claim the title of widow once more; she would bear her loss with Christian resignation."

"I would never have married you, if I had known you would insult me with nick names," said Margaret, with angry tears in her eyes. Mr. Meldrum turned suddenly and looked her keenly in the face.

"Have you been examining my account book," he asked, "or is Smith the only person you have dunned?"

"Yes. I felt it[104] was my *duty*," said Margaret, "I have presented bills to all the people that owe you in Cromaboo, and visited all your creditors here, and told them I would pay as soon as possible."

Now it was that Mr. Meldrum was seized with a desire to take his wife by the collar, and shake her out of the dove-coloured silk gown that became her so well. A flush came into his face, and he had to walk to the window to regain self-command. His long silence half frightened Margaret, and made her feel nervous. At last he turned and spoke.

"When you cease to meddle with my affairs, and mind your own business, I shall cease to call you Peggy, not before." He left the room as he spoke, and went to his surgery and walked about there; he was so angry at his wife's conduct and so angry with himself for being angry, that he felt he must get away from her, at least for a time; if he stayed in the house he might say things he would regret, perhaps

---

[104]The 1878 edition has "I felt is was..."

be tempted to lay his hand upon her. So when tea was announced he entered the parlour in riding dress, whip and hat in hand.

"I am going to Hamilton," he said, "and you need not expect me back for a week, – or till you see me."

"On horseback?" exclaimed his wife, in surprise. "Is it a consultation?"

"No," said Mr. Meldrum, "it is not. I wish you good night, Peggy," and he left her without a kiss or a shake of the hand.

He did stay a week, and having speedily recovered his temper, enjoyed himself very much. The day before he left Hamilton he found by accident a memorandum in his pocket book, that told him that tomorrow would be Margaret's birthday, and he went into Murray's[105] and purchased a dress piece – a shepherd's plaid silk, – Margaret being very fond of shepherd's plaid. "It is great folly," he argued "to quarrel with one's wife, though she is a fool; I will make it up." He thought of the only quarrel he had ever had with his first wife, – it could scarcely be called a quarrel, only a[106] little squabble, – and how he had taken her a pretty shawl as a peace-offering, and asked her to forget and forgive, and how she had cried and kissed him more times than he could count, and said it was all her fault, and she would never be so naughty again. He was too apt to judge all women by that one he had known so intimately, and being away from Margaret for a week he had half forgotten what she was like, yet remembered enough to regret with a half sigh that it was not Mrs. Meldrum number one, instead of number two, that awaited him at the end of his journey.

Perhaps if he had returned the day after he left, Margaret might have made it up; for she felt lonely and thought of Mr. Llewellyn's advice, and indulged in a long fit of weeping; but as the days passed, her heart hardened, and she took to dunning again, and visited all her husband's country debtors who were within walking distance, and gave them their bills. The day before her birthday Mary arrived by coach, and Margaret poured her troubles into her sister's ears, stating in conclusion that her husband was an unprincipled wretch, and "Mr. Moorhouse thought so too, and he is a Christian, a dear, Gaudly man, Mary."

---

[105] Apparently, a clothier local to Hamilton.
[106] The 1878 edition has "...only a a little..."

"He may be," said her sister, "but I can't bear the look of him; he is like a weasel – perhaps he has some private grudge at Mr. Meldrum." She was not at all surprised at Margaret's statements, remembering many a fierce battle between her sister and the Reverend Francis Hurst, deceased; but she made no remark on her conduct, fearing it would harden her in the course she had taken.

Late in the evening of the following day, Mr. Meldrum arrived, having put his handsome horse to its mettle, and ridden sixty miles since the morning – the dress piece safe in his saddle-bag – to be at home on his wife's birthday. He was flushed with exercise and looked very handsome as he entered the room; he was very glad to see Mary, and said so, which was a false step at the very beginning of his overtures for peace. Then he advanced to Margaret – it cost him an effort, but this did not appear on the surface, and he did it gracefully – and stooping, kissed her on the cheek, and wished her many happy returns of the day, putting the parcel in her hand with a hope that it would please her, and adding in a whisper, "Forgive and forget, Maggie." Mrs. Meldrum liked the nick-name of "Maggie" as much as she hated Peggy. Mary, who was near the door, slipped away.

Margaret would not have been a woman if she had not been pleased with the present and the handsome face of the giver, but she was a foolish one, and therefore not content with gaining so much of a victory; she was determined to conquer him at all points, and justify herself.

"Thank you, Thomas," she said, with a flush of surprise and pleasure, as she opened the parcel; "it is very pretty, and it is kind of you to think of my birthday; of course it's only right that you should, but I did not think that you would do it."

"Will you have it made up for Christmas to please me," said the doctor, "and kiss me – and forgive and forget?"

She did not refuse the kiss, and said she hoped, as a Christian, she knew how to forgive, and she was glad he was sorry for his past conduct; "but, Thomas," she said, "there is *one* question I feel it my *duty* to ask - *is it paid for?*"

Of course it was not paid for, but what *could* have been the doctor's reason for telling the truth? He had often lied to his wife before to avoid a squabble; why could he not lie now, when his object was peace? Because he had been a week away from her, and it had partly restored the freedom of his unmarried days; he did not feel afraid of her tongue to-night, and he answered, "*not yet.*"

"Then, Thomas, I shall *never* wear it, I *could not* wear it," said Mrs. Meldrum, decisively. "I have been thinking lately that till you are out of debt I ought to wear my shabbiest dresses; it would be more in keeping with our position, and I like consistency in all things, there is something inconsistent and improper in flaunting about in rich silks and merinos,[107] when you are over head and ears in debt."

"I wonder how long you would keep to that resolution?" said her husband, with a satirical curl of the lip. Again he judged her by his first wife, who loved pretty costumes, and would not have been thought a dowdy for the world. Mary returned at this point, and the *tete a tete* was at an end. Soon Mr. Meldrum had supper, and begged the ladies to join him, and they all sat down together. They were scarcely seated before a timid tap came to the door.

"Come in," said the doctor, and the door was pushed slowly open, and a thin old woman with a shawl over her head hobbled a step or two forward, and then paused, dazzled and awed by that pretty home picture; the bright fire, the richly dressed ladies, the neat supper, yet a little encouraged by seeing the doctor.

"Well, Biddy, what is it?" asked the gentleman.

"Sure, it's the bit o' money, sir. I'm very sorry, ma'am," turning to Mrs. Meldrum in a deprecating way, "but I've only fifty cents for ye to-night, – next week I hope I'll save more."

Mr. Meldrum's good resolutions took flight; he could have thrown his wife out of the window, in the presence of her sister. He rose and took the old body by the shoulders and put her into a chair.

"What's all this, Biddy?" he asked. The old woman's hand trembled, she tried to command herself, but the tears rolled down her cheeks, – or perhaps she didn't try very hard, being an Irish woman, and knowing she had a friend in the camp.

"It's so hard to get money, sir," she said, "I ought to have paid ye long ago."

"Put the money back in your pocket, Biddy, and I give you a full receipt in honor of Mrs. Meldrum's birthday; and you must have a glass of wine and drink her health."

---

[107] merino = a breed of sheep prized for its fine soft wool.

So he took his revenge, and Mrs. Meldrum felt it as such; she could hardly keep her tongue still till the old woman's back was turned, then she opened fire at once.

"What have you had from that old woman as an equivalent for the five dollars you have given her? Is that the way you are paid for your services?" she asked, almost fiercely. "I *know* you went to see her nearly every day for two months, last winter. She told me so, so it's useless to deny it."

"He is well paid that is well satisfied," quoted Mr. Meldrum, with provoking calmness.

Not much was said after this, and soon the gentleman pleaded weariness after his long ride, and retired for the night. He was up early in the morning, having promised Mary to see her off by the stage. "I am sorry I cannot drive you myself," he said, "but the horse is too tired."

"It's just as well," she replied, "it might have vexed Maggie."

"I am sure to do that in any case," returned her brother-in-law. "I am like that unfortunate Irish gentleman who never opened his mouth without putting his foot in it. I do not understand your sister at all, or know how to please her, – perhaps you could advise me."

Mary felt very uncomfortable; she had just taken leave of her sister in bed, and Maggie had told her with a burst of tears, that she and her husband had quarreled half the night, and then he had left her and slept on the dining room sofa. She had never been able to get on with Margaret herself, except by submitting in everything.

"Love never faileth," she said uneasily, and without looking at Mr. Meldrum, "if you care for each other, that is everything; you will come to be happier in time, I hope," and she was delighted to catch a glimpse of Robert coming to meet them and carry her bag; it was impossible to pursue the subject with him there.

The next day Mr. Meldrum had a visit from the bailiff, and Mrs. Meldrum took to her ugliest and shabbiest gown, her oldest breakfast shawl, her worst slippers; she laid aside her watch, – the doctor's gift, – she wore no jewelry, and her husband called her Peggy again, and said she was dressed in character.

Mr. Meldrum used rather to enjoy these visits from these living instruments of the law, in his first wife's time; she would be so indignant with those "greedy, heartless creatures," as she called them, and sympathise so entirely with her husband, that it quite amused him; and he would sometimes feign a headache to have her cool little white hands about his face, patting and petting him; now he often had a real headache from want of sleep and ceaseless domestic bother, and Mrs. Meldrum number two said, "Serve you right."

Chapter Twenty-One

"I choose her for myself;
If she and I be pleased, what's that to you?"
          – *Taming of the Shrew*[108]

"Gone to be married! Gone to swear a peace!"
          – *King John*[109]

W**E MUST** go back a little in our story. Mary Paxton and her friend Lavinia had gone to Hamilton, after St. Andrew's ball, as the guests of Mrs. Frank Llewellyn. Mary could only stay two days, but Lavinia remained for a fortnight. While Mary was there, Mrs. Frank was sweet and gracious to her little kinswoman, but as soon as she had turned her back, she began to snub Lavinia and clearly intimated that her absence would be more acceptable than her company. But Harry paid her unremitting attention, and this made up for Eleanor's rudeness; and at first Eleanor was as pleased as Miss Lavy herself, and praised Harry privately for his "good nature" in taking his cousin for walks and drives, and frankly told him it was a great relief to her to be rid of "the little blackie," but at last she grew suspicious and her manner changed towards him. She imperatively beckoned him into her little boudoir one afternoon, and said she hoped he was not "such a fool" as to think of falling in love with that "little darkie. Let me tell you," she went on, "she is a very artful little creature, as artful

---

[108]William Shakespeare, *Taming of the Shrew*: Act 2, Scene 1. These lines are spoken by Petruchio.
[109]William Shakespeare, *King John*: Act 3, Scene 1. These lines are spoken by Constance.

as she is ugly; she may hook you into a promise of marriage, so you had better be careful with your hand-kissing and nonsense."

"I might do worse," said Harry; "she's a nice little thing, and my own flesh and blood, and all that sort of thing, you know."

Mrs. Frank flashed her dark eyes at him to see if he was in earnest. "If you dared to do such a thing," she said, "I would disown you forever, and you need not think you would be long in partnership with Frank, if you married that ugly, little black thing. Nobody with taste would look at her twice after seeing Miss Paxton – now if you could get *her* for a wife, that would be quite different, that would be a match that would please me."

"Suppose I prefer Lavy," said Harry; "every one to his taste, you know."

"The hateful little thing; but she's going to-morrow, thank heaven, and you're only talking nonsense to tease me; even you are not quite such a fool, I should think, as to think of such a match seriously."

"Well, I haven't asked her yet," said Harry, laughing, "but we're just going up the James street steps to see the view, so that will be a chance of popping the question; and you can get a telescope and watch us if you like, when it comes to embracing, and all sort of thing, you know," and so he departed.

Eleanor went to sleep after he had gone, but when she wakened after an hour's nap, and found the cousins still absent, she fell to wondering what could possibly keep them, and thought of Harry and the James street steps. It wanted but twenty minutes to five, and at that hour they dined; she felt better tempered than when she lay down, and was glad it was Lavy's last evening. She daudled from room to room in pure idleness, glancing at herself complacently in various mirrors, till she came to the apartment which Frank dignified by the name of study, and there she saw his telescope lying on the table. She thought of Harry's last words, drew it out, fixed it to her eye, and turned it towards the James street steps.[110] She had hit the right focus; there they were, Harry and Lavy, seated side by side, and very near together. She could see their faces quite distinctly, both were smiling, presently they drew together in a long kiss, and Harry's

---

[110]In Hamilton, it would have been a very great distance from the Ocean House Hotel to the James Street steps.

fat white hand closed over his cousin's. Eleanor's hand shook, she dropped the telescope in a tumult of passion; presently she took it up again, and this time she could not get the right focus, and when she succeeded after many efforts, nothing human remained on the James street steps; only a solitary bird and dark shadows covered the mountain side. If Eleanor could have heard what the guilty pair were saying, this is what she would have heard:

"By George, you know, Lavy, dear, I'm your kinsman, and all that sort of thing, and I'm very fond of you, I am really, and marriages between cousins are generally the happiest, because their heads are the same shape,[111] you know, and they have the same tastes; and its all fudge about such marriages being unhappy; just let you and I try, that's all. Uncle and aunt can come and live with us, and it will be like the garden of Eden, now really, with you for our little house-keeper – love in a cottage, and all that sort of thing. You won't refuse me, now really, will you?" he said, in conclusion.

Lavinia was greatly touched; tears came to her eyes, and a sense of humility to her heart.

"It's very generous and kind of you, cousin Harry," she said, "and I'm not half good enough for you."

"Oh! that's nonsense, now," said Harry, and truly it was, and here he kissed her, and after that they chatted about their plans, and tears gave way to smiles on Lavinia's face, and then came another kiss to seal the compact – which salute Eleanor saw – and as they descended the steps they arranged that the wedding should take place before Christmas, if possible. Neither of them saw the view, the beautiful blending of light and shadow, other views were before them and shut it out; Harry saw a vision of wealth and power, and life-long prosperity; Lavinia a vision of perfect conjugal happiness, her wildest dream was realized, the hero she had longed for was her own; not once did she think of Bob Smith, the Cromaboo mail carrier. Eleanor scarcely spoke at dinner and watched the young people during the evening with jealous eyes and an angry heart; their little occasional billing and cooing gave her great offense, and she was steadily working herself into a tremendous passion. When Lavinia had gone to bed, she commanded Frank into her boudoir, and relieved her feelings to him,

---

[111] A probable reference to Phrenology, a pseudo-medical concept primarily focused on measurements of the human skull.

and then waylaid Harry – when, candle in hand, he was retiring for the night – and said that she *must* speak to him. He tried to excuse himself and escape.

"Really, Eleanor," he said, "I'm very tired, rather overdid it to-day rowing on the Bay, – won't to-morrow do?"

But Eleanor told him sternly that to-morrow would *not* do, and he entered her little gem of a room reluctantly, indeed, but resolved to put a bold face on it. Eleanor closed the door.

"I saw you kiss that girl," she said, looking down on him with blazing eyes and flushed cheeks. "*I saw you through the telescope.*"

"Did you though, by George?" said Harry, laughing, "said I would do it, and I thought you would be disappointed if I didn't."

Mrs. Frank stamped her foot. "Don't you *dare* to kiss her when you part with her," she said. "Frank shall go with her to the station."

"That he won't, by George, though, for I mean to do it myself, and kiss her too if I please. Frank is your lawful prey, Eleanor, and you may dictate to him if you like, but not to me," said Harry, with spirit.

"You idiot," retorted Mrs. Frank, with great scorn, "you will compromise yourself with the girl, if you haven't done it already."

"I have," said Harry, "I've been and gone and done it; I've popped, you know, and been accepted, and you ought to be pleased, Eleanor, with Lavy's choice, it's not a disgraceful connection like Bob Smith, anyhow."

Eleanor took up a china vase and dashed it to the ground in the vehemence of her passion.

"My dear, dear Eleanor," expostulated her husband, in great alarm.

She heeded him not, but turned savagely upon the offending Harry, who opened his round eyes with surprise indeed, but stood his ground with a calmness that did him credit.

"You leave this house this very night, sir, you and that infamous girl, and never dare to enter it again, *never*," she said, with great vehemence.

"If you insist on that," said Harry, coolly, "I must look up a parson and be married right away, for the sake of Lavy's character, and all that sort of thing, you know; though we didn't mean to do it till Christmas."

"Do you stand there, Frank, and see me insulted?" said Eleanor, shaking with passion, "turn that fellow out."

"Oh! you needn't trouble, Franky," said Harry, in an off-hand way, "sorry to have made a row, old fellow, good night to you both," and he went at once; not into the street, however, but up to his own bed-room, turning the key in Lavinia's door as he passed it, and putting it in his pocket. In a few minutes Lavinia heard a stormy rustling of silks, and her door was shaken violently.

"I cannot open it, Eleanor," she said piteously, "it's locked on the outside."

Eleanor shook it again and cried, "open it instantly, you shall leave the house this very night, you wicked, bad girl."

The door opposite was wide open, and Mr. Harry called out, "I locked her in, and have the key under my pillow, and we're not going till the morning, 'twill be more respectable, and all that sort of thing, you know – if you make such a row you'll wake the servants. Oh! it's no use coming here, I've got my pants off," added this practical young gentleman, as the silks came towards his door with a swishing kind of rush. She contented herself with closing the door upon him with a violent bang, and descended the stairs defeated.

Lavinia left Hamilton by the earliest train, having first break-fasted with her cousin at the Royal, and Harry went to look up a lodging house.

Three days later Mr. Meldrum came to Hamilton, and to Frank's request did his best to make up matters between Mrs. Frank and Harry. He called on that lady, who received him very coldly at first, for was he not Mary Paxton's brother-in-law, and Mary was, in her opinion, the author of all this mischief, by inveigling Lavinia into her house. He gently sympathised with this magnificent fine lady, who did not even rise to receive him when he entered her presence, but lay back in her large cushioned chair like a sultana, and played with a screen in her hand with a haughty affectation of langour. He said it really was a very singular choice Mr. Harry had made, and enough to surprise anybody, but perhaps it was contradiction because he had been advised against it; "and, my dear Mrs. Llewellyn, I hope you will pardon me for speaking so plainly – but I think you are very in-judicious in opposing him so strongly; if he was let alone this fancy might die a natural death – now, if you dissembled a little –"

"I dissemble!" exclaimed Eleanor, with scorn, "it is not my way; I dissembled when I asked that girl to my house, it was a false step, and I will never take another. How could I guess he would prefer that little blackamoor[112] to a pretty, fair woman like Miss Paxton?"

"It seems incredible," said Mr. Meldrum, with a sympathising shrug of the shoulder, "but love's blind."

"*Love*! I have no patience with him – he's the greatest fool in Canada. What has she to recommend her to any man; can you tell me one virtue, one grace in her to love?" asked the lady, extending her white jeweled hands in appeal to heaven and earth.

"Well, the little lady is of excellent birth," said Mr. Meldrum, "and very fair education, her accounts are most beautifully kept, and she is a skillful house-keeper and good cook."

"A good cook," echoed Eleanor, with supreme scorn; "that is just a man's reasoning all the world over. She is all the cook he is ever likely to have, if he marries her, the ugly, presuming, vulgar little creature; for I will make Frank turn him out of the firm – and he has neither sense nor perseverance to make a living for himself – I will disown them both if they don't give up this wretched idea of marriage; I will never look upon that hateful girl again, *never*."

"Do not make rash vows, dear Mrs. Llewellyn, remember Jephthah,"[113] said Mr. Meldrum, in his most suave, courteous voice. "Mr. Harry may change his mind, or Miss Lavy may pick up another beau, the marriage may never be consummated, and a betrothal does not stand in law – who can tell what may happen – young men and maidens are so fickle?"

"I shall never respect him again whether he marries her or not, I shall always think him a fool, a creature of no spirit, to want to marry a girl that a low boy like Bob Smith had kissed – actually kissed – yes, it's a fact, and I have told Harry so again and again. If she had been as beautiful as Mary, Queen of Scots, *would* any man of spirit have married her after that, I ask?"

"Ahem!" said Mr. Meldrum, "you ladies are so severe in virtue. Bob is a great pet of mine; I believe I have kissed him myself when he was younger, and foreigners – Miss Lavy is half a foreigner – are

---

[112]The 1878 edition has "blackamore."

[113]Jephthah appears in the *Book of Judges* (12:7). He fulfilled a rash vow by sacrificing his daughter.

more lenient in their construction of these little gallantries than we who are descended from the English, a – a very proper nation. I am sure Miss Lavy is a *very* virtuous, exemplary young lady, notwithstanding little Bob's kiss."

"Bah! I am tired of the subject," said Eleanor, with disgust, "talk of something else, or go away, – do;" but notwithstanding her words, her face had a look of softening.

"I will go away, Mrs. Llewellyn, but not till you have promised that you will be lenient to Harry; though the stupid fellow has such bad taste. Give him a chance, – I ask it as a personal favour, – do not turn him out of the firm till he *is* married."

"Well, I don't mind promising that much, I will give him another chance, though he is a fool, – if you tell me something that I wish very much to know, – you know women are all inquisitive and I have a passion for knowing secrets."

"I will tell you anything and everything that I know," said Mr. Meldrum, with great gallantry.

"Well then, why did you marry Mrs. Hurst instead of Mary Paxton? Now, the truth and nothing but the truth?" said Eleanor, tapping his hand playfully with her screen. N.B. – She had seen Mrs. Meldrum before leaving Cromaboo, and the ladies had measured lances.

"Ah! if my friend Frank had died opportunely, I would never have thought of either," said the doctor.

"That is not answering my question," persisted Eleanor.

"Because, – as I said just now, love's blind, you know, – I preferred Mrs. Hurst to Miss Paxton, and –"

"I don't believe it," said Eleanor, "so spare yourself the trouble of telling stories, and I will not spare Harry."

"Well, then, in *very* truth," said the doctor, "it was because Miss Paxton preferred little Bob Smith to me."

"Really?" but, after a little pondering, she added, "I believe you; how her face glowed when she was defending him. The little wretch, he ought to be shot, – you would never allow her to marry him, now tell me?"

"I only promised to answer *one* question," said the gentleman, smiling, and pressing her fingers gently, as he bowed himself out of the room. "Adieu, for the present, dear Mrs. Llewellyn."

"Come back to dinner," said Eleanor, "we shall be so glad, – but do not bring Harry."

"Thank you very much, but I did not anticipate such a pleasure, and I have promised to dine with that naughty prodigal at the Royal."

"Well, then, to-morrow," said Mrs. Frank, graciously, and so he departed, and when he left Hamilton he was the bearer of another silk dress, besides that unlucky shepherd's plaid, that failed so signally in its mission; a rich white watered silk, to be made up immediately, a note accompanying it, to tell Lavy to be ready any day.

"Got it on tick, you know, at Murray's," explained Harry to his friend, "to be paid for out of the fortune."

But as the weeks passed and no word came from the Brazils to Frank, Harry grew nervous and restless. He received daily little loving notes from Cromaboo, which made him uncomfortable; he wrote more and more seldom; he had put off the wedding till after Christmas, then he deferred it till after New Years, when he received a letter from Mr. Meldrum telling him in plain English he was a fool, and would lose the lady and her fortune, and deserve his fate for his tardiness.

He answered this note by a telegram, asking Mr. Meldrum to meet him in Gibbeline, and say "nothing to nobody," so he expressed it.

Mr. Meldrum did meet him on a stormy winter's day, and did his best to persuade him to return with him to Cromaboo, and be married before he went back to Hamilton. Harry refused.

"Hang it, you know," he said, "I am beginning to doubt if we shall ever hear of the money at all; you expected we should hear before Christmas, and you can't account for our not hearing, can you?"

"No, except on the principle that fortune favors fools – if Frank had heard, my young friend, your chance would have been over forever. I cannot account for the silence, but I believe in the fortune."

"Meldrum," said Harry, walking the room and much disturbed, "I'll tell you the truth if I never tell it again – I don't half believe in the money- - sometimes I do and sometimes I don't, you know – and by George, you know, I *wouldn't* marry Lavy without it, I'd rather turn monk."

"A very jolly little monk you would make, Harry – but why do you dislike your cousin?"

"I don't dislike her, but hang it, you know, she's *so queer*; I would never have chosen her without the money. By George, you know, when we were driving in Waterdown she asked me to let her drive, and I did to please her, and she cocked up her little fat leg, and put her foot on the brake like a man; she did really, and said she would like to drive four-in-hand. And when I asked if she objected to tobacco, she said not at all, she could smoke a cigarette, the ladies all did it in Brazil, and last year I saw her cross the High street in Gibbeline at a run, and tap Bob Smith on the back with her fan as if he had been an equal. By George, you know, *anything* will go down when people have money, and it doesn't matter if they are a little queer, and I *do* like her; but when it comes to working hard for a woman, and straining every nerve, and all that sort of thing, for a living, you need love as an incentive, and if you don't love a woman you are a fool to marry her, by –"

"By St. Andrew," said Mr. Meldrum. "Well, Harry, I will persuade you no further, but if you lose Lavy, you will regret it."

"She's good-natured, and all that sort of thing, and with plenty of money I know we should get on," said Harry, "but without it, hang me, you know, I'd rather be hanged."

"And what of Miss Lavy's feelings," said Mr. Meldrum, "have you thought of that?"

"Let her marry little Bob Smith, he's better looking than I am, and it would be a step up the social ladder for him with the money or without; they could run a big hotel, or a little wayside inn at first; she'd make a splendid landlady, and he wouldn't be a bad landlord, if he didn't take to drinking."

"Perhaps Bob wouldn't care for her without the fortune any more than yourself."

"Hang his impudence if he didn't, he might feel honoured," said Harry, all the Llewellyn alive in him in a moment.

"He might, *but he mightn't*," said Mr. Meldrum, dubiously.

A tap at the door, and Robert's bright young face peeped in. "Beg pardon, gentlemen, but I must be up to time with the mail, I cannot wait a minute longer."

"I am ready, Bob," said Mr. Meldrum, rising. "Will you come with me Harry?" looking at him keenly.

"Not this time," he replied, "but I may turn up in a day or two."

"Then you will turn up like the deuce of spades instead of the ace of hearts, you will be too late. There is a tide in the affairs of men –"

"Oh! confound it, Meldrum, go away with you; you know I'm in a deuce of a pickle, and don't know how to decide," said Harry, really impatient in his perplexity.

So Mr. Meldrum returned to Cromaboo, and Harry returned to Hamilton in a great state of indecision and doubt. Stepping out of the cars at the station, he fell almost into the arms of a slight, dark very singular looking little gentleman, evidently a foreigner. He had a little wizened brown face, and Harry was grasped by a thin, naked hand with half a dozen rings on it, which the gentleman stretched out to save himself from falling. The rest of his person was covered by an immense fur coat.

"Beg pardon," said Harry, "nearly had you down."

"I am but just arrived," said the person he addressed, smiling, and bowing. "I speak your Ingliesh not well, will you show me to pronounce this name, if you please?" and he handed Harry a card on which was written Mr. Frank Llewellyn's name and address. Harry instinctively drew his cap over his eyes, his heart was in his mouth. It flashed upon him that the gentleman was a Brazilian or Portuguese, and had come about Lavy's fortune. He told him how to pronounce the name, said he was in a great hurry, sprang in a cab, and gave the driver double fare to take him like the wind to his lodgings, having made up his mind to make, in the name of an old play, "a bold stroke for a wife."[114] He left Hamilton by the midnight train for Gibbeline, never went to bed at all, but as soon as it was daylight hired a horse and cutter, and started for Cromaboo.

It had been the most severe Christmas known for many a year, and more than four feet of snow had fallen since New Year's day, then the wind had risen, and blown it into drifts, so that the sleighing was anything but good. Not a breath of air stirred the day Mr. Meldrum met Harry, but the snow fell heavily and steadily, from morning till night; so bad were the roads that the mail did not reach Cromaboo till ten at night, and when Harry started the next morning the snow was still falling. His horse was not a very good one, and the roads

---

[114] *A Bold Stroke for a Wife* was a satirical English play developed in 1717 by Susanna Centlivre, known also as Susanna Freeman or Susanna Carroll (c.1667 to 1670 - 1723).

grew worse as he advanced; at noon he had only made ten miles, and had ten still before him; he tried to hire another horse but failed, and was obliged to push on with the one he had.

He stopped to take tea at Ostrander and rest his weary beast; it was dark when he left, and the wind had risen and faced him, the air was piercingly cold, the drift nearly blinded him, and the poor horse plodded on through soft snow that was breast deep in some places. Harry had to get out once or twice, to try and see where he was going, and to keep his cutter from upsetting, and he soon became very cold; his most comforting thought was that the mail could not get through to-morrow, and all communication with Hamilton would be cut off for some days. He began to get drowsy, and walked in front of his horse – or rather *waded* – with his hand on the bridle to keep himself awake; and in spite of himself his thoughts reverted to the poor boy frozen to death in carrying the mail on this very road not so many years before. He saw a light glimmering ahead and made up his mind to turn in there and go no further to-night – suddenly he made a false step and rolled down a bank in the soft snow head first; he laughed a little, but felt so weary that it cost him a great effort of will not to lie there for a minute or two to rest, but, a Canadian by birth and education, he knew that such a weakness would be fatal to him; a Welshman by descent, he had that indomitable pugnacity and pluck that will fight to the last. He rose, and forsaking horse and cutter, stumbled forward towards the light; determined to die on his legs if he must die. He felt a violent pain in the forehead, and had the greatest difficulty in keeping awake. There were no fences to impede his progress to the house, he walked over them without knowing they were there, though he waded through three feet of soft snow that had fallen to-day and yesterday. The house was on a hill, but he walked to it to-night as over level ground, for the snow had filled up all the valleys and made an even field. The light was near at last, and he stumbled against a door and knocked loudly.

The door was opened by a tall man, and a stream of welcome light poured out upon poor, half-frozen Harry, who tried to speak and explain his case, but found his mouth too stiff to utter a word. For some minutes his lips were too swollen even to take a drink; he was sick and giddy from the sudden warmth, but he had a vision of two men, a woman and children all busy about him, helping him off with his overcoat, chafing his hands, pulling off his boots, and wrapping a warm blanket round him. They would not let him near the fire, but it was good to see it; after a cup of hot coffee, the aching was easier to bear, and he could tell them of his horse and cutter. The two men sallied forth with a lantern to look after it, and Harry raised his *Te Deum*[115] in his own fashion.

"I'm thankful to you, ma'am," he said, addressing the little red-haired woman, who ministered to him, "and I'm thankful to God; I am, you know, by George. It was a squeak for life, a narrow squeak, and hang it, I know I don't deserve it, and I'm thankful, by George, I am."

"We deserve nothing but hell," replied the little woman, with a clearness and sharpness of tone that made Harry start and look at her in astonishment. "I mean it," she added, with a quick nod, as she rapidly buttered a piece of toast for him. "I don't know your sins, and you don't know mine, but God sees both our hearts, and knows what we deserve."

"Hell's a warm place, by George, you know, a trifle too warm, and it's not the thing, you know, to talk about; it's strong language, you know," said Harry, who was shocked in his propriety by her remark, "and a woman shouldn't talk about it, you know, it's not proper, and all that sort of thing, and people won't respect you if you talk in that way."

She glanced at him quickly, and something in his appearance softened and touched her. "Poor boy," she said, compassionately, "the cold bed in the snow might have been the best thing for you; you would never have sinned more, or caused others to sin; now you will forget the escape and go on in the old track."

"You are an uncomfortable kind of little woman, you are, though, by George," said Harry, "and make me feel as though I was up to something wrong, you know." And troubled by the sight of her, for she said no more, and heartened by her coffee, eggs and toast, he determined to push on to Cromaboo to-night, if the men would help him, so when they returned with his valise, and the information that his horse was stabled and rubbed down, and wrapped in blankets, he asked the taller one what he would take to drive him on to Cromaboo to-night, adding, "I'll give you five dollars cheerfully."

---

[115] *Te Deum* (Latin) = literally, "Thee, O God," the first words of an early Christian hymn of praise.

"Faith, then, you're in a divole of a hurry to get to Cromaboo," he replied, looking down on him good humouredly, "I thought ye'd be plazed to have a roof to cover ye, and stay undther it till daylight."

"Important business, you know, – anxious to get on," said Harry.

"Is it love or revenge, that pushes you?" asked the shorter man, speaking for the first time. There was something in the question, in the tone of the speaker, and his incisive, well-featured face that nettled Harry.

"You go to the dickens with you," he replied, with great spirit, "and don't be impertinent; it isn't generous, by George, when you see the fix I'm in, or manly either, and I won't stand it. If it's your own roof, by George, you don't know much about hospitality, and if it's the other fellow's and you are his servant, you deserve a licking."

The little man smiled; the big one laughed a jolly sounding laugh at this speech.

"No offense," said the little man, "we are farmers on shares, and you are welcome to a bed, but *I* won't help you to Cromaboo to-night. I might turn out for love, but never for money."

"Faith, that's just what I'm thinking," said the big man. "The divol a foot will I stir to-night, though it is but three miles."

"Well then, will you lend me a pair of horses and a sleigh?" said Harry, "and I'll drive myself and pay you anything you ask. You may trust me, my name is Llewellyn, my uncle lives in the village."

The tall man gave a long whistle. "Is it the ould masther's nephew, Misther Harry, that is to marry the young lady?" he exclaimed. "Faith, I'll drive ye myself, wid all the pleasure in life, and ye *must* go, but if ye stay ye'll be as welcome as the flowers in May. Sure, I'm Robbie's brother, and my name is Smith, and this is my partner Root, and I hope ye'll forgive him for hitting the mark, for it's love, sure enough, that's driving ye."

Harry would go on, and soon all was bustle at the farm-house; the two elder boys clamoured to go with their father, but the mother opposed this and so did Root; Chip, however, overruled them both, and took the boys.

"Bundle them up, Fanny, and let them come along – bring them up hardy, I say, and not like slips of girls or ould women," quoth John James William Smith.

A great farm sleigh, with a heavy box on it, was brought out, and great heavy farm horses were harnessed to it; hot bricks were put in for the children's feet, and plenty of clean straw and four warm buffalo robes completed the arrangements.

"I may not come back to-morrow, or the next day ayther," said Chip, as he departed, "so don't be onaisy, Fanny."

Harry shook hands warmly with Fanny, and thanked her again for her kindness, and he offered a bill to Root, who brought out the horses.

"Not a stiver," said the German, sententiously, "pay in the same coin when I need it – good night."

Again they faced the drifting snow, the driving wind; the little boys cuddled down to their hot bricks and played beneath the buffaloes, the horses plodded on at a foot pace, breaking the track at each step, and Harry and his brawny companion were very cold before they saw the lights of Cromaboo. The horses were covered with frozen sweat and fairly exhausted by the time they arrived at Mr. Llewellyn's door, but Canada against all the world for a warm welcome on a cold night; men, children and horses were soon well cared for, and forgetting their troubles in a sound sleep. Lavinia cried when she saw her cousin, and said she felt heart-broken when she heard he had been in Gibbeline and had not even sent her a line or his love, "but I see the reason now," she said. "Ah! if I had known you were on the road I should have been so anxious."

"Let me go to bed, there's a dear girl," said Harry, kissing her, "I am drunk with weariness, I never closed my eyes last night."

But the next morning he was abroad by eight o'clock, on his snowshoes – or rather Robert's – in search of Mr. Meldrum, and delighted to find Miss Paxton at the doctor's house.

"By George, you know, fortune seems to favour me," he said; "you'll be bridesmaid, of course."

"Of course," said Mary, "I expected to be bridesmaid before Christmas; why did you defer the wedding, sir, without assigning a reason for it?"

"Pressing business, you know, and all that sort of thing," said Harry, but he looked rather out of countenance at the questioning bright eyes that regarded him so keenly. "I was awfully sorry, you know, by George," he added with a scarlet face.

Miss Mary nodded gravely. "I am glad to hear it," she said.

Harry and the doctor went to procure a license and engage the parson, and Robert drove Mary Paxton to Mr. Llewellyn's in Chip's big sleigh to help her little friend. That day was a busy day in doors and out, for scores of men were ordered abroad by the path-masters to dig snow and make tracks, and Chip employed his horses in getting an enormous back-log from the woods for the wedding fire. Lavinia wanted to defer the marriage till the following week, but Harry coaxed her to let the next day be the happy day, and prevailed.

Chapter Twenty-Two

"Wooed and married and a'
Wooed and carried awa'."
— Joanna Baillie[116]

"There was a charm I did not know, –
The simplest pipe a clown can blow,
The rudest harp is touched, and lo!
It was in vain I willed! I see
The cabinets of memory
Are all unlocked by harmony!"
— W.B.R.[117]

A STORMY morning, a furious north-east wind driving the snow in blinding drifts, and blowing great masses of clouds across the cold, blue sky, now obscuring, now partially revealing the stormy winter sun; a piercingly cold morning, a morning to freeze your nose and ears, and make your toes and fingers ache; a morning when only the strongest and healthiest have any pleasure in battling with the elements, and the timid and ailing and lazy cling to the fireside: the wedding morning of Lavinia Llewellyn and her cousin Harry.

Mr. Meldrum and Mary Paxton – who was sole bridesmaid – were early astir at the doctor's house, and by their joint efforts, and not without great difficulty, induced Margaret to don the cream-coloured

---

[116]Leslie has 'Joanna Baily.' This is Joanna Baillie (1762-1851), Scottish poet and dramatist.

[117]W.B.R., "The Player and the Listeners" in *Good Words* (1864): 168.

satin gown in which she had been married. It was extremely unbe-
coming, she said, for her to dress in satin and her husband in debt,
she would rather wear her old print, *that*, at least, was paid for –
and more to the same effect. She made a stand against the diamond
broach her father had given her, when she became Mrs. Hurst; ought
she, as an honest woman, to wear it; ought she not rather to sell it
and pay her husband's debts? It belonged to her poor old grandmother, who little thought her son's daughter would ever come to
this. Her husband stood waiting, with his great coat on, outwardly
calm enough, coiling and uncoiling his whip lash, the wild cat within
him suggesting a wish to lay it across his wife's shoulders, but he
only shrugged his own as Mary entered with her wrappings on.

"Oh! the broach is it, Maggie? If you have scruples of conscience
about wearing it, lend it to me; it's just the thing I want to complete
my toilet."

"Diamonds are more becoming to a married lady than a single
one. Everything that I possess which is valuable *you* covet," and she
pinned it into her own bosom.

"I covet that great fur cloak the good man has bought you; shall
I help you on with it?"

"Mary Paxton, *do* you know that it is bought on credit? It is the
next thing to stealing, for he *never* means to pay for it."

"I wish he had stolen two while he had been at it," said her sister,
"the next time you rob a fur shop remember me! my brother. How
lovely and warm! If you don't mean to wear it, Maggie, I will, and you
can have the shawls. Come, hurry, don't let us delay the wedding."

"If you say much, I shall not go at all," said Margaret, sitting down
obstinately.

"*Much* – now do as you like, Maggie, I *must* go, you know, as I am
bridesmaid, so I might have both the broach and the fur cloak, and
it will be a great deal pleasanter without you," said Mary, with great
gravity.

"I *shall* go, my young lady," said Margaret, angrily, "if only to
disappoint you," and she proceeded slowly to put on the fur cloak;
they got her into the sleigh finally, but it was a ticklish business even
to the last, like driving a pig to market.

Mr. Meldrum relieved his chafed feelings by passing the parson
on the road, in a narrow place, and upsetting him. So he arrived at
Mr. Llewellyn's first. The bridegroom helped the ladies out himself.

"By George, you know, Meldrum," he said, "I was afraid you wouldn't come, I was afraid Mrs. Meldrum wouldn't let you, you know, for fear you'd take cold. *Such* a morning for a fellow's wedding."

"You thought me an old woman, aye, Harry? It was Mrs. Meldrum's toilet that delayed me, but I'm before Mr. Moorhouse, as it is; we left the reverend gentleman in a large snow drift. You must really forgive me, Harry, for I forgot when I upset him that he was necessary to the ceremony."

It was half an hour after the time appointed for the nuptials, and the bride was in all her bravery – the white silk dress and a rich veil purchased by Harry, in a desperate hurry, the evening he left Hamilton. Miss Lavinia's dress was made by Miss Paxton and Mrs. Smith, assisted by the Cromaboo dress maker; she looked almost pretty in her elation and happiness, and not the famous man-milliner of Paris could have fashioned her costume with greater taste. Mrs. Llewellyn was dressed in her best, too, a faded purple satin gown, and snowy cap; Mr. Llewellyn in his handsomest skull-cap and dress coat, to give away the bride; Mrs. Smith in her best gown and clean white apron, to wait upon the guests, and Tommy in his Sunday tartan, to see the ceremony. Robert, too, was in his Sunday clothes, which being black scarcely looked like a wedding, and made him seem much smaller than he did in his every day garments, but not less at his ease, – all were ready, and waiting for the parson.

There was no gentleman in Cromaboo but Mr. Moorhouse, so Robert was Mr. Harry's groomsman, because he could get no other.

"By George, you know, I wish he wore anything but black, it looks like mourning," said Harry, in an aside to his friend, Mr. Meldrum.

"He *will* mourn when he hears of Miss Lavy's good fortune, and see what he's lost," was the reply. "Coming events cast their shadows before."

A huge log fire blazed in the wide chimney, the long table was covered with a snowy cloth, and an ample feast was spread; the bride's cake was home made, the pumpkin pie and cheese cakes were a sight to see, and Prince Llewellyn himself would not have disdained the chickens and ham; that is if that royal personage was gifted with a grain of common sense. The rafters were decked with evergreen, and so were the pictures in the little parlour, where the ceremony was to take place. Rich coffee and strong green tea took the place of wine at the entertainment, and the whole house had a festive look and odour. Before the parson arrived, Miss Paxton had decorated everybody with a wedding favour of orange blossom and mountain ash berries. They were all growing nervous, – especially Harry, and the ladies, – when that indispensible gentleman turned up; he was very cold and somewhat sulky, and apologised for being late; he had been upset and broken a shaft, he said, and looked straight at Mr. Meldrum as he spoke, and bowed very coldly. Mr Meldrum returned the salute, with his usual grace, but without speaking; Mrs. Meldrum was "so sorry," and Miss Paxton decorated him with a wedding favour. Mrs. Llewellyn treated the disaster very lightly.

"Upset, aye!" she said, "*we* have all had our tumbles; if you had delayed much longer, we should all have been upset, sir."

The bride and bridegroom stood up, and the ceremony began. Mr. Moorhouse read it with great emphasis, laying particular stress on the most trying passages. "I require and charge you both," he said, in a grating, stern, awful voice, "as you shall answer at the *dreadful* day of *judgement*, when the secrets of all hearts are disclosed," – here he fixed poor Harry with his eye, and cold as the day was the happy bridegroom burst into a profuse perspiration, and the wind suddenly blew a mighty blast, as if to give additional emphasis to the parson's words, and shook the old frame house to the foundation. When he came to question the bride – "Will *you obey* him, and *serve* him?" he said in a voice that gave Lavinia a desire to box his ears. "I will," she retorted, shortly and snappishly before he had well finished the sentence. It was quite a marvel the expression he threw into the sentence, "Lord have mercy upon us," as if they were criminals, and he the jail chaplain, interceding for them at the last pinch, and he pronounced the final benediction as though they were just going to be hanged, and he begged God to have mercy on their souls. "Amen!" said Mr. Meldrum, sweetly, in echo to the clergyman's stern "amen."

So nervous had Harry become at this juncture that he required a pinch from his friend, and a whispered reminder, before it occurred to him to kiss the bride.

"Permit me to present my congratulations – may I be allowed the privilege of an old friend?" said Mr. Meldrum, stooping gracefully and saluting the cheek of the dark little lady; and then her uncle kissed her, and then her aunt, and then Mrs. Meldrum, who delighted the parson by saying, "I hope you may never repent it, my dear;" and then came Miss Paxton, and the little bride kissed Mrs. Smith and Tommy, and shook hands with the best man, and the register was produced and signed; and they all went into the great kitchen to partake of the wedding feast, Robert made happy in that short transit because Mary Paxton's hand rested on his arm. Mr. Meldrum offered his arm to Mrs. Llewellyn, but the old lady said, "Go along with you," and nimbly dodging her guests, ran into the dining-room first, and placed herself at the table in her usual seat, eyeing the feast with great satisfaction. Mrs. Smith waited on them, but her son sat as a guest at his master's table, and that fact gladdened her heart as much as the sight of Tommy seated in his own little chair by the great fire-side, quietly munching his part of the feast, and complacently admiring his plaid stockings.

There was a good deal of pleasant chat, but no attempt at speeches; and the meal at an end, the ladies did a great deal of talking, as ladies generally do everywhere, and it was decided that Miss Paxton should stay at Mr. Llewellyn's that night, instead of returning with the Meldrums, as it would save her an additional cold mile when she left by stage in the morning, and that Mrs. Smith should send Tommy home, and stay all night and sleep with her and get the breakfast. Mr. Harry talked very affably to his best man about dogs and horses, and Mr. Llewellyn entertained the doctor and the parson with an account of the siege of Babylon until it was time for the bride to change her finery for a traveling dress, when Mr. Moorhouse took his leave. Harry followed him to give his fee, and Robert to open the door, – John Smith brought out the horses to-day to spare "Robbie." Harry, in his nervousness, slipped a fifty-cent piece into the parson's hand, in mistake for a twenty dollar American eagle.

"Sir?" said the clergyman, sternly regarding the happy bridegroom, as he held the coin in his palm. The best man – who I am afraid was laughing in his sleeve at them both – gently pointed out the error, but not before poor, blundering Harry had said, apologetically, "I am sure you deserve twice as much – such a cold day – made me the happiest of men, and all that."

Then Mr. Llewellyn had a private interview with his nephew, in which he told him his duties as a husband – which I spare the reader, feeling sure his mother-in-law will instruct him fully on those points, without any assistance of mine – and Robert and Mr. Meldrum were left alone, the ladies having all accompanied the bride to her chamber. After a reasonable time had elapsed, Robert, who was to drive them to the station, put on his great coat and grew impatient.

"You need not expect them yet, Bob," said Mr. Meldrum, "they won't be here for half an hour or so; suppose you play something; you can play, I hear."

Mr. Meldrum had never heard him. Robert opened the instrument at his request and began one of those strange melodies, wailing voluntaries, in which he delighted. As the wind howled without, and Bob's fingers touched the ebony and ivory keys within, memory struck strange chords in Mr. Meldrum's bosom. He had never heard the tune before, and could not account for the feeling within him, or why the melody brought old scenes to his mind with bitter pain and regret.

It brought back the birth of his first child; he remembered pacing the dining-room floor, while one dear to him indeed, but who should have been far dearer, was lying in pain and danger in the room above. He was not nervous, but he was greatly interested; he listened attentively for sounds. Presently he heard the cry of a child, with a sense of relief, soon followed by a footstep, and a brother practitioner, an old school-fellow entered the room, and congratulated him upon being the father of a fine boy, and told him, in answer to his question "was it an easy birth, – did she suffer much?" that she had suffered greatly, and when the nurse advised her to cry out, as it would relieve her, she had asked where her husband was. In the room below, they told her. "Then I'll die before I cry and distress him," she said, and fainted. He felt a little flattered at the time, and it amused him greatly, and his fellow practitioner still more, for he had known Tom Meldrum as a hard boy at school, who always took his palmies[118] without a tear; and he doubted very much whether any woman's cries had power to distress him. But, as Robert played, the memory of that scene smote his hearer with remorse and pain.

Mother and son were gone for many a day; the grave had shut them away forever, but oh! if he had them back how he would love and value them. He felt the worth of his lost jewels, and the reality that they would never return to his possession. Who cared to spare

---

[118]palmies = blows on the palms with a ruler or other instrument, formerly used by teachers to punish misbehaving pupils.

him now, who cared whether he was vexed or pleased, who in all the world would suffer a pang for his sake? His wife's dying face came back to him vividly; the wistful look in her eyes, when she could no longer speak, the pitiful quiver of the silent lips, as she put her weak wasted arms about his neck for the last time. He could bear it no longer; he laid a hand on the player's shoulder, he did not know how roughly. "Stop that, and be damned to you," he said, in a voice that astonished Robert as much as if he had discharged a pistol at him. The music ceased suddenly, and the lad turned and looked at the doctor's usually calm face, disturbed enough now, the eyebrows drawn together, with a frown of pain.

"What is the matter?" asked Robert, in alarm, "are you ill, sir?"

"No," returned the gentleman, "but why do you play like that? You will make the bride weep on her wedding day, – what the – the dickens do you play like that for?"

Robert's face flushed, he was greatly hurt and annoyed at the effect of his music. There was a short silence, then the doctor's face relaxed, he touched the lad again, but this time kindly.

"Come, Bob," he said, "don't be offended; not an oath has passed my lips since my student days till now, and it's a greater compliment to you than Miss Paxton's tears, which flow easily, because she's a woman, but I am a thick-skinned fellow, with self-command enough, I have thought, till lately, and you have probed and ruffled me, and – and made me swear. You have brought the dear lost dead to life, but only as the Witch of Endor raised Samuel to shock and frighten Saul. You will make Miss Lavy remember and regret some half forgotten lover, instead of rejoicing in her wedded lord."

The lad laughed his soft musical laugh. "It is hard to be forgotten quite," he said, – "I – I wanted Miss Lavy to remember if only for a little while, a minute or two."

"You did, you young dog in the manger," said Mr. Meldrum, eyeing him keenly. "If she had possessed ten thousand pounds, let us say, – would you have let her go?"

"Yes, if she had all the money there is on the outside of this round world, and if Miss Mary had nothing but her own pretty self, I would be content to work all my life as her servant, without pay, only to be near her."

He touched the keys again, and sang the sweet words of another Robert, who loved fair women so well, that he ought to have treated them better:

> "Oh! were I on the wild side,
> Sae bleak and bare, sae bleak and bare,
> The desert were a paradise
> If thou wert there, if thou wert there.
>
> Oh! were I monarch of the globe,
> Wi' thee to reign, wi' thee to reign,
> The brightest jewel in my crown
> Wad be my queen, wad be my queen."[119]

The sweetest Scottish music penetrated not only the ears, but to the heart of the little bride, as she received the finishing touch to her traveling toilet above stairs, and she led Mary into another room and earnestly addressed her:

"*Do* keep an eye upon Robert," she said; "those dreadful Cromaboo minxes have too much influence on him, and he is a weak boy. I could not bear him to marry one of those creatures. Do you know I saw him playing in a yard the other day - yes, auntie dear, I'll be back in a minute."

"Playing upon what," said Mary, "the bag-pipes?"

"No, but an impudent girl had snow-balled him and knocked his hat off, and he threw the reins to me and jumped off the sleigh, and chased her into a yard and kissed her - it was what she wanted, no doubt, the bold minx - yes, auntie, I am coming, how you *do* tease - and all this actually before my face."

"I'll do my best to take care of him - I'll be faithful," promised Mary, laughing, as the music ceased below.

A smile of calm amusement played on the doctor's face as the lad warbled this ballad, he was himself again, and stepped forward with his usual quiet gracefulness to hold the door open as the ladies entered.

There were kisses, good byes, last words, good wishes; there were tears on Lavy's cheeks, and her uncle's, as he held her in his arms and blessed her fervently.

---

[119]Robert Burns, "Oh, Wert Thou In The Cauld Blast," *The Poets and Poetry of Scotland, From the Earliest to the Present Time,* James Grant Wilson, ed. (Blackie and Son: 1876): 371.

"My dear child, my brave little helper," he said at last, gently releasing himself from her embrace; "take care of her, Harry, and God bless you both."

"I will, uncle, by – George," said Harry, greatly touched by this scene, and very much in earnest.

Then they were packed in warm buffalo robes, old slippers were thrown after them, the sleigh bells jingled, and they were off.

Chapter Twenty-Three

"If of herself she will not love, nothing will make her,
The devil take her!"

– Sir John Suckling[120]

JOHN SMITH and his son Chip stood at their door to see the bride depart, and to wave their hats and shout "good luck go wid ye wherever ye go," and when the sound of the sleigh-bells had died away, it entered into the heart of Chip to step into Mr. Llewellyn's house and see Robert's divinity, or as he expressed it, "Bob's girl."

He had never even caught a glimpse of her, though he had been walking about the house all the day before, because the lady had avoided him; but he had formed an idea of her beauty based on his experience of the Cromaboo lasses, who, to borrow Sidney Smith's[121] comparison, were "made like milestones," and were for the most part strapping, red-cheeked, and loud voiced. Among these he had made many conquests, and though he fancied the unknown beauty, straighter, bigger, better dressed and haughtier, or as he would have said, "with more of the devil in her," he had no fear of winning her if he made up his mind to it. His father, who was more than half drunk, encouraged him in the idea, for John Smith drunk and John Smith sober were quite different men.

"Sure," said he, "she might fancy ye for a husband, since she doesn't mane to take Robbie, and she has a dacent bit o' money that ye'd find handy."

---

[120]John Suckling (1609-1641), from "Why So Pale and Wan, Fond Lover?"
[121]Most likely Sidney Smith (1823-1889), a lawyer and political figure in Canada West.

"Faith she might," returned Chip, complacently, "any way I'll have a look at her."

John James William Smith was a comely giant, standing six feet in his stockings; like his father in figure, but with straight features, eyes large and black as midnight, and curling hair inherited from a handsome mother; and he had cultivated a magnificent beard that reached nearly to his waist. His step-mother was the only woman in the world for whom he had a respect, and her he did not like. He had no belief in the virtue of women, yet he was not without virtue himself, with all his faults. He was generous, good tempered, and honest. He loved his father, brother, and his partner Root better than either; indeed if put to it Chip would have laid down his life for Root. He was clean in person and civil in manner, and he scorned a lie as much as his father did.

He knew it would be useless to try and put his plan into execution while Mr. and Mrs. Llewellyn were up, so he lingered about the house for a couple of hours, after Harry and his bride had departed; lingered till his father went to bed, till after his step-mother had come in with Tommy and put him to bed.

"Are you going home to-night, Chip?" asked Mrs. Smith, sharply, "if you mean to stay, these boys should go to bed."

"They may go to bed," said Chip, "it's a rough night, I'll stay till morning."

But the boys utterly refused to go to bed, and after a sharp contest with them, Mrs. Smith returned to Mr. Llewellyn's, and left them up. She had longed for an hour or two alone with Miss Paxton. Our heroine's pretty face had a great charm in it for the mother as well as the son, and Mrs. Smith had made up her mind to tell Mary her history. Who is without a history? Uneventful as many lives are, every man and woman born into the world has a tale to tell, and it is only a very few who go to the graves and leave it untold. Do we not all, at times, bore our friends with the story of our past joys and sorrows, and are we not bored by them in return, "many's the time and oft?"[122] Mrs. Smith had fully made up her mind to tell Mary her history.

Chip waited for ten minutes after his step-mother had gone, and then banged the door behind him, and strode off through the falling

---

[122]Charles Dibdin (1745-1814), from "Poor Tom! Or, The Sailor's Epitaph."

snow. "When the gods plot our ruin they answer our prayers."[123] He lifted the latch of Mr. Llewellyn's kitchen door, and his wish was gratified. He found Miss Mary alone, seated quietly in the bright fire light, arrayed in her bridesmaid's dress of white lustre, ornamented with swan's down, and covered, but not concealed by a long tulle veil, fastened above the forehead by a coronet of blue and white forget-me-nots. There was a brilliant colour in her cheeks, left there by the recent excitement, and, as she turned to look at the new comer, he thought it the most lovely face he had ever seen, and scarcely earthly. She was not in the least what he expected her to be, and her calmness under the scrutiny of his conquering black eyes, flustered and abashed him.

"Good evening," she said, in return to his salutation of "God save all here," and he, half from policy, half by the instinct of reverence, removed his hat, for the first time in his life in civility to a woman. Miss Mary knew who he was at a glance, and recognized his great bass voice, which had been sounding through the house, half the day before.

"You wish, I suppose," she said, "to see Mrs. Smith?"

Now Chip had not, in reality, the least desire in the world to see his step-mother, but he said, in describing the scene to his partner, Root, "I was that bothered wid her beauty, for she's like an angel drissed in white moonshine, thrimmed up wid new fallen snow, that I said 'if you plaze ma'am.'"

Immediately the lady tripped across the kitchen and disappeared, and Chip, to his dismay, heard her clear voice calling up the narrow stair, "Mrs. Smith, your eldest son wishes to see you," and when she returned to the kitchen, she was not alone.

Mrs. Smith knew John James William of old, and guessed the object of his visit far better than Miss Mary did, and felt very angry at the intrusion; Mary preceded her, and seating herself calmly in the low rocking chair as before, began turning over the leaves of a large

---

[123]Perhaps from Horace (*Od.* iii. 5.5): "Whom the gods wish to ruin they make mad" (*Quem deus vult perdere prius dementat*). A variation appears in Longfellow's *The Masque of Pandora* (1875): "Whom the gods would destroy, they first make mad." Oscar Wilde later, in 1895, reworded this in his comedic play *An Ideal Husband* (Act II), where the character Sir Robert Chiltern says: "...I remember having read some-where, in some strange book, that when the gods wish to punish us they answer our prayers" (London: Methuen, 1899:84).

illustrated Bible she had brought back with her, having picked it up on the parlour table as she passed. Mrs. Smith said not a word, but looking her big step-son straight in the eyes, she made an imperative sign to the door, as if she would say, "march out of it,' " a sign which roused all the latent obstinacy in the character of John James William.

Some minutes passed, and Miss Paxton hearing no sound, looked up. "I fear I am intruding," she said gently, addressing Chip, "you wished to see your mother alone?"

"Faith then I didn't, ma'am, said he, plucking up courage, "I would rather see yourself alone."

The lady looked at him with a calm kind of surprise that brought the blood to his face, and Mrs. Smith, who stood behind her, frowned at him with another imperative sign to the door. As if in answer to that sign it suddenly burst open, and two boys came in, with a rush of cold air, and banged it after them.

"What do *you* want, boys?" asked Mrs. Smith, sharply.

"We want to see the lady," said the eldest, a handsome, dark-haired lad of eight, in a long great coat and big boots, who was unmistakably the son of John James William, bearing the stamp of his paternity in his face. The younger lad was better dressed, in Knickerbocker trousers, and a blouse with a sailor's collar, turned up with purple. He had bright red hair, and a little coaxing, cherub face, half shy, half saucy.

"To see me, is it?" said Mary, extending her hand, "come here and let me look at you."

I have said that she hated nothing that God had made, but she *loved* little children and animals, and the boys knew it without being told, just as the cats and dogs did; they came shyly, yet with confidence, and shook hands with her. She looked at them keenly, kindly, with interest, and noted that both were clean and well-kept.

"What are your names?" she asked.

"Johnnie Smith, and he's Joey," replied the dark-haired lad.

"What made you wish to see me?" was the next question.

"Because daddy said he was going to marry you."

"He has a wife already," said the lady, calmly and distinctly – both boys nodded – "and that is all he has a right to." A pause. "Would you like to see some pictures?" They nodded again, eagerly. Laying one hand on Johnnie's shoulder as she sat, and passing the other round Joey's waist, she told them to open the book, and turn the leaves nicely. They opened at the picture of Christ blessing little children. "Oh!" exclaimed both boys, and looked long and evidently with great pleasure.

"That is our Saviour, do you know who he is?" she asked.

"God," said Joey, reverently, the first word he had spoken.

"Who told you that, my dear?"

"Mother."

"And you say your prayers to Him?" Both boys nodded. Mrs. Smith felt her anger evaporating, and Chip, to use his own expression, "mighty uncomfortable." Twenty minutes passed, the leaves softly rustled, and the lads asked questions and returned answers with growing confidence; meanwhile their father twirled his hat, and looked very sheepish indeed at this unexpected interruption to his love-making, and Mrs. Smith stood erect by the chimney-piece. The group with the Bible were perfectly at their ease, the little fellows quite happy and unconscious that they disturbed their father's arrangements; they not knowing and Miss Paxton not caring, or glad to confound his politics. The boys exclaimed with delight at the miraculous draught of fishes, they admired Ruth; they paused a long time at Jonah issuing from the mouth of the whale, they lingered lovingly over Hannah presenting Samuel with his little coat.

"She made it for love, Joey, as your mother made this for you," said Miss Mary.

"How do you know she made it?" said Joey.

"Because it is so pretty, and has such nice work on it. I do not know, but I think she did, Joey."

"Yes, she did," said Johnnie, with a nod, "he's the pet."

"Have you any more brothers?"

"One, and a sister, she's going three, and her name is Frances Elizabeth Anne," said Johnnie, with great gravity.

"And your brother – what is his name?" asked their new friend.

"James Thomas, and the baby was Robert, but he's dead."

"Happy Robert," said the lady, with a sigh; "how old was he when he died?"

"Just six weeks and three days," replied Joey, promptly.

Again they turned the leaves; they found Samson, and criticized him, they found Queen Esther in Royal apparel, and approved of her, – "but she isn't as nice as you," said Johnnie, sturdily, – at last they came to father Adam and mother Eve, and closed the book.

"Well, boys, you came to see me, what do you think of me?" said Miss Paxton, taking Johnnie gently by the ear, and smoothing back one of Joey's red curls.

"I think you are nice," said Joey, "and so pretty," added Johnnie, with a blush.

"I have a great mind to come and see your mother."

"Oh! do," said both boys, in a breath, and Joey added, "I'll show you my puppies."

"And I have a lamb, – a pet lamb," said Johnnie, as an additional inducement, "he drinks out of a tea-pot like anything, – I'll give him to you."

"And I'll give you my cat, though I love it," said Joey.

"You are generous little fellows to promise me so much," said Miss Mary, with a smile. "You have reason to be proud of your sons," turning to the father and addressing him.

"They're well enough," he replied, clearing his throat.

"They are," pursued the lady, "a credit to your wife."

"I have no wife, ma'am, and never had," returned John James William, determined not to damage his position by the admission of an encumbrance; "faith, I'm as much a bachelor as ever I was," and he slapped his thigh as he concluded.

"Poor little boys," said the lady, and her eyes softened, and grew humid as she looked at them, while Mrs. Smith's darkened, and flashed fire at the offending Chip. Two great tears gathered and fell on the cover of the Bible.

"Oh! don't cry," said Johnnie, in a half whisper, standing very close to his new friend, and Joey drew down his lip, and looked as if he would cry for sympathy. Chip felt *he* was the cause of the tears, but was puzzled and annoyed at the sight of them; his step-mother he could understand, but this lady was a mystery to him. An awkward pause ensued, broken at last by Miss Paxton saying gently, "I think you had better go now, little boys. If I do not come to see you, my dears, I shall send you some picture papers by Robert."

She rose, she kissed the red-haired lad, and shook hands with Johnnie, she opened the door and told them to "take hands, and run fast to John Smith's," and go to bed at once, and bade them say their prayers to-night, as they sped away. They obeyed implicitly. She stood for a moment looking out at the stormy night, then closing the door and returning stood before Chip as he sat. Her features had sharpened and hardened, her face had a grave kind of scorn in it; her eyes flashed. She stood looking at him steadily for full a minute before she spoke.

"I don't know whether I scorn or pity you most," she said, "I despise you for despising the mother of those children, for making use of her, and then disowning her, and putting shame upon her sons, your own flesh and blood; I pity you for your blindness that you do not see that those dear boys are a blessing sent from God; you do not feel their worth, you are not proud of them, yet God has given them to you – *you*," with unmeasurable scorn, "like pearls before swine. You, with your good looks, and your bone and muscle, and your six feet of strength and impudence, are a very poor creature after all, and I am sorry from my heart that Robert has such a brother, and those poor little boys such a father, – heaven help and pity them all."

She turned and walked swiftly from the room.

"I think you had better go, John James William," said Mrs. Smith sternly.

"Faith, I think so, too," he replied, and he did without even the ceremony of good night, and so ended the wooing of John James William Smith.

Chapter Twenty-Four

"You came beneath my tent with friendly greeting,
Of all my joys you had the better part,
Then when our eyes and hands were oftenest meeting
You struck me to the heart.
No less a murderer that your victim living
Can face the passing world, and chat and smile,
No less a traitor for your show of giving
Your friendship all the while."

– Anonymous[124]

THOUGH excited, elated and happy beyond compare, Lavinia had, as we have seen, an eye to Robert. He had behaved so nicely, so unselfishly, she thought, that he deserved a reward, and she would give him a word, if possible, before she left. An opportunity occurred at the station; Mr. Harry wanted a smoke to quiet his nerves, and asked if he might leave her for twenty minutes.

""Oh! certainly," said his bride, "I want to have a chat with Robert."

The happy bridegroom did not feel jealous, he was grateful to Bob for not acting as his rival, and giving him trouble, and for the way he had behaved to-day, so he said "all right," and left them the sole occupants of the waiting-room.

"Mr. Harry is out in his time," said Robert, looking at his watch – who so poor as to be without his watch in Canada? – "but I suppose as he's just married, it's not to be wondered at; your train's due in five minutes."

---

[124]From "Dust And Ashes" Part II, *Littell's Living Age* 128 (1876): 66.

"Just a word, Robert," said Lavinia, "and then you must go and see after the luggage, and look up Harry. You don't feel hurt, I hope, because I left you – you know you were fickle first, so you ought to forgive me – we are friends, I hope," she concluded in a sentimental tone, with her head on one side and her lashes drooping.

"I am proud to be called your friend," replied our hero, heartily; "I wish you every happiness, and I shall never forget how you saved my life. I got this for you," producing a little gold broach, "if you will do me the honour to take it – and I want you to give me something at parting, just for the sake of auld lang syne like, if you will," here he became very sentimental, too, lowering his voice and speaking very softly.

"Oh! thank you, it's a little beauty," said his little mistress; "I *did* feel hurt that you hadn't given me anything, but what *can* I give you?"

"Will you give me one kiss?" in the softest and most persuasive tone.

She blushed, she lifted her face half shyly, half slyly, this bride of half a day, and looked in his face, and then condescended to offer her cheek. He had taken the first kiss unasked, but he received the last as a great favour. Uncovering his head, and putting a forefinger lightly on either shoulder, he stooped and kissed, not the offered cheek, but the pouting, red lips that were to be Mr. Harry's henceforth and forever. The coming train shrieked as if shocked at such an impropriety, and Robert, with a hasty good bye, went off in search of the absent bridegroom. There was a bustle with the luggage, and he only returned in time to place the checks in Harry's hand as the train was moving, to wish them all happiness, and wave his hat as it steamed away. Then he turned the ponies' heads towards Cromaboo, a bitter north wind blowing in his very teeth as he started on his solitary journey; but he was used to dreary drives and more hardened to wind and weather than Harry Llewellyn; happiness in the form of Mary Paxton waited for him at the end, and he didn't mind it.

The road was more sheltered by woods than that from Gibbeline, and had been dug out in the last two days, the snow forming a wall on each side of the track; he just made fast the reins to the dashboard, wrapped himself in the buffaloes, and lay down in the bottom of the sleigh, turning his back to the wind and the ponies, and guessing rightly that he would meet no one on so stormy a night. He used neither whip nor rein, only chirrupped to the cattle to keep them on the trot, yet his hands and feet were aching, and his face was numb, as he drove into Cromaboo, and dimly discerned through the drifting snow, a tall figure striding away from Mr. Llewellyn's. He recognized his brother, and shouted out, "Chip, old boy, put up the horses for me, I'm half frozen. You'd better not go home to-night; groom the ponies for me and bed them down, there's a good fellow."

Chip assented with a growl. It took him some time to do his allotted task, and as he rubbed the weary beasts, and turned over the straw for their beds, he turned over the night's adventures in his mind. He was used to success and no novice in love-making, and therefore not so much discouraged as another man might have been in his place. "Sure, if she hadn't an inthrest in me," he argued, "she would never be that angry," and it occurred to him, as he banged the stable door, that he might peep in at Mr. Llewellyn's uncurtained kitchen window, before he put away the lantern, and see what sort of a reception Robbie met with. They had helped the lad off with his overcoat, brushed the snow from him, rubbed his hands and made much of him, and now, as Chip peeped in, Miss Paxton kneeled beside his brother before the fire, making a piece of toast for him, while his mother stood at the table pouring out a cup of steaming hot coffee. As she turned to bring it to Robert, who sat before the blaze in the rocking chair, she caught a glimpse of the lurking, handsome face of her step-son. She said nothing, but she regarded that good-looking visage with secret anger, and thought it fraught with all evil, and the sight of it strengthened her in her resolution to tell her history to Miss Paxton and Robert.

"It's worth a longer drive on a colder night to have such a welcome," said the lad, as he basked before the fire, sipping his coffee and crunching his toast with a relish, and listening to the howling of the wind. "What are we to do to make this evening forever remarkable to you two as it is to me? It's only half past nine; I vote we don't go to bed yet."

"Let us tell stories," said his mother, "I have one to tell that I think Miss Paxton ought to know."

"I hope it's a pleasant story, mother."

"It's the story of my early life, and it will be more new to you, my boy, than to Miss Paxton."

"Dear Mrs. Smith," said Mary, cordially, "I never heard a word of your life in my life, so it will be new to me, too, and a great pleasure to hear it."

"I doubt of its being much of a pleasure to either of you," she replied; "but you shall hear it when Robbie has finished his supper."

So accordingly when the crockery was cleared away, she began her tale by asking Miss Paxton, "Did you never see my face till you came to see Robbie in his sick bed? Take a look at me and think."

"I am sure I never saw you till last summer," replied Mary, with surprise at the question, "I know no face like yours except Robert's; *he* is like you in expression sometimes, and about the mouth."

"You see nothing *familiar* in my face – nothing that you ever saw before?"

"I see that you are agitated and stirred by some strong impulse, that is new to me in your face; but it touches no chord, it awakens no memory," returned Mary.

"Miss Mary, when I was fourteen years old, I lived with my parents on a wild, uncultivated farm twenty miles back o' this place; our nearest neighbour lived six miles away, and there was no road; the only way of traveling was by a blazed track. I was born in Ireland, and have a dim memory of the sea and the ship we crossed in. I was six when they brought me to the backwoods. My parents were Roman Catholics, but we never saw a priest all the time I lived there, and the church was forty miles away. They could not read a letter, and there was no school; so at fourteen I knew very little; I could only sew in a rough way, plait straw, knit open-work stockings, milk, and do a bit o' coarse housework."

"Pardon me for interrupting you Mrs. Smith, but that was a good deal to know," said Mary, "and many a middle-class English woman is more ignorant of useful things at forty, though she can read and write, – but go on."

"Our house was a large shanty, with only two rooms in it; the floor hewn timber, the roof bark. I had seven brothers and sisters younger than me. When I was thirteen my father hired Smith to help him clear the land, and he brought Chip with him, a little slip of ten. They were just out from Ireland and Smith's wife died coming up the country. He was a Roman Catholic."

"I like him none the worse for that," said Mary, "I am no Orange woman."

"Better and more respectable than a Methodist, isn't it, Miss Mary?" said Robert.

"Hush! hush! Robin Adair, boys should be seen and not heard," replied the lady, tapping him with the screen she held, "now we won't interrupt you any more, Mrs. Smith."

"Smith had been with us a year," she resumed, "when two gentlemen came up the country shooting and fishing. Mr. Meldrum was one, and the other was named Robert Hardacre. They stayed about a month, and Mr. Hardacre came back the next spring to see the sugar making; and when he left he said he would come again, at the end of the summer, and he did in July. He came on horse-back the last time with a large knapsack full of books and clothes, and he stayed six months, or more. He was ten years older than me, and seemed to me, in my ignorance, to know everything. He danced beautifully, and taught us children to dance; he played the flute and sang as sweet as any bird, and he would work too, and help my father and Smith, when the fit was on him, and he paid his board liberally, and as money was scarce it was a great help to us. His voice was sweet, and he never said anything harsh or rude to one of us, but I was his favorite. He taught me how to read and sing, he corrected me in speaking, and showed me how to speak nicely, but so gently that he never offended or hurt my feelings. All days were alike to us till he came, but he would do nothing on Sunday but read and play the flute and sing hymns. He used to sing the evening hymn as the sun was setting, but he made no pretense of religion, and I never heard him name the name of Jesus. He often read to me, and told me Robinson Crusoe,[125] and other tales. He would milk for me on rough nights and help me with the cooking; he tried to please me and make me love him, and I did with my whole heart; I was completely under his influence, like a poor bird under the eye of a cat, only I felt no fear of him beyond a pleasant shyness, which was not fear. I believed in him, I worshipped, everything he did was right in my eyes; I had no conscience but his will. He used to call me his 'little wife,' and I never doubted but he would be my husband."

She paused. Robert had been looking attentively at his mother, but at this point he turned away from her, and leaning his face on his hand, gazed at the fire. Both women noticed a bright ring sparkling

---

[125]Daniel Defoe, *Robinson Crusoe* (1719).

on his little finger. Mrs. Smith resumed her story.

"He did not leave when the fall came, but stayed on through the winter. He was still very kind to me, very civil to all, but I began to be a little afraid of him, I did not understand him; he was quieter, and sang and talked less as the months passed. I feel sure, since, that his conscience troubled him, and he was on the wing. One stormy afternoon, towards the end of March, he and my father quarreled, and he left us suddenly. I did not hear what passed, I was out milking at the time, – he did not help me so often now, – and when I came in he was gone. They were talking very loud when I lifted the latch, but stopped when they saw me. I saw something had happened, and asked what, and said, 'Where is Robert?' My mother said, 'He is gone, and sorrow go wid him.'

"I ran out, and saw him with gun on shoulder, and knapsack on back, disappearing in the wood. I ran after him, and called his name, and he waited for me. I asked how long he would be away. 'Not long,' he said lightly, 'a day or two perhaps, it's quite uncertain, – it may be a week or a fortnight, at the furthest.'

"Tears rushed to my eyes, I couldn't bear to lose him for so long. He rested the gun on one arm, and put the other round my waist and kissed me, and told me to go back at once and not take cold. His manner, though kind, was commanding, and I did as he bid me, only begging him to come back soon, and putting up my mouth for another kiss. 'You silly, little Nelly,' he said, and smiled as he kissed me. When I turned away, he called me back, and gave me a paper. 'What is this?' I asked. 'Money,' he said, 'to buy clothes for your baby – now run away home.' He did not say *my* baby, or *ours*, I thought of that bitterly afterwards. I kept the note in my bosom and told no one, I have it yet unchanged."

"Burn it," said her son, with a sharpness that startled them both, but he did not change his position or look up.

"Four weeks passed and he did not come; they were all very un-kind to me, it seemed as though their hearts had changed and gone from me; all but Smith, who was kind in a gruff way. Robert had left his horse, and one night my father said he had given it to him because he had no money left to pay his board, and he went on to say 'that Hardacre is a scoundrel.' I spoke up hotly for Robert – for I knew he had given my father gold the very day he left – then he struck me and put me outside the door, and told me never to come back. I never crossed his threshold again. 'Twas a fine spring evening and I stayed all night in the woods, and started next morning by the blazed track for Gibbeline, where I knew Robert had stayed the year before. It was forty miles, and it took me four days to get there. I stayed one night in Cromaboo; there were six houses in it, no more. I thought it a large place. I passed your house, Miss Paxton, on a warm spring day at noon; I wore a navy blue frock, and had a coarse straw hat on my head; I was barefoot – I see you remember me now."

"Yes," said Mary, with gathering tears in her eyes, "I remember you."

"'Twas four in the afternoon when I reached Gibbeline, for I was very tired and sat long to rest on the road. It was not a large town then, and I soon found out the best inn and asked for Mr. Hardacre. The waiter said he was staying there, and was in the house at that minute, and took me upstairs to his rooms. He was sitting at a table writing. I'll never forget how shocked and annoyed he looked to see me, he who had never received me before but with smiles and open arms. Yet he was gentle, he closed the door on the waiter, and seated me in an arm chair, and listened to my story. The room we were in opened into another, where a table was set out with glasses and silver, and a snowy cloth. He went through, and got a glass of wine and water for me, telling me imperatively to 'drink it at once.' I could not drink it. I remember his hand shook as he placed the glass in mine. 'It's very perplexing,' he said, 'I am expecting some guests to supper, – you must go to the kitchen, Nelly, and get something to eat,' putting some silver in my hand, – 'to-morrow I will see about you. I hear their voices, and you must go at once.' He put his hand on my shoulder, and spoke the last words impatiently. I felt my heart breaking. I set down the glass, I rose and the silver dropped on the floor.

"'Don't you love me any more, Robert,' I said, 'even a little?'

"'Nonsense, Nelly,' he replied sternly, 'go at once, I will see you in the morning.'

"I did go at once, but he did not see me in the morning; he will see me no more till we meet before the Great White Throne. I went down stairs and out of the house; I scarce knew what I was doing, yet by a kind of instinct I turned back the road I came. I longed to die, for I knew now that he loved me no more. When I reached your house the sun was setting, I wished it would rise on me no more. I sat down on a stone, and heard sweet young voices singing the evening hymn that Robert loved, 'Glory to Thee my God, this night.' I shed no tears; I was past that; I had no knowledge of God; I was bitter and despairing. I listened to the hymn till I could bear it no longer, it hurt me so. Then I rose and went down a side road, slowly, for I was nearly spent. I had no object but to get away from the hymn. I had tasted nothing since the morning. I went down a hill, and came to a log bridge that crossed a rapid stream;[126] I sat down on it and looked into the water; it was nearly dark now. Soon a hand was laid on my shoulder, and a sharp voice asked what I was doing there. I saw a man and a young girl standing beside him; it was your father and your sister, Miss Maggie. An ox team was coming onto the bridge. I think your father told me to stand up; then I lost all consciousness and fainted. When I came to myself I was in a large room, and your mother was calling sharply to a servant to come and wash my feet, saying I was not fit for a decent bed with feet like that. The girl refused, she said she was not hired to wash the feet of such 'a dirty drab.' 'I'll do it, mamma,' said a clear voice near me, and you knelt before me, Miss Mary, and did it. I can feel your soft hands about me yet, and see your large eyes looking at me compassionately. Then you grew dim to my eyes, and I fainted again. When I came back to life I was in bed. I laid there till the next evening, and, as I grew stronger, my misery grew sharper. I got up and your sister helped me to dress, and your mother took me down to a large clean room, and questioned me alone. I felt very weak and ill; I told her the whole bitter truth; I concealed nothing. I ended by saying I longed to die. She did not express much sympathy; she said I ought to have known better, and my mother was much to blame, when Mr. Paxton, (who was close to me, though I didn't know it when I was telling my tale, for he came in in his slippers,) burst out with 'No, no, Prissy, how *could* she know better, woman? She's only a child, and not to blame, and Hardacre is a damned young scoundrel, and ought to be shot, and I'll go to Gibbeline before the week's out and tell him so. And her father and mother deserve a bullet, too, for turning her out o' doors, – why, she's a year younger than Maggie, hardly older than Polly and Emmy, – it's a shame altogether, mother, a shame, and you

---

[126]Possibly referring to the Speed River in Guelph, or to the now overgrown bridge mentioned in the Introduction (page xxi).

must look up some clothes for her baby.'

"Your father did see Robert, but I never knew what passed between them. He was very angry when he came home, and the next day he rode up to my father and mother, but they wouldn't have me back, they disowned me forever. I waited at your house till Mr. Paxton came home again; he was four days away, having lost the blazed track; he was obliged to camp out one night; and Mrs. Paxton endured me all that time, though sore against her will, and did give me things for the baby; but you, young ladies, I shall never forget your kindness. Miss Maggie read Scripture to me, – I had never heard a line from the Bible before, – about God being love, and cut out little things for the baby, and you brought me flowers and ginger bread nuts, and Miss Emmy, your dear little fairy of a sister, sang for me, and danced before me, and tried to make me smile; and you made a little pudding between you just for me, and I sat like a stone, hard and cold, and scarcely thanks you, and could not shed a tear, or give a smile; but often since I have thought of it, and blessed you all. At last Mr. Paxton returned, and John Smith with him."

"'If ye'll marry me, Nelly,' he said, 'I'll be a thrue and kind husband to ye, and if ever I desert you, may God desert me, and if ever I cast u this trouble to you may God remember my sins forever.'

"I consented to marry him, for I didn't care what I did; I hoped to die. Mr. Hurst came from Gibbeline that evening and married us."

"And Emmy and I were your bridesmaids," said Mary, "and wore our white frocks, and curled our hair; mamma didn't wish it at all, but we battled for it and papa upheld us, – how proud we were! Ah! how near the old time seems, and yet it is so long ago. Did Smith keep his word, – was he good to you?"

"He never reproached me; he was always kind when sober, and never struck me, or spoke of my past shame, even in drink. You kind happy little girls kissed me, and wished me joy, – wretched me, – and that broke me down, and made me cry, and I cried till the next day when Robbie was born. Mr. Paxton would have kept us all night, but your mother would not listen to it; your brother drove us six miles on our way to a little inn, and we stayed there a month."

"And we came to see you when the baby was three weeks old, - papa and Emmy and I," said Mary, "it was a lovely drive."

"You looked like an angel to me," said Mrs. Smith, "with your plump white shoulders and bright eyes, and cool, clean muslin frock;

and your little sister – how she danced at the sight of the baby, and she told me of another baby born at an inn, in a manger, and she would have this one in her arms all the time she was there, and took it out for your father to see, as he stood outside talking to Smith, and made him feel how heavy it was, and he kissed Robbie's hand. I think it's little things make people dear to us. Mr. Paxton lent Smith a hundred dollars, to begin the world with, but it touched me more than anything to see him kiss my child, and I'm sure it was the way Smith behaved to Robbie the first week of his life that made him dear to me, and not because he protected me and covered my shame. He used to sit with Robbie in his arms, by the bedside, day after day, and say he was the prettiest little fellow he ever saw, and the Queen herself might be proud of him, and he didn't believe Albert Edward, Prince of Wales, was half such a beauty when he was born.[127] When Robbie was two years old, Smith paid back part of the money to your father; he met him in Gibbeline by appointment, because Mr. Paxton feared his wife would know about it if he went to the house."

"Poor papa," said Mary, with a little laugh, "that's just like him."

"I thought you like him to-night, when you broke out upon Chip and told him your mind," said Mrs. Smith, with a smile.

"Perhaps I am a little, but I don't swear, and I'm not so much afraid of mamma as he was."

"He wouldn't take interest for the money, and that was kind, but what touched my heart most of all was his giving back two dollars to buy Robbie a frock, and when Smith said he had no taste in such things, being in truth afraid he would drink the money if 'twas left to him, Mr. Paxton bought it himself, scarlet French merino, and black braid to trim it, and a lovely little frock it made; I wish he could ha' seen him in it, with a little white bib over it. I'm sure if the Queen herself had seen him, she couldn't but ha' kissed him, for though the highest lady in the world, she is but a woman after all, and never a woman saw him at that age, but picked him up and hugged him. He had no shoes, but his little bare feet looked as pretty without, and to see him running to meet Smith at night, with his teeth gleaming, and his little rings of hair flying, every inch of him alive with joy, 'twould have moved anyone with a heart in their body. Do you mind this?" and she took from her pocket a worn and ragged baby's sock.

---

[127]King Edward VII was born 9 November, 1841.

"The very shoe – the first I ever made," said Mary, "he has worked his toe through the end of it. What a pleasure it was to make it, and Emmy made him a bib, and Maggie read Queechey[128] to us while we worked. We sat in the orchard under the trees; it seems like a vivid pleasant dream of another life – ah! it was another life indeed," and she sighed and rubbed the little ragged sock against her cheek.

"Where is your little sister?" asked Mrs. Smith, in a low voice.

"Dead, and my brother, too; and Maggie is not the Maggie of old, she is changed and soured; she formed such exalted ideas of people, and expected too much of them, more than it's in human nature to give, and then was disappointed when her idols fell; but as soon as one is down she sets up another, and will to the end, I suppose." She held the little sock to the light and straightened it out. "How proud we were of our work, Emmy and I, and she held him in her arms while I put them on, and he slept, the little warm bundle, unconscious of his honours, and we kissed the rosy, perfect toes before we covered them."

"And you kissed me, too," said Mrs. Smith, in a tremulous voice, "and so did your sister; you didn't despise the like o' me. And you brought me flowers, early roses and lilies o' the valley. Them flowers were the sweetest I ever saw, I couldn't bear to throw them away when they withered, and I dried them and laid them in my box; I have them yet."

"Ah! you are right, Mrs. Smith, there are no such roses now; they belong to by-gone, happy days, days of youth and hope for me, and not wholly miserable days for you, either; for that dear little baby was your first born, your very own, and though it brought you pain, it brought pleasure too; it seems incredible, impossible, that that tiny, pink, mouse-like creature could be this fellow here," laying her hand on his shoulder, "that I have held in my arms, and kissed his toes, and speculated about the colour of his eyes."

Robert turned his head and kissed the hand that touched him. He was strangely stirred and moved, the tears had been very near his eyes for a long time, and now they fell. He rose and put his arm about his mother, and pressed his lips to her cheek.

---

[128] *Queechey*, an 1852 novel by Elisabeth Wetherell, pseudonym of Susan Bogert Warner (1819-1885).

"I am glad you told me, mother," he said, "I *couldn't* love you more than I did before, that's impossible, you couldn't be dearer to me than you always have been, but if my birth disgraced you, mother dear, my life shall not; though I was born with shame, I will live with honour, God helping me; I will try and be worthy of you two good women; I wonder you didn't hate me, mother, because I'm the son of that man who deserted you – may evil haunt him all his days."

His mother shivered.

"Hush! Robert," said Mary. "I have been thinking of him for the last half hour, and I feel very sorry for him. Half the tears I have shed have been for him, poor hard-hearted, worldly, short-sighted man, who turned his back upon his blessings; who gave up his babe, his own flesh and blood, at once and forever, and despised the love of a woman. True love is so rare, Robert, and children such a source of pride and pleasure, that, seeing all he lost, I pity your father from the bottom of my heart, and so should you."

Mrs. Smith broke into sobs and sat down, and her son kneeling beside her, begged her to forgive him. "I will never speak ill of him again, mother; it was because he was so cruel to you, and not on my own account, and now I have been cruel too."

"I have sometimes wished he could see his son," said the mother, stroking his hair with her rough hand.

"God forbid, mother."

"You are so like him," she murmured.

"God forbid," said her son again, from his heart.

"It's only the shell, Robert," said Mary, soothingly, "and not the inner man, and even outwardly you are not altogether like him, for you have your mother's mouth," – he took her hand and kissed it gratefully – "but you do not use it with discretion, as she does," the lady went on. "I think that habit of kissing must be a trick of your father's; just think of that when you are tempted, Robin Adair."

"You hoped my son would be a blessing to me," said Mrs. Smith, wiping her eyes, "when you kissed him so long ago."

"And I am sure he has been," answered Mary, quickly.

"Yes he has, but once I wished him dead. He was just five, and that year Smith was hardly ever sober, and he used to take Robbie out of his bed and wrap him in a bit o' blanket, and take him into the tavern next door to sing to the men in the bar-room, and he would stagger in at three or four in the morning, with Robbie in his arms, and the little mite would be flushed with excitement, and too tired to sleep – excitement, not drink, for he promised me not to drink, and he kept his word, my poor, little, half-starved boy; and he would have his little fists full o' coppers the tipsy fellows had given him for singing, and would say 'dot money for you, mother.' God knows it was needed bad enough, for I had a babe scarce a week old, and little of anything in the house, but it went nigh to break my heart to take it, for I hated the way it was earned; I hated the life for him, and I prayed to God that he might die. Smith heard me one night, and it sobered him; he's never been on the spree for so long a time together since – it's not him that's bad, but the drink; that whisky is the curse of Canada, and there's no way of curing the evil till they give up making it."

"You had another child, Mrs. Smith? – I thought Tommy was the only one except Robert."

"I had four others. Three were carried out o' the house in one day with scarlet fever, and after two weeks of suffering Nelly died too – my only girl – and Robbie was as weak as a baby, but Smith and I cried to God for him, and it was like as if our prayer was answered, for that very day the trains were blocked with snow at Bezar,[129] where we lived then, and couldn't go on, and Mr. Meldrum was one of the passengers, and Smith fetched him to see Robbie, and he stayed three weeks at Bezar, and lent us money for comforts Robbie needed more than physic – may God reward him for it – and John James William was kind too, I never forget it. I lay it against his sins when I feel hard to him. He spent his wages for us, and stayed till I could get about after Tommy was born."

"Oh! Chip is a good fellow in many ways," chimed in her son, "though he's rough like."

"What kind of a person is Chip's wife?" asked Mary, "tell me."

Robert's face flushed with shame and annoyance. "He has no wife, Miss Mary."

"Well, the mother of his children, then," she said, a little impatiently, "do you know her? I am thinking of going to see her, and I will tell you why. Your brother has been here to-night with his boys; they are nice little fellows, – I like them. I think them well cared for,

---

[129]Bezar is Leslie's fictional name for Acton. See Introduction, page xxiv.

and not ill-taught. I think the mother of such children cannot be *all* bad, – what think you, Robert? Have you seen her?"

"More times than I can count." He paused for full a minute, and then looked up in Miss Paxton's face. "Miss Mary, you trusted me once, you took my advice, wasn't it for the best? Will you trust me once again, in this matter?"

His voice had a coaxing pathetic sound.

"I don't know, Robin, you are prejudiced against this woman, and think ill of her with reason, I doubt not, – and God forbid that you should ever think lightly of sin, – but I fear you would consider my feelings rather than her good. She has a soul to be saved as well as you and I, and she is not the only sinner in the case; your brother is much to blame, and the children, heaven help the poor little creatures, my heart bleeds for the children. I promised them some books, poor little things."

"I'll take them anything you like to send," said Robert.

"You hard boy, you don't want me to go."

"I'm not hard, Miss Mary, but I know them all better than you do, and I'm heart sorry that Chip forced his company upon you."

"Nothing happens by accident, Robert; it may be that God directed him here to get a rubbing up, and have things put before him in a new light. Perhaps I could do her good, poor, lonely, sinful woman. Why do you wish me to stay away, – is it for my sake only?"

"Yes," replied Robert, in a low voice, "just for your sake. I'm a poor ignorant fellow, as you know, but I love you, you cannot guess how much; you are as far above me as heaven is above the earth, I know, but I love you. I live for you; I could, if need be, die for you. If you had been married to-day, instead of Miss Llewellyn, I should lie down to-night with a broken heart. The highest castle I ever built, the sweetest dream I ever had was the hope of calling you my wife; but not to have you for my wife to-morrow would I consent to let you go to Chip's house; I am that set against it. I love you too well to think of it with patience. Don't go, dear Miss Mary. I don't ask anything but that, except that you'll forgive me for speaking so plainly, and not cut me out and out for loving you, for indeed I can't help it."

"Well, Robin, I won't go, since you are so much in earnest, and as for your love you'll get over that soon enough, and I hardly know whether to be glad or sad at the thought of it. Where did you get that ring on your little finger?"

"It's out o' place, Miss Mary, and you don't like to see me in it, do you? A brown rough fist and a ring don't look well together."

"It's the hand of a friend, it has fought for me, and helped me many a time. I do not despise it for being brown and rough with honest labour, but I am a daughter of Eve, Robin, I want to know the history of the ring; it looks like a handsome one."

He held out his hand, and she slipped off the ring with her slender white fingers, and took it to the light to examine it. It was of massive gold, beautifully chased with a large ruby for a knob, and inscribed within the circle were the words, "Her price is far above rubies."

"Is it your mother's ring?" she asked, with a startled look, "did it belong to your father?"

"It belongs to you, if you will accept it, and it never belonged to anyone else but me."

She put the ring on the middle finger and held it up to the light, then took it off and laid it in her open palm.

"How much did it cost you, extravagant boy?"

"Never mind," said Robert, "It's money well spent if it pleases you."

"Robert," she said, leaning against the mantle-piece and looking at him as he sat beside his mother, "a ring is a kind of fetter that implies much, and I can make no promise to love you better than I do now, for I do love you as a brother, a dear younger brother that I have held in my arms as a baby. I am but two years younger than your mother; I am fourteen years older than you, and that is too great a difference in age on the wrong side, setting aside other differences."

"*Other differences*," repeated our hero, with a keen glance of his brown eyes; "*Such as?*" inquiringly.

"You told me your story, Mrs. Smith," said Mary, suddenly turning to his mother, as if moved by a new impulse, "and I will tell you mine, and afterwards we will talk about the ring."

But we will leave Miss Paxton's story for another chapter.

Chapter Twenty-Five

"Dreams of my youthful days! I'd freely give,
        Ere my life's close,
All the dull day's I'm destined yet to live
        For one of those."

— Berenger[130]

MRS. SMITH, when Robert here was six years old, a gentleman
loved me and asked me to marry him, and I loved him – aye,
and do still. This ring of opals that I always wear he gave to me,
it has an inscription too, 'Ralph's love.' You shall see the extent of
'Ralph's love,' and mine. He was six years older than you are now,
Robert, when I first knew him, and just as unlike you as it's possible
to be. He was tall, with a quiet manner, a gentle voice, and an eagle
face, very dark eyes that flashed and sparkled when he was angry,
while yours, Robin, turn red and glow like a coal. His face was of
that kind that expresses much without speech, and he used to say little satirical, saucy things in dispraise of me, that were after all very
complimentary. He had a noble face, and the man himself was noble though proud and obstinate. I was very sad and lonely when I
first made his acquaintance, my little sister Emily had just died – she
married unhappily and died the first year of her marriage – John was
dead too, and Maggie away with her husband.

"My father had imbibed a prejudice against matrimony, he was
very cautious and careful about his last ewe lamb, and did not wish
me to marry, and mamma did not wish to lose my services. She

---

[130]Pierre-Jean de Béranger (1780-1857), "Garret," Father Prout a.k.a. Francis
Sylvester Mahony (1804-1866), trans.

thought if I married I ought to live with my parents all the same, and do their bidding. I was their last child, and she could keep my husband in order and rule me as of old. They had no reasonable reasons for objecting to Ralph as a suitor, but they sanctioned the engagement reluctantly, and they wished it to be a long engagement; whereas Ralph wished to be married at once, having more than a competency at his command. He was always urging the old Scotch proverb, 'Happy is the wooing that's not long a-doing;' but papa would shake his head in reply, and answer with the wise English saw, 'Marry in haste and repent at leisure.'

"I was not the Mary Paxton of to-day, or the Mary Paxton you knew so long ago, either, Mrs. Smith, but a very reserved young lady, shy with all gentlemen, but especially with Ralph. I never tried to converse with him in the daylight, only when I could not see his face could I talk to, or before him freely. Our habit of chatting by twilight, and singing duets by moonlight, annoyed both papa and mamma; they had very little patience with my shyness, their youth was so far away that they had forgotten the feeling, and made no allowance for it. The bloom is off the plum now, and really I had forgotten what it was to feel shy myself, till this young rogue of yours kissed me in the summer, and renewed the old, half painful sensation. In my heart I did not like the thought of living at home after marriage, but both parents decided that it should be so.

"Ralph was the engineer of the first railway that passed through Gibbeline,[131] his work lay near us at the time, and if we were married, he might come and see me once or twice a week as before; so they arranged that if he would marry me on those terms he should have me at once, if not he must wait after their death. Ralph, when mamma first spoke to him about it, would not agree to either proposal, but he differed from her respectfully, and did not lose his temper. We had been engaged six months; he had given me many a present and many a long drive and ride, but never alone. Whichever way we went, papa always found his business lay in that direction, and cantered along

---

[131]The first railway ran through Guelph in 1856. As Robert was six years old when Ralph proposed marriage to Mary, this places Robert's birth in 1850. We have already learned in Chapter 3 that Mary Paxton is 32 years old, and later, in Chapter 24 that Mary is fourteen years older than Robert. Therefore, Mary Paxton was born in 1836. From these details, the main actions of the novel are set in 1868 (see Introduction).

beside us, or took a seat in the same conveyance, if we were driving, or else mamma thought a drive would make her sleep better. We were never alone for more than ten minutes at a time, till one sunny autumn afternoon, when Ralph came unexpectedly to take me for a drive, and papa was out, and mamma had a needle-woman to look after, and could not get away. She let me go reluctantly, and made Ralph promise to bring me back before dark.

"At first I was so shy that the pleasure of being alone with him was almost pain; but his gentleness and delicacy soon set me at my ease; he avoided trying subjects, talked of the horse we drove, the scenery we passed, and told me of pretty places he had seen. Never shall I have such an afternoon again till I reach Hades, and have great strong wings to bear me through the sweet air of paradise, with the dear spirits gone before. Our horse was a good traveller, but we did not hurry; we drove fast or slow, as it pleased us; once we stopped outright, a bird sang so deliciously, and we sat at our ease and drank in the sweet melody, while the horse champed his bit, and pawed the ground, and a brook near by gurgled a soft accompaniment. We had started on a side line, but at last we turned into the main road to Cromaboo;[132] then Ralph told me he had bought a farm over-looking the railway track, and built a house upon it, that we were going to see it, and that it was to be my home for the next three years, while he superintended the railway. I timidly mentioned the wish of my parents that I should live with them.

"'Do you wish that?' he asked very gently. 'Would you rather be with them than with me alone?'

"'I would rather be alone with you,' I said simply and truly, but looking up at him, and catching the sparkle of the laughing dark eyes, I was instantly afraid of my own temerity, and ashamed of my avowal.

"You remember a very high hill before we reach Ostrander, crowned at the summit with a clump of maple trees? Not a vestige of a human habitation is there; but when I first saw it a large log house stood in the centre of the maple group; a little garden was fenced off at the back, and a spring in the hill side, forced through a wooden tube, played in the garden as a little fountain; aster and candy-tuft

---

[132]There are a number of side line roads that intersect with the main road (now Highway 124).

and mignonette bloomed thick about it. From that house you could see the then new line of the railway winding away for miles to the left, and the men at work upon it, now plainly seen, now hidden by the trees. All the hill in front is bare and smooth now, but then there were many stumps, and we had to wind our way slowly among them to reach the house. Not a soul was there but ourselves, the door stood hospitably open, and we went in. The house was furnished; every little wish of mine had been attended to, as if I had known about it and ordered it all; every whim in furniture or decoration was gratified. It was fairy-land to me. I ran from room to room, peeped into cupboards and closets, examined pots and pans with an interest I had never felt before.

"I had always thought I should like to live in a log house; here it was. I had always wished for a house without blinds, or carpets, where the sun might shine in freely, and yet so far away from other houses as to be quite private; – my dream was realized. I had longed, in a childish way, for an Indian basket rocking-chair; here it was. I thought I should like a tiny French clock under a glass globe, and a great Dutch clock to hang on the kitchen wall; and there they were, ticking away. I had wished for a little round table with a claw, a writing desk that stood on four legs, a great open fire-place, where you could burn whole cordwood logs without cutting; and now my wish was gratified. In my vanity, I had often wished for a looking-glass that would show me myself from head to foot, and a hand glass to see the back of my head; and when I went up stairs and peeped into the bed-room, there they were. I was startled at my own image, with Ralph behind me, but he took me by the shoulders and made me walk forward, and said it was not a true glass, – the reflexion did not equal the reality. I found a rustic book-case, with all my favourite authors, my pet stories and ballads, and others I had never read, which promised pleasure. I pried into cupboards, with exclamations of delight, finding a spice-box, and tins of rice and coffee, and sugar, and at last I came to pink egg-shell china. Such china as I had dreamed of, but never hoped to see; I caressed the cups like a baby with a new toy; they made my cup of happiness almost too full. I cried a little, and laughed a great deal; I lost all fear of Ralph, and felt at ease with him.

"'How good of you to think of me in everything,' I said, 'how did you come to know me so well? It is like a castle in the air, brought down to the earth.'

"He exacted a kiss as payment, – the only one I ever gave him, – and drew me gently within his arms, and begged me to come and be lady of the castle before the bloom wore off my new possessions; we talked about it till the setting sun shone red on our faces, and I promised to marry him that day fortnight, – 'I just want to come home here, I love this place so much.' I sighed as the sun disappeared that this sweet day was over.

"'You are tired, my pet,' he said, turning the face of his watch for me to see, 'it is tea-time.'

"'Let us light the fire and have tea,' I exclaimed. I had forgotten the promise to return home before dark; *he* remembered and should have reminded me, but who can love and be wise? He knelt before the fire and put a match to the dry wood, and in an instant it was crackling up the wide chimney. He fetched water from the fountain and filled the kettle, and hung it on a hook above the blaze; while I set forth cups and saucers, plates and knives and inquired for the caddy, and exclaimed with delight when I found the caddy spoon was just a scallop shell Ralph had stolen from my work box, only now it had a silver handle and my name engraved on it, and the tea spoons were tiny scallop shells to match, taken from the same place by the same thief, and I had never missed them. I gave him a bite for punishment. The bread was dry, so we made toast, cream we had none, or butter either, but we opened a pot of marmalade, and in searching for it came upon an owl that was a pepper box, and a cupid whose quiver contained salt instead of arrows. We were hungry, we were happy, but above all we were *young*; everything was *couleur-de-rose* to our eyes. The world was a dear old world, notwithstanding its thorns and thistles; the people in it were well meaning creatures on the whole, and, happily, far away from us just then; care and sin and sorrow were unknown, or forgotten for the time, and the log house was an Eden, the fabled happy valley perched on the top of a hill, with all trouble shut out and all happiness within it forever. We lingered till the moon rose, and brought a sudden remembrance of home before me.

"'Oh! Ralph,' I said, 'we promised mamma, – she will be angry; do get the horse at once.'

"He did not delay, and I was soon wrapped up and seated in the buggy. He led the horse down the hill, through the stumps, and not till he was seated by my side did I look back at the house, now far above us. The light of the fire shone bright through the windows as we drove swiftly away.

"A chill fear came over me, the tears rose to my eyes. I felt I had seen it for the last time and said so.

"'You dear superstitious little goosey,' said Ralph, 'you will spend many a happy day there, and you shall not be scolded tonight either, I will explain everything to them; they shall not say a harsh word to my pet,' and he put his arm about me, and drew my shawl closer to keep me from the chill night air. I wished the drive would last forever, but it came to an end all too soon. Papa and mamma were very angry because we were so late, and spoke harshly and rudely to Ralph, and he lost his temper and returned their remarks in kind. He went away at last, unable to convince them that we were not very much to blame. He called two days later, in the evening; we were all in the parlour when he came; he enclosed my hand in both of his for a minute, and was polite to papa and mamma, but cool and grave; he did not offer to shake hands, nor did they. He declined to sit down when asked, but leant against the chimney-piece, and throughout the interview commanded his temper, and so did my father, but mamma said very bitter things. Ralph began by saying he had come with an object; I had promised to become his wife in a fortnight, and he was most anxious that the marriage should take place; he was willing to make a very liberal settlement on me, but entirely unwilling to live with papa and mamma, and he said plainly, but courteously, that he would never consent to such an arrangement. I had told mamma about the house on the hill, and she scorned it; she would not let papa speak, but answered sharply:

"'You would take her to that log cabin on the hill, I suppose, to be left by herself and neglected, and frozen to death in the winter, and half starved – for where would you get provisions? Never, with my consent.'

"'Never, madam,' said Ralph, coolly, 'with your consent, or without it, for the house was burned to the ground the night Mary and I were there, and everything in it destroyed. I suppose a spark from the hearth kindled it.'

"I could not help crying for the loss of my castle in the air; both papa and Ralph were sorry for me, and I think my tears quenched the fire of their tempers; but mamma, who loves property better than people, was angry at Ralph's loss and the calm way in which he took it; she said it was clearly a stroke from Providence, and a plain warning to him not to teach children to disobey their parents. My father spoke then in a measured civil way, and said he was sorry for Ralph's loss, and that he had no objection to the marriage taking place at once if Ralph would consent to live with them and not take me away; he did not consider the condition a hard one. Ralph replied quietly and firmly that he would *not* consent to that, and he would not consent to an indefinite engagement, when there was no urgent reason to prevent an immediate marriage, nothing, indeed, but 'the whim of an unreasonable old lady,' – so he expressed it – and unless he could be married at once and take me away *quite to himself,* he would break off the engagement. I looked at him in an agony. He came and stood beside my chair and softly stroked my hair.

"'I should be unjust, unfair to you, Mary, if I married you on the condition your father and mother propose, you would have three people to obey. I want my wife to be my wife, and in taking up new duties to leave the old as the Scripture commands; I want you all to myself. If you love me as I love you, only death can separate us. You will marry me?'

"I pleaded for a longer engagement, and asked time to think of what he had said. He replied that he would come again to-morrow, or give me a week to consider it if I liked, but he refused to consent to a longer engagement, 'and though I love you dearly,' he added, 'better than I shall ever love another woman, I cannot promise to live single for your sake, if you decline to marry me now.'

"He said no more, but mamma said a great deal that I scarcely heard, so confused and stunned was I. He came the next week at my request, and I saw him alone. Youth had left me forever in the interval, I had become a woman all at once and had made up my mind. I told him the truth quite calmly, that I loved him so well I would never marry another man, but I would not take him on his terms, though I would live single for his sake all my life. He stayed an hour and urged me to marry him in defiance of papa and mamma, and said in that case he would wait till I was twenty-one years of age; but when he saw my mind was made up, he said 'then our engagement is at an end,' not angrily, but sadly. He would not take back his gifts, or give me mine. I took the ring from my finger, but he put it on again with a kiss; he held my hands in his at the last, and as the old sweet ballad says, 'looked in my face till my heart was like to break,'[133] then he went without a word. He turned at the gate and lifted his hat with a grace peculiar to himself. I watched his figure as far as I could see it; he walked rather slowly, but steadily; he never looked back.

"Three months later he married a lady of fashion, a Roman Catholic. She lived in Toronto, and his work still lay in our neighbourhood. In taking a long walk, one gloomy spring day I met him face to face. He was riding, he uncovered his head and checked his horse, and I - I could not meet him as an ordinary acquaintance, he had put an insuperable barrier between us - I bowed and walked on. I have never seen him since. After that walk I was very ill, and I was sent to England and France for my health, they had to part with me to save my life; I was away three years, and when I returned Ralph and his wife had left the country.

"When I told papa that I had rejected Ralph, he said 'you will never regret this, Polly, I shall always remember that you stood by your old father and mother,' and when he died he made no special provision for me, but left me to the tender mercies of mamma. And that, Mrs. Smith, is all my story."

"I have no patience with that man," said Robert, "he was not worth a hair of your head, he had no faith in him and no pity; he was worse than old Jacob, who, for all he was a cowardly two-faced chap, was yet man enough to serve fourteen years for his Rachel."

"Do not think lightly of Jacob, Robert. God met him by the way; he wrestled in prayer with his Maker and prevailed; he saw the ladder that reached from earth to heaven. And as for Ralph, poor fellow, I have heard his marriage is not a happy one; he has sown and must reap like the rest of us."

"I can't comprehend him; how could he leave you knowing that you loved him? He is a monster, and deserves the worst that can happen to him," said Robert, but turning his eyes as he spoke on the tired sad face of Miss Paxton, he was stricken with compunction, and added, "I didn't ought to have said that to pain you, but it is hard that you should care for him yet, and despise my love. I that would be content to work as your servant all my life, rather than marry another woman."

---

[133] by Lady Anne Barnard, née Anne Lindsay (1750-1825), "Auld Robin Gray," *The Universal Songster; or, Museum of Mirth* Volume 1 (1825): 141.

"I do not despise your love, dear Robert, or any love, God forbid that I should; there's little enough in the world. You are very dear to me, you jealous, naughty boy; you have brightened my life and made it happier, and I do not like to refuse your ring, but I can make no promise, you understand, if I take it, no promise but to be your friend always – your elder sister – and I claim no promise, Robin Adair; you may, and I hope will, love somebody better than me and make her a happy woman."

"Oh! do take it," said Robert, eagerly, "let me put it on your finger," and she did, with a smile and a sigh.

Chapter Twenty-Six

"A man's a man for a' that."
— Robert Burns[134]

"Turn Fortune, turn thy wheel, and lower the proud."
— Tennyson[135]

L ET any man who thinks the age of chivalry is past, come to Canada and see the gallant offices, and the pretty duties assigned to any cavalier who has charge of a lady, young or old, on a stormy winter day. First, he leads the lady forth, who – whatever the beauty of her figure upon ordinary occasions, – is now an unwieldy bundle of shawls and furs. He must lead her carefully, for her face is covered with several layers of silk and worsted in the form of veils and clouds, and she is, therefore, nearly blind. If the lady be young and active, like our heroine, she will, probably, scramble into the sleigh without much help, but if otherwise, he must hoist her deftly and cannily into her seat, and this requires some bodily strength, and great skill and delicacy of touch. This feat accomplished, he must arrange the hot bricks beneath her feet, and swaddle her up carefully and tightly in buffalo and bear skins, and if such are not to be had, a large patchwork quilt will answer the purpose, – and the first of his duties are at an end. I do not say that it is necessary to do all this with uncovered head; on the contrary, the gentleman in attendance may have his fur cap fastened firmly beneath his chin, and surmounted by an extinguisher hood, without any imputation on his gallantry, or good

---

[134]Robert Burns (1759-1796), "A Man's A Man For A' That" (1795).
[135]Lord Alfred Tennyson (1809-1892), "Enid's Song."

manners. Conversation is next to impossible till you arrive at the first halting place, some wayside inn, which even a temperance man will hardly disdain on a winter day, when the thermometer stands at twenty degrees below freezing point. Having conveyed his fair burden to the sitting room, and stirred the fire, and ordered something for her refreshment, and assisted her in undoing her voluminous clouds and veils, and hung them on chairs to dry, – for they will be frozen stiff with the fair one's breath, – having helped her off with her outer wraps, and removed her snow-stockings, – I know a lady who wears three pairs, – and placed them beneath the stove, or before the blazing fire, he must proceed to the kitchen, or bar-room, and see that the bricks are carefully re-heated. If the lady is prudish, and refuses to have her foot coverings removed, he must borrow a corn broom, and brush every particle of snow from them, or she will have cold feet for the rest of the journey, and that may affect her health, and will certainly affect her temper. All this accomplished, he may remove his capote and cap, and entertain his fair charge to the best of his ability, till the horses are refreshed and ready for the road again.

The lady in this case was Miss Paxton, and her cavalier the Cromaboo mail carrier, and as he was removing her over-socks, on bended knee, – Mary holding firmly by the chair in which she was sitting, for it required a smart tug to pull them off, – he said, "Why don't you wear cloth overshoes, Miss Mary, – they are very warm?"

"I detest them," she replied, "they make one's feet look like a Methodist parson's."

"I think you detest the Methodists too," said Robert, good temperedly.

"No, no, I am only acquainted with one, and that is yourself; how did you become a Methodist, by the bye?"

"To please mother. She likes the parson in Cromaboo, and he is a nice gentleman. I go with her, but I guess they wouldn't call me a Methodist now; I have been turned out, or suspended, or something, for bad conduct."

"Tell me about it please," said Mary, and don't say *guess*, Robin, it's a Yankee vulgarism, and I detest it as much as I do cloth overshoes."

"It was a bit of a row I had with a Methodist fellow, a painter. I lent him two dollars, and he didn't want to pay me back, and when I went to dun him, one night, he painted my best hat one side red and the other blue. I never knew, till I picked it up and stuck my fingers in the fresh paint. That put my Irish up, and I pitched into him, and they had me up about it at the next class-meeting, and when I said I wasn't sorry, they all agreed I was in a bad frame of mind. The other fellow said *he* was sorry, so I told him he had better pay the two dollars and give me a new hat, but he didn't, of course; he said he would pray for me. So they suspended me, or something of the kind, but I go to the Sunday-school yet, and Mr. Crutch, the parson, is very good to me, though he says I should have turned the other cheek."

"A new way of paying old debts," said Mary, laughing, "I approve of your conduct, Robin Adair."

They did not delay beyond what was absolutely necessary, as the mail had to push through in a given time if possible, and they were soon on the road again, a part of which was not yet dug out, though a gang of men were busy at work on it. At last they came to a part still impassable, but where two gangs of workers would soon meet. Robert stopped, seeing that it would not take more than ten minutes to make a passage for them, but a gentleman in a cutter on the other side was more adventurous; he assayed to push through, getting half way with great difficulty, and there he stuck. It occurred to him to get out of the cutter, for what purpose it is hard to say, and in doing so he upset, and was buried in buffalo robes and soft snow, amid a roar of laughter from the two gangs of workmen, who however went to his assistance. He was rescued and placed for the present in the Cromaboo stage to recover breath, while the men returned for the horses and cutter. Miss Paxton, seeing the poor gentleman in such a sad case, struggled to get her nose and eyes out of their many wrappings, and addressed him in a strain of polite condolence, hoping that he was not hurt, and saying that traveling was at present very unpleasant.

The stranger – who was encased in an immense fur coat – replied in very bad English with many bows and gesticulations, that he was not hurt, that he was on his way to Cromaboo in search of "Mees Lolwon, a lady he should see on beezness."

"Miss Llewellyn?" said Mary, inquiringly.

"Ah! yees, that is the name," he replied, with more bows.

"Then I am afraid you will have your journey for nothing, for she was married yesterday to her cousin Mr. Harry Llewellyn, and is gone to the States for the honeymoon."

The gentleman threw up his hands in great dismay and hoped she had been misinformed.

"Oh! no, I was bridesmaid," said Miss Paxton, smiling, "but you will find her uncle if you go on."

Senor Pedro Diaz was sorely disappointed, for he had brought the news of Miss Lavinia's fortune in person, because he was a bachelor, and intended proposing for the heiress himself, and carrying her back to her native Brazil, if possible. It was vain to keep the secret any longer, so he told the bright-eyed, sympathetic lady that he had come to give Miss Llewellyn joy of a great fortune, and had hoped to make his compliments in person, and condole with her on the death of her aunt.

Miss Paxton regretted that he had not arrived in time for the wedding festivities, and advised him to go on, as the track was now clear, and see Mr. Llewellyn; which he decided to do.

When they reached the next stopping place, and were warming themselves by the parlour fire, Robert said, "I am glad Miss Lavy is to be so rich, but I wonder if Mr. Harry could have had a hint of the fortune?"

"Robert, I am almost ashamed to admit it, but I had the same thought. It seems so strange that he delayed the wedding so many times without assigning a reason for it, and came in such a hurry at the last. Is that your reason for thinking – for being suspicious?"

"No, it was something Mr. Meldrum said yesterday. If Mr. Harry knows, Mr. Meldrum knows too."

"For the honour of manhood, I hope they don't know," said Mary, "it would be dreadful to be married for money – the very thought of it troubles me – I hope she may be happy – I know Frank Llewellyn can act meanly, but I thought better of Harry; perhaps it's only the wickedness of our own hearts, after all, to think so."

"It may be," said Robert, doubtfully, "I hope so. It's done, anyway, and can't be undone; I think women have a poor time of it in this world and are often very badly used."

Mary, who was standing near him, turned and looked in his face at this remark; the lad seemed weary, and had dark circles beneath the eyes.

"You didn't sleep last night," she said quickly, "your mother's story kept you awake."

"Her story and yours did, Miss Mary."

"Well, dear Robin, don't be unhappy about it, no man can help his birth or change his parents, but he *can* make his life what he will, he can live a noble life and be a gentleman in spite of the bar-sinister."[136]

"I am so ignorant that I do not know what a bar-sinister means, and for being a gentleman, that takes education, Miss Paxton, and a different life from mine."

"There are some kinds of wood that will not take a polish, Robert, and there are men in the world that no kind of education or example could turn into gentlemen; but I am sure there is the right material in you, and even though the history of your birth is a sad one, and I cannot respect your father, yet I think your position happy after all – let us look at the bright side. You are young and healthy, and you have a noble mother, and you live in a country where if a man is ignorant, it is just his own fault and he has nobody else to blame, for there are good schools, and cheap books, and good wages. You have a great talent for music, and a fair ability, I do not doubt, for other things as well, you have refined tastes and a warm heart, and friends who love you dearly – what more would you have, Robin Adair?" kindly patting him on the shoulder, "many a nobleman would gladly change places with you, I doubt not, to have your fresh unsoiled youth; many an old weary, worthless man would be glad to take your young life and prospects, even though a patched coat went with it. Now for the bar-sinister – you were telling me about the Free Masons, the other day, and their symbols, their compasses, death's heads, and other rubbish – well, a gentleman's coat of arms, or shield, is simply a symbol or sign telling those who understand heraldry the noble families into which he has married, or the deeds he has done; oftener the deeds his ancestors did long before he was born. Very likely your father had a shield; many a craven and many a scamp is entitled to bear arms, as well as many noble and good men. Well, the baton sinister is a line, or band, running through the middle of the shield, and marking the gentleman who bears the coat of arms as illegitimate, or some

---

[136]bar-sinister = from *barre sinsiter* (French), a heraldic term for a narrow strip running from the upper right to the lower left of a coat of arms, sometimes used to indicate fatherless birth. Sir Walter Scott is credited with giving literature the phrase "bar sinister," which has become a metonym for bastardy.

ancestor before him. Many a noble coat of arms is marred by that line of shame, the baton sinister. Did you ever hear of William the Conqueror?"

"Yes, the first king of all England together, that's about all I know of him."

"Our Queen is descended from him. He was illegitimate, yet a very successful man in a worldly point of view, though a merciless and evil one; and, Robert, to come nearer to our own day, the natural son of that worthless bigot, King James the Second, was as noble a soldier as ever buckled on a sword – you must read about him. And there is another case that always touched me greatly; a wee, sickly child was born to a worthless French woman of noble birth; its father was a nobleman, and it was a child of shame, and they, cruel, heartless wretches, deserted it and left it on a church door step to perish, yet it lived, though grudged its life, and became a celebrated scholar. When this despised child was a man, colleges bestowed honours, and foreign sovereigns invited him to their courts, and pensions and favours were heaped upon him, and D'Alembert[137] was worthy of it all, for he was more than a scholar, he was a grateful and honest man. Then there is Jeptha,[138] I read his story in the Old Testament, and see that God himself did not disdain to use him for his service, and answered his prayers. Take courage, dear Robert, and believe me, though men are willful and wicked, God never makes mistakes, and being here, you have just as much right to enjoy life and improve it as the Governor General. Only the hopelessly wicked are born in vain, and only a very narrow-minded and foolish person would think worse of you because of your birth, or your mother, either. See how John Smith and my father and Mr. Meldrum regarded your mother; the good opinion of such people is worth having; and for the rest of the world, let them go. Besides I don't suppose many people know the history of your birth."

"More than you would think, Miss Paxton, I have been taunted with it more than once. One time Chip licked a man well for making

---

[137]Jean-Baptiste le Rond d'Alembert (1717-1783), a noted French mathematician, physicist and music theorist. He was the illegitimate child of writer Claudine Guerin de Tencin and the chevalier Louis-Camus Destouches. He was abandoned immediately after his birth by his mother on the steps of the Saint-Jean-le-Rond de Paris church. According to custom, he was named after the patron saint of the church.

[138]In Chapter 21 the name is spelled correctly, Jephthah.

me angry; he said" – Robert stopped in time, – he was going to say, "he said I was born on the wrong side o' the blanket."

"Well, never mind what he said, Robin Adair, *I* say you are to be an honest man, and a gentleman, and make your foster father a proud man, and comfort and bless your mother, and help to educate Tommy, and be happy and useful, and manage my money matters when I am old, and be my best and dearest friend always, you won't disappoint me, will you?" and she took his brown hand in both her own, Tears welled up to his eyes.

"Ah! you know how I love you," he said, "if it rested with me you should never be disappointed again."

"Well, then you must sleep well to-night, and be cheerful to-morrow, and not let your mother see how this thing has pained you, and be true to her, because your father was false; and be yourself again, and do your best for the sake of a better Father, who permitted your birth, and died for you in love. It doesn't matter how a man comes into the world; how he lives in it, and goes out of it, is the test. Every man is made in the image of God, and there is a spark of Deity in him. God has 'a desire to the work of His hands,' and will help those who ask him."

Robert was dumb for a time, from excess of feeling, but he kissed the thin fingers that held his many times, and when he spoke at last, it was only a muttered "God bless you," as he went out to his horses.

A week later the news of Mrs. Harry Llewellyn's fortune appeared in the *Hamilton Spectator*,[139] and was read by hundreds of families in "that great little city," as Mary Paxton termed it. Mr. Frank Llewellyn read the paragraph to his wife at breakfast, and she screamed as if the house had been on fire. A week later, and Mrs. Harry returned from her wedding tour, and after a flying visit to Cromaboo, took up her abode in Hamilton, and made a great sensation there. She called on Mrs. Paxton as she passed her house, and the old lady kissed her on both cheeks, and gave her a glass of wine, out of her best cut-glass decanter, never brought out but upon the most state occasions, and said she had always seen something very remarkable in the girl; and when the train stopped at the Hamilton station, there stood Mr. Frank Llewellyn, with uncovered head, ready to assist her from the car; and before she had recovered breath, from

---

[139] *The Hamilton Spectator* newspaper began in 1846.

this surprise, Eleanor clasped her in both arms, exclaiming, "You dear, dear little creature, can you ever forgive me for my wicked conduct, when I last saw you? Believe me, dear Lavy, it was nothing but neuralgia that made me so cross, and I have been heartbroken about it ever since, and ashamed to write and ask your pardon." And after this Eleanor would have carried bride and bridegroom home to dinner, but that Lavinia was determined to go to her own house; and only a few days succeeding this public reconciliation, Eleanor called on the bride, who kept her half an hour waiting before she would see her. Harry described the scene to Mr. Meldrum in great delight.

"By George, you know," he said, "I began to grow nervous, least Eleanor should get mad and smash something, but, do you know, she was as sweet and civil, and begged dear Lavy not to rise, – she had stretched herself on the sofa, through pure insolence, – and treated me with the greatest respect, not patronizing me a bit."

Then he went on to tell about the visit of the Portuguese gentleman. "I couldn't see him, you see," he said, "lest he should recognize me, and, by George, he came so unexpectedly, that I was obliged to pop into a closet in the drawing room, to avoid him, and Lavy thought I was out, and asked him to dinner, and delayed it for me, hoping I would return; but I didn't, and precious hungry I was, I can tell you. I heard all they said, but couldn't understand a word, for they spoke Portuguese all the time, and Lavy laughed and cried too, and she told me it did her heart good to hear 'the dear old music,' meaning his jabber. You were right, Meldrum, if that wizened little beggar had turned up earlier, I should have been just no where; she'd have married him and gone off to Brazil. By George, you know, it made me feel awfully queer to hear them. I realized the whole thing, and how nearly I missed it, and I felt like the fellow in the story, who fainted, you know, who passed over a precipice, or something of that sort, in the night, you know, without knowing it; I'll be hanged, if I didn't," said Harry, quite earnestly.

Mr. Meldrum laughed till the tears rolled down his cheeks. "You'll never be hanged now, Harry," he said, "I shouldn't wonder if they make a judge of you yet, and then you will hang others, my boy."

Four hundred people left their cards for Mrs. Harry Llewellyn, and desired the honour and pleasure of her acquaintance; the little body was radiant with joy and pride, every step was one of triumph.

Week by week Mary Paxton received letters asking her advice about silks, laces and ribbons, and begging her to come to Hamilton and spend a month with her loving Lavinia; but Mary steadily declined, mamma was ailing, she said, and didn't wish it; in the summer she would come.

Chapter Twenty-Seven

"Life is a frost of cold felicity
And death the thaw of all our vanity."

– Old Author[140]

A FEBRUARY thaw, a soft, south wind blowing, every tree and branch and twig covered with rime, and the bright sun shining and converting the cold hoar frost to thousands of sparkling diamonds and opals.

As Robert drew near Mrs. Paxton's and blew his horn, the glittering frost work made the country before him look like fairy land. "What a day it would be for a wedding," he said, as he took the horn from his mouth, "all the world in white and every bush in bridal attire."

"You have marriage on the brain, Bob," said Mr. Meldrum, who was his sole passenger, "but the reality will take the romance out of you."

Mrs. Paxton's door opened, and Mary ran down the steps with an anxious face; the sun was shining in her eyes, and she did not for the moment see her brother-in-law.

"Good morning, Robert; mamma is not well, and I want you to send Mr. Meldrum to see her, just as if he came by accident."

"Here he is by accident," said the doctor, lifting his hat, "how is my pretty sister this morning?"

"Well enough, thank you; could you come in and see mamma now, or have you pressing business in Gibbeline?"

---

[140]John Marston (1576-1634), *The Malcontent* (1603/4): Act 5, Scene 6, Lines 44-46, spoken by Aurelia.

The doctor's only business was to get away from the tongue of his Margaret, but after a thoughtful pause, he said, "I will set aside all my business for to-day and come in."

"That is very kind," said Mary, gratefully, and Mr. Meldrum went in and chatted with his mother-in-law, and felt her pulse, and professed to regret that he had not brought Margaret, as the day was so fine. He was rather a favourite with the old lady, though she abused him behind his back, and disapproved of his debts as much as Mrs. Meldrum herself. His healthy manly beauty pleased her, the very calves of his legs were in his favour, and a kind of letter of recommendation to Mrs. Paxton, who hated sickly people, and pale people; in whose opinion there was only one invalid who had any business in the world, and that was herself. Mr. Meldrum's visit cheered her, but it excited her, and the arrival of Dolly's mother to borrow a flat iron annoyed her greatly. She kept her temper until the stage arrived, and Mr. Meldrum had gone, then she proceeded to scold Mary in no measured terms.

"This place might as well be a tavern at once," she exclaimed, "it *is* a tavern without the profit, if one person comes another comes; we might as well put up a sign and call it the Blue Boar, or the Red Lion, and be paid for our pains."

"But you were glad to see Mr. Meldrum, mamma," said Mary.

"Glad! what good did he do me? He ate half a bottle of Governor's sauce,[141] and more beef than we would consume in a week, and these things cost money; you will know that when you are without both money and food, and let me tell you that will be pretty soon when I am gone. It is nothing but wicked extravagance, and selfishness to burn the large coal in the parlour; there will be nothing but small coal to burn, when I am well enough to sit there again; and there is wood enough used in this house in one week to last a poor family the whole winter. I don't know where the money is to come from, I am sure, for the people don't pay their interest as they used to, and that dawdling wench, Dolly, is another nuisance, and a great expense. If you were a proper woman instead of being the poor, miserable, sickly thing you are, you could do all the work of this house, and find it a pleasure; I should, when I was your age. Accomplish-

---

[141] Green Tomato Pickle was known as "Governor's Sauce," traditional in most provinces of Canada.

ments! what's the good of them? If I had to bring up children again they should read nor write, they should not know so much that they know nothing. You may amuse yourself once too often, with your fires late at night, to warm you while you draw and write, and be burnt in your bed when I am gone. Are you sure that you didn't put out hot ashes; It would be a good thing for you if you were carried out feet foremost before I died, and you may be, for you are a miserable looking wretch; no wonder you never married, a man must have a taste for a bag of bones, who looked twice at you. No wonder Ralph Oliver changed his mind."

Mary made no answer, and there was a long pause.

"What is that noise?" said Mrs. Paxton, sharply, at last, "oh! Dolly turning out the cats, I suppose; one of them ought to be shot, they eat as much as a child, and never catch anything. Go and send that dawdling girl to bed, and give her a snuff, and not a whole candle to burn, – I can tell you that if either you or Dolly Trimble lived in an English house you would be dismissed in three days, – yes, in three days, – for extravagance, – and when you have got rid of her, come back and help me off with my clothes, for I'm very tired of them."

Mary obeyed, and when she returned found her mother scolding about her gown. "I will rip it out, every stitch to-morrow," she said, "and have it made over again, you and that fiend of a needle-woman laid your heads together to make me look ridiculous, and she professes to be religious too; all I can say is if such people as *that* go to Heaven, I don't want to go, – a woman who doesn't know how to make a gown, Heaven would be no heaven to me, with such creatures."

"In my Father's house are many mansions," quoted Mary, with a sigh.

"I'm glad of it," the old lady retorted sharply, "for I am sick of these hateful people, and God would not be a just God to put me with them. I *couldn't* do the things they do. I couldn't rob and cheat and take money I had never earned for work that has to be done over; and you conspire with these people to waste my substance; you were lending that woman the flat iron to-day, without consulting me, you would never have told me if I had not caught you."

Mary began to brush her hair, which had fallen down when she took off her cap, and this diverted her a little.

"Nobody would pronounce me a coarse old woman, who saw my hair," she said, "see how fine it is; it is like a hank of floss silk, although it's white."

"I think white hair very pretty," said the daughter.

"Yes, it's only fools who wear wigs – there, that will do – go to bed at once, and don't sit up and waste the coal oil; and give me toast for my breakfast to-morrow, toast and coffee, with *very little* sugar mind, I grudge the sugar for I don't know where the money is to come from to buy it. Have you locked the doors?"

"No, but I will at once," replied her daughter.

"Do, I don't want to be knocked on the head; and throw down the mat at the door, for I feel a draught. Don't wake me before nine – good night."

As Mary re-entered the parlour she encountered Mr. Meldrum, and could scarcely refrain from uttering a cry of astonishment.

"What has brought you back?" she asked in alarm.

"I did not like Mrs. Paxton's symptoms to-day, and I thought I would return and stay the night," he replied. "If she sleeps well I will go away in the morning without seeing her, not to alarm her. I had tea at Thompson's Inn[142] and walked back."

"If you think her life in danger she ought to be told," replied Mary, "it's a dreadful thing to go into eternity unprepared."

"If you told her suddenly it might bring on a paralytic attack," replied the doctor; "the least ill could do would be to keep her awake all night."

"But to-morrow?" said Mary.

"We will see about it," he returned, "I do not think it advisable."

"As the tree falls so it must lie through all the days of eternity," said Mary, with solemn eyes.

The doctor shrugged his shoulders. "A gloomy thought, quite unfit for the ears of an invalid; only cheerful things should be talked of in a sick room."

"Cheerful things," she echoed. "Do you know, Mr. Meldrum, you shock me? You are like the woman who nursed Sir John Falstaff,[143]

---

[142] The location of Thompson's Inn is unknown.

[143] Sir John Falstaff is a fictional character who appears in three plays by William Shakespeare; *Henry IV*, Part 1 and Part 2, and *The Merry Wives of Windsor*.

and told him he should not think of God *to comfort him*, no need to trouble himself with any such thoughts yet."

"I feel the full force of the compliment," said Mr. Meldrum, with a smile.

"If she had a fit, could you do anything for her?" asked Mary, presently.

"Not much at her age; it was for your sake I returned that you might not be alone. You had better go to bed, if I hear the least sound I will waken you. I have locked the doors."

"You cannot lock out the King of Terrors – poor mother. I will not go to bed, I couldn't sleep after what you have said; but we mustn't talk," she added.

This dialogue had been carried on in the lowest possible tone. Mr. Meldrum took a volume of Scott's poems from the book case.

Mary opened the Bible, having first opened the door wide opposite to her mother's room. The hours passed slowly; the clock struck nine, ten, eleven – absolute stillness reigned. Mary took a rag she had got for the purpose, and softly fed the fire with more coal; the outer air grew warmer, the eaves began to drip – the clock struck twelve. As it ceased striking they both heard a slight, gurgling sound. Mary took the hand-lamp, opened the door, and passed swiftly and silently into the bed-room. Mrs. Paxton's head had fallen over the side of the bed, her face had a strange, unnatural look. Mary set down the lamp, and lifted her head tenderly back to the pillow.

"Mamma! dear mamma," she said. There was a pitiful, startled look in the old woman's face as her eyes turned on her daughter's, as suddenly followed by blankness and vacancy. She never spoke again, and by six in the morning all was over.

Chapter Twenty-Eight

"I am going that way to temptation where prayers cross."
                                    – *Measure for Measure*[144]

AFTER Robert had set down Mr. Meldrum at Mrs. Paxton's door, on that soft, February day, which was to be her last in this world, he trotted gaily into Gibbeline, blowing his horn as usual in the high street, and unconscious of any good or evil that might await him on this day, more than any other that had gone before it. He knew indeed that his period of service would soon be at an end, as his master, on the strength of Mrs. Harry's good fortune, was going to give up the mail and retire to Hamilton, but this made him none the less zealous in the discharge of his duty, and when he saw two gentlemen regarding him curiously as he came out of the post office after delivering the mail, he took a second glance at them and advanced to meet them. One, who was short and stout, he knew to be Mr. Jackson, the most skillful and successful lawyer in Gibbeline; the other, whom he regarded as a probable passenger, was taller, and a stranger.

"Good morning, gentlemen," said Robert, with his brightest smile, displaying his white, even teeth, and a dimple, as he spoke.

"Are you Robert Hardacre Smith, the regular Cromaboo mail carrier?" asked Mr. Jackson, and the other gentleman touched his hat, rather to our hero's surprise, who felt it a point of politeness to return the compliment, and removed his cap and replaced it again with that quick, easy grace which was as much a part of him as his shining hair and bright eyes.

---

[144]William Shakespeare, *Measure for Measure*: Act 2, Scene 2.

"Yes, sir," he said, in answer to Mr. Jackson, "the stage leaves at two."

"Ah! does it?" said the lawyer. "Will you call at my office before two, then?"

"Certainly, sir – one passenger or two – any luggage?"

The gentlemen exchanged glances, and Mr. Jackson was about to reply, when Robert's horses, thinking it was time for their stable and oats, trotted briskly away. In vain he called "whoa" after them, it was a new illustration of the old proverb, "None so deaf as those who won't hear," they only quickened their pace, and trotted faster. So Robert, with a hasty "I will call without fail," ran after them. Swiftly, freely, gracefully the lad ran, notwithstanding the impediment of the old military great coat, now embellished with sundry patches of a brighter colour; and as he sprang to his perch, rewarded his ponies with a flick or two of the whip for their impudence.

Both gentlemen watched him till he disappeared round a corner, then Mr. Jackson said, "Well, I suppose he will come – would you like me to send a clerk to remind him?"

"No," replied the other, "he will come, I am sure," and they walked slowly on, Mr. Jackson looking like what he was, a well dressed, intelligent man, as dissimilar as possible from his companion, who was unmistakably a gentleman, yet remarkable for nothing at a first glance but grace of movement and ease of manner.

Dr. Johnson pronounces a gentleman "a man of birth," and the definition is well enough as far as it goes, but a man must be more than well-born to be a gentleman, and I have known men who were not men of birth, and yet gentle and noble men. But when a man is well-born and well-bred, when he is well educated, and polished in manner, as much above meanness of conduct as he is above rudeness of speech, then he is certainly a gentleman; and if you add to this that kindness of heart and thoroughness of principle which spring from a knowledge and love of God, you have a gentility that will last when the earth "is removed like a cottage," and "the heavens are no more." Such a gentleman was Mr. Llewellyn, but the one to whom I am about to introduce you was quite a different kind of gentleman. A difficult person to describe, because entirely free from point or angle of any kind, not even remarkable for being remarkably common place. Neither tall nor short, stout nor thin was he, neither plain nor handsome, neither young nor old. A fair man, with rather grey hairs, and slight side whiskers, a natural unaffected manner that you could not call either cool or warm, that claimed nothing from you and yet had a kind of command in it, from the fact that the gentleman seemed to expect courtesy as his due; a man you would no more think of taking a liberty with, than you would of pulling the Queen's nose; a man who, with all his careless courtesy of manner, impressed even obtuse and conceited people with a feeling that it wouldn't do to go too far with him; a man who expected obedience to his wishes as a thing of course, and exacted it without a word or an effort. Thus, when he intimated to Mr. Jackson's clerk, in his master's absence, that the fire needed more coal, and the young man replied, "I'll send Tom to put some on when he comes in, sir," he did not repeat his request, but simply placed his double eye-glass on his nose, and looked at the speaker, and John Anderson, without knowing why, immediately left the deed he was copying and put on more coal himself.

"Ah! thank you," said the gentleman, carelessly, as the clerk took another glance at him, rather wondering at himself for what he was doing. It was real, not studied carelessness, his mind being occupied with other things; presently he removed his outer coat, feeling the fire he had desired too warm, and at that moment Mr. Jackson entered.

"You are a little before the time, Sir Robert," he said with great respect.

"I suppose I am impatient," replied the other, with a smile, and they retired to the inner office, with a command to John Anderson to show in the Cromaboo mail carrier when he came. It was ten minutes to two before his arrival was announced by a great jingling of bells, and a blast of the stage horn. Then he appeared in the outer office with a quick, bright glance round the room, and the question, "Gentlemen here for the Cromaboo mail?"

"Yes, go inside," said the clerk.

He tapped at the door, a business-like, imperative tap, and entered immediately. Seeing both gentlemen without great-coats or hats, he felt a little annoyed at their tardiness, thinking in his heart, "It's nothing but pride and impudence in them." He said aloud, civilly, but imperatively, "Sorry to hurry you, gentlemen, but I must be up to time with the mail – any luggage? I leave at two sharp."

"Could you not wait a little longer?" said the stranger, with a smile.

"Not for the Queen herself," replied the lad promptly. "Mr. Jackson knows it's against the law to delay the mail."

"Well, it wants ten minutes to two yet," replied the gentleman, looking at his watch. "I am not going by the mail, but I had a word or two to say to you."

"An order," thought our hero.

"Shall I leave the room, Sir Robert?" asked the attorney.

"Oh! certainly not," returned Sir Robert, with easy civility, and yet he seemed to hesitate about the word he had to say, and pondered instead of speaking; and Mr. Jackson, stepping noiselessly behind Robert, turned the key, and removing it from the door hung it on its nail.

Our hero stood and waited, half blind with the sudden transition from the dazzling snow and sunshine to the dim office, and wishing the gentleman would hurry up. Presently his bright eyes grew accustomed to the light, and he caught the expression of Sir Robert's face.

"Well sir," he said, rather impatiently, "time's passing."

"I hope you will pardon me for what I am about to say," began Sir Robert, "I do not put the question from a spirit of impertinence, but I would like to know how you came by the name of Hardacre – I understand your name is Robert Hardacre Smith."

The lad's face flushed crimson with surprise and annoyance, but he answered at once, from a sudden angry impulse he could not have explained, "I was christened Robert Hardacre after a very worthless man who was once dear to my mother."

For a minute there was a silence that could be felt in its still intensity, then Sir Robert, who had been standing with his back to the window, came a step nearer to the stage driver, and leant with his arm against the mantle-piece.

"He is your father," he said.

"Well," retorted Robert, with sparkling eyes, and a fierceness that had something threatening in it, "I cannot help that, God knows! Who are you, and what do you mean by speaking in that way; I am not a-going to take insult from any man living."

Another instant of silence that seemed much longer, then Sir Robert said, "I am your father."

The lad recoiled a step, and turned so pale that he alarmed both Sir Robert and the lawyer, who hastened forward with a chair.

"Sit down, my boy," said the baronet, in his gentle tone of command, "and tell me how is your mother?"

This speech brought the blood back to Robert's face, he grasped the chair by the back and leant against it trembling. "I will neither sit nor stand at your command," he said. "How do you *dare* to ask for my mother, if you are the man who injured her, who basely deserted her and left me to be born on the road side, as I should ha' been but for the charity of a stranger – you" – he took a hard breath and then went on. "If you are my father, why do you seek me now? You never cared to look at my face when I was a helpless child, and I never thought – I hoped I should never see yours. Do you come to disturb my mother after all these years, and make her miserable again, you that destroyed her innocence when she was only a child, and nearly took her life? What is your object in coming back – tell me that, if you are Robert Hardacre?"

Sir Robert was a good deal disturbed by this attack, and his colour went and came almost as much as his son's; he answered with an effort to speak calmly, which was not quite successful, and his words sounded truthful.

"I came with no evil intent – I came to see you, and to see if I could help you."

"Help me!" echoed Robert, scornfully, "It's rather late to begin, I think. I can get my own living now, and need nobody's help; and if I did – if I was a helpless cripple – I would not take a penny of yours – I would not have your blood in my veins if I could help it."

His voice shook, his anger came from eyes as well as tongue, for it now took the form of two great tears, which he brushed from his cheeks scornfully. This culmination was so very boyish, that Mr. Jackson, an indifferent spectator, was tempted to smile at it, and it certainly gave Sir Robert an advantage he would not otherwise have had, for while the lump in the boy's throat choked him too much to let him bring forth more than a hard sob or two, his father spoke slowly, yet with a kind of eagerness that showed his earnestness. Well might David pray not to have the sins of his youth remembered against him; Robert, in his youth and his pain, did not know – could not guess, how bitter, how terrible were the words he hurled at his father, or the pain it cost the elder man to reply to him.

"I see you are much prejudiced against me," he said, "and I suppose it is natural. I do not wish to defend my conduct to your mother;

it was very bad, but there are two sides to every question. I did *not* desert her. She came to me and I would have taken care of her in her illness, but she deserted me. She left me and I did not know about her for four and twenty hours. I was very anxious and troubled about her. When I heard of her again it was through an old gentleman, a Mr. Paxton, at whose house she was; he told me harsh truths, much as you have now. I was young and hot headed; he made me very angry. When I heard of her again, a few days later, she had married Smith, whose name you bear." He paused and took a long breath. "I was so jealous that it is a matter of wonder to me since, that I did not put a bullet in him. I saw the man, and offered him money; I had little enough then, and he refused to take it, – you may ask him if I do not speak the truth. We quarrelled and fought. Your mother was very ill at the time, – it was the day after your birth, – the doctor, a lad named Meldrum, said it would cost her life if I saw her. I did not think much about you, though I saw you. I deserted you, – I admit that but remember I had no claim over you in the law after your mother had married Smith, and the doctor said she was so ill that her love for you was her sole chance of life. When I left the country I meant to return some day and look after you, – hell is paved with good intentions, they say, – I did not, till now."

Something of the bitterness and pain of this retrospection came from the man's heart to his face, as he concluded, and was seen by his son through his angry tearful eyes; it smote him with a compunction he could not account for, and softened him towards his father. There was another pause and the town clock struck two.

"Do you mean," asked Robert, "that you would have married my mother, if Smith had not?"

Another pause, and then Sir Robert said, "No, I had no such intention, but I would have taken care of her and you."

Robert turned to the door and gave it a slight shake. "Open that door, Mr. Jackson," he said in a low voice.

"If Sir Robert Hardacre wishes it," replied the lawyer.

"*I* wish it," said the lad, "and if you don't open it instantly, I'll crack your skull with your own ruler," and he seized that weapon as he spoke. The lawyer retreated behind his desk in alarm, and the baronet stepping forward took the key from its nail and unlocked the door.

"I think you had better come to me at two to-morrow," he said, "if you do not, I shall be obliged to see your mother."

"Is that a threat?" asked Robert, facing him fiercely.

"No, no, no, my boy, I would rather not see her if it could be avoided; I want to help, not to injure you, – I'm very sorry to pain you. I have no power to compel you to come, but I wish it, – it may be I have no right to ask it, – but I do wish it very much."

Robert looked at him with eyes full of anger and trouble, and left him without a word.

When the seed is in the heart I do believe that love will spring up as suddenly as a mushroom does from the earth. Sir Robert went to the window in an eager kind of way, and saw his son spring to his seat and drive off rapidly, and then he made a speech which astonished Mr. Jackson, who thought the young cub had offended past pardon.

"Poor boy," he said, with a sigh, "how happy he was this morning and now he is angry and sad at heart, – he is a lad of great spirit."

"He is a young devil," said the lawyer, with whom the scene of the ruler still rankled, and who was a crusty little man at the best, and no sycophant. Sir Robert laughed as if it had been a compliment.

"Very true, Mr. Jackson," he said, "your discernment does you great credit."

This was spoken with so much sincerity that Mr. Jackson was not sure whether it was satire or not, and he made no answer, not knowing in truth what to say; and presently Sir Robert donned his top coat and took leave.

"Do you think he will come to-morrow?" asked the lawyer, as the baronet took up his hat and stick to depart.

"I will walk down in case he should, and I think if he does I will see him alone. Good afternoon, Mr. Jackson – pray do not come out," and Sir Robert bowed himself out at the door, and closed it. Mr. Jackson went to the window, and watched him walk slowly up the street.

Robert's thoughts were in such a tumult, that for the first time since he knew her, he did not look out for Mary Paxton as he passed the house, and he scarcely understood Mr. Meldrum, when he dropped him at Thompson's Inn, and that gentleman charged him to call on Mrs. Meldrum as soon as he reached Cromaboo, and tell her that her mother was very poorly: he had to make him repeat the message before he could get it into his head. When his evening's work was done and he had called on Mrs. Meldrum, he went to his mother's, intending to see John Smith alone, and question him about Sir Robert Hardacre and take counsel with him. His mother met him at the door with an anxious face.

"Sure your father's been at the drink again," she said, "and Chip's brought him home."

And sure enough there lay John Smith before the kitchen stove, too drunk to know one thing from another; not asleep, indeed, but quite imbecile and stupid. Robert put his arm about his mother, and kissed her with great tenderness, but he did not say much to her, or stay long. He went back to Mr. Llewellyn's and to bed, but not to sleep; he heard the clock strike every hour till the daylight dawned. All night long he thought the matter over, and came at last to this conclusion: he would ask for a holiday, and trust to a chance ride to Gibbeline; he would call on Miss Paxton and tell her all about it, and ask her advice; then he would go to his father and try to listen to what he had to say calmly. He dreaded the meeting, because he detested Sir Robert's character, and yet, though he hated to admit the thought even to himself, he liked the man, and it seemed a sort of treachery to his mother to have even a kindly thought for him. Come what would, he would prevent him from seeing his mother; this ghost of the old too well remembered shame and pain should never rise before her to torment her.

Mr. Llewellyn made no objection to the holiday, and asked no questions, and a team overtook Robert before he had gone a mile, and picked him up. He ran up the steps at Mrs. Paxton's and raised his hand to the knocker before he saw the streamer of crape attached to it; he recoiled at this new shock, but guessed the truth in a minute at the sight of the black love ribbon. He went round to the back door and gently knocked. Dolly opened it, and told him, with tears, the particulars of the old mistress' death, and that Miss Mary had gone to lie down, having been up all night. He had not been alone in suffering, she had suffered, too, and counted the hours, he thought, as he turned away; for he could not disturb her, that would be too selfish; he felt he must stand alone, he must face Sir Robert again without advice or help, since this door, too, was shut in his face. Then the memory came to him of "the friend who sticketh closer than a brother," whose door is never closed against us, and whose ears are ever open to our cries for help, and he leant against the fence and prayed. If John Smith had been sober and in his right mind the night before, or if he had seen Miss Paxton in the morning, this prayer would never have been made; he would have leant upon human reed, and not have gone to the strong for strength.

He was fortunate in getting a ride the rest of the way to Gibbeline, and he went to the Western Hotel at once, and took a strong cup of green tea and some biscuits to steady him for the interview, before he repaired to Mr. Jackson's office. As he reached the door, he met Sir Robert Hardacre, who had come up another street.

"So you came," said the baronet, with a smile, and regarded the lad with a keen, yet kindly scrutiny.

"Yes," was Robert's brief reply. He looked weary, but calm and pale, quite unlike the excited lad of yesterday, who had threatened to crack Mr. Jackson's skull. Perhaps the elder Robert had not slept either, – I have no means of knowing, – but our hero thought he looked older than on the previous day.

"Shall we go back to the Royal," he asked, "or make use of Mr. Jackson's office?"

Robert was tired and wanted to get it over, so he said, "We will go in here, if you please."

"Did you walk from Cromaboo?" asked Sir Robert.

"No sir, I had a chance ride."

By this time they had reached the office door and tapped. Mr. Jackson opened it with a polite good day to Sir Robert.

"Good afternoon, Mr. Jackson," said Robert, "I'm glad I didn't break your head yesterday, and I'm sorry I was rude to you; but why did you lock me in like a thief?"

"I feared some one might intrude, and see your tears," was the reply. "You quite misunderstood me."

"We shall not have any misunderstanding to-day, I hope," said Sir Robert, politely. "Will you kindly allow me the use of your room for half an hour, Mr. Jackson?"

Mr. Jackson of course retired at once, and left them alone. Sir Robert placed a chair for his son, and sat down opposite to him, removing his hat, and resting his elbow on the table. Our hero took off his fur cap and sat in a waiting attitude, determined not to speak first; his eyes bent to the floor, his long lashes concealed them. A very boyish and rather injured individual he seemed to the father, who yet hesitated to address him. At last he began in a very gentle voice. "I hope you will not be offended at what I am about to say.

I don't speak with the intention of offending, and I wish, I beg that you will consider what I say quietly by yourself, and not make up your mind hastily, or decide finally to-day, but think about it for a day or two, and then come and tell me, when you have made up your mind."

Robert looked up, on the alert, and attentive in a moment. "I hoped this would be the last meeting," he said bluntly, but the flush of pain in his father's face, made him sorry as soon as the words were out of his mouth, and he added, "I beg pardon, I don't wish to offend either, and I won't get angry if I can help it, – go on please."

"I must begin by a question," said Sir Robert, "have you spoken to any one, taken counsel with any one since I saw you last?"

"About you? No, with no one but God," was the reply.

There was no doubting his sincerity, and Sir Robert felt secretly relieved. He took a turn about the room, before he began again.

"I have no right to dictate to you," he said, "and I suppose you have friends whose opinion, whose counsel you value far more than mine?"

"No mistake about that," said the son.

"Then why, may I ask, did you speak to none of these?"

"I don't think you've any right to ask that," replied Robert, "but I don't mind answering you. I couldn't consult my mother, of course about you, and the two dearest friends I have in the world except her, one was in trouble and couldn't see me, and the other was drunk, so I was driven to seek the best Helper."

The baronet smiled and took another turn about the room; he had dreaded some meddling third person between himself and his son.

"Robert," – the lad started to hear his name spoken by those alien lips, – "I hope you will believe me when I say I am sorry, heartily sorry for deserting and neglecting you all these years. I have no right to you, I know, except the right of blood. I *am* your father, and I hope you will listen patiently to what I propose, and seek alone that best Helper of whom you spoke, to help you to a decision."

"I cannot promise that," said the lad, sturdily.

"No? Well I cannot exact it, I must take what comes, that is my punishment; I can ask no more than a patient hearing. I am a wealthy man and have no near relatives; I have been married twice and am now a widower, but, except you, I have neither son nor daughter."

"You would never have looked me up if you had," said Robert, in a little spurt of indignation he could not repress.

"*Never,* God forgive me, it is too true. I seldom thought of you, never with pleasure, you were a mere shadow to me, rather a dream than a reality. I did not know if you were living or dead, or care, but I thought of your mother oftener than I wished; I would, when it was too late, have given my right hand and half my fortune to undo the injury I had done to her."

"But you wouldn't ha' married her," said Robert, with an impatient movement of the head.

"I couldn't when repentance came, for she was another man's wife. Virtue that has never tripped is a hard judge of error, my boy, and you cannot – it is impossible for you, though you have suffered for my sin, to know the strength of my temptation. I had locked away a little sketch I made of your mother when I first knew her, and I came upon it some time since by accident; it was that impelled me to come to Canada and see you. I had made no plan with regard to you, except the determination to see and help you, if you were alive – till yesterday."

"I don't need it, as you see," replied his son, "and if I had been an ugly, awkward lout, or a cripple, I believe you would ha' gone back to England without looking twice at me."

"I hope not," said the father, gently, "if you wish to drain my blood from your veins, as you said yesterday, I cannot echo the wish, Robert, now I have seen you, even though you dislike me. I would not put you back into chaos if I could, and though I deeply regret the pain it cost your mother, I cannot regret your birth now," and he laid his hand lightly and kindly on his son's shoulder. Robert shrank under the touch with a mixture of feelings that made him tremble like an aspen leaf.

"Oh! don't," he said imploringly. Sir Robert instantly removed his hand and moved away, bitterly hurt by this rebuff.

"I do not dislike you as much as I wish to," the boy went on, "it seems like treachery to my mother to be here listening to you at all, but I do it partly for her sake, and partly –" he stopped abruptly.

"And partly for mine," thought the father, with a sudden warm thrill of pleasure at his heart, as he truly read the lad's real thought in his sensitive, speaking face.

"Now, I have seen you, I don't wonder she cared so much for you, I never did blame her, – poor mother, – but now I understand how she would feel for you, and I don't want to feel in the same way," – the baronet turned to the window to conceal the smile that rippled over his face in spite of his self command, – "and I will not have her hurt any more, understand that; I will not have her feelings played with; I will not have you see her or speak to her, for you are not to be trusted."

Sir Robert returned to his seat.

"I will do just as you wish, about that," he said. His object was to win the boy's confidence, and gain his affection, and he was far too good a diplomatist not to know the reconciling power of judicious concession. "I will not see her without your knowledge or consent, I promise you that, on my honour as a gentleman."

"Thank you," said the boy, "*that* is all I ask of you, or want of you."

"Ask more," replied the father, with a smile that expressed more tenderness than he was aware of, – "ask more and see if I refuse."

Robert had not the heart to ask him to go away and never come back; he thought of it but couldn't bring out the words, and against his will a half smile curled his lip in answer to his father's, making his mouth so like Sir Robert's memory of Nelly's half repelling, half pouting, and altogether charming mouth, that, near as he was, it cost the father an effort not to kiss him, for he was by nature a kisser and a very affectionate man, with all his faults; fond of young things, whether animals, birds or children; but especially fond of half-grown lads and lassies. A great admirer of beauty of any kind, and prone to express his affection, without any restraint, by free caresses with his plump white fingers, or tender pressures of his full red lips, the very man to spoil a son or dear daughter by over much petting. A hearty rebuff, a sound box on the ear, would have been the greatest benefit to him in his youth, but unfortunately for himself and others, he was too charming to receive any such check, and his attentions were all too acceptable. So many of the sweets of life had fallen to his share, that only his bright, keen intellect and real warmth of heart had prevented him from being an unprincipled deceiver and wholesale seducer of youth. As it was his foot had slipped more than once, bringing him complicated troubles and bitter repentance.

"I do not want anything but to protect and take care of my mother," said Robert, "that was my object in coming to-day, but if you have anything else to say, sir, I am willing to listen."

"I have a great deal more to say," replied the baronet, "but you have interrupted me so often, you rogue, that I am long in coming to the point."

"Well, I won't say another word if I can help it," and Robert locked his lips firmly.

"My property is entirely my own, my estate is unencumbered and unentailed, and I can leave it to whom I please, and I mean to leave it to you, the only living child ever born to me, my dear son; you cannot have the title, but you shall have the estate. You cannot alter my purpose in this, even if you refuse to let me help you while I live, but I wish very much that you would let me help you now, for one thing to a better education than you have. I could give you a sum of money at once for that."

Sir Robert made rather a long pause. The poor boy's colour came and went, his lips parted, but he did not speak; the offer was very tempting, it would enable him to be more worthy of Miss Paxton, and finally to lay a fortune at her feet; would it be right to refuse? As these thoughts passed rapidly through his mind, his father resumed.

"You might complete your education here in Canada, or you might travel with me; if you told your mother that you had a good situation, and wrote and sent her remittances constantly, she would be satisfied, and it would be a great pleasure to me to be your teacher."

Robert started up as if he had been stung.

"You would rob my mother of what is dearer to her than life, and you think to pay her in money," he exclaimed indignantly. "I would not desert her for any man living, *you* last of all; nay more, if she was in her grave I would not leave her husband," he added, determined to stand up for John Smith, none the less – perhaps all the more – because last night he had felt inclined to kick him.

"Do you care so much for that half-savage man-beast?" said Sir Robert, a little disgusted at the last part of this speech.

"If he is a beast, I am his cub," replied Robert, "and it would be base to desert him for you of all others, for he has been a true father to me. He has denied himself and worked hard to give me schooling. He carried me in his arms night by night, walking the room for hours when I had the fever, to rest me and get me to sleep; he protected my mother and covered her shame, and never cast it up to her or me. It isn't many men would have such a cuckoo's egg in their nest, and never regret it."

Skillful as Sir Robert was in the art of winding people around his finger, he sometimes lost his point by losing his temper, and sometimes gained it by the very same weakness, and that was the case now. If there was a man in the world he thoroughly detested it was John Smith, and to hear him praised by Robert was more than he could bear patiently.

"He is an old villain," he said, speaking with great heat, "he robbed me of Nelly, pretty wild flower that she was, *he* an Irish ruffian, past middle age, a grossly ignorant, coarse peasant; and he has robbed me of you. Do you think I couldn't have walked the room with my little son, and nursed him tenderly for the pure selfish pleasure of cooling his hot cheek against my own and soothing him to rest. Do you think the baton sinister could ever have been a bar between us, Robert, or the marriage ceremony with your mother have made you dearer to me, – or made her dearer either, for that matter?"

He spoke bitterly, not caring to conceal the pain he felt, as he would if Mr. Jackson had been present. His son did not reply, and for a long time there was a painful silence.

"Well, well, Robert," said the father, at last, "I have sown and I must reap; if you cannot give me love and confidence, at least give me credit for an honest meaning, and let me help you in your own way, – in any way you please. There is money at your command, at any time you like; there is property you must have, *you* and no other when I am in my grave; this is what I had to say, think about it, and let me know your decision to-morrow."

"I cannot come to-morrow, because it is mail day, but I will come on Saturday," said Robert. "I am sorry to hurt you, and I don't doubt you mean kindly, but – but – I am afraid of myself, because I – I do like you."

"You've an odd way of showing it," said the baronet, secretly pleased in spite of his ill-humour, by this unwilling confession, "will you come to the Royal on Saturday, and dine with me?"

"No, sir, thank you, – I must go now."

"Do you think I would poison you, or perhaps you won't take salt with me on principle, – is that it? You might, at least, shake hands, it needn't prevent you from doubling your fist the next time we meet."

Robert, after a minute's hesitation extended his brown paw. "Won't you forgive me," he said rather tremulously; he was worn out with excitement and want of rest, and could scarcely keep from tears. Sir Robert was greatly touched by the apology, and the lad's wan face; he could have taken him in his arms, and kissed him, but resisted the impulse within him lest he should scare him away like a frightened bird.

"My son," he said in a tone that went to the lad's heart, it expressed so much love and tenderness, "it is *I* that want forgiveness, and you find it hard to forgive."

Robert did not reply, for the simple reason that he could not without a burst of tears, so with a long hand shake, they parted.

Chapter Twenty-Nine

"We'll talk it over by the bed-room fire
And come to our conclusions."

– Old Play[145]

MARY would like to see you," said Mrs. Meldrum to her husband, on the day following Robert's interview with his father. "She thinks of sitting up for a time, but I do not think her fit to be up," added Margaret, who would have liked to keep Mary prisoner, till she had arranged the funeral and mourning in her own way.

"Well, I will go up, if you like," he replied.

"I think you had better go at once, then, and hear what she has to say, and persuade her to go to bed again, if you can."

The doctor made no promise, but ran lightly upstairs and tapped at the bed-room door. Dolly opened it and placed a chair for him beside Mary's, and then left the room. Miss Paxton, who was wrapped in a dressing-gown of Turkey red cotton, and leaning back in a large rocking chair, looked haggard and hollow eyed, and older than her age. Blinds were down, and curtains drawn; a small wood fire burned sleepily on the hearth, enough for the day, which was warm and thawing.

"Well?" said Mr. Meldrum, kindly, "how are you to-day, – did you sleep?"

"A little, and I feel better, I mean to go down stairs to-morrow; it was not myself I wished to speak of, but other things; Maggie will tell me nothing, she says I am not strong enough to bear it. When will the funeral be?"

---

[145]Unidentified source.

"To-morrow afternoon. I had a telegram from your uncle to say he could not come till after the funeral, so I must be chief mourner."

"I will go too," said Mary, "mamma shall have one of her own blood to follow her to the grave."

"Well, I see no objection to that if you feel strong enough," replied Mr. Meldrum. "Is there anything else you wish to ask about?"

He felt like a hooded hawk in the darkened room, and was anxious to get out of it as soon as possible.

"Yes, you might put up that blind towards the garden while you stay, it is unpleasant to be so much in the dark, and it doesn't do poor mamma any good, but Maggie says it's respectable, and we mustn't vex her."

"I suppose I can bear it if you can," he returned, "but it's not good for you."

"I have had a letter from Robert this morning," said Mary, turning her large grave eyes on Mr. Meldrum's face, "and I wanted to consult you about it. It is full of kindly thoughts and –" she paused.

"Bad spelling," suggested her brother-in-law.

"Well, yes, but I won't have you make fun of Robin Adair."

"I promise to be very discreet if you show me the letter," he replied, with a smile.

"I cannot do that, it would not be honourable, but you can help me greatly, if you will, by telling me all you know about Robert's father," – Mr. Meldrum opened his brown eyes with surprise, – "Miss Llewellyn's wedding," the lady went on, "and Robert too. If you will tell me all you remember of Mr. Hardacre, and what you really thought of him, it would be a great help to me in giving advice to Robert. His father is in Gibbeline now, and he saw him to-day and yesterday. I want you to tell me all you remember of him."

"I will, my dear child, with pleasure," said Mr. Meldrum, and he added thoughtfully, "it is a great responsibility to advise in such a case."

"What kind of a man was he when you knew him?" she asked, "Was he handsome, – do you think he had any principle at all – any worth?"

"He was well looking enough as to the outside, not unlike Robert, but taller, and not so bonnie, and he was certainly one of the pleasantest fellows I ever met, charming company at all times and never out of temper at trifles. He was some years older than me; I was only a boy when I met him, had just passed my first examination at college, and had come to Gibbeline for a holiday after my studies, and we were fellow-travelers in the coach together. We stayed at the same inn, and arranged a hunting expedition to the backwoods – Croma-boo was the backwoods then, but the place we went to was twenty miles beyond it. We camped out many a night together, and told stories and sang songs by the watch fire. I, as a youngster, felt flat-tered by Mr. Hardacre's gay, good humour and friendliness. He had those accomplishments which tell with every kind of person. He was an excellent shot, a good singer, and a clever, amusing talker, who seemed to say just the right thing always, and knew how to take people. He never gave offense except when he meant to – little Bob is like him in that – and then no man knew how to do it better. I remember the first night he ever saw Nelly Connel, Bob's mother. We did not know there was a human habitation near, when she sud-denly peeped round a tree at us; I never saw a prettier creature, quite a child, a young unformed thing as graceful as a deer, and erect as a ramrod; with wonderful eyes and teeth, and very little clothing.

"'A wood nymph, by St. George and the dragon,' Mr. Hardacre exclaimed, as she ran away. A minute after we came upon her father and Smith sitting on a log smoking. They gave us a warm welcome, invited us to the shanty, gave us their best, and asked us to come back every night while we stayed in the woods; and we did. There was game in plenty and we stayed a good while. Mr. Hardacre made a great pet of Nelly from the first, and did not disguise his fondness for her; but I never thought harm of it, nor did anybody. I don't believe he meant evil himself at first, but there was no excuse for him, it was a heartless business, she was such a young, helpless thing in his hands. I remember he taught her the alphabet, and gave her a little seal from his watch guard as a reward for learning so quickly, and coaxed her to give him a kiss for teaching her. And he used to coax her to sit on his knee, and bribe her by the offer to show her his watch and the contents of his purse – she had never seen gold or a watch before – and she would perch herself there with shy confidence, though I could never persuade her to come near me; whereas the younger imps were free enough with me. One night we came in late after a very successful hunting expedition, and found little tired Nelly stretched in front of the fire in a sound sleep. Connel and Smith were with us, but Hardacre stopped all our noise with an imperative "Hush!" saying he wanted to make a picture of the sleeper, and he did, a very life-like little Crayon sketch, and took it away with him, 'the prettiest spoil of our expedition,' as he truly said.

"Another afternoon Hardacre and Smith shot two fine bucks, and the wolves pursued us, and pressed us so severely that it was precious hard work to get our spoil into the shanty safely; I brained a wolf at the very door, and they stayed about all night, howling most drearily. Mrs. Connel – prudent woman – hearing them afar off, had taken the cow and the pig into the family mansion, lest the wolves should break into their little shanties and devour them, so that with these animals, and Hardacre's deer hounds, and my beagles, we were thickly packed that night. The younger brood of Connels had literally gone to bed with the chickens, but Nelly was up when we arrived, and very much frightened. Mrs. Connel finding her lord safe, said 'Glory be to God and the blessed Virgin,' and then gave us our supper of poached eggs and new potatoes, which Hardacre insisted upon saying grace over, and pronounced 'food for a king.' The meal over, she slipped behind the curtain which divided the room, and went to bed, and Connel soon followed, and in a minute or two they were snoring loudly in spite of the howls of the wolves.

"Smith, – who had given up his bed to us, on our first arrival, which we shared with little Chip and a black hen that roosted over our heads, and used to slip into the bed every day when we vacated it, and lay an egg there, – Smith, I say, lay down before the fire with his head on a bag of feathers, promising to stay awake and keep little Nelly company; but he was asleep as soon as his head touched the pillow, and added his snores to the general discord. At last, at a dismal and prolonged howl, answered within by the dogs, in spite of our efforts to keep them still, Nelly put her trembling hand into Hardacre's and begged him not to go to bed and leave her alone. He wrapped her in his plaid from head to foot, and took her in his arms without a word, and presently began to sing softly, 'Hush my dear, lie still and slumber,' and she nestled close to him, comforted by his protection, not knowing that he was more dangerous than any wolf. We felt it would be useless to go to bed, so sat by the fire all night, and a cold night it was, though in September. At last Nelly went to sleep with her head on his shoulder, and towards morning I went to sleep too. When I woke, the wolves had gone and Hardacre was sitting in the same attitude, with the sleeping girl in his arms; he was still wide awake, and gazing into the remains of the great wood fire, now one mass of glowing coals. I said if the old mother bird caught them in that attitude, she would be angry with Nelly, and he took the hint at once, and woke little Nelly with a tender whispered word and a kiss, and she slipped from his knee, and ran behind the curtain blushing.

"All the next day, we were busy patching the cow's house, and building a new pig-stye, to make those valuable animals safe against another inroad[146] of the wolves, and Hardacre worked as hard and sang as gaily as if he had slept the night before instead of watching. He proposed that the Connels should have another room to their shanty, and we helped them so effectually that they actually got it up and roofed in before we left. If he had never gone back 'twould have been all right, we should have done them nothing but good. Hardacre asked Nelly for a kiss at parting, and she gave him one, and then burst into tears and ran away.

"We returned to Gibbeline together, and I parted with him there. I knew nothing of his return to the backwoods till I saw him in the spring nearly two years later. I thought he was not very glad to renew the acquaintance, though we had parted on the most friendly terms, but he invited me to sup with him at the tavern where we boarded, and I went. At the foot of the stairs I met Nelly Connel; I could scarcely believe my eyes when I saw her. She did not recognize me, she never even saw me, and I never saw such despair in a human face as in hers that evening. I was nearly stopping her, but I didn't from the feeling that she had seen Hardacre and was going somewhere by his direction. As soon as I met him all my suspicions were confirmed, I saw the whole thing; a duller man might have guessed the truth from his face, for he was never an adept at the art of concealing. He was silent, almost morose, at first, till the wine warmed him, then he was uproariously gay and jolly. There were two other guests, and we did not separate till midnight.

"I called the next morning early to see if I could find out anything about Nelly. Hardacre was up and in a most disturbed state of mind. He opened his heart to me just from the necessity of speaking to somebody, I think. He could find no trace of Nelly, and the people at the inn had not seen her go out. I have no doubt they had quarreled,

---

[146]The 1878 edition has "inrode."

but he did not tell me so. I told him I met her the night before, and that I saw the print of her naked feet in the dust as I came up the street, and we went out to follow the footprints. We lost the trail once and found it again, and then traced the little naked feet to the river bank; we tried in vain to find another footmark; she had gone off on the grass, I suppose. Hardacre was in a frantic state, and I felt very much alarmed, remembering the expression of the poor child's face. I had great difficulty in persuading him to go back to the inn. We wandered about all day looking for further footmarks, and he abused himself so bitterly that I felt it unsafe to leave him.

"'If little Nelly has been driven to take her life through my unkindness,' he said, 'I'll shoot myself and go down quick into hell.'

"When at last we got back to Murphy's Inn,[147] we found your papa waiting for Hardacre, and with every respect for him, in a general way, I must say he was much too fiery and combustible to be a skillful diplomatist. He burst upon Hardacre like –" he was going to say "like a turkey cock," but in consideration to his hearer, checked himself, and though he regretted it, changed the apt comparison into another simile – "like an avalanche, and with much strong language, asked him if he meant to marry the girl, or not, after telling him that he ought to be shot for a heartless young scoundrel. It seemed unreasonable in Hardacre to be angry, for Mr. Paxton said no worse than he had been saying of himself all day, but he was very angry; I really didn't think it was in him to lose all self command, and get into such a rage. He would have struck your father, in spite of his grey hairs, if I had not stepped in between them, and to do the old gentleman justice, he would have liked nothing better. I shared the fate of all people who get into bad company, and came in for a share of abuse from Mr. Paxton, who would gladly have fought us both. At last he went away, after forbidding Mr. Hardacre to set foot in his house, and telling us he meant to let the Connels know that Nelly was there. We never dreamt that he would go and see Connel in person, for we knew he came from London, and was altogether a city man in habits, and quite unaccustomed to backwoods traveling and blazed tracks. If Hardacre had known he was away I am sure nothing would have kept him from seeing Nelly, and if your mamma had been willing to give her up, it might have changed her fate. He wanted me to go and

---

[147]The location of Murphy's Inn, Guelph, remains unidentified.

get Nelly away, but I would not, because I knew that if she was once in his possession, he would never either marry her, or part with her again. That was my feeling at the time; I hope I didn't do him injustice. I did not absolutely refuse to go, but I said I would think about it. After four days Hardacre told me plainly that if I didn't go and see what had become of Nelly, he himself would go to Connel and 'make some arrangement,' he said, and take her out of Mr. Paxton's house, whether he liked it or not.

"'Do you mean to marry her?' I asked, but he made no reply, and I thought silence meant no, so I said I would ride up to Mr. Paxton's at once, and make inquiries about her. I tapped three times at the front door, but nobody heard me, so I marched straight into the dining-room, where I found little Nelly weeping bitterly, and John Smith looking at her with great compassion, and your papa much softened, and trying his hand as a comforter. I also had a glimpse of Mrs. Paxton driving you little girls out of the room before her, and the parson and Maggie billing and cooing in the garden beyond. Mr. Paxton flew at me like a bull at a red rag; he called me 'a colleague of that young blackguard Hardacre,' and asked me what the devil I wanted?'

"Poor papa," said Mary, "we often blushed for his violence," and a little tinge of colour, and a half smile came to her pale face as she spoke.

"Poor Nelly saw me through her tears and sobbed afresh, but Smith's respect for me made your father more respectful, and we went out into the chip-yard and talked it over; Smith and I – your father was present, but made no remark. Smith told me he had married Nelly, and that he would take care of her and her child, 'poor crather,' and 'never even ask a kiss,' he said, if she did not give it voluntarily, and I believe he kept his word; he behaved very wisely and kindly.

"Kindness is wisdom," said Mary gently, and added with a little hesitation, "if you would only believe that about Maggie, and not be so satirical with her, I think you would be happier."

"Do you?" said Mr. eldrum. "Well, I will try and command my tongue. I never found it a difficult matter till I married your sister."

"And pay your debts now, when the property is divided, it would be much easier to live with her if you did – and there is something else I would like to say before you finish the story, only I am afraid you will think it impudence in me."

"Not at all," replied Mr. Meldrum, "it is kind, very kind to give your advice, and I thank you. You know I once asked you to advise me about Maggie."

"Well, then, if you are patient with her, and put up with her peevishness now she is ailing, when the baby is born she will be quite satisfied and happy if it lives; she is so fond of little babies that she will be wholly absorbed, and quite forget there is such a person as Mr Meldrum in the world. Maggie is a good mother to little things, it is only when they grow older she expects too much of them."

"I will do my very best – will you not help me by becoming a member of my household?"

"I will come when Maggie is ill, certainly," said Mary, "but I can make no further promise – now go on with the story, please."

"Well I went back to Hardacre and told him, and I could judge how much he cared for Nelly by his violent jealousy of Smith. If hatred and the wish for his death could have killed him, Smith would have died that night. He had told me the inn where they were to stay for a day or two, and I went up, by Hardacre's wish, to see Nelly, as he was afraid to trust himself. I arrived just in time to be of use. It was a dangerous case, she had a fever and was delirious for some days; more than once she attempted to take her life. I tried the effect of Hardacre's name to see if it would soothe her, but it made her quite frantic. I could not leave her, so I sent a messenger to Hardacre to tell him he had a son and that Nelly was very ill; but I did not tell him the full extent of the danger for I feared if she lived she would become a lunatic. I thought if I alarmed him too much he would come; and sure enough the next day he *did* come. I would not let him see Nelly, for that day she had again attempted to take her life; I tried to persuade him that now it would be best for him to see her no more, as the excitement of such a meeting might kill her.

"'I would rather she died than lived to be that man's wife,' he said, and I believe meant it.

"I showed him the child, but he scarcely looked at it; the sight of it seemed to annoy him 'Poor little devil,' he said, 'take it away, take it away.'

"Going out of the inn he met Nelly's husband; he had no weapons but his fists, luckily for Smith, but being a good boxer he knew how to use them, and put in his blows straight. Not a word did he say, but the double fist went out with such steadiness and force that it made Smith stagger. The Irishman, though the strongest man, was not Hardacre's equal in a fight of that kind; after a few blows, I got between them, and begged them to hear reason, then they took to their tongues, those wicked weapons, and used them most unsparingly. Hardacre took out his purse before leaving, and offered Smith money to pay the expenses of Nelly's illness, but the Irishman's blood was up, he would not take a penny, though he had not a coin in his pocket, or in the world.

"Hardacre stayed in Gibbeline for more than a month, and I sent him daily accounts, or took them myself, till Nelly was out of danger. One day when I was away, your father and two of you young ladies went to see her; that visit did her a great deal of good, did much to calm her mind and give her hope; and Smith was very kind and judicious, for when Nelly said the baby must be called Robert Hardacre, he made no objection, and when he went up to Connel's for his clothes and his son, and she asked him to bring her the books Mr. Hardacre had given her, he replied very kindly, 'That I will, Nelly, wid pleasure,' and he seemed really fond of her brat, from the first day of his birth.

"The last time I saw Mr. Hardacre was in Toronto, the fall of the same year, just before he went to England, two years after our happy hunting expedition. He looked thin, and more than two years older, he was grave in manner, all his old spirit gone; he told me his elder brother was dead, and his father had written for him to return home. He asked after Nelly. I told him she was well, except her eyes, which were incurably weak from over much crying.

"'You might have spared me that,' he said coldly.

"I told him the name of the child; he sighed and said, 'Poor little devil.' He said he had only enough money for his expenses home, but when he was richer he would send me my fees for attending to Nelly. I told him, of course, that I required no fees, and he retorted sharply that he would have nothing at my hand, I had connived with 'those wretches' who robbed him of Nelly. He did not offer to shake hands at parting, but simply bowed. Four years later I received a brief letter from him enclosing two hundred pounds sterling as a fee for me. He did not ask me to write, but enclosed his address. I wrote at once, telling him that Nelly was well, and had another son, and that as I wanted no fee, I would apply the money, as no doubt he had intended I should, for the benefit of Nelly and his boy. I helped Smith in every way I could, without telling him or his wife that the money was not my own. The lot they live on in Cromaboo was bought with Mr. Hardacre's money. I have no doubt he received my letter, but he never wrote again, and soon after I saw his father's death in the *Times*, and his own marriage with a lady of title. Smith is not a hard man to deceive in money matters, as he scarcely knows a shilling from a sixpence, and he has no pride where I am concerned; he has had more than that two hundred pounds from me."

"Thank you very much for telling me," said Mary, "and that is all you know about Mr. Hardacre?"

"Absolutely *all*, I know nothing more."

"Robert is to see his father to-morrow evening, but as I am very tired, I will not attempt to write to him, but send a message by you instead. Give my kindest regards to him, and tell him to come in after the funeral to-morrow, and I will see him for a little while. I am really grateful for what you have told me."

"I should like to be a rat in the wall," said Mr. Meldrum, "and hear what passes between little Bob and his father."

Chapter Thirty

"Aye, sooth, we feel too strong in weal to need Thee on that road,
But woe being come, the soul is dumb, that crieth not on God."

– Elizabeth Barrett Browning[148]

T HOUGH ROBERT had asked Miss Paxton's advice, and promised
to follow it implicitly, he had fought his battle alone, and made
up his mind how to act, before ever he saw her face. The fact that
Sir Robert had promised to make him his heir, was to the son by no
means a proof of his sincerity, but the varying tones of his voice, the
expression of his face, carried conviction to the lad's heart. Mr. Meldrum had said truly that Sir Robert was not adept in the art of concealing whatever he felt, good or bad appeared plainly enough in
his face, in spite of his self-command, and that polished hypocracy
which good breeding teaches, and his real love for his son, and longing for the lad's affection and confidence; had come out far more
clearly in look and accent than he himself knew. Thinking of his last
look, Robert's heart softened towards the lonely father, now bearing
the burden of his old sins, none the easier to carry after all, because
he deserved it.

"And I'm not the one that ought to cast them up to him, for all
he's been wicked," thought our hero, "and though I'll have none of
his help I'll speak kindly and fairly to him, and tell him I *do* forgive
him, and tell him the truth that I love him better than any person I
ever saw, except mother and Miss Paxton, far better than John Smith
that has done so much for me, – and I *won't* be angry and impudent
again."

---

[148]Elizabeth Barrett Browning (1806-1861), "The Lay of the Brown Rosary."

To strengthen himself in this good resolution, he knelt by the bed-side and asked God's help to make him kind and respectful to this newly found parent, who was quite unlike the hard cold father he had imagined. As distrust and doubt took wing, happiness and peace came back into the boy's heart once more, and when he laid his head on the pillow, it was to sleep soundly and quietly till the morning.

The next day Sir Robert could not resist the temptation of going into the high street, with the hope that he might meet his son, or at least catch a glimpse of the active free young figure. In turning a corner he met him face to face. He lifted his hat and smiled, and as Robert returned the salute, a bright, shy answering smile of recognition, that was certainly expressive of anything but dislike or fear, came into his face. To him the meeting was unexpected.

"You will not forget to-morrow?" said Sir Robert in passing.

"Oh! no sir," was the reply.

Having seen him, the father returned to his hotel satisfied, but when the time came for the mail to start, he grew restless, and went into the high street and watched it off at a distance, and heard the departing toot, as it drove away.

There were more than one hundred people gathered at Mrs. Paxton's grave on the following afternoon, for though, not a popular woman, she was an old settler, and well known; but there was not one happier or more peaceful than Mr. Llewellyn's servant, who stood beside his master and listened to the service feelingly, and with great attention, understanding, as others there did not, that "man walketh in a vain shadow, and disquieteth himself in vain," that "he heapeth up riches, and knoweth not who shall gather them." He secretly joined in the prayers with his whole heart.

As they were returning from the burying ground, he asked his master if he might go back to Gibbeline and stay all night, and drive home on Sunday morning with Mr. Meldrum.

"Two holidays in one week, Robert," said Mr. Llewellyn, in some surprise, "what are you after – a concert or a ball?"

"No sir, a friend that is going to leave for another country asked me to meet him; father will put away the ponies for you, if you don't mind driving home from Mrs. Paxton's alone."

"Well, Robert, this is the last holiday I shall give you while you are with me; a lad of your age should be in his bed by ten, and large towns are bad places at night – but you may go."

"Thank you, sir," said the servant, "I'm not up to anything bad, Miss Paxton knows where I am going and who I am to meet. I would tell you, but 'twouldn't be honourable."

"Oh! it's all right if Miss Paxton knows," said the old gentleman, much relieved, "and you are right in not breaking a confidence of hers. I am very willing to do without your services to oblige her."

And thus it was that Robert got his leave of absence, his master rather misunderstanding the tenor of his last speech.

Miss Paxton had just reached home before Robert arrived; she was still in her crape bonnet and heavy veil and cloak when he was conducted into her presence. Never had he seen her so unnerved, so unlike herself, her hands trembled, her lips quivered, she could not speak at first. Mr. Meldrum, who met the lad at the door, gave him a chair and left them alone, but they had not exchanged a sentence, when Dolly burst into the room with small ceremony, for she was concerned for her mistress, and regarded the mail carrier as a mere servant like herself.

How tired and sick you *do* look, Miss Mary," she said, "and nobody to take care of you. I've got a hot cup o' tea ready, will you drink it if I bring it in?"

Miss Paxton was touched with the girl's kindness, and the tears rolled down her cheeks.

"My, if you cry, I shall cry too," said Dolly, instantly putting the threat into execution; "let me take your bonnet off."

"It seems there is somebody to take care of me," said Mary, smiling through her tears, "you are very kind, Dolly. You can bring two cups of tea, and some biscuits for Robert."

Dolly was gone and back again in a minute with a little tray. Never had the dawdling little girl been so expeditious, and her mistress was pleased with her efforts to comfort even though she spilt the biscuits on the floor and dropped a tear into Robert's saucer. When she had made up the fire, with a good deal of noise, she began to talk.

"Mrs. Meldrum's gone to bed to have a good cry, and just after she went, a tall old lady came from Gibbeline, in a cab, a Mrs. Marshall. She said she had traveled from Montreal, and was tired, so I made her some strong tea, and lots o' toast," said the little maid boldly, though she would have shaken in her shoes to take so much upon herself in Mrs. Paxton's time; "and if she didn't eat it every bit, and then she said she was very sleepy, and I made up the old missises bed with clean sheets, and the best quilt, and put her in there, and she's asleep."

"You are a very good girl, Dolly," said her young mistress, "and you did quite right; and now go and prepare tea for Mr. Meldrum, and then get something for yourself, and leave me alone for half an hour, as I wish to speak to Robert on business."

But Dolly, having tasted the sweetness of a brief authority, felt the spirit of power within her, and was disposed to exert it.

"I'm sure you ain't fit for business to night," she said, "couldn't he come to-morrow?"

"No, no, Dolly, run away, there's a good girl."

Dolly, however, instead of obeying, lingered till Robert, who knew how to use his lips for punishment as well as reward, rose and opened the door wide for her.

"Come," said he, "if you don't be off out o' this when your mistress tells you, I'll give you a kiss," which had the effect of expelling her, exclaiming as she went against "the impidence o' them boys."

He closed the door and sat down and stirred his tea.

"Won't you try and take a mouthful, Miss Mary?" he said, persuasively; "it will do you good."

She lifted the cup to her lips and sat it down again. "Dear Robert," she began tremulously, "I have been so troubled and shaken by mamma's sudden death that I hardly know how to advise you, but I feel for you," and she extended her hand to him, which the boy lifted to his lips as the best mode of expressing his feelings. "I think your father's offer to make you his heir is a mark of penitence, and – he cannot be young now, – I feel sorry for him."

"So do I," said Robert, heartily.

"But yet Smith has been a kind father to you, and a good father, so far as he knew how to be; and, dear Robert, the basest of all sins is ingratitude. Then there is your mother to think of."

"She must never know," said Robert, "and she *would* know if I let him help me now. I think I must just say good bye to him from to-night, for her sake; that's what I've made up my mind to."

"Do – do you like him, Robert?"

"Very much, I never loved anyone as much except you and my mother. There's something so frank and sincere in his way o' saying

things, that I couldn't help believing him even when I fought against
it. He looks honest and kind, and I don't wonder mother loved him,
and I am sure he is sorry he was so cruel. If I lived with him long
'twould be hard to do without him, but I mean to say good bye, and
stick to duty, God helping me."

"He never forsakes those who prefer duty to their own worldly
interest," said Mary. "I have formed no plan yet, with regard to my
future life, except that when Mr. Llewellyn had done with you, I want
you to become one of my household, – at least you shall if you like."

"If I like!" said the boy, with sparkling eyes, "why, 'twould be
happiness to serve you any way I could."

"My poor dear boy," she said, smiling through her tears, "what a
boy you are; and your father at last sees what he has lost, – do you
think he is proud of you?"

"I don't think he could be proud of such a patched chap as I was
in my working duds, but he wasn't ashamed o' me, and that says a
good deal for him; and I know he is fond o' me, I could see it in his
eyes."

"Poor man, he has done what he cannot undo, by neglecting you
so long; there are some paths we cannot go back upon," she said with
a sigh, then added, after a pause, "I spoke to Mr. Meldrum about your
father, Robert, and he told me what he remembered of him. I told
him nothing of the contents of your letter, or your father's promise
to make you his heir, only that he was in Gibbeline, and that you had
seen him, and would see him again. I thought it would help me in
coming to a conclusion about him."

"Well, and has it, Miss Mary?"

"I should think him a man of more feeling than principle. You
and your mother, and Mr. Meldrum all concur in one thing, that he
is a very pleasing man. I think your resolution a right one if you can
carry it out, about seeing the last of him, – better for your mother's
peace of mind. But be kind, do not be hard to him, dear Robert, as he
was to her in that last interview. When you come to your death bed,
– as we all must, – it is not your kind acts you will regret."

This was the substance of their conference, and presently Robert
took his leave, but looking back after he had opened the door, he
was moved to a sudden impulse of compassion by the sight of Miss
Paxton's face, which looked older than he had ever seen it, and very
weary. He turned back; he had come to be counseled and comforted,

but it was she who needed help, and his warm boy's heart was stirred to the core at the sight of her unhappiness. He stooped and kissed her on the forehead, saying, "It just goes to my heart to see you looking so tired and ill, Miss Mary; do lie down and try and rest and be comforted about the old lady. The great and good God is not a man to bear hardly upon the peevishness of a poor old lady, that was childish from old age, and not rightly able to command her words and thoughts. Don't you mind when you told me that 'God is love,' just think o' that now, and cheer up."

She murmured a "thank you," as he went away, though the tears came again to her eyes at his words and caress.

Mr. Meldrum, who was standing at the front door to conduct our hero out, saw the leave taking and strongly disapproved of it. He closed the door gently behind them, and as he walked to the gate, opened his mind on the subject in these words.

"You are an impudent young dog Bob, to take advantage of Miss Paxton's present weakness and grief, as you did just now. You took a liberty that I *could* not and would not take, though I am nearly related to her."

"If you don't take such a liberty," replied the offender promptly, "it's because you know if you did you'd put your foot in it past pardon. Don't be a humbug, Mr. Meldrum, I believe you'd ha' married her if you could, let alone kissing her."

"Indeed," said the doctor, with his usual calmness, "who's your authority for that statement?"

"Oh! nobody told me so, it's just my own thought, and I'm pretty sure it's a right one. I have a feeling that you put the question and got no for an answer, and then you turned to Mrs. Hurst. Miss Mary may marry some day, you know, and she's free to choose who she pleases, I suppose."

"I suppose so, Bob," said Mr. Meldrum, quite unmoved by the question, "and you think she will choose you, but you may find yourself mistaken, my young man, for she regards you as a mere boy or she would never permit you to take such liberties. However, there is another subject I wish to speak about. Miss Paxton told me that you were going to see your father to-night, and I must tell you in justice to him, that I heard from him when you were four years old, and he sent two hundred pounds as a fee for me, he said, for attending to your mother when you were born, but I thought he meant it to be spent on you, and I have spent it all at different times in helping Smith, and all of you in helping to buy the lot, and building the house your mother is in; but I never told them who the money came from, lest they should refuse it. I let them think it came from me."

"That was very delicate and kind in you sir," said Robert, repenting his late impudence.

"I hope you are not going to-night with hostile intent, Bob," the doctor went on, "for your father must be an old boy now, and you are his own son, or you would never have kissed Miss Paxton to-day; you ought to have charity for him, for in the same position you would have acted just in the same way."

Robert flushed angrily. He was outside the gate, and the doctor leaning on it; he moved a step or two away.

"Never," he said. "It isn't in me to cruelly seduce an ignorant young creature, no better than a child. You must think me a devil, if you think that of me."

"Oh! no, Bob, a mortal man, or rather boy. It's difficult to make you understand, you are such a young one," said Mr. Meldrum, not unwilling to pay him off for his impudence by patronizing him a little; "but it was a real passion on your father's part; he did love little Nelly; only when he had injured her, it was a natural consequence that he should be a little harsh and unkind; his conscience troubling him would make him worse, of course. You have only had sentimental fancies, and don't know what a real passion is."

"And never shall," said Robert, hotly, "for what you call a real passion is just sin and selfishness."

"Ah! of course, I knew you would answer in that way," retorted Mr. Meldrum, coolly, "you are like the young Jewish ruler who said, 'Is thy servant a dog that he should do these things?' and yet after all he did them just as the prophet said he would."

"That prophet was inspired by God," said the lad, "but you are inspired by old Hob, to put me in a bad temper with my father just when I wished to think the best of him. I won't hear another word – I wish you good night, sir," and he walked rapidly away.

Chapter Thirty-One

"The child of love, though born in bitterness."
– Byron[149]

S IR ROBERT had waited till long after his appointed dinner hour,
hoping his son would change his mind and come. Disappointment succeeded hope. He had set the door ajar to hear the sound of
the boy's footsteps when he came, and now, as he moved towards
it with a sigh, to ring the bell for the long deferred meal, he heard a
woman's voice exclaim, "Is that little Bob Smith? Well, I never."

"Yes, it's me," replied the clear tones he loved to hear; "how are
you Molly? You look charming, anyway." Then presently followed
the question, "Where is Sir Robert Hardacre's room? – show me,
please – I have an appointment with him."

"Then I guess you're too late or too early, for he's expecting a
gentleman to dinner, and that'll be right away. I'm listening for his
bell every minute; so I guess you'd better come and have a cup o' tea
with me, instead of intruding upon that big swell before he wants
you. I'll get Alvira to wait on him."

"No, Molly, thank you all the same; show me the room, please,"
and then came the quick, advancing footsteps.

Sir Robert opened the door and extended his hand with a smile
of welcome.

"I am very glad to see you, Robert," he said. "I hope you have not
dined?"

---

[149]Lord George Gordon Byron, "Childe Harold's Pilgrimage": Canto CXVIII.

"No, sir, but I've had a cup o' tea. I had to go to Mrs. Paxton's funeral with Mr. Llewellyn, and that delayed me. I hope you have not waited dinner for me?"

"Yes I did," said the baronet, ringing the bell, "you will not refuse to dine with me, I hope."

"You are very kind, sir – I'm rather hungry." He had come for peace to-night, and his three miles walk[150] had given him an appetite.

The maid who waited at table was the very Molly who had shaken hands with Robert not ten minutes before, but though surprised at Sir Robert's guest, she was too much awed at the presence of a live baronet to take liberties; and Robert made no blunders, he had been too thoroughly drilled by Miss Llewellyn in table etiquette for that; and his father's real kindness set him at his ease. He enjoyed his dinner, but declined wine.

"Perhaps you would like a glass of ale," said the father.

"No, thank you, I never take it, or anything intoxicating; I haven't the head for it."

"I am disappointed, I hoped to drink a cup of kindness with you to-night."

"I will take wine with you, sir, if you wish it, by and bye," said Robert; "I think I could stand half a glass of sherry without being tipsy."

Then the conversation turned to general topics; Sir Robert asked Mrs. Paxton's age, if her husband was still living, and other things about the family; then it melted off in a natural easy way to other matters; he talked of hunting, shooting, skating and snow shoes, and was pleased with his son's ready answers and bright interest in what he said. When Molly had disappeared with the cloth, and they were left alone over their wine, their eyes met with another meaning in them.

"Are you pressed for time to-night?" asked the father.

"No, sir, I am at liberty for the evening."

"I am very glad. You will stay and bear me company, will you not?"

"If you wish it, sir," said Robert.

---

[150]Therefore, the Paxton house is situated three miles from Gibbeline, on the Eramosa Road (Highway 124).

"You know I wish it, you rogue," replied the father, with a fond, bright smile, "are you going to shut me out of your heart altogether?"

"No, sir, I can't if I would," the boy spoke sturdily, but with a deep blush, "for I love you a deal better than John Smith, though he's done fifty times as much for me, and I owe him duty and respect." – Sir Robert put his white hand upon Robert's brown paw, which lay upon the table, and the lad did not resist the kindly pressure, or remove it. – "I don't see that there's harm in caring for you, seeing you're my father; and I can't help it, anyway, and I'm not going to try; I've given up fighting against the feeling. I have confidence in you, and don't fear you as I did at first."

"You need not fear me, God knows. What did you fear in me, Robert?"

"That you would trouble my mother. Her comfort is my first thought, my pleasure as well as duty, but I think I did you some injustice. Mr. Meldrum told me to-day that you sent two hundred pounds out, he thought for me; anyway he spent it that way, getting a town lot and house for mother, not telling her you sent it, which was delicate in him; and fruit trees, and other things he bought."

"Why did you speak to Mr. Meldrum?" asked Sir Robert, by no means pleased by this revelation.

"I didn't, he spoke to me. I wrote to Miss Paxton and told her you were in Gibbeline (she is my dear friend and I love her), and she spoke to him; he married her sister, you know, and she knew he was acquainted with you. I asked her advice, but I had made up my mind how to act before I saw her, and it was well I had, for she was so shaken by her mother's death that she was quite broken down and ill; she couldn't say much to me."

"To what had you made up your mind, my son?"

"To tell you I loved you before I said good bye, and though I cannot take your money, that you are dear to me, – *father*."

The last word was added to heal the pain given by the first part of the sentence, and in some measure it did.

"Then you mean to leave me, Robert, – you mean to give me up, I am to lose my newly found treasure?"

"I hate to speak and pain you, but the truth is best; you cannot give up and keep, you know, and you gave me up long ago when you left me. Smith, and more especially mother, have had their dreams about me; they have worked hard for me, and brought me up, and have a right to me; if I left them for you, the truth would leak out somehow, and cause them bitter pain and disappointment. Why, mother cannot bear me out of her sight for a week. She must see me every day, and comes to Mr. Llewellyn's if I do not go to her; and not a day passes without her kiss and fond touch, I am that dear to her. You are not jealous of *her*, – father?"

"No, my dear boy, no, – but do you mean that I am to go away, – that I am to part with you forever?"

"I don't mean any such thing; you might write through Mr. Jackson, and it would be a pleasure to get your letters, and a profit, for I'd know how a gentleman ought to write, and when you got mine it would reconcile you to part with me when you saw the bad spelling in 'em.'"

"Every misspelt word, every ill-constructed sentence would be a keen reproach to me, Robert; it would tell me of my own neglect."

"Then I'll look in the dictionary for every word, and study grammar, we won't have any more reproach. I cannot bear to give you pain, I hurt myself as much as you the other day when I was angry. It would be a better help to me than money if you would write to me sometimes, and your love for me is a better help too," giving emphasis to his words by a pressure of the brown fist. The half glass of sherry had brightened his eyes, loosened his tongue and given him a brilliant spot in one cheek; he spoke freely and without fear. The father was pleased with the lad's confidence and encouraged it.

"But surely, Robert, you do not wish to be a servant all your life?" he said.

"No, sir, I hope not, but I have heard that some of old Boney's[151] best generals fought in the ranks and rose from them, and why shouldn't I? You wouldn't love your son the less for fighting his way up, would you?"

"Nothing could make me love my son either less or more, Robert; last week I was a lonely man, and now I have an interest in life. Tell me your plans, if you have any. Do you think of going into trade – do you like trade?"

"That depends – I don't think I would make a good salesman, I couldn't crack up a thing and sell it for more than it was worth – as I have seen some of those fellows do. I think it shabby, even

---

[151]Napoleon Bonaparte

dishonest; but if there was such a thing as *fair trade*,[152] I would like it well enough, if nothing better offered; but I like the fresh air, I like horses and animals of all kinds, and I like out-door exercise, and don't like to be shut up."

"Would you like a farm," said the father, "do you know anything of farming?"

"Not much. I have lived at a tavern, and with the Cromaboo parson, and worked a a day labourer, and for a little while in a saw-mill, and I was a cook for the volunteers, but I never liked anything so well as driving the mail. It suits me. I used to wait in the shop the other day at Mr. Llewellyn's, but since his niece's marriage is closed; I never liked the job much. I often went to fish for the family; Mr. Llewellyn called it work, but I thought it fun to fish, and so it was to gather raspberries. If I finish that glass of wine I shall be tipsy. I'm talking too much, as it is."

"Not too much to please me; I take an interest in all you say, but we will go into the other room, if you are afraid to finish the glass," said Sir Robert, and he rose and opened the door. It was a large, well-furnished cheerful parlour, with a bright glowing fire in the grate, and an open piano facing them.

"I love music," said Robert, "do you play, sir?"

"Yes, I will play for you presently, but it's music to me to hear you talk." Sir Robert leant against the mantle-piece as he spoke, and his son stood opposite to him. "You are like your mother, and yet so unlike, – what a boy you are, not the shadow of a whisker, not the least down on the upper lip."

"And yet I've tried everything to make 'em grow," said Robert the younger, with a blush and a grin.

"Have you tried the cat?" said Robert the elder, laughing, "why don't you get pussy to lick you?"

"Oh! she often does of her own accord, but that's a fallacy, there's nothing in it," and he shook his head, "but I don't mind," he added, "Miss Paxton says she likes me better without whiskers."

"How did you become acquainted with Miss Paxton? She must be many years older than you, if she is the lady I remember as a child.

---

[152]With the advantage of hindsight, we see here what could be interpreted as a prophetic vision by Leslie.

But do not answer if you would rather not," he added quickly. "I take an interest in all that concerns you, that is why I asked."

"I will tell you anything about myself or mother that you like to hear," the son answered, frankly. "She was very kind to mother when I was born and held me in her arms as a baby, but we passed out of her life, till I met her on the stage about a year ago, and fell in love with her. And then I had a fever in the summer, and she came to see me, and mother was so glad to see her again, and she lent me books, and took me in hand about my grammar, and made me give up smoking; and then the night of Miss Llewellyn's wedding, when all the guests were gone, mother told us both about my birth. It hurt me, of course, but Miss Paxton comforted me, and spoke so kindly and wisely, and – and I love her. I hope one day to make her my wife."

"She must be years older than you," said the father.

"Only fourteen years, but when you love a sweet, dear woman like that, you never think about her age," was the reply, "and what does it matter?"

Sir Robert had great difficulty in repressing a smile. "I remember two pretty little girls at Mr. Paxton's," he said, "and I remember them quite distinctly, though I never heard their names. I was at the house only once, I went with Dr. Catternach, when young Paxton got some sand in his eye, and was turned into the garden to amuse himself while the doctor saw his patient. I found two little girls playing with a kitten; I wonder which is your Miss Paxton. One had long, fair curls, and a slight cast in the eye that was not a blemish, but a beauty. I asked her for a kiss, and she kissed her hand at me and ran away laughing. She was dressed in a white frock and blue tippet, and looked like a little blue butterfly as she ran. The other was a very grave little person, and eyed me suspiciously at a safe distance; she had beautiful eyes, like the German fairy's 'a barley corn bigger' than other people's eyes. She did not smile, and said discreetly that she never kissed men, and when I tried to get near her she was gone like a lap wing."

"That is Miss Mary," said Robert, "I have her photograph; would you like to see it? The other one married and died," and he took the picture from his pocket.

Sir Robert looked at it critically, and pronounced it, "A sweet, gentle face; but she is like her father," he said, "and I do not like that in her, for I did not like him, though prejudice apart, he was a handsome old man. And so this is your first love, Robert?"

"Oh! no, sir, Miss Llewellyn was my first, or I thought so. I didn't really know what love meant till I saw Miss Paxton. I was engaged to Miss Llewellyn, and it worried me no end, but she went and married her cousin, Mr. Harry, and never asked my leave."

"Perhaps Miss Paxton may do the same," said Sir Robert, smiling.

"Oh! she won't promise to be anything but my friend," said the lad, with a big sigh, "that's the worst of it; we're not engaged, you know."

Sir Robert was secretly glad to hear it, but he didn't say so, he only smiled. His son catching the expression, said "You think its nonsense about Miss Paxton, but I'm quite in earnest, my happiness depends upon her."

"How long is it since the engagement with Miss Llewellyn?" asked the father.

"It was last winter," Robert admitted, rather unwillingly, "but it doesn't take ten years to fall in love, you know; a sun picture like this photo only takes a few minutes to make, and lasts a long time. You didn't love me last week," he added, with a half saucy smile.

"And do you tell your mother all your little affairs of the heart, my boy?"

"Yes, and she loves Miss Paxton as well as I do."

"And John Smith – is he your confidante, too?" asked the baronet, with a comic elevation of the eyebrows.

"I should think not," said Robert, laughing. "I'd as soon think o' telling a stump fence."

The father laid a hand on each of his son's shoulders, and gave him a little shake, and looking into his face, said "You are about as tall as your mother."

"Not near so tall, she grew six inches after I was born."

"That would make a difference indeed. Robert, do you know I've been resisting a strong impulse within me ever since I saw you?"

"What is that, sir?"

"I have wanted to give you a kiss."

"Well, I don't see why you shouldn't; I like kissing myself, though Mr. Llewellyn calls it 'a meaningless habit.' I kissed his niece last winter, and some busy body told him, and if I didn't catch it. And this afternoon Miss Paxton looked so sad and broken down, that it went to my heart to see her, and I couldn't help kissing her. Mr. Meldrum saw me, and he said I had taken a liberty, he said I was my father's own son.'

"Meaning *mine*," said Sir Robert, delighted, "and not John Smith's? Do you like Mr. Meldrum?"

"I do, but he often rubs me up the wrong way, and I don't know whether it's intentional or not."

"That's just my feeling about him," assented the father, "he seemed to delight in making me wretched when you were born; he told me every pang poor Nelly suffered; he extenuated nothing."

"He would," said Robert.

"Do I tire you, my son – do you wish my hands away?"

"No, I like you to touch me, though if it was any other man I should be ready to knock his head off," replied Robert.

His father stooped and lightly kissed his forehead. "John Smith never kisses you, does he?" he asked.

"I don't remember that he ever did, but I've kissed him many a time when I was a little chap."

"Devilish bad taste," said Sir Robert, with a grimace.

"You didn't ought to swear," said Robert junior, looking his father straight in the eyes, and forgetting his grammar in his earnestness. "It's lucky you're not in my coach."

"What would you do with me?"

"Have you out of it for bad language, if you didn't give in to moral suasion."

"The dickens you would. You speak like a Methodist."

"I am a Methodist," said Robert.

"Really? What kind of a one – Wesleyan?"

"I believe we are the sort called ranters; I don't know the right name. The reverend Peter Crutch is our minister. I went at first to please mother, she finds great comfort there. But now I'm on probation," he added, with a grin, and related his fight with the painter, at which his father laughed heartily.

"Won't you play for me," pleaded Robert, presently, "I should like so much to hear you play," and Sir Robert at this sat down to the piano, saying as he did so, "I am such a selfish old fellow that I would rather hear you talk than play to please you." He was master of the instrument, and played in a sparkling, brilliant way, and seeing the pleasure in his son's face, he played longer than he would have done; at last with a long, sweet, shivering trill of harmony, he ceased.

"Oh! do play that bit again," pleaded Robert, "it's like the wild note of a robin in the spring, a cry of joy."

He played it again, and gently glided off to a softer and more liquid melody, before he ceased, with the question, "Is that enough?"

"No, it isn't," said the son, "I could listen forever; that last piece was as sweet as falling water – oh! do play again."

And Sir Robert did, for a long time; at last he rose.

"Thank you," said his son, "I won't be selfish and ask for more but that *is* music. I wish I could play like that," and he softly touched the key with his brown fore-finger.

"Can you play at all, my boy?" asked Sir Robert.

"A little on the melodeon, not on the piano."

"Here is one in the corner," said the father, and he went across and opened the instrument, "let me hear you – what music would you like?"

"Any piece will do, sir," replied the lad, with a bright glance over his shoulder, "for I don't know one note from another."

He sat down and touched the keys, and his father stood aloof at a little distance, listening critically. Remembering the effect of his music upon Miss Paxton and Mr. Meldrum, Robert struck into one of his pet voluntaries, a sighing, mournful melody; he felt no nervousness in playing before a skilled musician, only a strong curiosity as to what effect his music would have upon him; would he approve, or disapprove? Would he shed tears, or would he swear? After a ten minuted performance, he turned to his father, who leant against the mantle shelf, looking grave enough and listening attentively. "That will do, Robert, thank you," he said.

"You don't like my music as I did yours," said the boy, rising.

"You have the inspiration of a true musician, you make the thing wail like a lost spirit; does it hurt and grieve you to draw out such sounds?"

"No, sir, it's a pleasure to me."

"The deuce it is! It only hurts the hearer, aye – and why should it, I wonder? There were no false notes, no uncertain sounds, no discord, but the combined effect is painful; I would as soon listen to a dying groan, my boy, as your music, if it's all like that. Can you play away the effect of the last piece? If you are at all uncertain don't attempt it, try the music of your tongue instead."

"I'm afraid to try," said Robert, secretly delighted with his own power, "so I'll talk till you're tired o' hearing me, and then maybe you'll play again, and I'll never be tired o' hearing you."

Whether it was the effect of Robert's music or not, his father was graver after this; he moved a chair close to his son's, and sitting down, took the lad's brown hand in his own.

"Tell me about your mother," he said, "she has other children; does she love them, as well as you, or is the first born the favourite of all?"

"I think I am; she has only one other now, he's six years old."

"But she had a son a year or two younger than you," said Sir Robert.

"Four years younger, he died of scarlet fever, and so did two more brothers in one day, and my little sister Nelly died a few days later. They were my playmates, and it half broke my heart to lose them. I would have died, too, but for Mr. Meldrum's skill and mother's love. Tommy was born just after; I'm very fond o' Tommy; he's the wisest, prettiest little thing you ever saw; his mouth is like a red rose bud, and his eyes are mother's over again."

"Nelly is less desolate than I," said Sir Robert, with a sigh. "I never had a living child but you, my son," – this with a liquid tenderness of tone and a sad softening of the eyes that met Robert's.

"Perhaps it was because you married in a worldly way and didn't love your wives," suggested the Cromaboo mail carrier.

"No, Robert, it isn't in me to make a worldly marriage. I couldn't take a woman into my bosom, if I did not admire and like her; they were both very dear to me. My first wife only lived two years after our marriage, and never had a child; the last had seven, but only one ever breathed, and that but for a few minutes, and he cost his mother's life. I never saw those still little bodies without thinking of the squalling bundle I had left in the backwoods that was so unmistakably alive. Ah! Robert, you do not know what it is to wander about a great lonely house as I did last year, when the death of the mistress has made it desolate, and it is empty of all fellow creatures but servants, and the spirit of home gone out of it forever. I suppose your Methodist parson would say I deserved all my troubles for the sins of my youth."

Robert looked straight into the eyes so near his own and answered gravely, "And if he did, wouldn't he say the truth, father?"

Sir Robert would not have taken such a reproof good temperedly from any other human being, and it was a great proof of his love for his newly found son, that though his face flushed, he laughed too, and gave the lad a little fond shake of the shoulder as he said, "You rascal, I thought you promised not to reproach me any more."

"I don't mean to, father, but I don't want to lose you again, I want you to take a right view o' things that I may meet you in heaven."

"My dear boy, I am glad – I am more thankful than you can think that you take a right view of things; you are like my youthful self come back, but without my bad breeding and lax morality; you have Nelly's sense of justice, your ideas are like hers. She would not let me rob the squirrel's hoard of nuts, and when I found a bird's nest and placed the warm, speckled eggs in her hand, she put them back reverently, saying 'Sure if we broke up the little home, how could we ask the Virgin to bless the nest we'll build ourselves when I am your little wife?' And yet after that I harried dame Connel's nest cruelly and by stealth, and took her callow fledgling from her forever. I don't think Connel cared, he would rather have the money I gave him than his daughter's honour; for after taking one hundred pounds in gold from me, to pay the expenses of Nelly's illness, he turned her from his door to sleep with the wild beasts in the woods. But the mother felt it, she cursed me as only an Irish woman could, and I have sometimes felt that the curse clave to me. Tell me, Robert, did she not come to see your mother? Connel would prevent her if he could, but I feel sure she would do it by stealth."

"I know she did, more than once, but I do not remember it, and she sent her presents of tea many times. She is dead now."

"The noble, ragged creature!" exclaimed Sir Robert, "she was a fit wife for an ancient Roman rather than a sordid creature like Connel. Did you ever see any of the Connels Robert?"

"Yes, one called Pat; he taunted me with my birth, and Chip gave him a licking for it. That was the first time I ever suspected that I was not Smith's son. I asked Chip if what he said was true, when the row was over, and he growled out 'Whether it's truth or not, Robbie, it's spite, and he deserved his sore bones.'"

"He did, the little devil," said Sir Robert, "I would have wrung his neck in his youth, and nipped him in the bud, if I could have dreamt of that taunt. How old were you, Robert – did it hurt you much – did it make you think less of your mother?"

"I was seventeen – it vexed me, of course, but nothing could make me love mother less, and she just living to please me."

"And you must not love her less, my son," said Sir Robert, with energy; "there is no woman in the world I have a greater respect for, and I should know her if anybody does. She was just a dear, innocent, ignorant child when I led her astray, feeling no fear in me, and not knowing why she blushed when I kissed her; rubbing her cheek against mine like a stupid, little harmless lamb, never dreaming of the effect her sweet caresses had on me, or the temptation she was to me. Those dear, wild slips of Irish lasses are more really innocent and ignorant of evil than the children of any other nation under heaven; and it is because their mothers are pure, and do not delight to dabble in dirty water, or rub the bloom from their sweet fruit before it is ripe. Nelly knew no more of the origin of babies, or where her little brothers and sisters came from, than she knew how the little birds got into the eggs; she was as pure as any snow drop, and therefore the most dangerous, the most tempting little charmer I ever saw. A modest, refined instinct she had, that made her shrink from coarseness and detest it, but no knowledge of evil. Little deceptions that would have been seen through in a minute by a coarser creature, were received as simple truths by her, and the sweet mysteries of nature were chaste mysteries in her pure child's eyes."

"Father," said Robert, with a shaking voice and tears in his eyes, "I cannot help saying it, if it was the last word I had to speak – it was worse than a murder serving her so; many a man has been hanged for a smaller sin." A great tear fell on the white hand that held his own, as he spoke.

"My boy, I admit it – I know it, and though I have suffered, though my punishment is hard, now that I have seen you, and know what I have lost, I acknowledge God's mercy to me; I feel that it might have been far worse for me. If I had a daughter and any man served her as I did Nelly, I would not be content with cursing, and leaving the vengeance to God, as dame Connel did, I must have his life if I forfeited my soul for it. But I make you unhappy, and you must not be unhappy, my dear, long neglected boy" – fondly stroking his hair as he spoke – "and I must and *will* help you; time may unfold a way, and you must let me know; I long to have yours a happy and pure life, far happier because better than mine; my dear son, my flesh and blood, my new and better self, my youth come back to me in the flesh without my sins and stains; the pride and glory of my old age – for the bar sinister is my disgrace, not yours, Robert, or your mother's."

Sir Robert spoke honestly, earnestly, and from his very soul, but if he had been the most artful schemer in the world, he could not have found a better way of winning his son's confidence, and creeping into his warm young heart; for when a man frankly confesses his faults, it breaks our self-righteous judgement and cuts away the ground of our anger. God had punished, vengeance was His, and He had opened the eyes of the sinner, and Robert forgave him with his whole heart, he more than forgave him, and he expressed his feeling by suddenly putting his brown paw on the penitent's shoulder and kissing him right upon the mouth as he might have kissed his mother. Sir Robert was greatly touched by the mark of love, and it drew a further confession from him.

"Ah! my son," he said, "I did not yield to sin without a struggle, and when you are tempted to do wrong you must not parley, you must fly, it is the only way of escape, for when it is in your heart to do evil, the devil will make an opportunity for you. I had gone to the backwoods for the third time before I really knew how strong my feeling was for Nelly, though I knew well enough it was her sweet face that drew me back, and not the wish to see sugar making, or the love of hunting. When the truth became clear to me, I went away for a week's solitary hunt to face the thoughts of my heart and conquer them. Dame Connel, who had grown suspicious of my love for Nelly, for I could not conceal it, asked me if I was sure I would be gone for a week. I answered her truly that I would. If she had confided her plans to me, I would not have returned before, I should have been armed against myself and conquered evil, my honour would have been touched had she told me, and I would have been forearmed. As soon as I left, she and her husband and Smith went to an Indian encampment ten miles away, to trade for baskets. They were away for two days and nights, and left Nelly to keep house by herself and take care of the children. She was left against her will, being very much afraid to stay, nor was it kind or altogether safe to leave her alone in the heart of a great wilderness, for there were Indians and wild beasts in plenty in those days to frighten, if they did not harm her. I knew nothing of this, and when I had gone a few miles my favourite dog staked himself against a snag in running, and was badly hurt. I took the creature in my arms and turned back, intending to leave him for dame Connel and Nelly to nurse, and start again, but as soon as we reached the friendly shelter of the shanty he died, and Nelly wept to see it, though she was delighted to have me back, and begged me not to go again till her father and mother returned. I stood face to face with my temptation, and was too much startled by it to care much for the death of the dog. I leant against the door post in the soft Indian summer sunlight, and tried to steady myself and think; when Nelly, who was surprised to see me so quiet, and thought I was grieving for my four-footed friend, came to my side and whispered sweet words of consolation, and for the first time gave me without asking a timid little kiss. Never did the devil present such a tempting bait to turn a wavering sinner into a down-right villain. I made a last faint fight with temptation. I took up my gun and turned to go, but the little creature followed me, and laid her hand upon my arm, and begged me not to leave her; and she asked if she had vexed me, with sudden tears in those wonderful dark eyes; and the brats seeing me going, added their entreaties and tears to hers; Mickey and Peter, and Judy and Mary, and Chip, and that little devil Pat, who was next to the baby. The baby was away, or that, from its very helplessness, might have been a protection to Nelly. Ah! if mother Connel had trusted me, and told me her intention, I would never have harried her nest – but the temptation came suddenly, I turned back with no ill-intent. You are not the result of lust alone, Robert, for cruelly, inexcusably as I behaved, I did love Nelly dearly, my little flower of the wilderness, and when she followed and begged me to stay, all power of resistance went out of me, I could but take her in my arms and kiss her. I was the devil's property for the time, and for many a day after, and the bitterness of parting with her, my pricks of conscience, my jealousy when she married Smith, gave me my first grey hairs. If Meldrum had got her away from Mr Paxton's, as I wished, I could not have resisted her entreaties, her tears, I must have married her."

"If it had depended on that alone, you would never have married her," said Robert. "My mother is a very proud woman, she would not have entreated, much as she loved you. There is a kind of hardness in her, and she does not forgive easily, though she never forgets a kindness. She loves Miss Paxton because she washed her feet for her, and kissed her, and did not despise her in her grief and shame."

"I could find it in my heart to love her for that myself," said Sir Robert.

"Oh! I know you would love her if you knew her," replied the lad, in his bright, eager way.

"Then I had better not know her," said the father, with a momentary return to playfulness, as he gently pulled his son's ear; "for it would never do for you and I to be rivals. Robert," he said presently, "I would like so much to see your mother once more, not to renew the old suffering, not to pain her by my presence – but could I not see her, and she not see me?"

"I think that could be managed," replied the son after a thoughtful pause, "and I see no harm in it. Are you equal to a twenty miles ride?"

"Yes, to sixty miles, if I had a horse to carry me, and it was necessary."

"Well, if you rode to Cromaboo, and got there after dark, and went to the Methodist chapel – mother always goes there to the evening service, – and if you sat back by the door, we would be some distance in front of you. Her sight is not good at night, and she never looks about her any way, she goes to worship God. You could leave before the service is quite over and ride back through the night."

"That will be forty miles. I will do it. Robert, do you think your mother a happy woman?"

"I think she is very happy sometimes, but she is a very quiet, grave woman, you hardly ever hear her laugh, though she has the sweetest smile in the world."

"She must think the worst of me if ever she thinks of me at all," said Sir Robert. "She is a woman now, and cannot regard me with her child's eyes; she has had a daughter of her own, and knows the full extent of my villainy to her old self, simple little virgin-hearted rose of the wilderness that she was, making the forest an Eden to me, and I rewarded her by being a very serpent in her path."

"She is a Christian," said Robert, "and knows we can't get into heaven by our own merits. I believe – indeed I know she prays for you night and morning, and she would have a clearer notion at her age, perhaps, of what she was to you in the way of temptation. She told me she always thought of you when I sang 'Sun of my Soul' – this is the verse: –

"If some poor, wandering child of thine,

Has spurned to-day the voice divine;
Lord, now the gracious work begin
Let him no more lie down in sin."[153]

Sir Robert walked to the window to hide his emotion from his son, and stayed there for what seemed to Robert a long time. When he returned he stood behind the boy as he sat, and put a hand on either shoulder.

"Is Smith still a Roman Catholic?" he asked.

"Yes, but he never interferes with mother, he'll walk to the chapel on stormy nights, and hold the umbrella over her head, and go to meet her when the meeting's over."

"If I detest a man in the whole world it's *that* man, said Sir Robert, bitterly, "and yet I should hate him more if he was unkind to Nelly."

"Do you know, father, it's ten o'clock," said Robert, "and they will be shutting up at the Western?"

"It's Saturday night, and they will not close till twelve. Stay with me till twelve, my boy, and I will walk with you to your hotel, and not only bless, but kiss you at parting. It's not English, but it's oriental and sensible. *Now* I know how old Abraham loved his Isaac."

"Mother would say, 'Not as well as Hagar loved her Ishmael.'"

"You are Ishmael and Isaac in one, my first born and my only one; you will never have a rival now. Do you like coffee? Then I will ring for some, I love coffee like a Turk. Ah! Robert, when shall we have another evening together again?"

"To-morrow night," said the son, "we'll worship in the same temple. It's a little log building, with a cow-bell to ring the folks in, and you will hear me prayed for by name, alongside o' the Queen, for Mr. Crutch always asks a blessing for all in power, and he approves o' me for putting down swearing, for all I fought the painter. Won't you play to me, father, while they make the coffee, and let us part in harmony?"

"I will, my dear boy; it makes me young again to see you while I play; you have a very happy face."

"I am happy to-night," said Robert.

---

[153]Richard F. Littledale and James E. Vaux, eds. "Hymns For The Sick," *The Priest's Prayer Book*, Part IX (1865): 128.

Chapter Thirty-Two

"For a cap and bells our souls we pay,
We wear out our lives in toiling and tasking;
It is only Heaven that is given away,
It is only God may be had for the asking."

– Lowell[154]

A LARGE room, low in the ceiling, and dimly lighted by tallow candles in tin sconces, that hung along the walls; a room filled
with rough benches without backs, and divided by a narrow passage that served as aisle; and twice every Sunday crowded with men
and women as thickly packed as herrings in a barrel. Such was the
chapel where the Rev. Peter Crutch officiated. He was a very popular
preacher, and the Rev. Paul Moorhouse attributed his popularity to
a rowdy love of vulgarity and noise on the part of the inhabitants of
Cromaboo, for did *he* not preach the most classical, the most fault-
less sermons to a handful of yawning people, whose orthodoxy could
scarcely keep them awake, whereas, there was hardly standing room
in the little log conventicle, and sleepers were quite unknown? Indeed, it would have been impossible for a grown man or woman to
sleep under the nose of Mr. Crutch, as they did under that of Mr.
Moorhouse, who, it must be said, was harsh, and by no means correct in his judgement of his dissenting brother. Peter Crutch was,
undoubtedly, sometimes coarse in speech, and he now and then ex-
ercised his lungs by roaring out his sentiments as if every member of
his congregation were deaf, and he had a bad habit of banging down
his great Bible with such force and energy as to make the reading

---

[154]James Russell Lowell (1819-1891), "The Vision Of Sir Launfal."

lamps beside him dance again; these were his defects, but his virtues were legion. He was honest, and thoroughly in earnest, and meant every word that he said, which is a great charm in a preacher; for a clever actor can never touch the heart like a sincere man.

The Rev. Peter was a bold man, and did not scruple to be personal in his remarks; and ignorant people like personalities much better than the more refined; he had a thorough knowledge of every day human nature, large sympathies, a warm heart; he was willing to take the whole world to his bosom, and anxious that every sinner in it should feel the love of God as he felt it. He was a healthy, temperate man, who could peel a potato with his fingers, and dip it in salt and eat it with a relish in the dirtiest house in Cromaboo; a man who knew nothing of dyspepsia, who had his teeth to extreme old age, when they dropped out of his head in a perfectly sound condition; a man whose laugh could be heard half a mile away on a clear day, and whose sneeze, as his wife said, "was enough to break a horse's leg." A white-haired, rosy, clear-headed old man, who could ride ten miles a day, in his seventieth year, and did not give up preaching till past eighty; a good tempered man who could enjoy a joke to the end of his days, a man who knew how to take people of his own class, and had great influence with them for good; a man who knew no foreign tongue, dead or living, but who understood the Bible thoroughly, according to the best translations, having the letter of it in his head, and the spirit of it in his heart. A self sacrificing man, who, if he promised, would not disappoint, though it were to his own injury; the happy husband of a handsome, large hearted, broad shouldered old woman, much above him in birth and education, though not in natural ability; a wife who had brought him a comfortable income and fourteen children; and who thought him superior as a preacher to the Apostle Paul. A man who gave sound practical advice in language that the most ignorant could understand, who knew a great deal about common subjects, and common people, and was never afraid to tackle the greatest reprobate in his congregation, or out of it, and take the wildest bull by the horns, so to speak; the happy head of one of the noisiest, jolliest households in Canada.

Such was the reverend Peter Crutch, a man who was rather too loud for my taste on ordinary occasions; but on a winter night when he was very weary with battling the elements, I have found it a pleasure and profit to listen to him. His voice was good and he read beautifully; his wife had taught him how to pronounce, and his right-thinking head and warm, throbbing heart, that pumped away in love to all humanity, made him throw feeling into every word and sentence, and it was a treat to hear him read when a hard day's toil had worked off his energy and fined him down. To-night he was very weary; he had ridden sixteen miles, he had preached twice with all his voice and heart and soul, and as his youngest son pertinently expressed it, "prayed no end;" his body was pretty well exhausted, and he was glad of a quiet moment to rest and think before the arrival of the congregation.

Sir Robert Hardacre came in early, and seated himself as directed in a quiet corner near the door. If it had been an English church he would have stood for a moment looking into the crown of his hat, but he did not know whether it was "the thing" in a Methodist chapel, and had no desire to attract attention by his eccentricities, so he omitted this ceremony. He sat back in the shadow, and though calm enough in exterior, watched with a good deal of eagerness for the arrival of his long lost Nelly, the well remembered pearl which he had rejected as if it had been a common pebble.

Mr. Crutch was quite unconscious that he had one of the upper ten thousand to hear him, but it would have made no difference if he had known, for he possessed a good deal of the spirit of another Methodist preacher, who told General Jackson that if he did not repent, "God would damn him as quick as he would a Guinea negro."[155] A good many people had poured in before Mrs. Smith arrived with Tommy by the hand, and as she was a little in advance of her eldest son, Sir Robert did not at first recognize her, though he remarked her as a *distingue* woman. Her pew – so called – was nearly full, and as Robert stooped to give her her hymn book and Bible, before turning back to look for another seat, she slightly turned her head, and the old lover knew it was Nelly; not from any likeness to her former self, but from her striking resemblance to dame Judy Connel, who had cursed him so bitterly, nearly twenty years before. It was only the profile he saw, surmounted by a black velvet bonnet, bought by Robert out of his wages; she wore a black dress and plaid shawl, and her shoulders were of that kind that look well in a shawl.

---

[155] Andrew Jackson (1767-1845), the seventh President of the United States (1829-1837).

Sir Robert thought the little innocent face of Tommy more like the Nelly of old than Mrs. John Smith. Robert had hidden away her spectacles lest she should turn by accident and recognize his father, and being half blind without them, she did not even attempt to look for the hymns, but gave herself up to listening. She had taken Tommy on her knee as the seat was crowded, and towards the middle of the service he grew sleepy, and in putting her arm about him and soothing him, she turned half round, and Sir Robert saw fully for the first time the worn, yet peaceful face of the old love. Her long lashes swept her cheeks, and a half smile played about her mouth, as she looked down at her little boy and patted his shoulder in a gentle monotonous way to soothe him off to the land of nod. Robert took the seat in front of his father, and gave him his hymn book, seeing that he had none. It was taken with a fond, bright smile, the last glance exchanged by them for many a month and year.

The service commenced, as Robert had predicted, by a fervent and loyal prayer for the Queen and all in authority under her, not forgetting the Cromaboo mail carrier, whom Mr. Crutch alluded to by name as "a stray lamb of God's flock," one day he heartily prayed to be gathered into the fold as a faithful and honoured servant of his Saviour. At this there were a few deep groans from the center of the building, whether of sympathy or derision it is impossible to say. Then the pastor went on to cry with heartfelt fervour to that God who, when He saw "a great multitude, had compassion on them," a cry for "the poor sinners enclosed in these four walls, unhappy, hard hearted, evil-minded, but not wholly God-forsaken sinners. "Have mercy on them, oh! my God!" he exclaimed, "and upon me, the poor crutch upon which they lean, help me to show them this night that I am but a broken reed, and that Thou alone art worthy of all trust and confidence. Every heart here is naked in Thy sight, Thou knowest their wants and the motives that led them to this house. Oh! grant that those who came empty and hungry for Thee may go away full, and that those who came full of pride and the lusts of the devil may go away empty, or filled with something better." He concluded with the Lord's prayer, which was responded to by loud amens from the congregation. Then followed the hymn, "All hail the power of Jesus' name," roared out by the united strength of the whole multitude, who sang with more vigor than harmony, and filled the building with a deafening volume of sound.

After a few minutes of silence, the clear, melodious voice of Peter Crutch poured out the parable of the lost sheep, with the commentary, "Do you *believe* it? Whether you do or you don't, it is simply and entirely true, and we all, like sheep, have gone astray, we have turned every one to his *own* way – which is far from being God's way – and the Lord hath laid on *Him* the iniquity of us all."

Then he turned to the fifty-third chapter of Isaiah, and read from the third verse to the end of the chapter. Perfect silence reigned in the densely packed house, not a sound was heard but the voice of the reader.

"Was it the Jews alone who despised and rejected Him?" he asked. "Do none among you all hide your faces from Him daily? Yes, you people of Cromaboo esteem Him not, though you say amen when I pray for the coming of His kingdom. You drink and smoke, and swear and gratify every lust, you see no beauty in *Jesus* that you should desire Him, my poor fellow-sinners, who should be saints in heart and life and practice. I pity – how I pity you all from my soul – and if I, a weak and feeble creature, can feel in this way, what is the sorrow of God, your Father, for the loss of so many of His children, who willfully reject His mercy day by day? I am tired to-night, and I cannot say much to you, but I *do* say, turn while it is time. *Now* is the accepted time. I have forgotten my spectacles, and I cannot see a face in this room, they are just so many blurred patches to me, but I know it is crowded with immortal souls, and I beg and beseech every one of you to turn while it is time. *Now* is the accepted time. Do not reject the message because you despise the messenger, do not say within yourselves, 'It is the voice of old Peter Crutch, the Methodist, who tells us the same thing over and over again every Sunday.' It is the voice of *God's messenger* to every one in this room, and it may be the last time that some of you will have the opportunity of hearing His message. He hath borne *our* griefs, and carried our sorrows. He – God – was wounded for *our* transgressions – I quote Scripture now – He was bruised for *our* iniquities, the chastisement of our peace was upon Him, and with His stripes we *are* healed, if we *will only believe it.* Not going to be healed, but 'we *are* healed.' Believe and your faith shall make you whole, believe *what*? Believe that God loves you, that He lived for you, and suffered and died for you, believe that He is most willing to help you, for He *is.* Only believe it.

Prisoners of hope, be strong, be bold,
Cast off your doubts, disdain to fear,
Dare to believe, on Christ lay hold,
Wrestle with Christ in mighty prayer.
Tell Him 'we will not let Thee go
Till we Thy name and nature know.
Hast Thou not died to purge our sin
And risen Thy death for us to plead?
To write Thy law of love within
Our hearts, and make us free indeed?
Thou wilt perform Thy faithful word,
The servant *shall* be as his Lord.'[156]

"Oh! reject Him no more, arise and go to your Father, how joyful He will be to welcome His dead to life, to find His lost. He is *satisfied* to bear your sins, He is most willing and anxious to write His laws in your hearts and make you happy. The great ones of the earth care nothing for you, poor, lost, insignificant backwoods sinners – insignificant means low, little, mean – but you are dear to God if you will only believe it; you will shine as the stars forever and not a hair of your heads shall perish, if you will only take His message and turn in time. Weary, lonely, desolate sinners, turn while it is time; for lonely you are, though you be packed as closely as pigs in a drum; alone you came into the world, and alone you must go out of it, unless God be with you, and takes you in His everlasting arms. God-rejecting sinners, reject Him no more, take Him to your hearts this night and forever; go to Him yourselves *every one* of you; and let no man who has heard me to-night dare to say he has never had the way of life pointed out to him, for if he makes *that* an excuse for his wickedness I will be a swift witness against him at the day of judgement."

During this address, there had been a few groans from the congregation and an occasional cry of "Glory, halleluia!" but when it was over there was a dead silence. After a few minutes rest, Mr. Crutch rose again.

"Let us now sing to the praise of God, our Maker, our dear elder Brother, our Saviour, if we will let Him save us by believing His word, our Lord and Master, who for *our sakes* became poor and took upon

---

[156]Charles Wesley (1707-1788), "Prisoners of Hope Be Strong, Be Bold."

Himself the form of a servant, to Him will we sing part of the 138th hymns. Lift up your hearts as you raise your voices, and be sure he hears and answers prayer.

> "Is there a thing too hard for Thee,
>> Almighty Lord of all?
> Whose threatening looks dry up the sea,
>> and make the mountains fall?
> Who, who shall in Thy presence stand,
>> and match omnipotence?
> Ungrasp the hold of Thy right hand,
>> or pluck the sinner thence?
> Sworn to destroy; let earth assail,
>> near to save Thou art;
> Stronger than all the powers of hell,
>> and greater than my heart.
> Bound down with twice ten thousand ties,
>> yet let me hear Thy call,
> My soul in confidence shall rise,
>> shall rise and break through all.
> Descend and let Thy lightning burn
>> the stubble of Thy foe,
> My sins o'er turn, o'er turn, o'er turn,
>> and make the mountains flow."[157]

To hear Peter Crutch give out this glorious old Methodist hymn was a privilege and a pleasure, that atoned in some measure for the ear-splitting screaming, roaring manner in which the congregation sang it. Mr. Crutch objected to their mode of singing, and often proved a check upon them by freely telling them their faults. To-night he would let them go no further than the fourth verse. "That will do my friends," he said, "I will read the rest, and God give you an understanding heart to take it in. If *that* is singing, then no more singing for me to-night, it may be the melody of the heart, but it's giving me a racking headache. Noise is not music, how often have I told you so, and yet you will not practice up and learn to do better. If I heard you sing every day it would soon break my constitution, and make an old man of me."

---

[157] Charles Wesley (1707-1788), "O That Thou Wouldst the Heavens Rent."

So he read the conclusion of the hymn, and then came to the last prayer; every head bowed but one, and that was Sir Robert Hardacre's; when Mr. Crutch was well off in his prayer, he softly rose and left the building. He could not forbear laying his hand fondly for a moment on the fair bent head of his boy, with a mental blessing upon him, ere he passed out into the darkness. He took the hymn book with him, and crossing the street, stood within the safe shadow of a dirty driving shed, – where the smell was rather strong than fragrant, – and waited till the service was at an end. It was a frosty starlight night, but the moon had not yet risen. "Lord dismiss us with Thy blessing," sounded much better where he stood than it did within the building, sweet and faint it was to the ears of the waiting man.

Presently the people poured out, and the tall stately figure of Mrs. Smith marched straight across the road towards the place of his concealment, followed by Robert with the sleeping Tommy in his arms. As they came near him she glanced over her shoulder, and said, "Is that your father, Robbie?"

It was not without a queer thrill that Sir Robert heard the question put by a sweet familiar voice, that he, at one time, thought never to hear again. "Yes, if he's going to the Harp of Erin[158] to get drunk, we'll stop him, that's all," replied Robert.

A minute later they met Smith, and his wife addressed him in a tone that reminded Sir Robert of the Dame Connel, who had cursed him in the days of his youth.

"And where are you going, John Smith?" she said, "you that promised me not to leave the house alone."

"Chip's there to take care of it. I am going to the Harp of Erin to get a dhrop o' whiskey," growled the person addressed.

"Then I think its very little to your credit," replied Mrs. Smith, with exceeding sharpness.

"Tommy wants you to carry him home, father," said Robert holding out the child, and placing himself so directly in John Smith's way that he nearly touched the lurking figure of his real father.

"How do you know what he wants when he's asleep?" retorted John Smith, wavering between the good influence brought to bear upon him, and his desire for a glass of whiskey.

---

[158] According to the author cited in Appendix B, "The Harp of Erin" was a tavern in Erin.

"People talk in their sleep, sometimes," said Robert, good humouredly, "and Tommy says he's worth more than a glass of whiskey, he's worth more than a hogshead of it; if you come to that he's worth more than all the distilleries of Canada."

"That's thrue for ye, Robbie," Smith admitted, taking the child in his arms, "may the divole fly away wid 'em all," and he wheeled about as he spoke.

Mrs. Smith had not waited to hear the end of the parley, but having spoken, marched on her way, with a steady unwavering stalk that delighted Sir Robert, it expressed so much of stately scorn.

"I should have had my own time if I had married her," he thought, "but after all the petticoat government of a noble creature like that is not to be despised. How magnificent she would have looked in diamonds and velvet," as John Smith and his foster son walked off side by side – "poor Nelly!"

He would not have said "poor Nelly," if he had seen the joy in her face when John Smith came in with the child in his arms; if he could have known the joy in her heart to think the rough man had overcome his temptation. Tears came into her dark eyes as she looked at him.

"Don't be crying, Nelly," he said kindly, "sure Robbie and Tommy turned me back, the crathers."

"Then it was God himself turned you back," she replied, "from playing the devil this Sunday night, when you ought to be praising Him for your blessings."

"Faith, then. I ought for the wife and childer," growled Smith, humbly; "where would I be this day but for ye and Robbie, that's the best son ever father had?"

"Well, I think I ought to be good to you, father," said Robert, putting his hand on Smith's broad shoulder, "so don't be cracking me up; and if you'll give up the drink at once and forever, I'll be better than good, I promise you; I'll work hard and educate Tommy, and he shall be Governor General yet."

"Sure it's you that always had the silver tongue, Robbie," said Smith, with a gruff, admiring laugh, "sit ye down, and stay a bit now, it seems fifty years since I saw you."

And Robert *did* sit down, following duty, not inclination, which would have led him to the Anglo-American to that other father, who was taking a solitary supper, under the name of Mr. Brown. Not till

Smith was safe in bed did Robert return to Mr. Llewellyn's, and he sat at the bed-room window in the moonlight, instead of undressing, listening for the sound of horses' hoofs, which he presently heard. Sir Robert paused for full two minutes before the door, hoping to get another word from his son, but Robert's heart was so full that he could not trust himself to take a second farewell, he stood behind the curtain with a beating heart and the tears rolling down his face. The father could see nothing but the closed blinds, but some instinct told him that his son watched him, he removed his hat and sat for a minute with uncovered head, before he replaced it; and if ever he prayed in his life, he prayed then. A minute more, and he rode slowly away in the light of the rising moon, turning his back upon his son with pain and reluctance, and leaving him for how long – who shall say? Perhaps forever.

Robert threw himself on the bed and wept bitterly, for the loss of that father, whose very name he had detested but a week ago.

Chapter Thirty-Three

"Let us be friends – life is not long enough for quarrels."
– Douglas Jerrold's last words to Charles Dickens[159]

M RS. MARSHALL had a headache that Sunday night and went early to bed, and Margaret had not risen that day, being determined that if Mary insisted upon getting up the house should not want an invalid. Mary sat up late, the clock struck eleven before she left the parlour, and Dolly sat up in the kitchen from a kind-hearted feeling that her young mistress would be lonely. They went out together, and removed the crape from the knocker before going up stairs; and Mary parted with her little maid, at the bed-room door, with a kindly hand shake. Dolly went down stairs again to put out the hall lamp, whose friendly light shone into the road, but feeling hungry, and thinking that "a little something," as she termed it, would be nice before going to sleep, she left the lamp burning and proceeded to the pantry, and selected a large wedge of Lent cake as her supper. This she was quietly and slowly finishing as the clock struck twelve, and it had scarcely ceased striking when a gentle double knock was heard at the front door by both Dolly and her mistress.

The little maiden was so startled that she gave a slight scream, but she jumped up without hesitation and ran to the door, and having across the chain and bolt as a precaution, opened it about an inch, and said in a voice that expressed a mixture of bravado and timidity, "Who are you, and what do you want at this time o' night?"

"Is Miss Paxton up?" asked a clear, pleasant voice.

"I think she is," said Dolly, "I don't know."

---

[159]Douglas William Jerrold (1803-1857).

"Give her that card, if you please, if she is up, and ask her if she will kindly see me for a few minutes," and a card was slipped through into her hand. "Shut me out if you are afraid," he added.

Dolly did shut him out, while she ran up stairs and with very round, wide open eyes, gave the card to her mistress. It bore the inscription, "Sir Robert Hardacre."

"Is it any one you know?" asked Dolly, in a mysterious whisper "I wouldn't let him in if you don't – his voice is something like Bob Smith's," and she gave his message.

"I will see the gentleman," said Mary, who was partly undressed, "ask him into the parlour, and light the lamp, and stir the fire, and ask him to excuse me for a few minutes."

"He might steal the silver spoons," said Dolly, doubtfully, "and the two great silver candle sticks is in that cupboard."

"He is a thief who steals hearts, not spoons, go Dolly, at once, and don't keep him waiting; and then come back to me," she added, fearing the suspicious little maid might think it her duty to stay in the parlour and keep an eye upon the stranger.

So strong was Miss Paxton's curiosity about Sir Robert, that had she been in bed she would have risen and dressed to see him; and the baronet's motive for calling was curiosity, too, but mingled with a more ignoble feeling, even jealousy; for his son had told him before they parted, his intention of becoming a member of Miss Paxton's household; and the further he left Cromaboo behind him, the stronger became his distrust to this unknown lady, the more suspicious did he grow of her influence on his son. He had promised Robert to leave Gibbeline on Monday morning, and had just decided to break his word, stay a day longer, and see this dangerous woman, when he arrived at Paxton's corner,[160] and saw the bright gleam of the fan light above the front door, and the fainter fire light through the carelessly drawn parlour curtains. In an instant he decided to call.

Dolly, having lighted the great lamp and taken a good look at the visitor, felt no further fear of him, but went up stairs to her mistress. She was no great observer of faces, and did not remark his likeness

---

[160]Possibly the intersection of Highway 124 and Watson Road, east of Kaine Hill Road.

to Robert; indeed a mere resemblance of features never strikes any beholder, as does the likeness of expression, voice, or manner.

Left alone Sir Robert glanced about the room with a quick observation and keen interest that would have done honour to a detective officer. He noted the well-stocked book case, the crayon sketches on the walls, the pretty paper, the rudely carved coat of arms above the chimney piece; the supporters were two griffins rampant,[161] not fiercer in aspect than Mr. Paxton had been the last time he saw his face. He noted a bright soft oil painting of the Bay of Naples, and the heads of two children in water colours, which he recognized at a glance as the little girls he had seen in the garden long ago; he noted the faded chintz curtains, the hand screens of peacock's feathers, the pretty card rack of pasteboard and bright wool; but above all, his attention was attracted by a spirited pen and ink sketch of a sleeping child. He took up the lamp and inspected it closely; two verses of Bishop Heber's sweet hymn[162] were inscribed beneath, the first verse in beautiful German text, the second in a large flourishing hand, expressive not only of bravado, but irresolution. He knew Mr. Paxton's hand writing and as he read the verses his lip curled. He read them more than once.

> "Ah! soon, too soon the wintry hour
>   Of man's maturer age
> Will shake the soul with sorrow's power,
>   Or stormy passions rage.
> Oh! Thou who givest life and breath
>   We seek Thy graces alone,
> In childhood, manhood, age and death,
>   To keep us still Thine own."[163]

"Bah!" he said, as he set down the lamp, and the monosyllable expressed much, yet his disgust was not for the author or the sentiments, but the man whose hand inscribed them there. "He could moralize about his own brat," he thought, "though he found no charity for me."

---

[161] An interesting play on Mary Leslie's mother's first married name of Griffin.
[162] Reginald Heber (1783-1826) was the Anglican Bishop of Calcutta (1823-1826).
[163] Reginald Heber, "Hymn 11 – First Sunday After Epiphany".

He picked up a book, "The Lady of the Lake,"[164] the very volume Mr. Meldrum had been studying the night of Mrs. Paxton's death; but laid it down again, and took up the lamp to have another look at the picture, when his attention was attracted by a large photograph of the very man about whom he had been thinking, and he paused, lamp in hand, and inspected it closely. There was nothing fierce or implacable in the face before him, a mild looking, handsome old man was Mr. Paxton in his photograph, who might have disarmed dislike by the gentleness and weakness of his appearance; but Sir Robert's face hardened as he looked at the picture, for this was the very man – older indeed, but still the very man who had called him a scoundrel and villain, and told him his conduct to Nelly was "worse than seething the kid in his mother's milk."[165] That comparison had touched a nerve in his conscience, and even though the offender was in his grave, the remembered expression hurt him, the sting of it had never been extracted yet.

A soft step coming down the carpeted stairs made him set down the lamp, and stand expectant, and he regarded the lady who entered the room with as keen a curiosity and sharp a criticism as he had her goods and chattels. Mary, though very weary, looked no longer haggard, but calm and peaceful; she had put up her hair hastily in a great loose knot, and donned the Turkey red dressing gown, turned up with white canton flannel. There was not a mark of mourning in her dress, though she wore no ornament but Ralph Oliver's opal ring, and Robert's ruby. She had considered hastily in dressing, that Sir Robert's visit was kind and friendly, and probably at his son's request. She knew where he came from for the lad had told her that morning, in passing, his father's intention of visiting the Methodist chapel in Cromaboo; and she was glad, though surprised that he had come.

She met him calmly, but very kindly; extending her hand with great courtesy, she said "You must pardon me, Sir Robert Hardacre, for keeping you waiting so long, I was partly undressed when you came."

The baronet's answering politeness was very gentle and impressive. "It is I that ought to apologize," he said, "for disturbing you at

---

[164] Sir Walter Scott, *The Lady of the Lake* (1810).

[165] Jonathan Bayley, *From Egypt to Canaan* (1867): 186.

such an hour, but I leave Gibbeline to-morrow; and as I saw a light I could not pass the house; I thought I would call for the mere chance of seeing one who is so very dear to my son."

"I am very glad to see you," said Mary, with truth, "will you not sit down?"

"Thank you," said her guest, and he wheeled forward the easy chair for her, and seated himself opposite her. He was not at all flurried by her calmness, as Chip had been, nor was he like Robert and Mrs. Smith, greatly impressed with her beauty; he had all his wits about him, and noted her resemblance to her father with no pleasant feeling. John Smith would have been extra respectful because she was her father's daughter, and Sir Robert Hardacre had a secret feeling of repugnance to her for the same reasonable reason. Mary, on her part, thought the baronet like his son, but as Mr. Meldrum said, "not so bonnie," for as yet he had not smiled, nor had Miss Paxton; their courtesy was of the gravest. Some sorrowful expression about the lady's mouth recalled her mother's recent death to Sir Robert's mind; an event he had entirely forgotten when he knocked at her door.

"A living grief is as hard to bear as a dead one, Miss Paxton," he said very gently, "and that is my only excuse for intruding upon your fresh sorrow; I am very anxious about my son. He told me last night, before we separated, that he was about to become a member of your household, and I would like to know on what footing, for he did not tell me. I did not tell him that I would see you, not knowing it at the time, but of course you are at liberty to do so, and I shall if you do not. In what capacity do you think of having Robert here – as a servant?"

"As a dear, younger brother, for as such I regard him; he would take his meals with me, of course, and I could teach him in the evenings. His education has been so much neglected that it would be very unpleasant for him, at his age, to go to school, and learn with others more advanced than himself; and love is not only a good teacher, but an apt scholar; he would learn better from me than from anybody else. I would pay him for his services, of course. I had formed this plan before I received Robert's letter telling me that you were in Gibbeline."

"What would your friends say to such an arrangement?" asked Sir Robert.

"I have not thought about that, and I do not care in the least what they say or think," was the reply; "I am a middle-aged woman and entirely my own mistress, and if I like to adopt Robert it is my own affair."

She began to feel by intuition Sir Robert's suspicion of her, which peeped out in spite of his grave courtesy.

"But Robert does not regard you as a dear, elder sister," he said, "on the contrary, he wishes to make you his wife, and says his happiness depends on you."

"Poor, dear boy, of course that is his present feeling, but he will get over all that; he may fall in love with someone else before the summer's over."

"Do you wish his present feeling for you to change?" asked the baronet.

"Yes," replied Miss Paxton, regarding him steadily with her grave, bright eyes; "I hope he may always respect and like me, of course, but I should be sorry to think that he would always wish to marry me."

"You take an odd way of converting him," said Sir Robert. "How can you hope that he will change, or forget you, if you take him into your family?"

This question was put with the greatest gravity, and contained no compliment, as the words would seem to imply. A bright smile broke over her face, and she slightly shrugged her shoulder.

"Oh! domestic life is very disenchanting," she said, "it is gold alone that can bear such a touchstone, and not lose its value; he will find out all my faults."

"No man ever loved his mistress the less for her faults," said Sir Robert, with a little bend of the head, "I think it a dangerous experiment, if you really wish him to change his mind."

"That speech would be very flattering," said Mary Paxton, "if it did not imply that I am a dangerous old maid, and not to be trusted."

"I love your sex far too dearly, Miss Paxton, to speak a harsh truth to any lady without pain to myself, but I have – pardon me – no reason to trust any one of your name or family. Not that I think you deceitful or hypocritical, – far from it, – I am sure you feel most kindly with regard to my son, but your father was hostile and implacable to me, in fact my enemy, and I am by no means sure his daughter is not equally my enemy."

Miss Paxton's pale cheek flushed. "And if I were," she said, "I would tell you as readily as ever my father did. Is it possible that you bear malice for the hard things he said to you so long ago, now that he is in his grave?"

"He told me nothing but the truth, and though it is not in human nature to feel grateful for such truths, Miss Paxton, I do not bear malice for his words; but his acts injured me. He was my implacable and most bitter enemy, and helped the devil in my heart more than any man I ever knew. When my father died, and I came into my inheritance, I thought of my son, not with affection, I admit, but I had a sense of duty towards the child, and I wrote to your father, having faith in him as an honest man, and enclosed a check for eight hundred pounds, on the Gibbeline Bank, to be spent as he should think best for the benefit of Nelly and her son, without letting her know from whom it came, to grieve her with old unhappy memories. I wrote to him in preference to Mr. Meldrum, from whom I parted in anger. That is his answer." He took a thin sheet of foreign note paper from his pocket-book and placed it in Miss Paxton's hand. "I deeply regret to say I acted on advice so harshly given; I never sought to help my son again till now, and he has worked as a servant, – a day labourer, – my dear son, the only child God ever gave me. Will you read that note, if you please, and see if I have reason to trust you?"

Mary unfolded it and read: –

> Sir, – I decline to be your emissary, your almoner, – I return the money. The kindest thing you can do for your son and his mother, in my opinion, is to leave them alone. It is better for the boy to be known as the son of an honest peasant, than as the illegitimate slip of a blackguard *gentleman, so-called.*
>
> I am, &c.,
>
> Yours sincerely,
>
> John Paxton.

The opal ring changed to many different colors, as Mary's trembling hands re-folded the letter.

"It was very bad advice," she said, "we ought not to disclaim the ties of kinship, we cannot wipe out blood even if we wished it, we have no right to separate a father and his child; but we are all poor blunderers. He acted harshly, unjustly, but as he thought for the best. He had daughters of his own, and your conduct seemed very bad in his eyes; but I cannot defend him in this. I see the evil of his conduct, as well as the good, and I am sorry. I can see that it injured you as well as Robert. The fact that you left the poor baby, and never inquired for him, or made an effort to take care of him, made me think more hardly of you, and perhaps others too, and – I am sorry. But, Sir Robert Hardacre, you do me injustice to feel distrust of me, and to blame me for what happened when I was a child, and for which I am in no way accountable; and you do yourself injustice to bear malice against a man who is in his grave, whose unrighteousness in this is, I trust, covered, whose sin is forgiven. Forgive my father, and think better of his daughter than to suppose she wishes to place a barrier between you and your son."

This was spoken with a tremendous kind of earnestness, and two or three great tears overflowed their channel and rolled down her cheeks as she concluded, and returned the slip of paper with her trembling fingers. He rose and dropped it into the glowing coals, and the thought flashed into his mind that it would be a painful kind of poetical justice, if Robert were reproached for his father's sins, when the family vault had shut that father in forever. He could kill a score of partridges without compunction; he had landed many a struggling fish with a hook in its gills without any regret; he could cut the throat of a wounded stag, or hear the scream of a hare, in coursing, without the slightest sense of pity, and had really enjoyed many a battue,[166] but, like Achilles, he had his vulnerable point; he did not like to see a woman in distress, and was especially touched when the tearful troubled eyes were of a beautiful colour, and as he had expressed it, "a barley corn bigger than other people's." He was stricken with compunction, and began to feel keenly that he had made a mistake, that it was not another addition of his old enemy, John Paxton, in petticoats, with whom he was contending, but a gentle delicate woman, with a very pretty personality of her own, and more than that she was dear to Robert and Nelly; and he had hurt her feelings and made her unhappy. If he had dared he would have expressed his contrition by taking her in his arms, like a child, and soothing her with gentle words and kisses, – father and son were so far alike, – but such behaviour was out of the question, so after a minute's pause, he just

---

[166]battue (French) = hunting method of flushing game by beating woods and bushes, or the indiscriminate slaughter of a defenseless crowd.

touched her hand with his white fore-finger to bring her eyes back to his face, and said, "Indeed I can forgive your father if his daughter will forgive me. I did you injustice, as you say, and it is more cruel in me to hurt you, now that your heart is sore. Forgive me, if you can."

This speech from some men would have been very offensive, but the baronet really meant what he said, and his words were borne out by his countenance, which wore its most tender softened look, all the Hardacre had gone, and left nothing but Robert there; he looked like an older addition of little Bob in a penitent mood. His face for the moment looked ridiculously like his son's, and Mary smiled involuntarily, turning a very April face upon Sir Robert, who smiled back, and said in a playful winning way, that made him quite unlike Robert, as by magic, "Well, are we to be friends, – will you forgive me?" and he extended his hand.

"Yes," she said simply, "and we will begin again."

"A fresh account," said Sir Robert, "on a clean white page, with the old ugly debts cancelled forever."

"Yes," said Mary, again, "and you must believe that I do not for a moment wish to stand between you and your son; but if he went with you just now it would be a heart-break to his mother, and I think she ought to be the first consideration with you as well as him."

"She is the first consideration with both," replied Sir Robert, "but the next with me is my son, and I still think you take the wrong way to make him love you less, though I am sure your society would be very beneficial to him, and he could not but improve under your tuition. It might become on his part a permanent attachment, and if you are sure you can never change your mind, it is scarcely fair to my boy."

"If I thought it possible that I *could* change my mind so far as to wish to marry him, it would be more unfair to your boy, and I would not have him in the house. But it is not possible, and he will change his, for he *is only* a boy; he will fall in love with some good girl who is worthy of him, and have a happier fate, I hope, than either yours or mine. I am not a very clever woman – not a blue stocking – but I know more than he does and can teach him many things; and I shall have an uncle staying with me shortly who is a good organist, he might give him lessons in music and Latin, if they like each other. I shall live a very quiet life, and we might read history together daily, I could teach him the elements of botany and practical gardening, and he could put up my brother's target and practice at that if he wishes to be a good shot."

"And you will," thought Sir Robert, "improve his manners as only a graceful, charming woman can, and keep him from mingling with low people, and making undesirable connections." That was his thought, but this is what he *said*:

"I am sure you will do him nothing but good, and I trust you entirely with what is dearer to me than life, or anything that life now offers. Having seen you, my dear Miss Paxton, I trust you without a doubt, I trust you entirely."

"You may," said Mary, "I would not injure you if I could, and I *could not* if I would, for Robert loves you so well already, that it is not in the power of any but yourself to turn his heart from you. If you are true to him, he will be true to you."

Sir Robert's face flushed with pleasure – they were both standing now – and as the readiest way of expressing his feelings, he lifted her hand to his lips.

If I wanted a convincing proof that the dead are dead to us indeed and return no more, this very fact would be one; for if anything could have brought John Paxton's body back from its grave, and his soul from Hades, it would have been that kiss; but no such shocking apparition appeared, and the photograph on the wall looked as mildly at them as if it meant a blessing, when Sir Robert said in his playful, pleasant way, "Well, I must not keep you longer from your rest, or run the risk of losing my own forever, after the example of Robert, by seeing too much of you; I must go. And if you *should* change your mind (for if he is '*only* a boy,' you are *only* a woman, he thought), there will be nothing left for me to do but to give you my blessing. Good bye, my dear Miss Paxton, and forget the pain I caused, since you forgive me."

"I will remember nothing but good of you, and I will be faithful to your son; I will *not* change my mind, Sir Robert Hardacre – good night."

Dolly had waited up to see him off the premises, and now came forward officiously to open the door.

"Thank you, little girl," said Sir Robert, in his gracious commanding way, as he placed a coin in her palm.

"What's this for?" asked the Canadian damsel, in amazement.

"For seeing me out," said the baronet, with a pleasant smile at her simplicity.

"Law sake, you needn't go to give me money for *that*," said Dolly, frankly, "I'm only too precious glad to get rid o' you – keeping us up to all hours – here, take it back."

But she was only answered by a not unmusical laugh as the gentleman disappeared like a ghost behind the bushes.

"Well, I never!" said Dolly.

Chapter Thirty-Four

"Who would pursue the smoky glory of the town,
That may go till his native earth,
And by the shining fire sit down
Of his own hearth."

– Sir Richard Fanshawe[167]

"I will collect some rare, some cheerful friends
And we shall spend together glorious hours,
That gods might envy."

– Joanna Baillie[168]

Hamlet – "Look here upon this picture; and on this."

– *Hamlet*[169]

THREE weeks after Mrs. Paxton's death, a family group were seated round her parlour grate, where such a jolly fire glowed and crackled that it was enough to make the old lady turn in her grave. Mary was the centre of the group, and her friends were discussing her future prospects and advising her. She had not asked counsel nor did she intend to follow it, but she leant back in her chair and listened patiently. Mr. and Mrs. Meldrum were there, and there were three other persons, all worth a description – we give the ladies precedence.

---

[167] Sir Richard Fanshawe, 1st Baronet (1608-1666), "An Ode" (1630).
[168] Joanna Baillie (1762-1851), *De Monfort: A Tragedy* (1798).
[169] William Shakespeare, *Hamlet*: Act 3, Scene 4.

The first was Mrs. Marshall, a tall, dark-eyed old lady of seventy, a widow for fifty years. She did not look more than sixty, her hair was scarcely grey, she had a healthy dark complexion, her cheeks were rosy, her teeth were her own. She wore a black lace cap, a white collar and bright crimson ribbon at the throat of a grey gown, from the skirt of which peeped forth a well shaped foot and ankle, encased in a snowy stocking and black slipper. Mrs. Meldrum had remonstrated with her aunt for not wearing mourning, but with no effect.

"I do not mourn Margaret," she replied calmly, "I never liked your mother, and she never liked me. It is for the sake of my brother's daughters that I am here now."

Margaret said it was "respectable" to wear black, and the bright ribbon was "indecent," under the circumstances, but the old lady went on calmly with her knitting, and was not to be moved from grey and black, and the neck ribbon remained unchanged. Mrs. Marshall was the only person in the family conclave who did not offer advice to Mary; she invited her to become a permanent inmate of her house, if she chose, and said it would greatly brighten her life to have her with her, but she did not urge the matter, but left her to accept or reject the invitation as she pleased. She was not a meddler by nature, nor would she be meddled with, but was thoroughly mistress of herself and her household, and had lived so long alone that she had grown in her isolation a little indifferent to the feelings of others. She was liberal, and her heart and purse were always open to distress. She was kindness personified in a case of sickness or poverty, but she had no mercy for self tormenters, – and of that class there are indeed too many in the world, – no tolerance for ordinary, common place, twaddling saints and sinners, and would not be bothered with them. She was a clever, intelligent, spirited old lady who could find no charity in her heart for either mediocrity or conceit.

Opposite to Mrs. Marshall sat a very different person, Mrs. Francis Paxton, the widow of her youngest brother, "my dear aunt Emma," as Mary often fondly called her. She was an American lady, and too entirely national ever to be mistaken for anything else. She was a small, slight, graceful woman about sixty-five years of age; her hair was dyed of the loveliest dark brown, and surmounted by a charming widow's cap with long streamers behind, her teeth were her own not quite in the sense that Mrs. Marshall's were, for she had bought them of the most skilled New York dentist; she had regular, delicate features, brilliant dark eyes, and not a shade of colour in her cheeks, but it was a natural healthy palour, and did not betoken disease. Gold-rimmed spectacles adorned her nose, and innumerable mourning rings her beautifully shaped, plump little fingers. Her voice was not unpleasant, though slightly nasal and drawling. She had been a beauty in her day, and would never be an ugly, because her heart was kind, her head was clear and her nature sound and wholesome. She had no greater love for the late Mrs. Paxton than Mrs. Marshall herself, but she would not for the world have hurt her niece's feelings, therefore she came in a perfect mountain of the handsomest crape, as much in fact as could be crowded on to the sable garment that covered her little person; her silk stockings were of the blackest, her quilted satin slippers adorned with such monstrous rosettes of crape and jet, that none but an American lady would have sported them. The very screen with which she toyed was as black as a crow, and glittering with jet beads.

Aunt Emma was liked by all her circle of acquaintance, she was dear to her servants, she was a favourite with every relative she had in the world, and loved for her own sake and not for her money; even Mrs. Paxton had not absolutely disliked her, but always spoke of her as "a good-natured fool," and she was right as to the good nature, but wrong as the the folly; at least if she was a fool, she was a very contented one, and commend me to the fool who can be happy anywhere, who wears his cap gracefully and never makes discord with his bells, but always jingles them kindly. Minerva herself could not have acted more wisely than Mrs. Francis Paxton did when the hearts of her relatives were sore, and their nerves ajar with the troubles and cares of this weary world. If she could not divert them, she would let them alone, which is surely the height of wisdom, and never by any chance caught their gloom.

The third figure in the group was Mr. James Paxton, the last man of his name and family. He was of medium height, but looked short from being so stout, he had a broad forehead and fair, compact, nobly-shaped head, the hair so closely cut and neatly brushed as to resemble a natural scratch; a fat face, reddish all over, light eyes, half closed from some weakness in the lids, very slight reddish grey whiskers, and a small, thick-lipped mouth that turned down at one corner and up at the other. All this does not sound attractive, yet James Paxton was attractive, and the longer people knew him the better they liked him, for though a man of strong prejudices, he was a genial, kind-hearted man, and a thorough gentleman. His movements were easy and graceful, his manner quiet, his step noiseless and stealthy; there was no self-assertion in the man, but he won upon the heart. In dress he was rather old fashioned, he wore a black stock, and dark clothes, and a watch without chain or guard. He was Scotch in appearance, and Scottish in the not amiable quality of remembering an injury forever, but to do him justice, he remembered kindness, too, and where he loved could see no faults, but was as blind as any bat that ever flapped his leathery wings in the twilight. He was about sixty years of age, being nearly the youngest of a very large family, as his brother John had been next to the eldest. He had perfectly detested the late Mrs. Paxton, as she had caused him to quarrel with his brother and kept them apart when her husband was dying. The photograph of the old white-haired brother, the coat of arms, the sketches drawn by the dead hand, were fraught with painful memories for James Paxton, as they had been for Sir Robert Hardacre. His brother's daughters were dearer to him than any relative he had in the world, they had always loved him, and had never forgotten his birthday. Margaret corresponded with him openly and in defiance of her parents, Mary by stealth and unknown to them, but both loved him; indeed, he was the only person in the world who could check Margaret's willfulness, or change her purpose, the only person who had the least power over her.

Such was the group collected round the parlour fire on a stormy March evening. Mrs. Meldrum, who had spread her ample robes in the most comfortable easy chair the room contained, introduced the subject they all had in their minds, by asking Mary whether she meant to rent the house they were in, or sell it.

"You will live with me, of course," she said, "but it's time you came to some decision about this property."

There was a pause. Some hope on the part of the elder ladies that their niece would choose to live with them, a better knowledge of her character on the part of uncle James kept these three silent; as for Mr. Meldrum, he knew there was no chance of Mary as a permanent resident in his house, but he felt interested and curious as to what her plans might be, and he spoke, as nobody else seemed inclined to speak, and said, "Of course you know I feel entirely with Maggie, and should be glad to have you as one of my household."

Then Mrs. Marshall spoke simply and plainly, as I have said, and told Mary what she herself wished, but offered no advice, and then aunt Emma.

"My dear Mary," she said, "if they monopolise you, and don't give me a little bit of you, I shall be jealous, and invite myself to the house you delight to honour, so take warning, Maggie and aunt Marshall. I *must* have my share of Mary, I want her altogether, but I suppose that is impossible, but I *will* have my share. I want to take her to Saratoga, and Newport and a dozen places, and make her fat and rosy. Think of all the years she has been shut up here, because poor, dear Pricilla disliked company so much; I am sure a little foreign travel would be delightful for her, but I won't dictate, I want her to do just as she thinks best," laying a fond hand on Mary's shoulder, "only I take the liberty of advising dear, and I advise you to be gay and happy, and not take life too seriously."

"And *I* advise her to do her duty," said Margaret, sternly.

"Oh! duty before all things," assented the American lady, amicably.

"I quite agree with you, Maggie, and our most serious and urgent duty is to make the best of everything, and be very happy, and so make everybody happy. Ah! what a very nice world it would be if everybody did their duty; remember, dear, it's your duty to shine on all your relatives a little, not forgetting aunt Emma," and she patted Mary with her screen.

"It's your *first* duty, in my opinion, to arrange about this property," said Margaret, dictatorially. "Of course no one would grudge you a holiday, but life is not all holidays as aunt Emma would seem to imply, life is a very sad, serious thing. Gaud sees fit to send us sorrow and disappointment as punishment, and we need not think to escape it by seeking pleasure and ease. The nearest relatives have the highest claim, let aunt Emma say what she will."

Mary made an effort. "It's very kind of you all to wish to have me with you," she said, "and I thank you gratefully; but I have formed my plan, if it can be called one – it's rather vague yet, though two or three things are quite distinct and settled in my own mind – like you, aunt Emma, I know what I want. For one thing – the most important thing in my plan – I want uncle James to give up his profession and bachelor's hall, and come and keep house with me. I don't want to part with uncle James any more," extending her hand to that gentleman, who stood near her.

He received it with a hearty pressure, and a smile, and said "That's good – I'm an important thing – well?"

"Whether you come or not – but I hope you will – I do not mean either to sell this place or let it; I mean to live in it and make it my home, and a home for more than me; for all of you, whenever you like to come and stay with me – for weeks – for months – for as long as you like – all of you. I mean to enjoy good fires and good dinners, and say grace at my meals, and eat the plums and pears instead of selling them, and give pennies to the beggars, and go to church every Sunday when it doesn't rain, and never trouble about trifles again, God helping me, no not if the pigs get into the garden, and Dolly boils the eggs as hard as a stone."

Mr. Meldrum approved of this speech, and a year ago would have applauded it, but time had taught him the wisdom of silence, so he said nothing, but uncle James said, "That's good," and patted Mary on the shoulder, "good, all but the beggars, Polly, don't give them pennies, give them a piece of bread and a tract."

"I will try and do my duty aunt Emma in making every body happy," the lady went on; "uncle will you come and live with me?"

"I must learn to play the fiddle or the Jewsharp, if I do," said uncle James, "for I can't exist without music, and there's not a room in the house large enough to hold my organ – and what are we to live upon, Polly, if I give up the law – *love?*"

"I have thought of that, and I have a plan. The barn is never used, now the farm is sold, and is no good to anybody. We might wainscot it and fill it with sawdust between the boards – there's plenty of sawdust in the old mill beneath the hill[170] – in a word, make it into a house, and build your organ in there, and you would always have a retreat when you wished to be solitary."

"Ah! and how much would that cost, think you?" asked Mr. Paxton.

"I do not know, that is to be proved."

"It would cost more than you think, Mary; it would take a slice out of your principle, and that would make your income much less,

---

[170]It is uncertain whether the author is referring to an actual mill previously near Kaine Hill road.

and you would be taking another in to keep, for I have laid by but little, – a solitary man, I had no one to save for. I think unless you had a larger capital you could not carry out that plan. I see difficulties."

"It is like all Mary's plans, poetical and impracticable," said Margaret, with a sneer.

"When did I ever form a plan before, Maggie?"

"Do you think we have forgotten that log house on the hill, that castle in the air, that you and Mr. Oliver were to live in?"

Mr. Meldrum was the only person present who did not understand this allusion, and not one of those who did approved of it. Aunt Emma looked at Margaret in an imploring way, and held up her slight forefinger to stop her. Mr. Paxton spoke:

"Come, I do not call that fair or kind, Maggie," he said. "Mary was under authority, perhaps not the best authority, or the wisest counsel; but we cannot judge the wisdom of a plan never carried out – marriage is a lottery in every case – and there is no merit in giving pain."

Mrs. Marshall knitted rapidly but was silent, and Mary, who had flushed deeply, was silent, too; as for Mr. Meldrum, he, with his usual thirst for information, made a secret resolution to have this love story out of the wife of his bosom as soon as he could accomplish it. There was rather an awkward pause, broken at last by Mrs. Marshall.

"You criticise before you hear the whole," she said; "perhaps Mary had some plan for making up the deficiency in the income. I never found you unpractical, my dear; have you thought of meeting the additional expenses you propose to indulge in?"

The kind old voice touched Mary. She had a plan, but was reluctant to enter upon it after what had passed. Her hands trembled nervously, and Mr. Meldrum observing this, suggested that they should wait for further information till to-morrow.

"And do you think I am going to wait all night in suspense, worrying myself and not knowing what she is going to do?" said Margaret. "Do, for goodness sake, tell us, and have done with it, Mary."

Mrs. Marshall's speech had softened her, but this hardened and set her up like a tonic. "Very well, Maggie, as well now as not. I have thought of turning this place into a market garden – not for vegetables, but flowers. I have not finally decided to do so, but I have thought of it. There is no flower market in Gibbeline,[171] and a good many wealthy people live there now, and there are flowers here from May till November. It would be a trifling expense to get a horse and light tilted wagon, and try – one can but fail. I would not, of course, sell them myself, but I would make up the bouquets, and Robert Smith is to live with me when Mr. Llewellyn has done with him, and he would be my salesman."

This project surprised everybody, and to tell the truth it seemed very foolish to all. Aunt Emma said, "Well, my *d-e-ar*, if that isn't poetry and romance," and Mr. Paxton laughed heartily.

"And so I am to live upon blossoms and clover blobs like the bees?" he said. "In all my life I never heard anything so funny, a substantial old fellow like me. You mean to rival Midas, and turn all your buds to gold. You should sell them yourself, Polly; with a Tyrolese hat,[172] and high-heeled slippers and a little lace apron, you would make a charming market woman."

"Robert will be more charming, especially with the ladies," said Mary, outwardly unmoved by this ridicule.

"You would never get on with Bob Smith," said Margaret, "you would have to have him at the same table or he would be offended, they spoiled him so at the Llewellyn's; and for selling the flowers, it's as mean as it is ridiculous; it's enough to make papa turn in his grave. All respectable people will cut you if you persist in such wicked conduct, – yes, I call it wicked, – and resist the advice of your friends."

"I hope not, Maggie, but if they do cut me I'll try and live without them. Of course I'll have Robert at my table, and treat him in all respects as an equal; he will be my man of business rather than servant. I shall not decide about the flower market till I have consulted him."

"Who is this Robert Smith?" asked Mr. Paxton.

"You may well ask, uncle," exclaimed Mrs. Meldrum, indignantly. "A vulgar, low boy, who till a week ago drove the Cromaboo mail; it's just an infatuation of Mary's because the boy is good-looking, and I *know* what the end of it will be. She will show him such favour that people will talk, and he will make the most of what they say for his own advantage, and work upon her feelings, and to stop their

---

[171]This explains Mary Leslie's plan of publishing her sequel to this novel – *The Gibbeline Flower Seller*. Evidence suggests this sequel was ever completed. See Introduction, page xxv.

[172]Tyrolese hate = a Tyrolean hat, also known as a Bavarian or Alpine hat.

mouths she will marry him – the crooked stick at last after all these years of waiting. And then she will not have the face to live in this neighbourhood with him – *he* will persuade her to sell – and he will take her somewhere to his wigwam – she loves the backwoods- - and she will be the squaw of that coarse little savage. I see it all plainly," she concluded bitterly.

"And mix his fire water and nurse his papooses," said uncle James, "this is prophecy indeed, Maggie."

"Well, Bob was certainly the prettiest papoose I ever saw," said Mr. Meldrum, much amused at his wife's prediction.

"Ah! you know him!" cried aunt Emma, "and what do *you* think of him, Mr. Meldrum – *do tell* now?" "Yes, let us hear your opinion," chimed in Mr. Paxton.

Mr. Meldrum, who wished to propitiate Margaret, and get that love story out of her, and who thought Mary was going rather too far in her liking for little Bob, chose to "damn him with faint praise," calling him "a nice little fellow enough," "a pretty boy," as if his face was his fortune, and the only thing to recommend him.

"I think you are coming to harsh and unkind conclusions concerning Mary," said Mrs. Marshall, "she may have excellent reasons for taking the boy into her household, and may wish to favour him, without a desire to put him out of his place, or marry him."

"I like him very much, aunt Marshall," said Mary, with exceeding calmness, "I regard him as a dear younger brother, and I mean to teach him and help him in any way I can, but you only do me justice in thinking I have no wish to marry him."

"You hear her," cried Mrs. Meldrum, "she's going to adopt this low boy as a brother. I tell you, Mary, it's madness, it's neither safe nor right that you should live alone and keep house, even if uncle came. You will get yourself talked about with your silly fancies, it isn't as though you were a widow, or a married woman, but a young unmarried person, it is neither right or proper."

Mrs. Marshall rose and laid her knitting in its basket. "Mary," said she, "has a perfect right to do as she pleases; I regret her decision because I shall lose so much of her company; but I cannot oppose it. As for impropriety, that's nonsense, Margaret; I was twenty years of age when I was left a widow, and I have lived alone ever since, except for my servants; Mary is more than thirty.[173] With regard to the gardening scheme, it seems to me romantic and impractical, but I may be wrong, and Mary has a perfect right to try it if she pleases; and for this young man, Robert Smith, I have never seen him, and therefore cannot judge, but I think as a general rule, it is foolish to put people out of the station in which they were born, unless in a case of great genius."

"Bob Smith a genius," said Mrs. Meldrum, "the little upstart, I should like you to see him, with his coat patched of three colours, and a hat without a rim."

"I *should* like to see him," said aunt Emma, "and I'm sure I should never think less of him for a patched coat; its a pity to think so much of the casket and so little of the precious jewel it contains."

"A jewel indeed," cried Mrs. Meldrum, with a toss of her head.

"I'm dying to see him," persisted aunt Emma, "how his ears must burn to-night – I don't care about his birth so long as he's nice, I believe in equality."

"A myth, my dear Emma, there's no such thing as equality in the world," said Mrs. Marshall, "but I am weary, and will say good night," and having kissed the ladies and shaken hands with her brother, she made a stately bend to Mr. Meldrum, and departed.

"How grave you look, Polly," said Mr. Paxton, kindly.

"You can't say it's not a wise thought this time," replied Mary, with a smile, "for it's one of Solomon's – 'He that considereth the wind shall not sow, and he that regardeth the clouds shall not reap.'"

"We will talk about all this to-morrow, Puss," said uncle James, "and you shall have the very best advice without paying a fee for it."

"And without asking for it," retorted his niece, as she kissed him and said good night.

---

[173]In Chapter 3 Mary celebrated her 32nd birthday.

Chapter Thirty-Five

"Like crowded forest trees we stand
And some are marked to fall."

– Cowper[174]

IT WAS not long before aunt Emma's desire was gratified, for the very next afternoon, as the little lady reclined luxuriously in a large rocking chair, and Mrs. Marshall was stepping up to the gate after her daily constitutional, hooded, cloaked and furred to the chin; a pair of pie-bald ponies, with a light cutter behind them, dashed up with a great jingling of bells, and a slight active figure sprang out, and opened the gate for the old lady, and the sweetest, most joyous young voice she had heard for many a day made a common-place in her ears, because of the tone in which it was uttered and the smile that accompanied it. Mrs. Marshall was conquered at the very first attack and struck her colours at once. She sailed into the parlour, bringing with her a blast of cold air, and innocently asking, "Who is that young gentleman that opened the gate for me so courteously, and is tying up his horse in the yard?" not dreaming that it was the obnoxious Robert Smith.

"Gentleman!" echoed Mrs. Meldrum, as Mary broke into a merry laugh, "it's that little upstart, Bob Smith, and I don't thank Mr. Llewellyn for bringing him here. Understand me, Mary, I do not choose to see Mr. Llewellyn unless he asks especially for me," and she departed to her own room forthwith, greatly to the relief of her husband.

---

[174]William Cowper (1731-1800), "Stanzas" (1787).

"Why, what has he done with his patched coat?" asked aunt Emma, who had been almost asleep a minute ago, but was now on the alert and wide awake enough, regarding Robert attentively through the double window, and her gold-rimmed spectacles.

The question was natural, for Robert was dressed in a top-coat of fine broadcloth, which his father had put upon him the night they parted at Gibbeline. Having only the old military garment, he had gone without a great-coat to see his father, who noticed the omission and guessed the truth, that he had no other.

"There is no mark on it, and your mother will never know it belonged to me, you will not pain me by refusing it, my son," said Sir Robert, with such pleading affection that Robert the younger could not say no, and allowed his father to help him on with it. He took it to a cunning Gibbeline tailor to make it fit, not, however, before he had examined the pockets, and found therein a twenty pound note and a photograph of papa; the note he would have returned had not Miss Paxton persuaded him to keep it, and the picture was locked into her work-box for safe keeping.

While we were making this digression, Miss Mary had run out in the snow to welcome Mr. Llewellyn; he had been brought in and divested of his wraps, had alarmed them all by a violent fit of coughing, had been introduced to Mrs. Francis Paxton, and renewed his acquaintance with Mrs. Marshall, whom he had met forty years before, and was now ensconced by the fire in a comfortable easy-chair, having a chat with that lady. Robert, who put the ponies in the stable, was ten minutes behind his master, and entered the room with Mr. Meldrum.

Mary rose and shook hands with him, saying "I am glad to see you, Robert, as I wished very much to ask your advice."

"I am sure you are welcome to it if it's worth having," he said, a pleased smile and fond brightening of the eyes showing his joy at seeing her.

She introduced him to Mrs. Paxton, saying "This is Robert Smith, aunt Emma."

The little lady graciously extended her jeweled hand and said, "It is a very cold day," and Mr. Paxton made the same statement to him, further offering some remarks about the distance he had come and the depth of the snow, and Mrs. Marshall, who was not introduced, acknowledged his presence by a bend of the head.

Mary sat down beside him and told him at once quite frankly about her flower scheme, saying "They have thrown so much cold water upon it, that I had almost decided to give it up, only I wished first to see what you thought of it."

Robert listened with a grave business face, quite different from his usual expression, and when she had finished Mr. Meldrum said, "Now advise her to give it up, Bob, and make us all your friends for life."

"Since Miss Paxton has honoured me with her confidence, I shall advise her honestly, even if I make you all my enemies," replied Robert. This answer pleased Mrs. Marshall, who though she appeared to be exclusively occupied with Mr. Llewellyn, could hear very well what every body in the room was saying.

"A week ago, Miss Mary," he went on, "I should have said give it up, but I don't say that now, for I hear there is to be a regiment of regulars quartered in Gibbeline,[175] and I noticed when I was with the volunteers that regular military gentlemen didn't mind a dollar for a good bouquet, and ten cents for a button-hole bud. Of course the military make a place gay, there will be balls and picnics, and parties, and flowers will be wanted for all. I can't say how it will succeed till it is tried, but if you like to try I will do all I can to make it a success. It shall not be my fault if you fail, and I think it's worth trying."

"Oh! buy, oh! buy, oh! buy, oh! buy my flowers!" warbled Mrs. Paxton just as the tea was announced, and the little lady paid Robert a good deal of flattering attention during the meal, and his modest pleasant replies pleased her greatly.

Mr. Llewellyn had come with an object, as he presently announced; he came to ask Miss Paxton to buy his ponies. "Lavinia has purchased a pair of silver tailed ponies, and doesn't want them," he said, "and I wish to provide a good home for my old friends, and I thought if you intended to keep horses they would suit you."

"I will take them, sir," said Mary, promptly, "and many thanks for giving me the first chance."

"Then, my dear, that is one matter settled, but I should like before I leave to see you alone, and speak about another subject I have at

---

[175]The Guelph Garrison Battery was organized in 1866 as No. 1 Company of the 30th Wellington Battalion of Rifles, and then in 1871 as an independent unit renamed the Wellington Field Battery of Artillery.

heart."

"You have bought and sold and never mentioned the price of the articles purchased," cried Mrs. Paxton, gaily.

"A bargain is an easy matter between honest people," said Mary. "It will give me great pleasure to have a private chat with you, sir," to Mr. Llewellyn.

"The last private interview we shall ever have in this weary world, this beautiful world which God himself pronounced 'very good,' before man marred its loveliness by sin and rebellion."

"Why the last, Mr. Llewellyn?"

"Because I am dying rapidly. Lavy thinks I shall go and live with her in Hamilton, but I shall never go; it is she who must come back to me for a little while. I intend writing her to-morrow."

"Oh! I hope you may be mistaken," said Mary, tears welling up suddenly to her eyes.

"Why, you ought to rejoice and be glad at my release, it will be like a bright, glorious morning after a long and dreary night, a night of troubled dreams and sore distress. You should rejoice, my dear, to think of my happy waking after this troubled passage of experiment and trial; I shall wake hale and well, refreshed and peaceful and *at home*."

Why is it that remarks of this kind always tend to chill and sadden good Christian people, who believe in God Almighty, maker of heaven and earth, and in Jesus Christ, his only Son and Our Saviour? I cannot tell the reason, but so it is, mention death and eternity, mention those glorious truths which we all profess to believe, and a sense of discomfort descends like a wet blanket, and everybody is ill at ease as by magic. I do not wonder at this when the speaker is a bit of a hypocrite, a worshipper of false gods, but when he is honest and earnest it is quite a different thing, and I am surprised that the result should be the same. I think the secret cause of this disquiet is a want of belief in the heart when the lip, and perhaps the understanding, says "I believe." A quietness and chill fell at Miss Paxton's tea table, and a short silence succeeded Mr. Llewellyn's remark, broken by the doctor, who said:

"I think you overrate your weakness, Mr. Llewellyn, you may live for many a year yet."

"I may, but I hope not, Meldrum, for I have had enough of it, and if God wills, I shall be glad to lay down my arms. I do not see that my life is of any use now; Lavy is happy and provided for, and my poor wife is growing so much worse mentally, that of necessity she must be placed under closer restraint; and I am no longer equal to the charge of her, as I am growing weaker every day, and more and more deaf. I wait the will of God, and I feel I shall not have long to wait ere he removes me."

"I shall miss you if you do die," said Mary, "I shall feel the world poorer."

"So much the better," he replied with a smile, "the poorer this world, the richer the one beyond to our eager longing," – and when Mary took him into her private sanctum after tea, he told her it was about Robert he wished to speak.

"I think I did him some injustice," he said, "I did not know the worth of the lad till I was left alone with him; he is everything to me, *everything*. Lately I have become so weak and infirm in body that I cannot dress without his help; he has been house-keeper and cook – for the Irish girl we have is a very bad one – and groom and stage driver, and *valet de chambre*; he has taken care of my wife as well as he could, and she has required constant watching, and is, I fear, becoming dangerous to herself and others."

"What a fearful affliction is insanity," said Mary, "it is like living death."

"It is worse," replied Mr. Llewellyn, "it is distorted and horrible life; God defend you and yours from such a calamity. But to return to Robert, I fear I underrated him because of his low birth; he is a *gentleman*, Miss Paxton; now, for the first time in my life, do I fully understand our Saviour's words – 'He that is highest among you let him be your servant.' In my prejudice of class I forgot that God, who makes all good and noble things, makes gentlemen; that a man without a pedigree may have the highest character, the greatest worth. I feared his love for you might injure you; now I have no such fear, you took a juster view of him than I did. I can say with Waller: –

> 'Stronger by weakness, wiser men become
> As they draw near to their eternal house.'[176]

"I am ashamed to say I used to have a prejudice against dissenters; all that is swept away forever; I feel that we cannot truly call

---

[176]Edmund Waller (1606-1687), "Old Age."

any denomination the church of God, His faithful people are scattered through all denominations; He has not left Himself without witnesses even in the corrupt churches of Greece and Rome; there are spiritual Christians in all. I acknowledge that even those greatly in error may not be without their use, even a narrow-minded bigot like Moorhouse may do some good, as well as a clear-headed, kindhearted, half ignorant fellow like Crutch. What a prejudice I had against Crutch last year, when he first came, because he was peasant born; I thought such as he should learn, and not presume to teach; and now I love the man as a brother, though he was never at school in his life; and I believe he has touched the hearts of some of the worst ruffians in Cromaboo, and may change their lives. I am a broader churchman than I was when you saw me last, and it is all owing to little Bob, the Methodist. No son could have done more for a loved and honoured father than Robert has done for me, no bishop could have preached Christ better than he has by his daily acts, though he seldom named Him."

Mary felt more than glad at this eulogy, and told Mr. Llewellyn so, with moistened eyes and a faltering tongue.

In the meantime Robert had been making himself friends in the parlour; seeing an open melodeon he asked Mrs. Paxton if she would play for him, and that lady, always good-natured and glad to give pleasure, sat down at once. She had been the favourite pupil of the celebrated Signor Twankipanni,[177] who made such a sensation in New York when she was a maiden, and to whom her papa paid fifty dollars for every lesson she received. This foreign celebrity was, as all musical people know, a pianist remarkable for brilliant and rapid execution, and Mrs. Paxton – who imitated him as well as she could – had never before touched a melodeon, and was surprised herself at the extraordinary jerking, squeaking sounds she elicited. Robert stood by her and turned the music for her, guessing with his usual apt instinct the right time. She did not play long, but begged Robert to take her place on the music stool, "And take the taste out of our mouths," she said, "and show us what music is," for the cunning little woman had been told he could play, and was determined to hear him.

---

[177] Signor Twankipanni is now an obscure figure.

Robert was by no means shy, as we know, but he held back for a time from the feeling that he played so much better than Mrs. Paxton that she might be vexed at his superiority; but seeing that she was resolved to hear him, and would take no excuse, he yielded.

He had never played before so keen a critic, for Mr. Paxton was a doctor of music, but Robert was quite unconscious of the genius of his listener, and thought rather of the ladies and Mr. Meldrum. As usual, he chose a sweet, plaintive voluntary, and its mournful beauty had double the effect from Mrs. Paxton's late spirited performance, which had greatly jarred the nerves of her brother-in-law. He stood at a little distance with folded arms, and head on one side, as he listened.

"Good," was his comment when Robert ceased, "do you practice much, and who is your teacher?"

"I practice a good deal, sir; I have no teacher," replied Robert, as his master and Miss Paxton returned from their private conference.

Mr. Paxton made no further remark, but turned away, and soon the ponies were ordered, and Mr. Llewellyn, as he took leave, remembered Mrs. Meldrum for the first time and expressed a hope that she was well.

"A little indisposed," replied her husband, complacently, as he gave the old gentleman his arm to assist him to his cutter.

Robert took a warm leave of Miss Paxton and aunt Emma, and was turning to Mrs. Marshall, of whom he stood a little in awe, when the old lady rose, and extending her hand cordially, addressed him for the first time.

"You have given me great pleasure with your music," she said, "and I thank you."

Robert blushed, and smiled his brightest smile, and said, "I am sure I am fortunate, I almost feared I was annoying you."

But when he was gone it seemed the effect of his music remained, for Mrs. Marshall's dark eyes wore their softest expression as she sat gazing dreamily at the fire, and she said at last abruptly, "I like that boy's playing, James, it is the music of memory, a sort of sweet dirge for past joys; it has brought back old scenes to my mind, things I have not thought of for years. What do you think of him – has he genius?"

"I cannot tell. The little beggar has music in him, and taste and feeling, but those fellows who play so well by ear are often too lazy to practice by note and make themselves perfect. He has one talent without doubt."

"And what is that?" asked his sister.

"A talent for creeping into old women's hearts," said Mr. Paxton.

"And young women's, too," added Mr. Meldrum.

"That sounds a little like envy," said the old lady; "I like your Robert, Mary," to her niece, who at that moment came into the room with Margaret and aunt Emma.

"Say *my* Robert, Bella," exclaimed Mrs. Paxton. "I have a great mind to adopt him for a son; he's a real nice boy; how can you say he is vulgar, Maggie? If he is vulgar, what are we?"

In the meantime Robert was rapidly nearing Cromaboo, quite unconscious that everybody was willing to take him up and make the best of him.

Chapter Thirty-Six

"Not heaven itself upon the past has power,
For what has been *has* been, and I have had my hour."
                                                    – Dryden[178]

AFTER turning it over in his mind for three weeks, Mr Paxton consented to keep house with Mary, and left Gibbeline to make his
arrangements, and Mrs. Marshall and Mrs. Paxton decided to make
a long visit to their nieces, and stay - one in Gibbeline, the other
in Cromaboo, till Mrs. Meldrum's confinement was over. As the
spring advanced Mrs. Marshall and Mary took long walks together
and though never out of temper and very fond of her niece, the old
lady was a somewhat still and taciturn companion. On returning
from a stroll one fine spring evening, towards the end of April, they
found Robert waiting to see Miss Paxton. He came with a note from
Mrs. Harry Llewellyn to say that her uncle was worse, and her aunt
almost unmanageable, and she begged Mary to come and stay with
her for a week. Robert had come on one of Chip's horses, as the
ponies had gone to the station to meet Mr. Harry, so Mary had to
wait for to-morrow's mail. He gave a sad account of "the master,"
whom he thought sinking fast. "Indeed, I think he's been sinking,"
he said, "ever since Miss Lavy got the fortune; he seemed to have
no further motive for exertion, and the old lady is a dreadful charge.
Biddy and I don't dare to sleep at the same time, but have to watch
her, turn about, for Mrs. Harry is quite worn out."

---

[178]John Dryden (1631-1700), "Translation of the 29th Ode of the 1st Book of Horace."

He looked very weary, and Mary ordered tea at once, and Mrs. Marshall asked, in her stately way, if he would play for her while the tea was making. He had been playing a great deal lately to soothe Mrs. Llewellyn and keep her quiet, and his practiced fingers made sweet music till Mary called him away. After he had gone, aunt Marshall and her niece went out into the orchard to enjoy the sweet spring air, and listen to the frogs, and speculate as to when the swallows would come. They sat down, side by side, on a large, flat stone, and the elder lady said, with a sigh, "It is singular the effect that boy's music has upon me; it brings back my youth, my happy marriage and its sad ending; it is a sweet, yet sorrowful pleasure to listen to him."

"Auntie, dear," said Mary, "will you tell me your story? I have heard it by bits, of course, but I would like to hear it from your own lips, if it is not too painful to tell it."

"The pain has died out of it many years ago," replied Mrs. Marshall, "I am no longer a rebel to the will of God. I will tell you, my dear, with pleasure, it will be like living the old life over again to relate it to so intelligent a listener. You know my parents died while I was yet at school, and when my education was completed I had no choice but to live with my eldest brother, who was married and didn't want me, or a maiden aunt who didn't want me either, though she had no nearer relative than myself. My father had settled fifty pounds a year on me, and for four years I lived alternately with my brother George and his wife in London, and my aunt Robina at Richmond. John had been in Canada some years, we heard from him twice a year, and his letters cost, I am afraid to say how many shillings each, but a great deal, they were diaries, rather than letters, and full of interest. He was married before he left England, but I had never seen his wife. She wrote, asking me to make her house my home; this invitation was warmly seconded by John, and was at once accepted by me, for I was young and romantic and tired of my humdrum life. There were no steamers in those days, and a voyage across the Atlantic was a great undertaking. What piles of linen under-clothing was bought for me, and two dozen pairs of shoes, no less, and twenty flannel petticoats. Aunt Robina opened her heart, feeling it was a life-long parting, and had her old silks made over for me, and gave me rich laces and a beautiful shawl, and many ribbons, and hoped I should get a good husband, and George gave me a handsome black silk gown, and a five pound note unknown to his wife, who was a very mean woman. I went to see my maternal grandmother, whom I had never seen before, by her own desire. She was a pensioner at Hampton Court, and quite childish. She gave me a beautiful piece of India muslin, which was afterwards made into my wedding dress, and a lucky guinea with two holes in it. She had been to India in her youth, and told me a strange, rambling story about her voyage, and blessed me because my eyes were like her mother's. Your father sent me the money for my passage. There were but two other cabin passengers, a clergyman's wife going out to her husband and Richard Marshall. We sailed from Portsmouth to New York; I was the last to reach the ship, going with the captain in his boat; I was swung up on board in an arm chair; how well I remember Richard's face looking over the side of the vessel.

"The captain, who was an Irishman, introduced us, and said when all other amusements failed we might fall in love to pass the time. The voyage was long, and a part of it very rough; it lasted nine weeks, it was the happiest part of my life, I was full of hope, joyous and free from care, and Richard and I *did* fall in love, but not merely to pass the time; we were alike in tastes, in principles, in youth and health. What a strange, dreamy idea we both had of Canada; quite unlike the reality. Richard brought with him two fowling pieces, a double-barreled gun, a case of pistols, four sword canes, and fishing tackle enough to furnish half a dozen disciples of Walton.[179] Not that he was at all blood-thirsty or a mighty hunter, but these equipments were considered the proper thing for Canada in those days. He also had the whole of Scott's novels and poems at that time published – for Scott was still alive and writing[180] – which he unpacked and we read many of them together.

"We were friends the very first day, for it does not take long at sea to become acquainted, people may live in an English house for a year and not know each other as well as in one week at sea. At the end of four weeks we were plighted lovers, in the fifth we planned our wedding tour to Niagara. It seems strange sometimes that a man I only knew six months of all my life should have had so strong and strange an influence upon me; yet now, in old age, I approve of my

---

[179] An obscure reference, and intriguing if this is Robert Walton, the fictional polar explorer in Mary Shelley's *Frankenstein*.

[180] Sir Walter Scott died 21 September, 1832. Therefore, Leslie has Mrs. Marshall journeying to Canada before that date.

choice, I feel sure we should never have tired of each other, even if we had lived together all these years.

"He was a tall, manly fellow – my Richard – over six feet in height, fair-haired, blue-eyed, sandy-whiskered. He was imaginative and romantic, and seemed for the time to live in the book he was reading. How happy we were, we did not feel the voyage long or desire it to end. We would stand together, side by side, watching the long, silvery track the vessel made, and chatting in low, happy whispers, we would pace the deck, arm in arm, or sit on our camp chairs for hours, Richard reading and Mrs. Budd and I listening. Happy dreamers, living in the bright, imaginary scenes of Scott, or in sweet thoughts of the future, building castles in the air as the sailors sang, and mended their sails or drew them in; moving on slowly, yet gaily, to meet our fate without a doubt or fear. We did not separate in New York, but he travelled up the country with me, and brought me to this very house, then but newly built; and he told John, before we had been in it five minutes, that he meant to come back two months from that day and marry me. Your father was anything but pleased, and your mother still more angry. She said it was a cheat, she had just dismissed her servant and counted upon me to fill her place, 'And my husband paid your passage,' she said, 'what do you mean?'

"'I mean to repay the money,' I replied, feeling greatly hurt at this reception.

"'Of course, *ma belle*,' chimed in Richard, in his jolly, hearty voice, 'and I'll give it to you at once,' and he took out his great pocket-book filled with notes and English gold.

"I assure you, all this occurred before I had been asked to take off my bonnet. Then John said Richard was a perfect stranger and he would not consent to the marriage without references, but Richard had some letters of introduction in his pocket which satisfied him as to his respectability, and he stayed four days, though he was not a very welcome guest. It was the month of May, I never remember such a spring as that, I have never seen such wild flowers since. That level, green field that you call 'the flat' was standing in woods, beech and maple, and the earth beneath the trees was carpeted with sweet squirrel corn and snowy blood-root, every rotten log and powdery stump had its decay covered and glorified by masses of fragrant loveliness. What velvety, living green mosses we found in our first stroll, and little, scarlet fungi-like cups, some as large as a tea-cup, others as tiny as a pin's head; and never have I seen such moccasin plants and cardinal flowers as we gathered later in the season when Richard came again. I suppose there are beauties in the woods still, but I never go in search of them; there is no Richard to carry my treasures and troll merry staves with his jolly young voice. There were stumps in your garden, with lovely flowers trailing over them; there was a pig stye over yonder entirely concealed by a lovely climbing plant with little prickly gourds on it, and delicate tendrils, and light green foliage; that pig stye was a mass of loveliness. Richard found it out the first night. 'Hold your nose, Bell,' he cried out, 'and come this way, I have something to show you.'

"I stayed six weeks with your mother – who had great taste with her flowers, I will say that for her – and it was the longest six weeks I ever spent, though I was very busy all the time. I just lived on Richard's letters. He had gone to Montreal to see his brother, and wrote once a week. I made all the baby linen for your brother John, who was expected in a little while, but your mother had to get her servant back, and was reconciled to part with me because I could neither cook, nor wash, nor make butter, or candles, or soft soap.

"There was no church in Gibbeline then,[181] so we were married in the house, and your father gave me back my passage money, and begged me to accept it, saying 'Upon my soul, I am ashamed, Bell, it's damned mean of Prissy, but don't tell her I gave it back, for God's sake – and may He bless you.'

"I told Richard about it that night, and he laughed heartily, and made a corkscrew of the bill and threatened to light his pipe with it. A pair of happy young fools we were; we sat up till midnight, and built castles and laid plans for the future by the light of the moon. He had bought a farm near Montreal, and there we were to live when our wedding tour was over. We went from Gibbeline to Niagara on horseback, it was the most comfortable mode of traveling over the bad roads; we rode by slow stages; we passed through the old Beverly swamp;[182] it took us ten days to reach Niagara. I shall never

---

[181]St. Andrew's Presbyterian Church was the first church built in Guelph, in 1831. This church property was sold in 1856 and replaced by the old city hall. Some of this congregation split and formed Knox Church in 1844. The present St. Andrew's church on Norfolk Street was completed in 1858.

[182]The Beverly Swamp remains a 2,400-hectare large forested wetland in south-central Ontario.

forget when, faint and far away, we first heard the sound of the Falls. We slept that night at Chippewa,[183] and the Falls roared in our ears, Richard said, 'Like the mighty voice of a giant fiend,' till we fell asleep. We woke very early, and decided to walk over and see that wonder of the world before breakfast, we would see the first glimmer of the rising sun upon it; but we lay quiet, listening to the sound of the mighty water in the happy, still night, for some minutes before we rose. An early bird made a faint, little twittering trill in the darkness.

"'I have such a strange, happy feeling, Bell,' said Richard, 'it seems like the beginning of a new life, in a new world,' and it was to him, poor fellow. He uncovered his head when he first saw the Falls, and I shed tears, I could not help it. He put an arm about me, but was still for so long that I said at last, 'Well, Richard, are you satisfied?' 'No,' he replied, solemnly, 'nor shall I be till I see the Maker of it all; *this* is His work, but what will it be to see the Author!' Then he carrolled out with his clear healthy young voice:

'We praise Thee, oh! God, we acknowledge Thee to be the Lord;
All the earth doth worship Thee, the Father everlasting!'

"'You sigh, Bell,' he said, at last; 'you are tired and hungry, and I am a selfish fellow to promise to cherish, and yet to starve you.'

"We looked up an inn and ate our breakfast with a relish. Day by day we explored, enjoyed, tramped, and rode about; we saw the Falls in rain and shine; we saw it by moonlight, by sunset; we saw it in the faint light of dawn and in the broad glare of day; we went under; we saw it from the American side, and from the Canadian; we saw it not as you see it now, but girdled by mighty forests; more than once we saw it with lightning flashing over it, and heaven's thunder mingling with its roar.

"I was a very strong, healthy girl, and never tired, and yet I found it harder to wake in the morning than Richard did. Once he took a long walk before breakfast without me, and wakened me by brushing my cheek with a handful of flowers he had gathered four miles away. I never missed him from my side.

"That last night! – how well I remember every minutiae of it. We sat up planning a row for the next day, far up on a safe part of the

---

[183]Chippawa was founded in 1850, but a loose settlement may have predated the official foundation.

river. I leaned my head against his shoulder, and we talked for hours. 'No more honey after to-morrow,' he said, gaily; 'it's the last day of our moon, *ma belle*, come and see it shining on Niagara,' and we looked out before lying down and saw it shimmering on the mighty restless water.

"I slept very soundly, but towards the morning I had a troubled dream: I thought I saw Richard nearing the Falls in the boat; he had no oars; he waved his hand to me, and was swept rapidly on to the cataract – many a night since I have dreamt of the dread enemy – I wakened with a start. I had thrown off part of the clothes and felt chilly. Richard was asleep, but was conscious of some movement, for he put his arm round me and drew me closer to him; my momentary fear was gone as I felt the brooding warmth at my back, the protecting arm; I was like a little chicken covered by its mother's wing. I felt safe and satisfied, and was asleep again in a moment. When I woke, the early sun shone in at the window, and I was alone. I rose and dressed quickly, the nervous terror of my dream had come back; I could not wait to take a good bath, but just washed my face and hands. I felt better when I got out into the air, and walked rapidly along by the river, but was still too anxious to meet Richard to admire the beauties of nature. I took but a casual glance at the Falls, hoping to meet him every minute. I saw an old man coming towards me, walking rapidly, with a wan and frightened face. He waved his hand to me before we met and pointed to the river. I looked, but at first saw nothing; then he took me by the arm and directed my eyes towards the Rapids. 'Look!' he said, '*he's your husband!*'

"There was Richard sweeping towards the Rapids in a tiny boat! He had lost an oar, and tried in vain with the only one he had to keep from the rocks; it snapped in his hand, and he was swept swiftly on. He saw me, poor fellow; he stood up and waved his hat, and sprang into the river, to try and swim, I suppose, but ah! the cruel water swept him away in an instant, and we never saw him after he sprang from the boat.

"I did not cry or faint, I stood watching eagerly, not entirely without hope, the cruel monster that had taken my husband forever. A crowd collected, and stood with me staring at the rapids, but after a couple of hours certainty took the place of hope; I returned to the inn. I have no vivid memory of the day, I sat in a stunned way unable to realize the blow. In the evening, a doctor, to whom I had been introduced, came to me and asked me if I had any friends to whom he could write. I said I would write myself; he brought me pen, ink and paper, but when I tried to frame a sentence, the hopeless truth came upon me in its desperate reality. I broke into a tempest of weeping. He wrote for me. Your father came, and was very kind in his way; Richard's brother came from Montreal, looking haggard and stricken, for Richard was dear to him; and Francis, who was yet a boy, came from the States with his wife, a very young bride, scarcely sixteen years old. She was very kind to me, she went to Montreal with me to Richard's farm, and stayed for four months.

"I left Niagara unwillingly, though now I hated it; like Naomi, I had gone full and I came away empty of all joy.[184] I think but for Emma, I should have died of loneliness; she took me back to New York with her, and I stayed for a couple of months, but I was more lonely there than on Richard's farm, where he had planned and arranged everything. His books, his clothes, his guns, were like old friends to me. He had made a will, it was signed the morning of our marriage; everything he died possessed of he left to me absolutely. It was against the advice of all my relatives that I kept house alone, but I think if I had been obliged to submit to other people's dictation in that first year of my grief, I should have gone mad. After the first few months the sense of utter loneliness left me and I was better alone. The servants Tom Marshall procured for me were very steady and unobtrusive, they never interfered with me. I would sit up all night when it was still and starlight, and I was restless, gazing out at the bright heavens, and having no light within but the wood fire. Tom Marshall came to see me sometimes, and does still; the sight of him pains me even now, though I have a great respect for him, he bears a kind of mocking-bird resemblance to his brother, there is likeness enough to renew my loss every time I see him.

"At the end of two years I went to England, but I only stayed a month; I could not bear it, the clouds were so near to the earth that they seemed to shut out heaven; in Canada I felt nearer to Richard. After six years I came to this place once more, 'the flat' was cut, denuded of all its beauty, and scarred with ugly stumps and weeds; the plough had passed through it, and not a wild flower remained. I felt an affinity to the rough field; like me, a ruthless hand had been laid

---

[184]Naomi, Ruth's mother-in-law in the Old Testament *Book of Ruth*.

upon it, and its glory had departed.

"Ten years after my bereavement, I went to Niagara, I went alone, telling no one of my intention. The first sound of the Falls shook me like the roar of an enemy, a merciless enemy who had taken my all. That night I slept in the same inn, in the same bed I had occupied with Richard, and I dreamt of him, but he was not alone; he came to me and with him that One who died that we might be saved. That dream comforted and soothed me. I recognized the Father's hand in all my woe. I began to work for others; I became a Sunday-school teacher, I dispersed tracts, I sought out distress and relieved it, I invited sick people to my house, and cheered and made them well again; I grew happy. I have been a happy woman for forty years, Mary, I am contented to wait till it's God's pleasure to take me home to Himself and Richard. I feel now that it was in kindness and love to me that God took Richard away. If he had been mine all these years, if we had been blessed with children, I should have been so tied and wedded to this world that I should have wanted to live on forever, and now I have nothing to leave that I greatly regret to leave, my ties are all on the other side. Some day when I feel the end is not far off, I shall once again visit the Falls.

"And now you have heard my story, Mary, from my own lips, and you are the only person to whom I ever told it. It was a fitting place to tell it, for I sat on this flat stone with Richard years before you were born, and listened to the far away frogs, and pronounced them musical."

The stately old lady rose as she concluded, and drawing her shawl round her, with a slight sign to Mary not to follow, she walked slowly back to the house.

Chapter Thirty-Seven

"Jesus, I cast my soul on Thee,
Mighty and merciful to save;
Thou wilt to death go down with me,
And gently lay me in the grave."

– Charles Wesley[185]

"There is a calm for those who weep,
A rest for weary pilgrims found;
They softly lie, and sweetly sleep
Low in the ground

The storm that wrecks the winter sky,
No more disturbs their deep repose,
Than summer evening's latest sigh
That shuts the rose."

– James Montgomery[186]

A STILL, small room, through which the early dawn is peeping, a narrow bed on which Owen Llewellyn has laid down to rise no more. Two are with him, the doctor and his nephew; his fingers have closed upon Harry's in a weak clasp, and he is speaking feebly and with an effort.

"My dear Harry, you are a comfort to me on my death bed; I am heartily glad that you are Lavy's husband; I know, my dear boy, that you married her from a sense of honour rather than love, because

---

[185] Charles Wesley (1707-1788).
[186] James Montgomery (1771-1854), "The Grave" (1804).

she was your poor, unprotected kinswoman, despised by many of her relatives, and only sheltered from the world by the feeble, failing arm of her old uncle; but it was a noble thing to do, and I felt in time that your virtue would be rewarded. You are like the Llewellyn's of old, you are worthy of the name, for you live for duty. Now you have ample wealth, and you and Lavy have no care but to make each other happy, and as the years pass your wife will become more dear to you, for she is kind and generous and has many virtues. May God bless you with children, as in mercy he denied me this wish of my heart, may they comfort your old age, as you have comforted mine. God send you a son to do by you as you have done by me – and Lavy." He paused exhausted. "You will take care of my poor wife, I know," – here his voice failed.

"I will, sir," said Harry, tears rolling down his cheeks, "I will, by George."

"God bless you with every blessing," replied the weakened voice of the sick man.

The doctor, who had a feeling finger on the feeble, fluttering pulse, gently suggested that he should rest now, and tell Harry the rest in the morning.

"Ah! Mr. Meldrum," he replied, with a smile, "we may not wake to the same morning," but he did not try to say more, and soon he was asleep, not the light, refreshing sleep of every day nature, but the last sleep of earthly insensibility before a glorious waking. So he lay for forty-eight hours; only once in all that time his lips moved, and he muttered the word "Jesus," to his hearers almost a word without meaning. Neither Mr. Meldrum nor Harry left the house, they shared the long, last watch together, yet they scarcely spoke. Harry was quiet, yet restless; his uncle's words had struck deep, and a sense of unworthiness and sin haunted him. "Undeserved praise is the most severe satire," and Harry felt the old man's last wish rather an awful one, that he might have a son to do by him as he had done by Lavy, a son to deceive him and value his money more than himself.

Towards the dawn of the second morning, Robert crept in and looked at the still face of his master. "Will he last long?" he asked, in a whisper.

"Not long now," returned the doctor, "the pulse in the wrist is gone, the feet are cold, only the heart pumps on. Are the ladies asleep?"

"Miss Mary is awake, the others are asleep at last." He glided away again. Half an hour later and all was over; the two gentlemen opened the door and went out into the chill dawn for a breath of air.

Something in the rising sun smote the conscience of Harry, as Moses smote the rock; he burst into tears, and leaning his head against the door-post, sobbed audibly. In a few minutes he recovered himself a little and could speak.

"Oh! we are blackguards, Meldrum, blackguards both," he said, sadly and bitterly.

"You should know yourself best, Harry," replied the other gentleman, with a calm smile and slight shrug of the shoulder, "and you may call me hard names if it's a relief to you; but if you mean that you are sorry for marrying Miss Lavy, all I can say is that I share your regret. If I had known of her fortune a little earlier you should not have had that to reproach yourself with."

"You don't know what blackguards we are, Meldrum, and I do, that is all the difference between us. I would change places with my uncle, how gladly, to be as good a man, as free from sin as he; I would, by George."

"So would not I," said the doctor. "He was a noble old man, certainly, – a little visionary and unreal in his ideas, though, – but he is dead, and I'm alive; there I have the advantage of him. I can see the sunrise, I can see the dandelions in the grass, I can feel the air – which is a little chilly – and hear the birds. I am hungry and shall enjoy my breakfast, weary and shall sleep sweetly; and all these things are over with him forever. You are over-tired and nervous, Harry, that gives you a wrong view of things; your bed is the best place for you."

"Ah! doctor, so you judge in your arrogance," said the low voice of his sister-in-law, at his elbow. "I heard the last part of your speech. But 'eye hath not seen, nor ear heard, neither hath it entered into the heart of man to imagine the glories prepared for them that love Him.' Mr. Llewellyn did love God and try to do His will. What glorious sight may now meet the eyes of the faithful servant; what music he may hear, such as mortal bird never made, though that in the tree carols his morning hymn very sweetly. You are tired and hungry, but he will never be weary again, he will hunger and thirst no more, he will eat the food of God's angels. You feel the air chill, but who can tell what warm delicious breeze fan his cheek? He is at home, as he never was on earth."

"I see there are two sides to every question," said Mr. Meldrum, with a kindly smile, – he liked Mary as he would a kitten or bird, or other pretty, inferior creature, and if she had married him would certainly have liked his second wife as well as his first; she amused him. "You look as though you needed some of that heavenly manna to refresh you, but I must set you to work, tired as you are. Will you try and persuade this young gentleman to go to bed, and rouse up Bridget to see about some coffee and something substantial – and in the meantime send Robert to me – and on no account wake the ladies."

"To wake Bridget would be to wake the whole house, – breakfast is ready; Robert prepared it when you told him your watch would soon be over. Come, Mr. Harry, and try and eat something before you lie down. We shall go to him, though he shall not return to us; be comforted, he is past all suffering and safe with his Maker and Father; in his case, death is swallowed up in victory. God never makes mistakes, as we poor mortals do continually, or gathers the unripe fruit; He never comes out of season to take back His treasures."

Poor Harry's tears broke forth afresh at this address, but when she laid her hand on his arm, he suffered her to lead him away.

Chapter Thirty-Eight

"Does it matter who comes to a man's funeral?"

– Ben Jonson[187]

"Britons never, never, never will be slaves!"

– Thomson[188]

"The sun parts faintly from the wave,
The moon and stars are beaming,
The corpse is covered in the grave,
And infants now are dreaming;
For Time conveys with rapid power
Alike the sweetest, saddest hour!"

– Prior[189]

M R. LLEWELLYN, was buried without ostentation in a quiet little
cemetery in Cromaboo, belonging to the Primitive Methodists.
This was according to a wish expressed in his will. "It is a lovely spot,"
he wrote, "for the body to rest in, and though the people buried there
were entirely wrong in the head with regard to church government,
their hearts were in the right place; they fixed their faith on the Rock
of Ages, and I would as soon rise with them as with a bench of bish-
ops." He also desired that no mourning should be used at his burial.

His unpopularity followed him to the grave, and the funeral was a
very small one; a few Irish attended it uninvited, but not a Scotchman

---

[187]Ben Jonson (1572-1637).
[188]James Thomson (1700-1748), "Rule, Britannia!" (1740).
[189]Matthew Prior (1664-1721), "Evening's Harping."

or a Dutchman was there, as a willingness to forgive and forget is not a national peculiarity with either Scotch or Dutch.[190] The younger Llewellyns were there, and some friends from Hamilton, and Mr. Meldrum and the Smiths, of course, and also Chip's partner Root, whom Mr. Llewellyn had lectured for his ill-living not a fortnight before his death. The German had listened so patiently that the old gentleman hoped his heart was touched, as perhaps it was, for when he concluded emphatically, "It is for your good I speak so plainly," Root answered "Aye, master, you mean well," and he certainly put on his best clothes and came to the funeral, not a little to the disgust of Mr. Moorhouse, who disliked him greatly. Only one person was offended at this quiet funeral, and that was Robert, the Irish half of him longing for a "big berrin;" he would have liked nodding plumes, sweeping cloaks, sable horses, in honour of the dear old master; it seemed to him a want of respect to have a walking funeral, with never a hat band or mark of mourning, and he expressed something of his feeling to Miss Paxton, as they were driving home together the day following the interment.

"You foolish Robert," she said, "didn't he tell us to rejoice and not mourn, to thank God that he is free. Mourning is very well for an unrepentant sinner – and the undertakers must live, poor fellows – no black is too deep for the loss of a soul, but for a suffering saint, who has escaped from his mortal prison, there is nothing to mourn about; our sorrow is just selfish."

"I know I am selfish, but I do miss him so much. I have such a respect for him, the dear old master, that it would have comforted me to have a black band."

"Then you shall have one, Robert," said Mary, with a smile, "and –" but at that moment they encountered Mr. Crutch, on his bay pony, and the sentence was never finished.

Robert drew in his horses and asked him if he thought they would find Mr. Jibb at home.

"Yes," replied the Reverend Peter, with a sly twinkle of his bright hawk-like eye, "I have just left him, and you will find him under his own vine and fig-tree what he planted," and he cantered on, and they turned up to Mr. Jibb's house, Robert explaining that he was "a first-

---

[190]With statements like this, it is no wonder that Leslie's novel didn't receive broader recognition from her contemporaries.

class hand at paneling but an ugly old beggar to deal with."

They found him standing at his door, with his arms a-kimbo; a short and burly man, clothes in a blue shirt, the sleeves rolled to the shoulders, displaying his hairy arms, which were as sturdy and muscular as a crocodile's fore legs. Brown derry trowsers, and a striped bed-tick apron, completed his dress. He had a short neck, and a large head covered with a thatch of thick iron-gray hair, a large, coarse face with a week's growth of stubbly beard upon it, the most remarkable feature being a very long upper lip. There he stood, John Jibb, the richest and most successful man in Cromaboo, looking at the new comers with more curiosity than courtesy.

"Good evening, Mr. Jibb," said Robert; "do you want a job?"

"I don't know as I do," returned the person addressed.

Mary now spoke, and courteously told him the nature of her business, her intention of turning the barn into a house, and what she would want him to do, asking what wages he would require, and if she should pay him by the day or by the job.

"Let me reckon," he replied, thoughtfully counting his stubby fingers – "four threepunces is two sixpuncies, twice two's four, and ought's ought, – you boards me of course, – now, how about the vittles?"

"Oh! I promise to feed you well," said Mary, with a smile.

"It ain't that," Mr. Jibb condescended to explain, "you knows I'm a Hinglishman, and I'm proud o' being a Hinglishman, I think Hingland beats all the countries in this yer world. I likes liberty; one man's as good as another, *I* say, but a Hinglishman is a deal better; I allays stick to that. Muster Crutch he says to me, says he 'It's your dooty to give to your poor neighbours;' says I 'If I likes to give I'll give, and if I don't I won't.' Them's my sentiments, and I'm a Hinglishman, none o' your dirty Irish," – here he looked at Robert – "and I must be sarved as sich. What I wants to know is *this*, do you keep two tables or *one*, that's what I asks?"

"I keep two tables," replied Miss Paxton, "you would not have your meals with me."

"Them there's a hend," said Mr. Jibb, with a wave of his brown arm, "I works for no fine lady as wun't sit to her wittles wi' me."

"Then I'll wish you good evening," said Mary, with a broad smile and a slight bend of the head; a courtesy which he in no way returned, and as they turned away, leaving him to enjoy his liberty, a shrill, female voice called from within, "Supper's ready, old man, come and hev the pudden while it's 'ot."[191]

"He's a rude, rough gem, deny it who can," said Robert, laughing merrily, and they soon forgot him, much sooner than he forgot them, for he thought of them all the evening and congratulated himself with many a chuckle upon telling "that fine lady what he thought on her."

"You are grave and still, Robert," said Mary, after a long silence, "what are you thinking of – may I know?"

"I was thinking of the old master, how we had parted for a long time, and were each beginning a happy, new life. His death gives me a solemn feeling, it stills my joy in being under your roof; I am glad past telling to be with you, yet sad that the old life is over and gone by forever. I can't but pity the old master, lying there in his fresh grave, while I have so much that I longed for before me, and my heart is too full between joy and sorrow."

"Dear Robert, it is only the shell we have buried in the little green churchyard, and his new life is certain joy and endless happiness; he has gone, in the words of our catechism, 'to glorify God and to enjoy him forever.' I think it is you that are to be pitied, Robin, because the new life is earthly and the new mistress full of faults, as you will soon find out; you are like the young bears, you have all your troubles before you."

"I have faults, too," said Robert, "But tell me of them by myself if ever I vex you. I don't mean to vex you, I mean to make you happy if I can, and I am happy in being here by your side to-night, but I realize that one day we must part; and God grant we may never be separate again till cruel death divides us."

"Time is as great a divider as death," said Mary, "only he does it more gently, but separate or together, we will always be fast friends."

"I am more than your friend," he replied, "you will *always* be dearer to me than any other woman in the world."

---

[191]By using the vernacular accents of these characters, Leslie is demonstrating that Jibb and his wife are East End London Cockneys, attempting to sound upper-class.

The End

www.ingramcontent.com/pod-product-compliance
Lightning Source LLC
Chambersburg PA
CBHW020838030726
47493CB00028B/307